SMALL WORLD

Zaps The Establishment!

"Very funny indeed." —*New York Times*

"A three-ring circus of academic drollery.... A delightful romance, that's what David Lodge has given us."
—*Newsday*

"A comic romp about the earth through the international literary conference circuit." —*Saturday Review*

"A wild party in prose." —*New Republic*

"Writing in a tone about midway between the elegant wittiness of Evelyn Waugh and the manic jocularity of Joseph Heller, Lodge follows his libidinous scholars from one conference center to the next.... The humor is the thing, and there is plenty of it.... *Small World* should be a boon for the humanities at the graduate level—and a boost for sagging spirits everywhere."
—*Cleveland Plain Dealer*

"Mr. Lodge's characters are those scholars...who flit from one international conference to another delivering, but not necessarily hearing, papers. These pedants errant are a wonderfully comic crew of blabbermouths.... They are all mercilessly satirized by Mr. Lodge, who is himself a professor of modern English literature and knows his enemies hilariously well." —*Atlantic Monthly*

"The most brilliant and also the funniest novel [Lodge] has written." —**Frank Kermode**

"This is a marvelous romp through academia; its nomination for the Booker Prize will not surprise captivated readers." —*Publishers Weekly*

"Grandly funny...juicy parodies of Barthes-style pedantry." —*Kirkus Reviews*

"Lodge's riotous novel deftly satirizes academic junkets and junketeers." —*ALA Booklist*

"Delightful." —*Library Journal*

"I doubt if any author has packed so many first-class jokes into his pages since the palmy days of Wodehouse and Perelman." —*Birmingham Post*

* * *

DAVID LODGE is Professor of Modern English Literature at the University of Birmingham in England, where he has taught since 1960. He is married and has three children. His novels include the award-winning *Changing Places* and the highly acclaimed *Souls and Bodies*. He is a fellow of the Royal Society of Literature and an honorary fellow at University College, London.

SMALL WORLD

An Academic Romance

DAVID LODGE

WARNER BOOKS

A Warner Communications Company

WARNER BOOKS EDITION

This Warner Books Edition is published by arrangement with
Macmillan Publishing Company, 866 Third Avenue, New York,
N.Y. 10022

Warner Books, Inc.
666 Fifth Avenue
New York, N.Y. 10103

W A Warner Communications Company

Printed in the United States of America
First Warner Books Printing: April, 1986
10 9 8 7 6 5 4 3 2

To Mary
With all my love

Author's Note

LIKE *Changing Places,* to which it is a kind of sequel, *Small World* resembles what is sometimes called the real world, without corresponding exactly to it, and is peopled by figments of the imagination (the name of one of the minor characters has been changed in later editions to avoid misunderstanding on this score). Rummidge is not Birmingham, though it owes something to popular prejudices about that city. There really is an underground chapel at Heathrow and a James Joyce Pub in Zurich, but no universities in Limerick or Darlington; nor, as far as I know, was there ever a British Council representative resident in Genoa. The MLA Convention of 1979 did not take place in New York, though I have drawn on the programme for the 1978 one, which did. And so on.

Special thanks for information received (not to mention many other favours) are due to Donald and Margot Fanger and Susumu Takagi. Most of the books from which I have derived hints, ideas and inspiration for this one are mentioned in the text, but I should acknowledge a debt or two which are not: *Inescapable Romance: Studies in the Poetics of a Mode* by Patricia A. Parker (Princeton University Press, 1979) and *Airport International* by Brian Moynahan (Pan Books, 1978).

Caelum, non animum mutant, qui trans mare currunt.

HORACE

When a writer calls his work a Romance, it need hardly be observed that he wishes to claim a certain latitude, both as to its fashion and material, which he would not have felt himself entitled to assume had he professed to be writing a Novel.

NATHANIEL HAWTHORNE

Hush! Caution! Echoland!

JAMES JOYCE

Prologue

WHEN April with its sweet showers has pierced the drought of March to the root, and bathed every vein of earth with that liquid by whose power the flowers are engendered; when the zephyr, too, with its dulcet breath, has breathed life into the tender new shoots in every copse and on every heath, and the young sun has run half his course in the sign of the Ram, and the little birds that sleep all night with their eyes open give song (so Nature prompts them in their hearts), then, as the poet Geoffrey Chaucer observed many years ago, folk long to go on pilgrimages. Only, these days, professional people call them conferences.

The modern conference resembles the pilgrimage of medieval Christendom in that it allows the participants to indulge themselves in all the pleasures and diversions of travel while appearing to be austerely bent on self-improvement. To be sure, there are certain penitential exercises to be performed—the presentation of a paper, perhaps, and certainly listening to the papers of others. But with this excuse you journey to new and interesting places, meet new and interesting people, and form new and interesting relationships with them; exchange gossip and confidences (for your well-worn stories are fresh to them, and vice versa); eat, drink and make merry in their company every evening; and yet, at the end of it all, return home with an enhanced reputation for seriousness of mind. Today's conferees have an additional advantage over the pilgrims of old in that their expenses are usually paid, or at least subsidised, by the institution to which they belong, be it a government department, a commercial firm, or, most commonly perhaps, a university.

There are conferences on almost everything these days, including the works of Geoffrey Chaucer. If, like his hero Troilus at the end of *Troilus and Criseyde,* he looks down from the eighth sphere of heaven on

> *This litle spot of erthe, that with the se*
> *Embraced is*

and observes all the frantic traffic around the globe that he and other great writers have set in motion—the jet trails that criss-cross the oceans, marking the passage of scholars from one continent to another, their paths converging and intersecting and passing, as they hasten to hotel, country house or ancient seat of learning, there to confer and carouse, so that English and other academic subjects may be kept up—what does Geoffrey Chaucer think?

Probably, like the spirit of Troilus, that chivalrous knight and disillusioned lover, he laughs heartily at the spectacle, and considers himself well out of it. For not all conferences are happy, hedonistic occasions; not all conference venues are luxurious and picturesque; not all Aprils, for that matter, are marked by sweet showers and dulcet breezes.

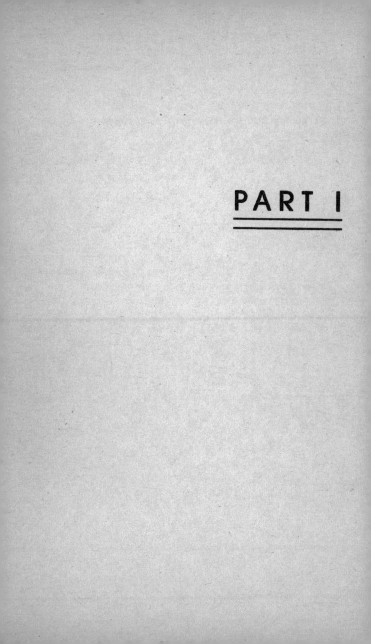

PART I

One

"APRIL is the cruellest month," Persse McGarrigle quoted silently to himself, gazing through grimy windowpanes at the unseasonable snow crusting the lawns and flowerbeds of the Rummidge campus. He had recently completed a Master's dissertation on the poetry of T. S. Eliot, but the opening words of *The Waste Land* might, with equal probability, have been passing through the heads of any one of the fifty-odd men and women, of varying ages, who sat or slumped in the raked rows of seats in the same lecture-room. For they were all well acquainted with that poem, being University Teachers of English Language and Literature, gathered together here, in the English Midlands, for their annual conference, and few of them were enjoying themselves.

Dismay had been already plainly written on many faces when they assembled the previous evening for the tradition-al sherry reception. The conferees had, by that time, acquainted themselves with the accommodation provided in one of the University's halls of residence, a building hastily erected in 1969, at the height of the boom in higher education, and now, only ten years later, looking much the worse for wear.

They had glumly unpacked their suitcases in study-bedrooms whose cracked and pitted walls retained, in a pattern of rectangular fade marks, the traces of posters hurriedly removed (sometimes with portions of plaster adhering to them) by their youthful owners at the commencement of the Easter vacation. They had appraised the stained and broken furniture, explored the dusty interiors of cupboards in vain for coat-hangers, and tested the narrow beds, whose springs sagged dejectedly in the middle, deprived of all resilience by the battering of a decade's horseplay and copulation. Each room had a washbasin, though not every washbasin had a plug, or every plug a chain. Some taps could not be turned on, and some could not be turned off. For more elaborate ablutions, or to answer a call of nature, it was necessary to venture out into the draughty and labyrinthine corridors in search of one of the communal washrooms, where baths, showers and toilets were to be found—but little privacy, and unreliable supplies of hot water.

To veterans of conferences held in British provincial universities, these were familiar discomforts and, up to a point, stoically accepted; as was the rather inferior sherry served at the reception (a little-known brand that seemed to protest too much its Spanish origins by the lurid depiction of a bullfight *and* a flamenco dancer on the label); as was the dinner which awaited them afterwards—tomato soup, roast beef and two vegetables, jam tart with custard—from every item of which all trace of flavour had been conscientiously removed by prolonged cooking at high temperatures. More than customary aggravation was generated by the discovery that the conference would be sleeping in one building, eating in another, and meeting for lectures and discussions on the main campus, thus ensuring for all concerned a great deal of tiresome walking to and fro on paths and pavements made dangerous and unpleasant by the snow. But the real source of depression, as the conferees gathered for the sherry, and squinted at the little white cardboard lapel badges on which each person's name, and university, were neatly printed, was the paucity and, it must be said, the generally undistinguished quality of their numbers. Within a very short time they had established that none of the stars of the profession was in residence—no one, indeed, whom it would be worth travelling ten miles to meet, let alone the hundreds that many had covered. But they were stuck with each other for three days: three meals a day, three bar sessions a day, a coach outing and a theatre visit—long hours of compulsory sociability; not to mention the seven papers that would be delivered, followed by questions and discussion. Long before it was all over they would have sickened of each other's company, exhausted all topics of conversation, used up all congenial seating arrangements at table, and succumbed to the familiar conference syndrome of bad breath, coated tongue and persistent headache, that came from smoking, drinking and talking five times as much as normal. The foreknowledge of the boredom and distemper to which they had condemned themselves lay like a cold, oppressive weight on their bowels (which would also be out of order before long) even as they sought to disguise it with bright chatter and hearty bonhomie, shaking hands and clapping backs, gulping down their sherry like medicine. Here and there people could be seen furtively totting up the names on the conference list. Fifty-seven, including the non-resident home team, was a very disappointing turn-out.

So Persse McGarrigle was assured, at the sherry party, by a melancholy-looking elderly man sipping a glass of orange juice into which his spectacles threatened to slide at any moment. The name on his lapel badge was "Dr Rupert Sutcliffe", and the colour of the badge was yellow, indicating that he was a member of the host Department.

"Is that right?" Persse said. "I didn't know what to expect. It's the very first conference I've ever been to."

"UTE conferences vary a lot. It all depends on where it's held. At Oxford or Cambridge you would expect at least a hundred and fifty. I told Swallow nobody would come to Rummidge, but he wouldn't listen."

"Swallow?"

"Our Head of Department." Dr Sutcliffe seemed to have some difficulty in forcing these words between his teeth. "He claimed it would put Rummidge on the map if we offered to host the conference. Delusions of grandeur, I'm afraid."

"Was it Professor Swallow who was giving out the little badges?"

"No, that was Bob Busby, he's just as bad. Worse, if anything. Been beside himself with excitement for weeks, organizing outings and so forth. I should think we'll lose a pretty penny on this affair," Dr Sutcliffe concluded, with evident satisfaction, looking over his glasses at the half-filled room.

"Hallo, Rupert, old man! A bit thin on the ground, aren't we?"

A man of about forty, dressed in a bright blue suit, hit Sutcliffe vigorously between the shoulder blades as he pronounced these words, causing the latter's spectacles to fly off the end of his nose. Persse caught them neatly and returned them to their owner.

"Oh, it's you, Dempsey," said Sutcliffe, turning to face his assailant.

"Only fifty-seven on the list, and a lot of *them* haven't turned up, by the look of it," said the newcomer, whose lapel badge identified him as Professor Robin Dempsey, from one of the new universities in the north of England. He was a broad-shouldered, thickset man, with a heavy jaw that jutted aggressively, but his eyes, small and set too close together, seemed to belong to some other person, more anxious and vulnerable, trapped inside the masterful physique. Rupert Sutcliffe did not seem overjoyed to see Professor Dempsey, or disposed to share with him his own pessimism about the conference.

"I dare say a lot of people have been held up by the snow," he said coldly. "Shocking weather for April. Excuse me, I see Busby waving urgently. I expect the potato crisps have run out, or some such crisis." He shuffled off.

"God!" said Dempsey, looking around the room. "What a shower! Why did I come?" The question sounded rhetorical, but Dempsey proceeded to answer it at some length, and without apparently pausing for breath. "I'll tell you why, I came because I have family here, it seemed a good excuse to see them. My children, actually. I'm divorced, you see. I used to work here, in this Department, believe it or not. Christ, what a retarded lot they were, still are by the look of it. The same old faces. Nobody ever seems to move. Old Sutcliffe, for instance, been here forty years, man and boy. Naturally I got out as soon as I could. No place for an ambitious man. The last straw was when they gave a senior lectureship to Philip Swallow instead of me, though I had three books out by then, and he'd published practically nothing. Now—you wouldn't credit it—they've gone and given him the Chair here, and he's still published practically nothing. There's supposed to be a book about Hazlitt— *Hazlitt*, I ask you—it was announced last year, but I've never seen a single review of it. Can't be much good. Well, anyway, as soon as they gave Swallow the senior lectureship, I said to Janet, right, that's it, we're off, put the house up for sale, we're going to Darlington—they'd been wooing me for some time. A Readership straight away, and a free hand to develop my special interests—linguistics and stylistics— they always hated that sort of thing here, blocked me at every turn, talked to students behind my back, persuaded them to drop my courses, I was glad to shake the dust of Rummidge off my feet, I can tell you. That was ten years ago, Darlington was small in those days, still is, I suppose, but it was a challenge, and the students are quite good, you'd be surprised. Anyway, I was happy enough, but unfortunately Janet didn't like it, took against the place as soon as she saw it. Well, the campus is a bit bleak in winter, outside the town, you know, on the edge of the moors, and mostly prefabricated huts in those days, it's better now, we've got rid of the sheep and our Metallurgy building won a prize recently, but at the time, well, anyway, we couldn't sell the house here, there was a freeze on mortgages, so Janet decided to stay on in Rummidge for a while, we thought it would be better for the kids anyway, Desmond was in his last year at junior school, so I commuted, came home every weekend, well, nearly every weekend, it was a bit hard on Janet, hard on me, too, of course, and then I met this girl, a postgraduate student of mine, well, you can appreciate that I was pretty lonely up there, it was inevitable when you come to think of it, I said to Janet, it was inevitable—she found out about the girl, you see . . ."

He broke off, frowning into his sherry glass. "I don't know why I'm telling you all this," he said, shooting a slightly resentful look at Persse, who had been puzzled on the same score for several minutes. "I don't even know who you are." He bent forward to read Persse's label badge. "University College, Limerick, eh?" he said, with a leer. *"There was a young lecturer from Limerick* . . . I suppose everyone says that to you."

"Nearly everyone," Persse admitted. "But, you know, they very seldom get further than the first line. There aren't many rhymes to 'Limerick'."

"What about '*dip his wick*'?" said Dempsey, after a moment's reflection. "That should have possibilities."

"What does it mean?"

Dempsey looked surprised. "Well, it means, you know, having it off. Screwing."

Persse blushed. "The metre's all wrong," he said. " 'Limerick' is a dactyl."

"Oh? What's 'dip his wick', then?"

"I'd say it was a catalectic trochee."

"Would you, indeed? Interested in prosody, are you?"

"Yes, I suppose I am."

"I bet you write poetry yourself, don't you?"

"Well, yes, I do."

"I thought so. You have that look about you. There's no money in it, you know."

"So I've discovered," said Persse. "Did you marry the girl, then?"

"What?"

"The postgraduate student. Did you marry her?"

"Oh. No. No, she went her way. Like they all do, eventually." Dempsey swilled the dregs of his sherry at the bottom of his glass.

"And your wife won't have you back?"

"Can't, can she? She's got another bloke now."

"I'm very sorry," said Persse.

"Oh, I don't let it get me down," said Dempsey unconvincingly. "I don't regret the move. It's a good place, Darlington. They've just bought a new computer especially for me."

"And you're a professor, now," said Persse respectfully.

"Yes, I'm a professor now," Dempsey agreed. His face darkened as he added, "So is Swallow, of course."

"Which one *is* Professor Swallow?" Persse enquired, looking round the room.

"He's here somewhere." Dempsey rather unwillingly scanned the sherry drinkers in search of Philip Swallow.

At that moment the knots of chatting conferees seemed to loosen and part, as if by some magical impulsion, opening up an avenue between Persse and the doorway. There, hesitating on the threshold, was the most beautiful girl he had ever seen in his life. She was tall and graceful, with a full, womanly figure, and a dark, creamy complexion. Black hair fell in shining waves to her shoulders, and black was the colour of her simple woollen dress, scooped out low across her bosom. She took a few paces forward into the room and accepted a glass of sherry from the tray offered to her by a passing waitress. She did not drink at once, but held the glass up to her face as if it were a flower. Her right hand held the stem of the glass between index finger and thumb. Her left, passed horizontally across her waist, supported her right elbow. Over the rim of the glass she looked with eyes dark as peat pools straight into Persse's own, and seemed to smile faintly in greeting. She raised the glass to her lips, which were red and moist, the underlip slightly swollen in appearance, as though it had been stung. She drank, and he saw the muscles in her throat move and slide under the skin as she swallowed. "Heavenly God!" Persse breathed, quoting again, this time from *A Portrait of the Artist as a Young Man*.

Then, to his extreme annoyance, a tall, slim, distinguished-looking man of middle age, with a rather dashing silver-grey beard, and a good deal of wavy hair of the same hue around the back and sides of his head, but not much on top, darted forward to greet the girl, blocking Persse's view of her.

"There's Swallow," said Dempsey.

"What?" said Persse, coming slowly out of his trance.

"Swallow is the man chatting up that rather dishy girl who just came in, the one in the black dress, or should I say half out of it? Swallow seems to be getting an eyeful, doesn't he?''

Persse flushed and stiffened with a chivalrous urge to protect the girl from insult. Professor Swallow, leaning forward to scrutinize her lapel badge, did indeed seem to be peering rudely down her décolletage.

"Fine pair of knockers there, wouldn't you say?" Dempsey remarked.

Persse turned on him fiercely. "Knockers? *Knockers*? Why in the name of God call them that?"

Dempsey backed away slightly. "Steady on. What would you call them, then?"

"I would call them . . . I would call them . . . twin domes of her body's temple," said Persse.

"Christ, you really are a poet, aren't you? Look, excuse me, I think I'll grab another sherry while there's still time." And Dempsey shouldered his way to the nearest waitress, leaving Persse alone.

But not alone! Miraculously, the girl had materialized at his elbow.

"Hallo, what's your name?" she said, peering at his lapel. "I can't read these little badges without my glasses." Her voice was strong but melodious, slightly American in accent, but with a trace of something else he could not identify.

"Persse McGarrigle—from Limerick," he eagerly replied.

"Persse? Is that short for Percival?"

"It could be," said Persse, "if you like."

The girl laughed, revealing teeth that were perfectly even and perfectly white. "What do you mean, if I like?"

"It's a variant of 'Pearce'." He spelled it out for her.

"Oh, like in *Finnegans Wake*! The Ballad of Persse O'Reilley."

"Exactly so. Persse, Pearce, Pierce—I wouldn't be surprised if they were not all related to Percival. Percival, *per se*, as Joyce might have said," he added, and was rewarded with another dazzling smile.

"What about McGarrigle?"

"It's an old Irish name that means 'Son of Super-valour'."

"That must take a lot of living up to."

"I do my best," said Persse. "And your own name . . . ?"
He inclined his head towards the magnificent bosom, appre-
ciating, now, why Professor Swallow had appeared to be
almost nuzzling it in his attempt to read the badge pinned
there, for the name was not boldly printed, like everyone
else's, but written in a minute italic script. "*A. L. Pabst*," it
austerely stated. There was no indication of which university she belonged to.

"Angelica," she volunteered.

"Angelica!" Persse exhaled rather than pronounced the
syllables. "That's a beautiful name!"

"Pabst is a bit of a let-down, though, isn't it? Not in the
same class as 'Son of Super-valour'."

"Would it be a German name?"

"I suppose it was originally, though Daddy is Dutch."

"You don't look German or Dutch."

"No?" she smiled. "What do I look then?"

"You look Irish. You remind me of the women in the south-
west of Ireland whose ancestors intermarried with the sailors
of the Spanish Armada that was shipwrecked on the coast of
Munster in the great storm of 1588. They have just your
kind of looks."

"What a romantic idea! It could be true, too. I have no
idea where I came from originally."

"How's that?"

"I'm an adopted child."

"What does the 'L' stand for?"

"A rather silly name. I'd rather not tell you."

"Then why draw attention to it?"

"If you use initials in the academic world, people think
you're a man and take you more seriously."

"No one could mistake you for a man, Angelica," Persse
said sincerely.

"I mean in correspondence. Or publications."

"Have you published much?"

"No, not a lot. Well, nothing, yet, actually. I'm still
working on my PhD. Did you say you teach at Limerick? Is
it a big Department?"

"Not very big," said Persse. "As a matter of fact, there's
only the three of us. It's basically an agricultural college.

We've only recently started offering a general arts degree. Do you mean to say that you don't know who your real parents were?''

.''No idea at all. I was a foundling.''

"And where were you found, if that isn't an impertinent question?''

"It *is* a little intimate, considering we've only just met,'' said Angelica. "But never mind. I was found in the toilet of a KLM Stratocruiser flying from New York to Amsterdam. I was six weeks old. Nobody knows how I got there.''

"Did Mr Pabst find you?''

"No, Daddy was an executive of KLM at the time. He and Mummy adopted me, as they had no children of their own. Have you really only three members of staff in your Department?''

"Yes. There's Professor McCreedy—he's Old English. And Dr Quinlan—Middle English. I'm Modern English.''

"What? All of it? From Shakespeare to . . . ?''

"T. S. Eliot. I did my MA thesis on Shakespeare's influence on T. S. Eliot.''

"You must be worked to death.''

"Well, we don't have a great number of students, to tell you the truth. Not many people know we exist. Professor McCreedy believes in keeping a low profile . . . And yourself, Angelica, where do you teach?''

"I haven't got a proper job at the moment.'' Angelica frowned, and began to look about her a trifle distractedly, as if in search of employment, so that Persse missed the crucial word in her next sentence. "I did some part-time teaching at . . .'' she said. "But now I'm trying to finish my doctoral dissertation.''

"What is it on?'' Persse asked.

Angelica turned her peat-dark eyes upon him. "Romance,'' she said.

At that moment a gong sounded to announce dinner, and there was a general surge towards the exit in the course of which Persse got separated from Angelica. To his chagrin, he found himself obliged to sit between two medievalists, one from Oxford and one from Aberystwyth, who, leaning back at dangerous angles on their chairs, conducted an animated discussion about Chaucerian metrics behind his back, while he bent forward over his roast shoe-leather and cast longing looks up to the other end of the table, where Philip Swallow and Robin Dempsey were vying to entertain Angelica Pabst.

"If you are looking for the gravy, young man, it's right under your nose."

This observation came from an elderly lady sitting opposite Persse. Though her tone was sharp, her face was friendly, and she allowed herself a smile of complicity when Persse expressed his opinion that the beef was beyond the help of gravy. She wore a black silk dress of antique design and her white hair was neatly retained in a snood decorated with tiny beads of jet. Her name badge identified her as Miss Sybil Maiden, of Girton College, Cambridge. "Retired many years ago," she explained. "But I still attend these conferences whenever I can. It helps to keep me young."

Persse enquired about her scholarly interests.

"I suppose you would call me a folklorist," she said. "I was a pupil of Jessie Weston's. What is your own line of research?"

"I did my Master's thesis on Shakespeare and T. S. Eliot."

"Then you are no doubt familiar with Miss Weston's book, *From Ritual to Romance*, on which Mr Eliot drew for much of the imagery and allusion in *The Waste Land*?"

"Indeed I am," said Persse.

"She argued," Miss Maiden continued, not at all deterred by this answer, "that the quest for the Holy Grail, associated with the Arthurian knights, was only superficially a Christian legend, and that its true meaning was to be sought in pagan fertility ritual. If Mr Eliot had taken her discoveries to heart, we might have been spared the maudlin religiosity of his later poetry."

"Well," said Persse placatingly, "I suppose everyone is looking for his own Grail. For Eliot it was religious faith, but for another it might be fame, or the love of a good woman."

"Would you mind passing the gravy?" said the Oxford medievalist. Persse obliged.

"It all comes down to sex, in the end," Miss Maiden declared firmly. "The life force endlessly renewing itself." She fixed the gravy boat in the Oxford medievalist's hand with a beady eye. "The Grail cup, for instance, is a female symbol of great antiquity and universal occurrence." (The Oxford medievalist seemed to have second thoughts about helping himself to gravy.) "And the Grail spear, supposed to be the one that pierced the side of Christ, is obviously phallic. *The Waste Land* is really all about Eliot's fears of impotence and sterility."

"I've heard that theory before," said Persse, "But I feel it's too simple."

"I quite agree," said the Oxford medievalist. "This business of phallic symbolism is a lot of rot." He stabbed the air with his knife to emphasize the point.

Preoccupied with this discussion, Persse failed to observe when Angelica left the dining-room. He looked for her in the bar, but she was not to be found there, or anywhere else that evening. Persse went to bed early, and tossed restlessly on his narrow lumpy mattress, listening to the plumbing whining in the walls, footfalls in the corridor outside his room, and the sounds of doors slamming and engines starting in the car park beneath his window. Once he thought he heard the voice of Angelica calling "Goodnight," but by the time he got to the window there was nothing to be seen except the fading embers of a departing car's rear lights. Before he got back into bed he switched on the lamp above his sink, and stared critically at his reflection in the mirror. He saw a white, round, freckled face, snub nose, pale blue eyes, and a mop of red curly hair. "I wouldn't say you were handsome, exactly," he murmured. "But I've seen uglier mugs."

Angelica was not present at the first formal session of the conference the next morning, which was one reason why Persse muttered "April is the cruellest month" under his breath as he sat in the lecture-room. Other reasons included the continuing cold, damp weather, which had not been anticipated by the Rummidge heating engineers, the inedibility of the bacon and tomatoes served at breakfast that morning, and the tedium of the paper to which he was listening. It was being given by the Oxford medievalist and was on the subject of Chaucerian metrics. He had heard the substance of it already, last night at dinner, and it did not improve on reacquaintance.

Persse yawned and shifted his weight from one buttock to another in his seat at the back of the lecture-room. He could not see the faces of many of his colleagues, but as far as could be judged from their postures, most of them were as disengaged from the discourse as himself. Some were leaning back as far as their seats allowed, staring vacantly at the ceiling, others were slumped forwards onto the desks that separated each row, resting their chins on folded arms, and others again were sprawled sideways over two or three seats, with their legs crossed and arms dangling limply to the floor. In the third row a man was surreptitiously doing *The Times* crossword, and at least three people appeared to be asleep. Someone, a student presumably, had carved into the surface of the desk at which Persse sat, cutting deep into the wood with the force of a man driven to the limits of endurance, the word "BORING". Another had scratched the message, *"Swallow is a wanker."* Persse saw no reason to dissent from either of these judgments.

Suddenly, though, there were signs of animation in the audience. The speaker was commencing his peroration, and had made reference to something called "structuralism".

"Of course, to our friends across the Channel," he said, with a slight curl of his lip, "everything I have been saying will seem vanity and illusion. To the structuralists, metre, like language itself, is merely a system of differences. The idea that there might be anything inherently expressive or mimetic in patterns of stress would be anathema . . ."

Some, probably the majority, of the audience, smiled and nodded and nudged each other. Others frowned, bit their lips and began making rapid notes. The question session, chaired by the Aberystwyth medievalist, was lively.

There followed a break for coffee, which was served in a small common-room not far away. Persse was delighted to find Angelica already ensconced here, fetchingly dressed in a roll-neck jumper, tweed skirt and high leather boots. Her cheeks had a healthy glow. She had been for a walk. "I slept through breakfast," she explained, "and I was too late for the lecture."

"You didn't miss much," said Persse. "Both were indigestible. What happened to you last night? I looked all over for you."

"Oh, Professor Swallow asked some people back to his house for a drink."

"You're a friend of his, then, are you?"

"No. Well, not really. I've never met him before, if that's what you mean. But he *is* very friendly."

"Hmmph," said Persse.

"What was the paper about, this morning?" Angelica asked.

"It was supposed to be about Chaucer's metre, but the discussion was mostly about structuralism."

Angelica looked annoyed. "Oh, what a nuisance that I missed it. I'm very interested in structuralism."

"What is it, exactly?"

Angelica laughed.

"No, I'm serious," said Persse. "What is structuralism? Is it a good thing or a bad thing?"

Angelica looked puzzled, and wary of having her leg pulled. "But you must know something about it, Persse. You must have *heard of* it, even in . . . Where did you do your graduate work?"

"University College Dublin. But I wasn't there much of the time. I had TB, you see. They were very decent about it, let me work on my dissertation in the sanatorium. I had a visit from my supervisor occasionally, but mostly I worked on my own. Then before that, I did my BA at Galway. We never heard anything about structuralism there. Then after I got my Master's degree, I went home to work on the farm for two years. My people are farmers, in county Mayo."

"Did you mean to be a farmer yourself?"

"No, it was to get my strength back, after the TB. The doctors said an open-air life was the thing."

"And did you—get your strength back?"

"Oh yes, I'm sound as a bell, now." He struck himself vigorously on the chest. "Then I got the job at Limerick."

"You were lucky. Jobs are hard to find these days."

"I *was* lucky," Persse agreed. "Indeed I was. I found out afterwards that I was called to the interview by mistake. They really meant to interview another fellow called McGarrigle—some high-flying prize scholar from Trinity. But the letter was addressed to me—someone slipped up in the Registry—and they were too embarrassed to retract the invitation."

"Well, you made the most of the lucky break," said Angelica. "They could have appointed one of the other candidates."

"Well, that was another piece of luck," said Persse. "There *were* no other candidates—not called for interview anyway. They were quite sure they wanted to appoint this McGarrigle fellow, and they were after saving train fares. Anyway, what I'm trying to say is that I've never been in what you might call the swim, intellectually speaking. That's why I've come to this conference. To improve myself. To find out what's going on in the great world of ideas. Who's in, who's out, and all that. So tell me about structuralism."

Angelica took a deep breath, then expelled it abruptly. "It's hard to know where to start," she said. A bell sounded to summon them back to the lecture room. "Saved by the bell!" she laughed.

"Later, then," Persse urged.

"I'll see what I can do," said Angelica.

As the conferees shuffled back towards the lecture-room for the second paper of the morning, they cast wistful glances over their shoulders at the figure of the Oxford medievalist shaking hands with Philip Swallow. He had his overcoat on and his briefcase in his hand. "That's the trouble with these conferences," Persse heard someone say, "the chief speakers tend to bugger off as soon as they've done their party piece. Makes you feel like a besieged army when the general flies out in a helicopter."

"Are you coming, Persse?" Angelica enquired.

Persse looked at his programme. " 'Animal Imagery in Dryden's Heroic Tragedies'," he read aloud.

"It could be interesting," Angelica said earnestly.

"I think I'll sit this one out," said Persse. "I think I'll write a poem instead."

"Oh, do you write poetry? What kind?"

"Short poems," said Persse. "Very short poems."

"Like *haikus*?"

"Shorter than that, sometimes."

"Goodness! What are you going to write about?"

"You can read it when it's finished."

"All right. I'll look forward to that. I'd better go." A vaguely smiling Philip Swallow hovered nearby, like a sheepdog rounding up strays.

"I'll see you in the bar before lunch, then," said Persse. He made a show of hurrying to the Gents, intending to loiter there until the lecture on Dryden had begun. To his consternation, however, Philip Swallow, accompanied by Bob Busby, followed him. Persse locked himself in a closet and sat down on the toilet seat. The two men seemed to be talking about a missing speaker as they stood at the urinal. "When did he phone?" Philip Swallow was saying, and Busby replied, "About two hours ago. He said he would do his best to get here by this afternoon. I told him to spare no expense." "Did you?" said Swallow. "I'm not sure that was entirely wise, Bob."

Persse heard the spurt of tapwater at the sinks, the rattle of the towel dispenser, and the banging of the door as the two men left. After a minute or two, he emerged from hiding and quietly approached the lecture-room. He peered through the little observation window in the door. He could see Angelica in profile, sitting alone in the front row, gracefully alert, a stainless-steel ballpen poised in one hand, ready to take notes. She was wearing spectacles with heavy black frames, which made her look formidably efficient, like a high-powered secretary. The rest of the audience was performing the same tableau of petrified boredom as before. Persse tiptoed away, and out into the open air. He crossed the campus and took the road that led to the site of the halls of residence.

The melting snow dripped from the trees, and ran down the back of his neck as he walked, but he was oblivious to the discomfort. He was trying to compose a poem about Angelica Pabst. Unfortunately some lines of W. B. Yeats kept interposing themselves between him and his muse, and the best he could do was to adapt them to his own case.

> *How can I, that girl standing here,*
> *My attention fix*
> *On Chaucer or on Dryden*
> *Or structuralist poetics?*

As he recited the words to himself, it occurred to Persse McGarrigle that perhaps he was in love. "I am in love," he said aloud, to the dripping trees, to a white-bonneted pillar-box, to a sodden mongrel lifting its hind leg against the gatepost of the halls of residence site. "I am in love!" he exclaimed, to a long line of depressed-looking sparrows perched on the railings that ran alongside the slushy drive. "I AM IN LOVE!" he cried, startling a gaggle of geese beside the artificial lake, as he ran up and down, round and round, in the virgin snow, leaving a trail of deep footprints behind him.

Panting from this exercise, he came up to the entrance of Lucas Hall, the tall tower block in which sleeping accommodation had been provided for the conferees. (Martineau Hall, in which they ate and drank, was in contrast, a low cylindrical building, confirming Miss Maiden's views on the universality of sexual symbolism.) A taxi was drawn up outside Lucas Hall, its engine churning, and a thickset man with a fat cigar in his mouth, and a deerstalker, with the flaps down, on his head, was getting out. Seeing Persse, he called "Hi" and beckoned. "Say, is this where the conference is being held?'' he asked, in an American accent. "The University Teachers of English Conference? It's the right name, but it doesn't look right.''

"This is where we're sleeping," said Persse. "The meetings are held on the main campus, up the road.''

"Ah, that figures," said the man. "OK, driver, we made it. How much?''

"Forty-six pounds eight, guv'nor," the man appeared to say, looking at his meter.

"OK, there you go," said the newcomer, stripping ten crisp new five-pound notes from a thick wad, and pushing them through the cab window. The driver, catching sight of Persse, leaned out and addressed him. "You don't wanner cab to London by any chance?''

"No thank you," said Persse.

"I'll be on my way, then. Thanks guv'nor.''

Awed by this display of wealth, Persse picked up the new arrival's suitcase, a handsome leather affair with the vestiges of many labels on it, and carried it into the lobby of Lucas Hall. "Have you really and truly come all the way from London by taxi?'' he said.

"I had no choice. When I landed at Heathrow this morning they tell me that my connecting flight is cancelled, Rummidge airport is socked in by snow. They give me a railroad ticket instead. So I take a cab to the railroad station in London and they tell me the power lines for the trains to Rummidge are down. Great drama, the country paralysed, Rummidge cut off from the capital, everybody enjoying every minute of it, the porters can hardly contain their joy. When I said I'd take a cab all the way, they said I was crazy, tried to talk me out of it. *'You'll never get through,'* they said, *'the motorways are covered in snowdrifts, there are people who have been trapped in their cars all night.'* So I go along the cab rank till I find a driver with the guts to give it a whirl, and what do we find when we get here? Two inches of melting snow. What a country!'' He took off his deerstalker and held it at arm's length. It was made from a hairy tweed, with a bold red check on a yellowy-brown background. "I bought this hat at Heathrow this morning," he said. "The first thing I always seem to have to do when I arrive in England is buy myself a hat.''

"It's a fine hat," said Persse.

"You like it? Remind me to give it to you when I leave. I'm travelling on to warmer climes.''

"That's very kind of you.''

"You're welcome. Now, where do I check in?''

"There's a list of rooms over here," said Persse. "What's your name?''

"Morris Zapp.''

"I'm sure I've heard that name before.''

"I should hope so. What's yours?''

"Persse McGarrigle, from Limerick. Aren't you giving a paper this afternoon?" he said. " 'Title to be announced'?''

"Right, Percy. That's why I strained every nerve to get here. Look at the bottom of the list. There are never many zees.''

Persse looked. "It says here that you're a non-resident.''

"Ah, yeah, Philip Swallow said something about staying with him. How's it going, the Conference?''

"I can't really say. I've never been to a conference before, so I've no standards of comparison.''

"Is that right?" Morris Zapp regarded him with curiosity. "A conference virgin, huh? Where is everybody, by the way?''

"They're at a lecture.''

"Which you cut? Well, you've learned the first rule of conferences, kid. Never go to lectures. Unless you're giving one yourself, of course. Or *I'm* giving one," he added reflectively. "I wouldn't want to discourage you from hearing my paper this afternoon. I went over it last night in the plane, while the movie was showing, and I was pretty pleased with it. The movie was OK, too. What size of audience am I likely to get?''

"Well, there are fifty-seven people at the conference, altogether," Persse said.

Professor Zapp nearly swallowed his cigar. "*Fifty-seven?* You must be joking. No? You're not joking? You mean I've travelled six thousand miles to talk to fifty-seven people?''

"Of course, not everybody goes to every lecture," said Persse. "As you can see."

"Listen, do you know how many attended the American equivalent of this conference? *Ten thousand*. There were ten thousand people at the MLA in New York last December."

"I don't think we have that many lecturers over here," said Persse apologetically.

"There must be more than fifty-seven," growled Morris Zapp. "Where are they? I'll tell you where. Most of them are holed up at home, decorating their living-rooms or weeding their gardens, and the few with two original ideas to rub together are off somewhere at conferences in warmer, more attractive places than this." He looked around the lobby of Lucas Hall, at its cracked and dusty floor tiles, its walls of grimy untreated concrete, with disfavour. "Is there anywhere you can get a drink in this place?"

"The bar will be opening soon in Martineau Hall," said Persse.

"Lead me to it."

"Have you really flown all the way from America for this conference, Professor Zapp?" Persse enquired, as they picked their way through the slush.

"Not exactly. I was coming to Europe anyway—I'm on sabbatical this quarter. Philip Swallow heard I was coming over and asked me to take in his conference. So, to oblige an old friend, I said I would."

The bar in Martineau Hall was empty except for the barman, who watched their approach through a kind of chrome-plated portcullis that stretched from counter to ceiling.

"Is this to keep you in, or us out?" quipped Morris Zapp, tapping the metal. "What's yours, Percy? Guinness? A pint of Guinness, barman, and a large scotch on the rocks."

"We're not open yet," said the man. "Not till twelve-thirty."

"And have something yourself."

"Yes, sir, thank you sir," said the barman, cranking the

portcullis with alacrity. "I wouldn't say no to a pint of bitter."

While he was drawing the draught Guinness, the other conferees, released from the second lecture of the morning, began to straggle in, Philip Swallow in the van. He strode up to Morris Zapp and wrung his hand.

"Morris! It's marvellous to see you after—how many years?"

"Ten, Philip, ten years, though I hate to admit it. But you're looking good. The beard is terrific. Was your hair always that colour?"

Philip Swallow blushed. "I think it was starting to go grey in '69. How did you get here in the end?"

"That'll be one pound fifty, sir," said the barman.

"By taxi," said Morris Zapp. "Which reminds me: you owe me fifty pounds for the cab fare. Hey, what's the matter, Philip? You've gone white."

"And the Conference has just gone into the red," said Rupert Sutcliffe, with doleful satisfaction. "Hello, Zapp, I don't suppose you remember me."

"Rupert! How could I ever forget that happy face? And here comes Bob Busby, right on cue," said Morris Zapp, as a man with a less impressive beard than Philip Swallow's cantered into the bar, a clipboard under his arm, keys and coins jingling in his pockets. Philip Swallow took him aside and urgent whispers were exchanged.

"I'm afraid you're landed with me as your chairman this afternoon, Zapp," said Rupert Sutcliffe.

"I'm honoured, Rupert."

"Have you, er, decided on a title?"

"Yep. It's called, 'Textuality as Striptease'."

"Oh," said Rupert Sutcliffe.

"Does everybody know this young man, who kindly looked after me when I arrived? "said Morris Zapp. "Percy McGarrigle from Limerick."

Philip Swallow nodded perfunctorily at Persse and turned his attention back to the American. "Morris, we must get you a lapel badge so that everybody will know who you are."

"Don't worry, if they don't know already, I'll tell them."

"When I said 'Take a cab,'" said Bob Busby reproachfully to Morris Zapp, "I meant from Heathrow to Euston, not from London to Rummidge."

"Never mind that now," said Philip Swallow impatiently. "It's no use crying over spilt milk. Morris, where is your luggage? I thought you'd be more comfortable staying with us than in Hall."

"I think so too, now I've seen the hall," said Morris Zapp.

"Hilary is dying to see you," said Swallow, leading him away.

"Hmm. That should be an interesting reunion," murmured Rupert Sutcliffe, peering at the departing pair over his glasses.

"What?" Persse responded absently. He was looking out for Angelica.

"Well, you see, about ten years ago those two were nominated for our exchange scheme with Euphoria—in America, you know. Zapp came here for six months, and Swallow went to Euphoric State. Rumour has it that Zapp had an affair with Hilary Swallow, and Swallow with Mrs Zapp."

"You don't say so?" Persse was intrigued by this story, in spite of the distraction of seeing Angelica come into the bar with Robin Dempsey. He was talking to her with great animation, while she wore the slightly fixed smile of someone who is being sung at in a musical comedy.

"Quite. 'What a set,' as Matthew Arnold said of the Shelley circle . . . Anyway, at the same time, Gordon Masters, our Head of Department, retired prematurely after a nervous breakdown—it was 1969, the year of the student revolution, a trying time for everybody—and Zapp was being mooted by some as his successor. One day, however, just when things were coming to a head, he and Hilary Swallow suddenly flew off to America together, and we really didn't know which couple to expect back: Zapp and Hilary, Philip and Hilary, Philip and Mrs Zapp, or both Zapps."

"What was Mrs Zapp's name?" said Persse.

"I've forgotten," said Rupert Sutcliffe. "Does it matter?"

"I like to know names," said Persse. "I can't follow a story without them."

"Anyway, we never saw her. The Swallows returned together. We gathered they were going to give the marriage another chance."

"It seems to have worked."

"Mmm. Though in my opinion," Sutcliffe said darkly, "the whole episode had a deplorable effect on Swallow's character."

"Oh?"

Sutcliffe nodded, but seemed disinclined to elaborate.

"So then they gave Philip Swallow the chair?" said Persse.

"Not *then,* oh goodness me, no. No, then we had Dalton, he came from Oxford, until three years ago. He was killed in a car accident. Then they appointed Swallow. Some people would have preferred me, I believe, but I'm getting too old for that sort of thing."

"Oh, surely not," said Persse, because Rupert Sutcliffe seemed to hope he would.

"I'll say one thing," Sutcliffe volunteered. "If they'd appointed me, they'd have had a Head of Department who stuck to his last, and wasn't flying off here there and everywhere all the time."

"Travels a lot, does he—Professor Swallow?"

"Lately he seems to be absent more often than he's present."

Persse excused himself and pushed his way through a crowd at the bar to where Angelica was waiting for Dempsey to bring her a drink. "Hallo, how was the lecture?" he greeted her.

"Boring. But there was an interesting discussion of structuralism afterwards."

"Again? You've really got to tell me what structuralism is all about. It's a matter of urgency."

"Structuralism?" said Dempsey, coming up with a sherry for Angelica just in time to hear Persse's plea, and all too eager to show off his expertise. "It all goes back to Saussure's linguistics. The arbitrariness of the signifier. Language as a system of differences with no positive terms."

"Give me an example," said Persse. "I can't follow an argument without an example."

"Well, take the words *dog* and *cat*. There's no absolute reason why the combined phonemes *d-o-g* should signify a quadruped that goes 'woof woof' rather one that goes 'miaou'. It's a purely arbitrary relationship, and there's no reason why English speakers shouldn't decide that from tomorrow, *d-o-g* would signify 'cat' and *c-a-t,* 'dog'."

"Wouldn't it confuse the animals?" said Persse.

"The animals would adjust in time, like everyone else," said Dempsey. "We know this because the same animal is signified by different acoustic images in different natural languages. For instance, 'dog' is *chien* in French, *Hund* in German, *cane* in Italian, and so on. 'Cat' is *chat, Katze, gatto,* according to what part of the Common Market you happen to be in. And if we are to believe language rather than our ears, English dogs go *'woof woof'*, French dogs go *'wouah wouah'*, German dogs go *'wau wau'* and Italian ones *'baau baau'*."

"Hallo, this sounds like a game of Animal Snap. Can anyone play?" said Philip Swallow. He had returned to the bar with Morris Zapp, now provided with a lapel badge. "Dempsey—you remember Morris of course?"

"I was just explaining structuralism to this young man," said Dempsey, when greetings had been exchanged. "But you never did have much time for linguistics, did you Swallow?"

"Can't say I did, no. I never could remember which came first, the morphemes or the phonemes. And one look at a tree-diagram makes my mind go blank."

"Or blanker," said Dempsey with a sneer.

An embarrassed silence ensued. It was broken by Angelica. "Actually," she said meekly, "Jakobson cites the gradation of positive, comparative and superlative forms of the adjective as evidence that language is not a totally arbitrary system. For instance: *blank, blanker, blankest*. The more phonemes, the more emphasis. The same is true of other Indo-European languages, for instance Latin: *vacuus, vacuior, vacuissimus*. There does seem to be some iconic correlation between sound and sense across the boundaries of natural languages.''

The four men gaped at her.

"Who is this prodigy?" said Morris Zapp. "Won't somebody introduce me?"

"Oh, I'm sorry," said Philip Swallow. "Miss Pabst— Professor Zapp."

"Morris, please," said the American professor, extending his hand, and peering at Angelica's lapel badge. "Glad to met you Al."

"That was marvellous," said Persse to Angelica, later, at lunch. "The way you put that Dempsey fellow in his place."

"I hope I wasn't rude," said Angelica. "Basically he's right of course. Different languages divide up the world differently. For instance, this mutton we're eating. In French there's only one word for 'sheep' and 'mutton'— *mouton*. So you can't say 'dead as mutton' in French, you'd be saying 'dead as a sheep', which would be absurd."

"I don't know, this tastes more like dead sheep than mutton to me," said Persse, pushing his plate aside. An overalled lady with bright yellow curls pushing a trolley piled high with plates of half-eaten food took it from the table. "Finished, love?" she said. "I don't blame you. Not very nice, is it?"

"Did you write your poem?" said Angelica.

"I'll let you read it tonight. You have to come to the top floor of Lucas Hall."

"Is that where your room is?"

"No."

"Why then?"

"You'll see."

"A mystery." Angelica smiled, wrinkling her nose. "I like a mystery."

"Ten o'clock on the top floor. The moon will be up by then."

"Are you sure this isn't just an excuse for a romantic tryst?"

"Well, you said your research topic was romance . . ."

"And you thought you'd give me some more material? Alas, I've got too much already. I've read hundreds of romances. Classical romances and medieval romances, renaissance romances and modern romances. Heliodorus and Apuleius, Chrétien de Troyes and Malory, Ariosto and Spenser, Keats and Barbara Cartland. I don't need any more data. What I need is a theory to explain it all."

"Theory?" Philip Swallow's ears quivered under their silvery thatch, a few places further up the table. "That word brings out the Goering in me. When I hear it I reach for my revolver."

"Then you're not going to like my lecture, Philip," said Morris Zapp.

In the event, not many people did like Morris Zapp's lecture, and several members of the audience walked out before he had finished. Rupert Sutcliffe, obliged as chairman to sit facing the audience, assumed an aspect of glazed impassivity, but by imperceptible degrees the corners of his mouth turned down at more and more acute angles and his spectacles slid further and further down his nose as the discourse proceeded. Morris Zapp delivered it striding up and down the platform with his notes in one hand and a fat cigar in the other. "You see before you," he began, "a man who once believed in the possibility of interpretation. That is, I thought that the goal of reading was to establish the meaning of texts. I used to be a Jane Austen man. I think I can say in all modesty I was *the* Jane Austen man. I wrote five books on Jane Austen, every one of which was trying to establish what her novels meant—and, naturally, to prove that no one had properly understood what they meant before. Then I began a commentary on the works of Jane Austen, the aim of which was to be utterly exhaustive, to examine the novels from every conceivable angle—historical, biographical, rhetorical, mythical, structural, Freudian, Jungian,

Marxist, existentialist, Christian, allegorical, ethical, phenomenological, archetypal, you name it. So that when each commentary was written, there would be *nothing further to say* about the novel in question.

"Of course, I never finished it. The project was not so much Utopian as self-defeating. By that I don't just mean that if successful it would have eventually put us all out of business. I mean that it couldn't succeed because it isn't possible, and it isn't possible because of the nature of language itself, in which meaning is constantly being transferred from one signifier to another and can never be absolutely possessed.

"To understand a message is to decode it. Language is a code. *But every decoding is another encoding.* If you say something to me I check that I have understood your message by saying it back to you in my own words, that is, different words from the ones you used, for if I repeat your own words exactly you will doubt whether I have really understood you. But if I use *my* words it follows that I have changed *your* meaning, however slightly; and even if I were, deviantly, to indicate my comprehension by repeating back to you your own unaltered words, that is no guarantee that I have duplicated your meaning in my head, because I bring a different experience of language, literature, and non-verbal reality to those words, therefore they mean something different to me from what they mean to you. And if you think I have not understood the meaning of your message, you do not simply repeat it in the same words, you try to explain it in different words, different from the ones you used originally; but then the *it* is no longer the *it* that you started with. And for that matter, you are not the *you* that you started with. Time has moved on since you opened your mouth to speak, the molecules in your body have changed, what you intended to say has been superseded by what you did say, and that has already become part of your personal history, imperfectly remembered. Conversation is like playing tennis with a ball made of Krazy Putty that keeps coming back over the net in a different shape.

"Reading, of course, is different from conversation. It is more passive in the sense that we can't interact with the text, we can't affect the development of the text by our own words, since the text's words are already given. That is what perhaps encourages the quest for interpretation. If the words are fixed once and for all, on the page, may not their meaning be fixed also? Not so, because the same axiom, *every decoding is another encoding,* applies to literary criticism even more stringently than it does to ordinary spoken discourse. In ordinary spoken discourse, the endless cycle of encoding-decoding-encoding may be terminated by an action, as when for instance I say, 'The door is open,' and you say, 'Do you mean you would like me to shut it?' and I say, 'If you don't mind,' and you shut the door—we may be satisfied that at a certain level my meaning has been understood. But if the literary text says, 'The door was open,' I cannot ask the text what it means by saying that the door was open, I can only speculate about the significance of that door—opened by what agency, leading to what discovery, mystery, goal? The tennis analogy will not do for the activity of reading—it is not a to-and-fro process, but an endless, tantalising leading on, a flirtation without consummation, or if there is consummation, it is solitary, masturbatory. [Here the audience grew restive.] The reader plays with himself as the text plays upon him, plays upon his curiosity, desire, as a striptease dancer plays upon her audience's curiosity and desire.

"Now, as some of you know, I come from a city notorious for its bars and nightclubs featuring topless and bottomless dancers. I am told—I have not personally patronized these places, but I am told on the authority of no less a person than your host at this conference, my old friend Philip Swallow, who *has* patronized them, [here several members of the audience turned in their seats to stare and grin at Philip Swallow, who blushed to the roots of his silver-grey hair] that the girls take off all their clothes before they commence dancing in front of the customers. This is not striptease, it is all strip and no tease, it is the terpsichorean equivalent of the hermeneutic fallacy of a recuperable meaning, which claims that if we remove the clothing of its rhetoric from a literary text we discover the bare facts it is trying to communicate. The classical tradition of striptease, however, which goes back to Salome's dance of the seven veils and beyond, and which survives in a debased form in the dives of your Soho, offers a valid metaphor for the activity of reading. The dancer teases the audience, as the text teases its readers, with the promise of an ultimate revelation that is infinitely postponed. Veil after veil, garment after garment, is removed, but it is the *delay* in the stripping that makes it exciting, not the stripping itself; because no sooner has one secret been revealed than we lose interest in it and crave another. When we have seen the girl's underwear we want to see her body, when we have seen her breasts we want to see her buttocks, and when we have seen her buttocks we want to see her pubis, and when we see her pubis, the dance ends—but is our curiosity and desire satisfied? Of course not. The vagina remains hidden within the girl's body, shaded by her pubic hair, and even if she were to spread her legs before us [at this point several ladies in the audience noisily departed] it would still not satisfy the curiosity and desire set in motion by the stripping. Staring into that orifice we find that we have somehow overshot the goal of our quest, gone beyond pleasure in contemplated beauty; gazing into the womb we are returned to the mystery of our own origins. Just so in reading. The attempt to peer into the very core of a text, to possess once and for all its meaning, in vain—it is only ourselves that we find there, not the work itself. Freud said that obsessive reading (and I suppose that most of us in this room must be regarded as compulsive readers)—that obsessive reading is the displaced expression of a desire to see the mother's genitals [here a young man in the audience fainted and was carried out] but the point of the remark, which may not have been entirely appreciated by Freud himself, lies precisely in the concept of displacement. To read is to surrender oneself to an endless displacement of curiosity and desire from one sentence to another, from one action to another, from one level of the text to another. The text unveils itself before us, but never allows itself to be possessed; and instead of striving to possess it we should take pleasure in its teasing.''

Morris Zapp went on to illustrate his thesis with a number

of passages from classic English and American literature. When he sat down, there was scattered and uneven applause.

"The floor is now open for discussion," said Rupert Sutcliffe, surveying the audience apprehensively over the rims of his glasses. "Are there any questions or comments?"

There was a long silence. Then Philip Swallow stood up. "I have listened to your paper with great interest, Morris," he said. "Great interest. Your mind has lost none of its sharpness since we first met. But I am sorry to see that in the intervening years you have succumbed to the virus of structuralism."

"I wouldn't call myself a structuralist," Morris Zapp interrupted, "A post-structuralist, perhaps."

Philip Swallow made a gesture implying impatience with such subtle distinctions. "I refer to that fundamental scepticism about the possibility of achieving certainty about anything, which I associate with the mischievous influence of Continental theorizing. There was a time when reading was a comparatively simple matter, something you learned to do in primary school. Now it seems to be some kind of arcane mystery, into which only a small élite have been initiated. I have been reading books for their meaning all my life—or at least that is what I have always thought I was doing. Apparently I was mistaken."

"You weren't mistaken about what you were trying to do," said Morris Zapp, relighting his cigar, "you were mistaken in trying to do it."

"I have just one question," said Philip Swallow. "It is this: what, with the greatest respect, is the point of our discussing your paper if, according to your own theory, we should not be discussing what you actually *said* at all, but discussing some imperfect memory or subjective interpretation of what you said?"

"There is no point," said Morris Zapp blithely. "If by point you mean the hope of arriving at some certain truth. But when did you ever discover *that* in a question-and-discussion session? Be honest, have you ever been to a lecture or seminar at the end of which you could have found two people present who could agree on the simplest précis of what had been said?"

"Then what in God's name *is* the point of it all?" cried Philip Swallow, throwing his hands into the air.

"The point, of course, is to uphold the institution of academic literary studies. We maintain our position in society by publicly performing a certain ritual, just like any other group of workers in the realm of discourse—lawyers, politicians, journalists. And as it looks as if we have done our duty for today, shall we all adjourn for a drink?"

"Tea, I'm afraid it will have to be," said Rupert Sutcliffe, clutching with relief this invitation to bring the proceedings to a speedy close. "Thank you *very* much for a most, er, stimulating and, ah, suggestive lecture."

" 'Suggestive and stimulating'—the old fellow hit the nail on the head," said Persse to Angelica as they filed out of the lecture room. "Does your mother know you're away out listening to that sort of language?"

"I thought it was interesting," said Angelica. "Of course, it all goes back to Peirce."

"Me?"

"Peirce. Another variant spelling of your name. He was an American philosopher. He wrote somewhere about the impossibility of stripping the veils of representation from meaning. And that was before the First World War."

"Was it, indeed? You're a remarkably well-read young woman, Angelica, do you know that? Where were you educated at all?"

"Oh, various places," she said vaguely. "Mainly England and America."

They passed Rupert Sutcliffe and Philip Swallow in the corridor, in urgent consultation with Bob Busby, apparently about theatre tickets. "Are you going to the Repertory Theatre tonight?" said Angelica.

"I didn't put down to go. It didn't say on the form what the play was."

"I believe it's *Lear*."

"Are you going, then?" Persse asked anxiously. "What about my poem?"

"Your poem? Oh dear, I forgot. Ten o'clock on the top floor, wasn't it? I'll try and get back promptly. Professor Dempsey is taking me in his car, so that will save time."

"Dempsey? You want to be careful of that fellow, you know. He preys on young women like yourself. He told me so."

Angelica laughed. "I can take care of myself."

They found Morris Zapp drinking tea alone in the common room, the other conferees having left a kind of *cordon sanitaire* around him. Angelica went boldly up to the American.

"Professor Zapp, I did so enjoy your lecture," she said, with a greater degree of enthusiasm than Persse had expected or could, indeed, bring himself to approve.

"Well, thank you, Al," said Morris Zapp. "I certainly enjoyed giving it. I seem to have offended the natives, though."

"I'm working on the subject of romance for my doctorate," said Angelica, "and it seemed to me that a lot of what you were saying applied very well to romance."

"Naturally," said Morris Zapp. "It applies to everything."

"I mean, the idea of romance as narrative striptease, the endless leading on of the reader, a repeated postponement of an ultimate revelation which never comes—or, when it does, terminates the pleasure of the text . . ."

"Exactly," said Morris Zapp.

"And there's even a good deal of actual striptease in the romances."

"There is?" said Morris Zapp. "Yes, I guess there is."

"Ariosto's heroines for instance, are always losing their clothes and being gloated over by the heroes who rescue them."

"It's a long time since I read Ariosto," said Morris Zapp.

"And of course, *The Faerie Queen*—the two girls in the fountain in the Bower of Blisse . . ."

"I must look at that again," said Morris Zapp.

"Then there's Madeline undressing under the gaze of Porphyro in 'St Agnes' Eve'."

"Right, 'St Agnes' Eve'."

"Geraldine in 'Christabel'."

"—'Christabel'—"

At this point Philip Swallow came bustling up. "Morris, I hope you didn't mind my having a go at you just now—"

"Of course not, Philip. *Vive le sport*."

"Only nobody else seemed inclined to speak, and I *am* very concerned about these matters, I really think the subject is in a state of crisis—" He broke off, as Angelica politely backed away. "Oh, I'm sorry, have I interrupted something?"

"It's quite all right, we've finished," said Angelica. "Thank you very much, Professor Zapp, you've been most helpful."

"Any time, Al."

"Actually, you know, my name is Angelica," she smiled.

"Well, I thought Al must be short for something," said Morris Zapp. "Let me know if I can give you any more help."

"He didn't give you any help at all," said Persse indignantly, as they helped themselves to tea and biscuits. "You provided the ideas *and* the examples."

"Well, his lecture provided the stimulus."

"You told me he cribbed it all from the other fellow, my namesake."

"I didn't say he cribbed it, silly. Just that Peirce had the same idea."

"Why didn't you tell Zapp that?"

"You have to treat these professors carefully, Persse," said Angelica, with a sly smile. "You have to flatter them a bit."

"Ah, Angelica!" A bright blue suit interposed itself between them. "I'd like to discuss that very interesting idea of Jakobson's you mentioned this morning," said Robin Dempsey. "We can't allow McGarrigle to monopolize you for the duration of the conference."

"I need to see Dr Busby, anyway," said Persse, retiring with dignity.

He found Bob Busby in the conference office. A young man from London University, whom Persse had overheard making the remark about generals deserting their armies at the coffee break that morning, was waving a theatre ticket under Busby's nose.

"Are you trying to tell me that this ticket isn't for *Lear* after all?" he was saying.

"Well, unfortunately, the Rep has postponed the opening of *King Lear*," said Busby apologetically. "And extended the run of the Christmas pantomime."

"Pantomime? *Pantomime*?"

"It's the only production in the whole year that makes a profit, you can't really blame them," said Busby. *"Puss in Boots*. I believe it's very good."

"Jesus wept," said the young man. "Is there any chance of getting my money back on the ticket?"

"I'm afraid it's too late now," said Busby.

"I'll buy it," said Persse.

"I say, will you really?" said the young man turning round. "It costs two pounds fifty. You can have it for two quid."

"Thanks," said Persse, handing over the money.

"Don't go telling everybody it's *Puss in Boots*," Busby pleaded. "I'm making out it's a sort of mystery trip."

"It's a mystery to me," said the young man, "why any of us came to this Godforsaken hole in the first place."

"Oh, it's not as bad as all that," said Busby. "It's very central."

"Central to what?"

Bob Busby frowned reflectively. "Well, since they opened the M50 I can get to Tintern Abbey, door to door, in ninety-five minutes."

"Go there often, do you?" said the young man. He fingered Persse's pound notes speculatively. "Is there a good fish-and-chip shop near here? I'm starving. Haven't been able to eat a thing since I arrived."

"There's a Chinese takeaway at the second traffic lights on the London Road," said Bob Busby. "I'm sorry that you're not enjoying the food. Still, there's always tomorrow night to look forward to."

"What happens tomorrow night?"

"A medieval banquet!" said Busby, beaming with pride.

"I can hardly wait," said the young man, as he left.

"I thought it would make a rather nice climax to the conference," said Bob Busby to Persse. "We're having an outside firm in to supervise the catering and provide the entertainment. There'll be mead, and minstrels and''—he rubbed his hands together in anticipatory glee—''wenches.''

''My word,'' said Persse. ''Life runs very high in Rummidge, surely. By the way, do you have a streetplan of the city? There's an aunty of mine living here, and I ought to call on her. The address is Gittings Road.''

''Why, that's not far from here!'' Busby exclaimed. ''Walking distance. I'll draw you a map.''

Following Busby's directions, Philip left the campus, walked through some quiet residential streets lined with large, handsome houses, their snowy drives scored by the tyre tracks of Rovers and Jaguars; crossed a busy thoroughfare, where buses and lorries had churned the snow into furrows of black slush; and penetrated a region of older and less well-groomed property. After a few minutes he became aware of a figure slipping and sliding on the pavement ahead of him, crowned by a familiar deerstalker.

''Hallo, Professor Zapp,'' he said, drawing level. ''Are you taking a stroll?''

''Oh, hi, Percy. No, I'm on my way to visit my old landlord. I spent six months in this place, you know, ten years ago. I even thought of staying here once. I must have been out of my mind. Do you know it well?''

''I've never been here before, but I have an aunty living here. Not a real aunty, but related through cousins. My mother said to be sure to look her up. I'm on my way now.''

''A duty call, huh? I take a right here.''

Persse consulted his map. ''So do I.''

''How d'you like Rummidge, then?''

''There are too many street-lights.''

''Come again?''

''You can't see the stars properly at night, because of all the streetlights,'' said Persse.

''Yeah, and there are a few other disadvantages I could tell you about,'' said Morris Zapp. ''Like not a single restaurant you would take your worst enemy to, four different kinds of electric socket in every room, hotel bedrooms that freeze your eyebrows to the pillows, and disc jockeys that deserve to have their windpipes slit. I can't say that the absence of stars bugged me all that much."

"Even the moon seems dimmer than at home," said Persse.

"You're a romantic, Percy, you know that? You ought to write poetry. This is the street: Gittings Road."

"My aunt's street," said Persse.

Morris Zapp stopped in the middle of the pavement. "That's a remarkable coincidence," he said. "What's your aunty's name?"

"Mrs O'Shea, Mrs Nuala O'Shea," said Persse. "Her husband is Dr Milo O'Shea."

Morris Zapp performed a little jig of excitement. "It's him, it's him!" he cried, in a rough imitation of an Irish brogue. "It's himself, my old landlord! Mother of God, won't he be surprised to see the pair of us."

"Mother of God!" said Dr O'Shea, when he opened the front door of his large and gloomy-looking house. "If it isn't Professor Zapp!"

"And here's your nephew from the Emerald Isle, Percy McGarrigle, come to see his aunty," said Morris Zapp.

Dr O'Shea's face fell. "Ah, yes, your mammy wrote, Persse. But I'm afraid you've missed Mrs. O'Shea—she left for Ireland yesterday. But come in, come in. I've nothing to offer you, and surgery starts in twenty minutes, but come in." He ushered them into a chilly parlour, smelling faintly of mildew and mothballs, and switched on an electric fire in the hearth. Simulated coals lighted up, though not the element. "Cheerful, I always think—makes you feel warm just to look at it," said the doctor.

"I've brought you a little duty-free hooch," said Morris Zapp, taking a half-bottle of scotch from his raincoat pocket.

"God love you, it's just like old times," groaned Dr O'Shea. He got down on his knees and groped in a sideboard for glasses. "The whisky flowed like water," he confided in Persse, "when Professor Zapp lived here."

"Don't get the wrong idea, Percy," said Morris Zapp. "It's just Milo's way of saying I usually had a bottle or two of Old Grandad in the cupboard. Here's looking at you, Milo."

"So where's Aunty Nuala?" Persse enquired, when they had sunk the whiskey, and O'Shea was refilling their glasses.

"Back in Sligo. Family troubles." Dr O'Shea shook his head gravely. "Her sister is very bad, very bad. All on account of that daughter of hers, Bernadette."

"Bernadette?" Morris Zapp cut in. "You mean that black-haired kid who was living with you when I had the apartment upstairs?"

"The same. Do you know your cousin Bernadette, Persse?"

"I haven't seen her since we were children. But I did hear rumours of a scandal."

"Aye, there was a scandal, all right. After she left us, she went to work in a hotel in Sligo Town, as a chambermaid in a hotel there, and one of the guests took advantage of her. To cut a long story short, she became pregnant and was dismissed."

"Who was the guy?" said Morris Zapp.

"Nobody knows. Bernadette refused to say. Of course, when she came home, her parents were very shocked, very angry."

"Told her never to darken their doorstep again?" said Morris Zapp.

"Not in so many words, but the result was the same," said Dr O'Shea. "Bernadette packed her bags and left the house in the middle of the night." He paused impressively, drained his glass, and drew the back of his hand across his mouth, making a rasping sound on his five o'clock shadow. "And niver a word has been heard of her since. Her mother's gone into a decline with the worry of it. Of course, what we all dread is that Bernadette went to London to get rid of the baby in one of them abortion clinics. Who knows, she may have died that way, in a state of mortal sin." Jumping rather hastily to this sad conclusion, Dr O'Shea crossed himself and sighed. "Let us hope that the good Lord gave her the grace to repent at the last."

In the hall a telephone began to ring.

"That'll be the surgery, wanting to know what's become of me," said Dr O'Shea. He stood up, and stooped to switch off the illumination of the electric fire.

"We'll be on our way," said Morris Zapp. "Nice to see

you, Milo." Outside the house, he turned and surveyed the
top storey of the house with a sigh. "I had the apartment up
there—Bernadette used to clean it. Poor kid, she was kind
of cute, even if she had lost all her teeth. It makes me mad
to hear of girls getting knocked up in this day and age.
You'd think that the guy, whoever he was, would have taken
precautions."

'You can't obtain contraceptives in Ireland," said Persse.
"It's against the law to sell them."

"Is that right? I guess you'll be filling your suitcase with,
what do they call condoms here, Durex, right?"

"No," said Persse. "I believe in premarital chastity for
both sexes."

"Well, it's a nice idea, Percy, but if you want my
opinion, I don't think it will catch on."

They separated at the corner of Gittings Road, since
Morris Zapp was going to the Swallows' house, not far
away, and Persse was returning to the halls of residence.
"Will you be going to the theatre tonight?" Persse asked.

"No, Philip Swallow warned me against it. I guess I'll
have an early night, catch up on my jet-lag. Take care."

Persse hurried back to Martineau Hall, but found that he
was too late for dinner, which had been brought forward
because of the theatre outing. "Never mind, love, it wasn't
very nice," said the lady with yellow curls, laying out
breakfast things in the empty dining-room. "Shepherd's
Pie, made from lunchtime's leftovers. There's some biscuits
and cheese left if that's any use to you."

Gratefully cramming cream crackers and cheddar cheese
into his mouth, Persse hurried to the foyer of Lucas Hall.
Dempsey, spruce and expectant in a dark brown blazer and
grey flannels, was standing near the door.

"Are you going to the theatre?" Persse asked. "I need a
lift."

"Sorry, old man, my car's full. There's a coach leaving
from the bottom of the drive. If you run, you'll probably
catch it."

Persse ran, but did not catch it. As he stood at the gates
of the hall site, wondering what to do, Dempsey swept by at
the wheel of a Volkswagen Golf, spattering Persse with

slush. Angelica was in the front passenger seat. She smiled and waved. There was nobody in the back seat.

It was cold, and growing dark. Persse turned up the collar of his anorak, thrust his hands into his pockets, and set off in the direction of the city centre. By the time he found the Repertory Theatre, a large futuristic concrete structure near the Town Hall, the performance of *Puss in Boots* was well under way, and he was ushered to his seat while a man, dressed apparently as Robin Hood, was coaching the audience in hissing whenever they saw the wicked Baron Blunderbuss appear. There followed a duet for the Miller's son and the princess with whom he was in love; a slapstick comic interlude in which two incompetent decorators, who were supposed to be papering the King's parlour, covered each other with paste and dropped their implements repeatedly on the King's gouty foot; and, as a finale to the first act, a spectacular song and dance number for the whole company, entitled "Caturday Night Fever", in which Puss in Boots triumphed in a Royal Disco Dancing competition at the Palace.

The lights went up for the Interval, revealing to Persse the bemused countenances of his fellow conferees. Some declared their intention of leaving immediately and looking for a good film. Others tried to make the best of it—"After all it *is* the only *genuinely popular* form of theatre in Britain today, I think one has a *duty* to experience it oneself"—and some had obviously been enjoying themselves immensely, hissing and clapping and joining in the sing-songs, but didn't want to admit it. Of Angelica and Dempsey, however, there was no sign.

Searching for them in the crowded foyer, Persse encountered Miss Maiden, who presented a striking figure among the drab provincial throng, wearing a fox-fur stole over a full-length evening dress, and wielding opera glasses mounted on a stick. It struck Persse that she must have been a very handsome woman in her prime. "Hallo, young man," she said. "How are you enjoying the play?"

"I'm finding it very hard to follow," he said. "What is Robin Hood doing in it? I thought *Puss in Boots* was a French fairy tale."

"Pooh, pooh, you mustn't be so literal-minded," said Miss Maiden, tapping him reprovingly with her rolled-up programme. "Jessie Weston describes a mumming play performed near Rugby in Warwickshire, of which the *dramatis personae* are Father Christmas, St George, a Turkish Knight, a Knight's mother Moll Finney, a Doctor, Humpty Jack, Beelzebub and Big-Head-and-Little-Wit. What would you make of that?"

"Nothing very much, I'm afraid."

"It's easy!" Miss Maiden cried triumphantly. "St George kills the knight, the mother grieves, the Doctor brings him back to life. It symbolizes the death and rebirth of the crops in winter and summer. It all comes back to the same thing in the end: the life-force endlessly renewing itself. Robin Hood, you know, is connected to the Green Man of medieval legend, who was originally a tree-god or nature spirit."

"But what about this show?"

"Well, the gouty King is obviously the Fisher King ruling over a sterile land, and the miller's son is the hero who restores its fertility through the magic agency of Puss in Boots, and is rewarded with the hand of the King's daughter."

"So Puss in Boots is equivalent to the Grail?" Persse said facetiously.

Miss Maiden was not discomposed. "Certainly. Boots are phallic, and you are no doubt familiar with the vulgar expression 'pussy'?"

"Yes, I have heard it occasionally," said Persse weakly.

"It is a very ancient and widely distributed metaphor, I assure you. So you see the character of Puss in Boots represents the same combination of male and female principles as the cup and spear in the Grail legend."

"Amazing," said Persse. "It makes you wonder that they allow children to see these pantomimes. By the way, Miss Maiden, have you seen Angelica Pabst and Professor Dempsey this evening?"

"Yes, I saw them leaving the theatre just before the performance started," said Miss Maiden. "They'll be sorry when they hear what they've missed. Ah, there's the bell. We must get back to our seats."

Persse did not return to his seat, but left the theatre and

made his way back to Lucas Hall. He took the lift to the top floor, which was dark and deserted, since it had not been necessary to accommodate anyone so far from the ground. The building consisted of twin tower blocks, connected at alternate floors by glassed-in walkways. The walkway on the top floor, as Persse had already ascertained, gave a fine aerial view of the grounds of the two halls, the artificial lake between them, and the south-western suburbs of Rummidge. He stared at the sky: there were wisps of cloud about, but generally it was clear, and the moon was rising.

After nearly an hour had passed, Persse heard the whine of a lift climbing the shaft. He ran to the doors of the lift and stood there, smiling expectantly. The doors opened to reveal the frowning figure of Dempsey. Persse rearranged his features.

"What are you doing here?" Dempsey demanded.

"Thinking," said Persse.

Dempsey stepped out of the lift. "I'm looking for Angelica," he said.

"She isn't here."

The doors of the lift closed automatically behind Dempsey. "Are you sure?" he said. "It's very dark up here. Why haven't you got the lights on?"

"I think better in the dark," said Persse.

Dempsey switched on the landing lights and looked around him suspiciously. "What are you thinking about?"

"A poem."

Dempsey's frown momentarily dissolved into a leer. "I've been working on that limerick," he said. "What about this for a start:

> *There was a young fellow from Limerick*
> *Who tried to have sex with a candlestick . . .*"

"It scans better than your last effort," said Persse. "That's about all I can say in its favour."

Dempsey pressed the button to open the lift doors. "If you see Angelica, tell her I'm in the bar."

As the lift descended, the door of the emergency Exit opened and Angelica stepped out on to the landing. Her beauty looked a little tousled, and she was out of breath—

indeed her bosom was swelling and sinking in the most amazing fashion under the high-necked white silk blouse she was wearing. It looked to Persse as if a button was missing from the blouse.

"Has that fellow been annoying you?" he said fiercely.

"Who?"

"That Dempsey. Big-Head-and-Little-Wit."

Angelica grinned. "I told you, I can look after myself," she panted. She put a hand to her bosom. "I'm out of breath from the stairs."

"Why didn't you make Dempsey stop his car when you passed me in the drive?" he said accusingly.

"You told me you weren't going to the theatre."

"I changed my mind. So did you, apparently. I couldn't find you there."

"No, when we discovered it was *Puss in Boots* instead of *King Lear,* we went to a pub instead. Robin wanted to go on to a discothèque, but I explained that I had an appointment back here. So here I am. Where's the poem?"

"It's a one-word poem," said Persse, somewhat mollified by this account. "The most beautiful word in the world, actually. And you can only read it in the dark." He turned off the landing lights. "Here, take my hand." He led Angelica out on to the glassed-in walkway, and showed her the view. "Down there," he said. "By the lake."

The snow-covered landscape brilliantly reflected the light of the nearly full moon, now high in the sky. The lawn that sloped gently upwards from the margin of the artificial lake was an expanse of dazzling whiteness, except where a trail of footprints, that had melted in the day's slow thaw, spelled out in huge, wavering script a name:

"Oh, Persse," she whispered. "What a lovely idea. An earth poem."

"Why do you call it that? I would have said a snow poem."

"I was thinking of earth art—you know, those designs miles long that you can only appreciate from an aeroplane."

"Well, it's also a sun poem and a moon poem, because the sun melted the snow in my footprints, and the moon lit them up for you to see."

"How bright the moon is tonight," Angelica murmured. She had not withdrawn her hand from his.

"Have you ever thought, Angelica," said Persse, "what a remarkable thing it is that the moon and the sun look to our eyes approximately the same size?"

"No," said Angelica, "I've never thought about it."

"So much mythology and symbolism depends on the equivalence of those two round disc-shapes in our sky, one presiding over the day and the other over the night, as if they were twins. Yet it's just a trick of perspective, the product of the relative size of the moon and the sun, and their distance from us and from each other. The odds against its happening like that by chance must be billions to one."

"You don't think it was chance?"

"I think it's one of the great proofs of a divine creator," said Persse. "I think He had an eye for symmetry."

"Like Blake," Angelica smiled. "Have you read Frye's *Fearful Symmetry,* by the way? An excellent book, I think."

"I don't want to talk about literary criticism," said Persse, squeezing her hand, and drawing closer. "Not alone with you, up here, in the moonlight. I want to talk about us."

"Us?"

"Will you marry me, Angelica?"

"Of course not!" she exclaimed, snatching her hand away and laughing incredulously.

"Why not?"

"Well, for a hundred reasons. I've only just met you, and I don't want to get married anyway."

"Never?"

"I don't say never, but first I want a career of my own, and that means I must be free to go anywhere."

"I wouldn't mind," said Persse. "I'd go with you."

"What, and give up your own job?"

"If necessary," he said.

Angelica shook her head. "You're a hopeless romantic, Persse," she said. "Why do you want to marry me, anyway?"

"Because I love you," he said, "and I believe in premarital chastity."

"Perhaps I don't," she said archly.

"Oh, Angelica, don't torment me! If you've had other lovers, I don't want to hear about them."

"That's not what I meant," said Angelica.

"I don't mind if you're not a virgin," said Persse. He added, "Of course, I'd prefer it if you were."

"Ah, virginity," mused Angelica. "What is it? A presence or an absence? The presence of a hymen, or the absence of a penis?"

"God forbid it's either," said Persse, blushing, "for I'm a virgin myself."

"Are you?" Angelica looked at him with interest. "But nowadays people usually sleep together before they get married. Or so I understand."

"It's against my principles," said Persse. "But if you promised to marry me eventually, I might stretch a point."

Angelica tittered. "Don't forget that this is entirely *your* idea." She suddenly prodded the glass. "Oh, look, there's a little creature in the snow down there—can it be a rabbit, or a hare?"

"*'The hare limped trembling through the frozen grass',*" he quoted.

"What's that? Oh yes, 'The Eve of St Agnes'.

And silent was the flock in woolly fold.

I love that phrase, 'woolly fold', don't you? It makes one think of being snuggled up in a blanket, but it could also be a metaphor for a snowdrift, so that it sort of epitomizes the forcing together of the extremes of heat and cold, sensuousness and austerity, life and death, that runs through the whole poem."

"Oh, Angelica!" Persse exclaimed. "Never mind the verbal texture. Remember how the poem ends:

And they are gone: ay, ages long ago
Those lovers fled away into the storm.

Be my Madeline, and let me be your Porphyro!''
"What, and miss the rest of the conference?"
"I can wait till tomorrow night.

Awake! Arise! my love, and fearless be,
For o'er the southern moors I have a home for thee.

Angelica giggled. "It *would* be kind of fun to re-enact the poem tomorrow night. There's actually going to be a medieval banquet."

"I know."

"You could hide in my room and watch me go to bed. Then I might dream of you as my future husband."

"Suppose you didn't?"

"That's a risk you'd have to take. Porphyro found a way to make sure of it, I seem to remember," Angelica said dreamily, gazing out across the moonlit snowfields.

Persse looked doubtfully at her exquisite profile—the perfectly straight nose, the slight, unmanning droop of the underlip, the firm but gently rounded chin. "Angelica—" he began. But at that moment they heard the sound of the lift approaching the top floor. "If that's Dempsey again," Persse exclaimed, "I'll push him down the liftshaft." He hurried back to the landing and adopted a challenging posture, facing the doors of the lift. They opened to reveal the figure of Philip Swallow.

"Oh, hallo McGarrigle," he said. "I'm looking for Miss Pabst. Robin Dempsey said she might be up here."

"No, she's not," said Persse.

"Oh, I see," said Philip Swallow. He seemed to be considering whether to push past Persse and investigate for himself, but to decide against it. "Do you want to go down?" he said.

"No, thank you."

"Oh, well, goodnight then." Philip Swallow took his finger off the "Hold" button, and the doors closed.

Persse hurried back to the walkway. "That was Philip

Swallow,'' he said. ''What the blazes do all these old men want with you?''

But there was no reply. Only moonlight filled the grassy space. Angelica had gone.

So, by the next morning, had Persse's inscription of her name upon the landscape. The wind had changed direction during the night, bringing a warm rain which had melted and washed away the snow. Drawing back the curtains of his bedroom window, Persse saw damp green lawns and muddy flowerbeds under low, scudding rainclouds. And there, splashing through the puddles in the carpark, was the surprising figure of Morris Zapp, clad in a bright red track suit and training shoes, a dead cigar clenched between his teeth. Quickly pulling on a sweater, jeans, and the tennis shoes that served him for slippers, Persse ran out into the mild morning air and soon overtook the American, whose pace was in fact rather slower than normal walking.

''Good morning, Professor Zapp!''

''Oh, hi, Percy,'' Morris Zapp mumbled. He took the cigar butt from between his teeth, inspected it with faint surprise, and tossed it into a laurel bush. ''You jogging too? Look, don't let me hold you back.''

''I would never have guessed that you were a runner.''

''This is jogging, Percy, not running. Running is sport. Jogging is punishment.''

''You mean you don't enjoy it?''

''Enjoy it? Are you kidding? I only do this for my health. It makes me feel so terrible, I figure it must be doing me good. Also it's very fashionable these days in American academic circles. Success is not just a matter of how many articles you published last year, but how many miles you covered this morning.''

''It seems to be catching on over here, too,'' said Persse. ''I can see another runner in front of us. But surely, Professor Zapp, you don't have to worry about success? You're famous already.''

''It's not just a question of making it, Percy, there's also keeping it. You have to remember the young men in a hurry.''

"Who are they?"

"Have you never read Cornford's *Microcosmographia Academica*? I have whole chunks of it by heart. *'From far below you will mount the roar of a ruthless multitude of young men in a hurry. You may perhaps grow to be aware of what they are in a hurry to do. They are in a hurry to get you out of the way.'* "

"Who was Cornford?"

"A Cambridge classicist at the turn of the century, under the spell of Freud and Frazer. You know Freud's idea of primitive society as a tribe in which the sons kill the father when he gets old and impotent, and take away his women? In modern academic society they take away your research grants. And your women, too, of course."

"That's very interesting," said Persse. "It reminds me of Jessie Weston's *Ritual and Romance*."

"Yep, it's the same basic idea. Except that in the Grail legend the hero cures the king's sterility. In the Freudian version the old guy gets wasted by his kids. Which seems to me more true to life."

"So that's why you keep jogging?"

"That's why I keep jogging. To show I'm not on the heap yet. Anyway, my ambitions are not yet satisfied. Before I retire, I want to be the highest paid Professor of English in the world."

"How high is that?"

"I don't know, that's what keeps me on my toes. The top people in the profession are pretty tight-lipped about their salaries. Maybe I already *am* the highest paid professor of English in the world, without knowing it. Every time I threaten to leave Euphoric State, they jack up my salary by five thousand dollars."

"Do you want to move, then, Professor Zapp?"

"Not at all, I just have to stop them from taking me for granted. There's no point in moving from one university to another these days. There was a time when that was how you got on. There was a very obvious pecking order among the various schools and you measured your success by your position on that ladder. The assumption was that all the most interesting people were concentrated into a few institutions, like Harvard, Yale, Princeton and suchlike, and in order to get into the action you had to be at one of those places yourself. That isn't true any more.''

"It isn't?"

"No. The day of the individual campus has passed. It belongs to an obsolete technology—railways and the printing press. I mean, just look at *this* campus—it epitomizes the whole thing: the heavy industry of the mind.''

They had reached a summit which offered a panoramic view of Rummidge University, dominated by its campanile (a blown-up replica in red brick of the Leaning Tower of Pisa), flanked on one side by the tree-filled residential streets that Persse had walked through the previous evening, and on the other by factories and cramped, grey terraced houses. A railway and a canal bisected the site, which was covered by an assemblage of large buildings of heterogeneous design in brick and concrete. Morris Zapp seemed glad of an excuse to stop for a moment while they viewed the scene. "See what I mean?" he panted, with an all-embracing, yet dismissive sweep of his arm. "It's huge, heavy, monolithic. It weighs about a billion tons. You can *feel* the weight of those buildings, pressing down the earth. Look at the Library—built like a huge warehouse. The whole place says, *'We have learning stored here; if you want it, you've got to come inside and get it.'* Well, that doesn't apply any more.''

"Why not?" Persse set off again at a gentle trot.

"Because," said Morris Zapp, reluctantly following, "information is much more portable in the modern world than it used to be. So are people. *Ergo,* it's no longer necessary to hoard your information in one building, or keep your top scholars corralled in one campus. There are three things which have revolutionized academic life in the last twenty years, though very few people have woken up to the fact: jet travel, direct-dialling telephones and the Xerox machine. Scholars don't have to work in the same institution to interact, nowadays: they call each other up, or they meet at international conferences. And they don't have to grub about in library stacks for data: any book or article that sounds interesting they have Xeroxed and read it at home.

Or on the plane going to the next conference. I work mostly at home or on planes these days. I seldom go into the university except to teach my courses.''

"That's a very interesting theory,'' said Persse. "And rather reassuring, because my own university has very few buildings and hardly any books.''

"Right. As long as you have access to a telephone, a Xerox machine, and a conference grant fund, you're OK, you're plugged into the only university that really matters— the global campus. A young man in a hurry can see the world by conference-hopping.''

"Oh, I'm not in a hurry,'' said Persse.

"You must have some ambitions.''

"I would like to get my poems published,'' said Persse. "And I have another ambition too personal to be divulged.''

"Al Papps!'' Morris Zapp exclaimed.

"How did you guess?'' Persse asked, astonished.

"Guess what? I just said that's Al Papps running ahead of us.''

"So it is!'' The figure Persse had glimpsed earlier was indeed Angelica: she must have taken some detour, and had now reappeared on the path ahead of them, scarcely a hundred yards distant.

"That sure is some girl! She looks like a million dollars, has read everything you can name, and she can really run, can't she?''

"Like Atalanta,'' Persse murmured. "Let's catch her up.''

"You catch her up, Percy, I'm pooped.''

Morris Zapp soon fell behind as Persse accelerated, but the distance between himself and Angelica remained constant. Then she gave a quick glance over her shoulder, and he realized that she was aware of his pursuit. They were descending a long sloping path that led to the halls of residence. Faster and faster grew the pace, until both were sprinting. Persse narrowed the gap. Angelica's head went back, and her black hair streamed out behind her. Her supple haunches, bewitchingly sheathed in a tight-fitting orange track suit, thrust the tarmac away from under her flying feet. They reached the entrance to Lucas Hall shoulder to shoulder, and leaned against the outside wall, panting and laughing. The driver of a taxi that was waiting by the entrance grinned and applauded.

"What happened to you last night?" Persse gasped.

"I went to bed, of course," said Angelica. "In my room. Room 231."

Morris Zapp laboured up, wheezing stertorously. "Who won?"

"It was a dead heat," said the cab driver, leaning out of his window.

"Very diplomatic, driver. Now you can take me back to St John's Road," said Morris Zapp, climbing into the taxi. "See you around, kids."

"Do you usually jog by taxi, Professor Zapp?" Persse inquired.

"Well, I'm staying with the Swallows, as you know, and I didn't fancy running through the streets of Rummidge inhaling the rush-hour. *Ciao!*" Morris Zapp sank back into the seat of the taxi, and took from a pocket in his track suit a fat cigar, a cigar clipper and a lighter. He was busying himself with this apparatus as the taxi drew away.

Persse turned to address Angelica, but she had disappeared. "Was there ever such a girl for disappearing?" he muttered to himself in vexation. "It's as if she had a magic ring for making herself invisible."

Somehow, Angelica eluded Persse for the rest of the morning. When, after showering and dressing, he went to the Martineau Hall refectory for breakfast, he found her already seated at a fully occupied table, next to Dempsey. She was not a member of the little caravan of conferees who, with a conspicuous lack of enthusiasm, and buffeted by occasional squalls of rain, made their way down the hill from the halls of residence to the main campus for the first lecture of the morning. Persse, having watched them depart, and waited in vain for a few extra minutes, finally hurried after them, only to be overtaken by Dempsey's car, with Angelica in the front passenger seat. The pair contrived, however, to be late for the lecture, tip-toeing in after the proceedings had begun. Persse paid little attention to the lecture, which was about the problem of identifying the authentically Shakespearian portions of the text of *Pericles,* being preoccupied himself with the problem of exactly what Angelica had meant by her proposal, the night before, that they should re-enact "The Eve of St Agnes". By pointedly telling him the number of her room that morning, she seemed to have confirmed the arrangement. What he was not sure of was how she read the poem. Failing to spot her in the crush at the coffee break, Persse hurried over to the University Library to consult the text.

He skimmed quickly through the early stanzas about the coldness of the weather, the tradition that maidens who went fasting to bed on St Agnes' Eve would see their future husbands in their sleep, the abstractedness of Madeline, with this intention in mind, amid the feasting and merrymaking in the hall, the secret arrival of Porphyro, risking his life in the hostile castle for a glimpse of his beloved, his persuading of the old woman, Angela, to hide him in Madeline's bedroom, Madeline's arrival and preparations for bed. Persse lingered for a moment over stanza XXVI—

> *Of all its wreathed pearls her hair she frees,*
> *Unclasps her warmed jewels one by one;*
> *Loosens her fragrant bodice: by degrees*
> *Her rich attire creeps rustling to her knees*

—and, with flushed cheeks, read on through the description of the delicacies Porphyro laid out for Madeline, his attempts to wake her with lute music, hovering over her sleeping figure; Madeline's eyes opening on the vision of her dream, and her half-conscious address to Porphyro. Then came the crucial stanza:

> *Beyond a mortal man impassioned far*
> *At these voluptuous accents, he arose,*
> *Ethereal, flushed, and like a throbbing star*
> *Seen 'mid the sapphire heaven's deep repose;*
> *Into her dream he melted, as the rose*
> *Blendeth its odour with the violet—*
> *Solution sweet.*

It was all very well for Morris Zapp to insist upon the indeterminacy of literary texts: Persse McGarrigle needed to know whether or not sexual intercourse was taking place here—a question all the more difficult for him to decide because he had no personal experience to draw upon. On the whole he was inclined to think that the correct answer was in the affirmative, and Porphyro's later reference to Madeline as his "bride" seemed to clinch the matter.

This conclusion, however, only pitchforked Persse into another dilemma. Angelica might be inviting him to become her lover, but she would not allow him to make her his bride, not in the immediate future anyway, so a contingency had to be thought of, distasteful and unromantic as it was. Probably it would never have occurred to Persse McGarrigle if the sad story of his cousin Bernadette had not been fresh in his mind, together with the censorious comment of Morris Zapp: "It makes me mad to hear of girls getting knocked up in this day and age." Accordingly, though he shrank inwardly from the task, he set his features grimly and set off in search of a chemist's shop.

He walked a long way, to be sure of not being observed by any stray members of the conference, and eventually found, or rather lost, himself in the city centre, a bewildering labyrinth of dirty, malodorous stairs, subways and walkways that funnelled the local peasantry up and down, over and under the huge concrete highways, vibrating with the thunder of passing juggernauts. He passed many chemist's shops. Some were too empty, some too full, for his comfort. Eventually, impatient with his own pusillanimity, he chose one at random and plunged recklessly inside.

The shop appeared to be deserted, and he looked rapidly around for the object of his quest, hoping that, when the chemist appeared, he would be able merely to point. He could not see what he was looking for, however, and to his dismay a young girl in white overalls appeared from behind a barricade of shelves.

"Yis?" she said listlessly.

Persse felt throttled by his embarrassment. He wanted to

run and flee through the door, but his limbs refused to move.

"Kinoielpyew?" said the girl impatiently.

Persse stared at his boots. "I'm after wanting some Durex, please," he managed to mutter, in strangled accents.

"Small meedyum or large?" said the girl coolly.

This was a turn of the screw Persse had not anticipated. "I thought they were all the one size," he whispered hoarsely.

"Nah. Small meedyum or large," drawled the girl, inspecting her fingernails.

"Well, medium, then," said Persse.

The girl vanished momentarily, and reappeared with a surprisingly big box wrapped in a paper bag, for which she demanded 75p. Persse snatched the package—it was also surprisingly heavy—from her, thrust a pound note across the counter, and fled from the shop without waiting for his change.

In a dark and noisome subway, decorated with football graffiti and reeking of urine and onions, he paused beneath a lightbulb to inspect his purchase. He withdrew from the paper bag a cardboard box which bore on its wrapper the picture of a plump, pleased-looking baby in a nappy, being fed something that looked like porridge. The brand-name of this product, displayed in large letters, was "Farex".

Persse walked broodingly back towards the University. He had no inclination to return to the shop to explain the mistake, or to make a second attempt at another chemist's shop. He took the frustration of his design to be providential, an expression of divine displeasure at his sinful intentions. On a broad thoroughfare lined with motorcar showrooms, he passed a Catholic church, and hesitated for a moment before a notice board which declared, "Confessions at any time." It was a heaven-sent opportunity to shrive himself. But he decided that he could not in good faith promise to break his appointment with Angelica that night. He crossed the road—carefully, for he was undoubtedly in a state of sin now—and walked on, allowing his imagination to dwell voluptuously on images of Angelica coming to her bedroom in which he was hidden, Angelica undressing under his very eyes, Angelica naked in his arms. But what then? He feared that his inexperience would destroy the rapture of that moment, his knowledge of sexual intercourse being entirely literary and rather vague as to the mechanics.

As if the devil had planted it there, another notice, printed in bold black lettering on flame-coloured fluorescent paper, caught his eye:

> THIS CINEMA IS A CLUB SHOWING ADULT FILMS
> WHICH INCLUDE THE EXPLICIT AND UNCENSORED
> DEPICTION OF SEXUAL ACTS. IMMEDIATE MEMBERSHIP
> AVAILABLE. REDUCED RATES FOR OLD AGE PENSIONERS.

Persse swerved in through the doors, quickly, before his conscience had time to react. He found himself in a discreetly dim, carpeted foyer. A man behind a desk welcomed him suavely. "Membership form, sir? That will be three pounds altogether."

Persse put down the name of Philip Swallow.

"That's a coincidence, sir," said the man, with a svelte smile. "We already have a Mr Philip Swallow on the books. Through the door over there."

Persse pushed through padded doors into almost total darkness. He stumbled against a wall, and remained pressed to it for a moment while his sight accommodated to the gloom. The air was full of strange noises, an amplified mélange of heavy breathing, throttled cries, panting, moaning and groaning, as of souls in torment. A dim luminescence guided him forward, through a curtain, round a corner, and he found himself at the back of a small auditorium. The noise was louder than ever, and it was still very dark, impossible to see anything except the flickering images on the screen. It took Persse some moments to realize that what he was looking at was a hugely magnified penis going in and out of a hugely magnified vagina. The blood rushed to his face, and to another part of his anatomy. Bent forward, he shuffled down the sloping aisle, peering vainly to each side of him for an empty seat. The images on the screen shifted, close-up gave way to a wider, deeper perspective, and it became apparent that the owner of the vagina had another penis in her mouth, and the owner of the first penis had his tongue in another vagina, whose owner in turn had a finger in someone else's anus, whose penis was in *her* vagina; and all were in frantic motion, like the pistons of some infernal machine. Keats it was not. It was a far cry from the violet blending its odour with the rose. "Siddown, can't you?" someone hissed in the circumambient darkness. Persse groped for a seat, but his hand fell on a padded shoulder, and was shaken off with a curse. The moans and groans rose to a crescendo, the pistons jerked faster and faster, and Persse registered with shame that he had polluted himself. Perspiration poured from his brow and dimmed his sight. When what seemed, for one hallucinatory moment, to be the face of Angelica loomed between two massive hairy thighs, Persse turned and fled from the place as if from the pit of hell.

The man behind the reception desk looked up, startled, as Persse catapulted into the foyer. "Too tame for you?" he said. "You can't have a refund, I'm afraid. Try next week, we've got some new Danish stuff coming in."

Persse grabbed the man by his lapels and hauled him halfway across the desk. "You have made me defile the image of the woman I love," he hissed. The man paled, and lifted his hands in a gesture of surrender. Persse pushed him back into his seat, ran out of the cinema, across the road, and into the Catholic church.

A light was burning above a confessional bearing the name of "Fr Finbar O'Malley," and within a few minutes Persse had unburdened his conscience and received absolution. "God bless you, my son," said the priest in conclusion.

"Thank you, Father."

"By the way, do you come from Mayo?"

"I do."

"Ah. I thought I recognized the sound of Mayo speech. I'm from the West myself." He sighed behind the wire grille. "This is a terrible sinful city for a young Irish lad like yourself to be cast adrift in. How would you like to be repatriated?"

"Repatriated?" Persse repeated blankly.

"Aye. I administer a fund for helping Irish youngsters who have come over here looking for work and think better of it, and want to go back home. It's called the Our Lady of Knock Fund for Reverse Emigration."

"Oh, I'm only visiting, Father. I'm going back to Ireland tomorrow."

"You have your ticket?"

"Yes, Father."

"Then good luck to you, and God speed. You're going to a better place than this, I can tell you."

By the time Persse got back to the University it was afternoon, and the Conference had departed on a coach tour of the literary landmarks in the region. Persse took a bath and slept for a few hours. He awoke feeling serene and purified. It was time to go to the bar for a drink before dinner.

The conferees were back from the sightseeing trip, which had not been a success: the owners of George Eliot's childhood home had not been warned in advance, and would not let them inside the house, so they had had to content themselves with milling about in the garden and pressing their faces to the window. Then Ann Hathaway's cottage proved to be closed for maintenance; and finally the coach had broken down just outside Kenilworth, on the way to the Castle, and a relief vehicle had taken an hour to arrive.

"Never mind," said Bob Busby, moving among the disgruntled conferees in the bar, "there's still the medieval banquet to look forward to."

"I hope to God Busby knows what he's doing," Persse heard Philip Swallow saying. "We can't afford another cockup." He was speaking to a man in a rather greasy charcoal grey suit whom Persse had not seen before.

"What's it all about, then?" said this man, who had a Gauloise smouldering in one hand and a large gin and tonic in the other.

"Well, there's a place in town called 'Ye Merrie Olde Round Table,' where they put on these mock medieval banquets," said Philip Swallow. "I've never been myself, but Busby assured us it's good fun. Anyway, he's booked their team to lay it on here tonight. They have minstrels, I understand, and mead, and . . .''

"And wenches," Persse volunteered.

"I say," said the man in the charcoal grey suit, turning smoke-bleared eyes upon Persse and treating him to a yellow-fanged smile. "It sounds rather fun."

"Oh, hello McGarrigle," said Philip Swallow, without enthusiasm. "Have you met Felix Skinner, of Lecky, Windrush and Bernstein? My publishers. Not that our professional association has been particularly profitable to either party," he concluded with a forced attempt at jocularity.

"Well, it has been a teeny bit disappointing," Skinner admitted with a sigh.

"Only a hundred and sixty-five copies sold a year after publication," said Philip Swallow accusingly. "And not a single review."

"You know we all thought it was an absolutely *super* book, Philip," said Skinner. "It's just that there's not much of an educational market for Hazlitt these days. And I'm sure the reviews will come eventually, in the scholarly journals. I'm afraid the Sundays and weeklies don't pay as much attention to lit. crit. as they used to."

"That's because so much of it is unreadable," said Philip Swallow. "*I* can't understand it, so how can you expect ordinary people to? I mean, that's what my book is *saying*. That's why I *wrote* it."

"I know, Philip, it's awfully unfair," said Skinner. "What's your own field, Mr McGarrigle?"

"Well, I did my research on Shakespeare and T.S. Eliot," said Persse.

"I could have helped you with that," Dempsey butted in. He had just come into the bar with Angelica, who was looking heart-stoppingly beautiful in a kaftan of heavy wine-coloured cotten, in whose weave a dark, muted pattern of other rich colours dimly gleamed. "It would just lend itself nicely to computerization," Dempsey continued. "All you'd have to do would be to put the texts on to tape and you could get the computer to list every word, phrase and syntactical construction that the two writers had in common.

You could precisely quantify the influence of Shakespeare on T.S. Eliot.''

"But my thesis isn't about that," said Persse. "It's about the influence of T.S. Eliot on Shakespeare."

"That sounds rather Irish, if I may say so," said Dempsey, with a loud guffaw. His little eyes looked anxiously around for support.

"Well, what I try to show," said Persse, "is that we can't avoid reading Shakespeare through the lens of T. S. Eliot's poetry. I mean, who can read *Hamlet* today without thinking of 'Prufrock'? Who can hear the speeches of Ferdinand in *The Tempest* without being reminded of 'The Fire Sermon' section of *The Waste Land*?''

"I say, that sounds rather interesting," said Skinner. "Philip, old chap do you think I might possibly have another one of these?" Depositing his empty glass in Philip Swallow's hand, Felix Skinner took Persse aside. "If you haven't already made arrangements to publish your thesis, I'd be very interested to see it," he said.

"It's only an MA," said Persse, his eyes watering from the smoke of Skinner's cigarette.

"Never mind, the libraries will buy almost anything on either Shakespeare or T. S. Eliot. Having them both in the same title would be more or less irresistible. Here's my card. Ah, thank you Philip, your very good health . . . Look, I'm sorry about *Hazlitt*, but I think the best thing would be to put it down to experience, and try again with a more fashionable subject.''

"But it took me eight years to write that book," Philip Swallow said plaintively, as Skinner patted him consolingly on the shoulder, sending a cascade of grey ash down the back of his suit.

The bar was now crowded with conferees drinking as fast as they could to get themselves into an appropriate mood for the banquet. Persse squeezed his way through the crush to Angelica.

"You told *me* your thesis was about the influence of Shakespeare on T. S. Eliot," she said.

"So it is," he replied. "I turned it round on the spur of the moment, just to take that Dempsey down a peg or two."

"Well, it's a more interesting idea, actually."

"I seem to have let myself in for the job of writing it up, now," said Persse. "I like your dress, Angelica."

"I thought it was the most medieval thing I had with me," she said, a gleam in her dark eyes. "Though I can't guarantee that it will actually rustle to my knees."

The allusion pierced him with a thrill of desire, instantly shattering his "firm purpose of amendment". He knew that nothing could prevent him from keeping watch on Angelica's room that evening.

Persse did not intend to sit next to Angelica at dinner, for he thought it would be more in the spirit of her romantic scenario that he should view her from afar. But he didn't want Robin Dempsey sitting next to her either, and detained him in the bar with earnest questions about structuralist linguistics while the others went off to the refectory.

"It's quite simple, really," said Dempsey impatiently. "According to Saussure, it's not the relation of words to things that allows them to signify, but their relations with each other, in short, the differences between them. *Cat* signifies cat because it sounds different from *cot* or *fat*."

"And the same goes for *Durex* and *Farex* and *Exlax*?" Persse enquired.

"It's not the first example that springs to mind," said Dempsey, a certain suspicion in his close-set eyes, "but yes."

"I think you reckon without the variation in regional accents," said Persse.

"Look, I haven't got time to explain it now," said Dempsey irritably, moving towards the door. "The bell has gone for dinner."

Persse found himself an inconspicuous place in the dining-hall, half-hidden from Angelica's view by a pillar. It was no great sacrifice to be on the margins of this particular feast. The mead tasted like tepid sugar-water, the medieval fare consisted of fried chicken and jacket potatoes eaten without the convenience of knives and forks, and the wenches were the usual Martineau Hall waitresses who had been bribed or bullied into wearing long dresses with plunging necklines. "Don't look at me, sir," the yellow-haired lady begged Persse as she served him his drumsticks. "If this is 'ow they dressed in the middle ages, well, all I can say is, they must 'ave got some very nasty chest colds." Presiding over the festivities from a platform at one end of the dining-room were a pair of entertainers from Ye Merrie Olde Round Table, one dressed up as a king, the other as a jester. The king had a piano accordion and the jester a set of drums, both provided with microphone and amplifier. While the meal was being served, they entertained the diners with jokes about chambers and thrones, sang bawdy ballads, and encouraged the diners to pelt each other with bread rolls. It was a rule of the court that anyone wishing to leave the room was required to bow or curtsey to the king, and when anyone did so the jester blew into an instrument that made a loud farting noise. Persse slipped out of the room while the medievalist from Aberystwyth was being humiliated in this fashion. Angelica, sitting between Felix Skinner and Philip Swallow on the far side of the room, flashed him a quick smile, and fluttered her fingers. She had not touched the food on her plate.

Persse stole away from Martineau Hall, towards Lucas Hall, drawing in deep breaths of the cool night air, and gazing at the ruffled reflection of the moon in the artificial lake. The strains of a new song which the king and jester had just started, their hoarse and strident voices powerfully amplified, pursued him:

> King Arthur was a foolish knight,
> A foolish knight was he,
> He locked his wife in a chastity belt,
> And then he lost the key!

Lucas Hall was deserted. Persse trod lightly on the stairs, and along the corridors, as he searched for room 231. Its door was unlocked, and he stepped inside. He did not turn on the light, as the room was sufficiently illuminated through a fanlight over the door, and by the moon shining in through the open casement. Snatches of song still carried on the night breeze:

Sir Lancelot, he told the Queen,
"I soon will set you free."
But when he tried with a pair of pliers
She said, "Stop, you're tickling me!"

Persse looked round the small, narrow room for somewhere to conceal himself. The only possible place was the built-in wardrobe. The packet of Farex was heavy in the pocket of his anorak. He took it out and placed it on the bedside table, reflecting that it was a rather poor substitute for jellies soother than the creamy curd, and lucent syrops, tinct with cinnamon, even if those did sound like baby-food.

He heard in the distance the thud and whine of the lift in operation, and stepped hastily into the dark interior of the wardrobe, pushing clothing to one side as he did so. He pulled the door to behind him, leaving it open an inch, through which he could breathe and see.

He heard the lift doors open at the end of the corridor, and footsteps approaching. The door handle turned, the door opened, and into the room came Robin Dempsey. He switched on the light, closed the door, and went across to the window to draw the curtains. As he took off his blazer, and draped it over the back of a chair, his eye was caught by the box of Farex, which he inspected with evident puzzlement. He eased off his shoes, and removed his trousers, revealing striped boxer shorts and sock suspenders. He took off one garment after another, folding and draping them neatly over the chair, until he was quite naked. It was not the spectacle Persse had been looking forward to. Dempsey sniffed himself under both armpits, then pushed a finger down into his crotch and sniffed that too. He disappeared from Persse's line of vision for a few moments, during which he could be heard splashing about at the sink, cleaning his teeth and gargling. Then he reappeared, still naked, shiverying slightly, and got into bed. He turned off the light from a bedside switch, but enough illumination came through the fanlight above the door to reveal that he was lying on his back with his eyes open, staring at the ceiling, and glancing occasionally at a small digital clock whose figures glowed green on the bedside table. A profound silence settled in the room.

Persse coughed.

Robin Dempsey sat up in bed with the force of a released spring, his torso seeming to quiver for some seconds after achieving the perpendicular. "Who's there?" he quavered, fumbling for the light switch. As the light came on, an archly fond smile suffused his features. "Angelica," he said, "Have you been hiding in the wardrobe all the time? You minx!"

Persse pushed open the door of the wardrobe and stepped out.

"McGarrigle! What the fuck are you doing here?"

"I might ask you the same question," said Persse.

"Why shouldn't I be here? It's my room."

"*Your* room?" Persse looked around. Now that the light was on, he could see some signs of masculine occupation: an electric razor and a flask of Old Spice aftershave on the shelf over the sink, a pair of large leather slippers under the bed. He looked back at the wardrobe he had occupied and saw a bright blue suit on the solitary hanger inside. "Oh," he said weakly; then, with more resolution, "Why did you think Angelica was hiding in the wardrobe?"

"It's none of your business, but it so happens that I have an appointment with Angelica. I'm expecting her here at any moment, as a matter of fact, so I'd be obliged if you would kindly piss off. What were you doing in my wardrobe, anyway?"

"I had an appointment with Angelica too. She told me this was her room. I was to hide in it and watch her going to bed. Like in 'The Eve of St Agnes'." It sounded rather silly to his own ears when he said it.

"I was to go to bed and wait for her to come to me," said Dempsey, "Like Ruggiero and Alcina, she said. Couple of characters in one of those long Eyetie poems, apparently. She told me the story—it sounded pretty sexy."

They were both silent for a moment.

"It looks as if she was having a bit of a joke," said Persse at last.

"Yes, it does," said Dempsey flatly. He got out of bed and took a pair of pyjamas from under his pillow. When he had put them on he got back into bed and pulled the blankets over his head. "Don't forget to turn off the light when you leave," he said in muffled tones.

"Oh, yes. Goodnight, then."

Persse ran downstairs to the lobby, to look at the noticeboard which he had consulted for Morris Zapp. Angelica's name did not appear anywhere on the list of residents. He hurried back to Martineau Hall. In the bar the conferees, who earlier had been drinking heavily to get themselves into the mood for the medieval banquet, were now drinking even more heavily in an effort to erase if from their memories. Bob Busby was nursing a glass of whisky alone in a corner, smiling fixedly in a brave effort to pretend that it was by his own choice that nobody was speaking to him. "Oh, hallo," he said gratefully, as Persse sat down beside him.

"Can you tell me what is Angelica Pabst's room number?" Persse asked him.

"It's funny you should ask me that," said Busby. "Somebody just mentioned that they saw her going off in a taxi, with her suitcase."

"What?" exclaimed Persse, jumping to his feet. "When? How long ago?"

"Oh, at least half an hour," said Bob Busby. "But, you know, as far as I know she never had a room. I certainly never allocated her one, and she doesn't seem to have paid for one. I don't really know how she got on this conference at all. She doesn't seem to belong to any university."

Persse ran down the drive to the gates of the hall site, not because he entertained any hopes of catching up with Angelica's taxi, but just to relieve his frustration and despair. He stood at the gates, looking up and down the empty road. The moon had disappeared behind a cloud. In the distance a train rattled along an embankment. He ran back up the drive, and went on running, past the two halls of residence, around the artificial lake, following the route he had taken with Morris Zapp that morning, until he reached the top of the hill that afforded a panoramic view of the city and the University. A yellowish glow from a million streetlamps lit up the sky and dimmed the light of the stars. A faint hum of traffic, the traffic that never ceased, night and day, to roll along the concrete thoroughfares, vibrated on the night air. "Angelica!" he cried desolately, to the indifferent city, "Angelica! Where are you?"

MEANWHILE, Morris Zapp had been having a quiet evening, tête à tête with Hilary Swallow. Philip was at Martineau Hall, doing his medieval bit. The two eldest Swallow children were away from home, at college, and the youngest, Matthew, was out playing rhythm guitar in a school band. "Do you know," Hilary sighed, as the front door slammed behind him, "his sixth form has *four* rock groups, and no debating society? I don't know what education is coming to. But I expect you approve, Morris, I remember that you used to like that frightful music."

"Not punk, Hilary, which seems to be what your son is into."

"It all sounds the same to me," she said.

They ate dinner in the kitchen, which had been extended and expensively refitted since he had last been in the house, with teak veneer cabinets, a split-level cooker and cork tiling on the floor. Hilary cooked them a tasty steak *au poivre* with baby squash and new potatoes, followed by one of her delicious fruit puddings, in which a viscous fruit compôte lurked beneath and partly, but only partly, permeated a thick stratum of light-textured, slightly waxy sponge-cake, glazed, fissured and golden brown on top.

"Hilary, you're an even better cook than you were ten years ago, and that's saying something," Morris declared sincerely, as he finished his second helping of the pudding.

She pushed a ripe Brie across the table. "Food is one of my few remaining pleasures, I'm afraid," she said. "With the dire consequences for my figure that you can see. Do help yourself to wine." It was their second bottle.

"You're in great shape, Hilary." Morris said, but in truth she wasn't. Her heavy bosom looked in need of the support of a good old-fashioned bra, and there were thick rolls of flesh at her waist and over her hips. Her hair, a dull brown, flecked with grey, was dragged back into a bun which did nothing to hide or soften the lines, wrinkles and broken blood vessels in her facial skin. "You should take up jogging," he said.

Hilary snorted derisively. "Matthew says that when I run I look like a blancmange in a panic."

"Matthew should be ashamed of himself."

"That's the trouble with living with two men. They gang up on you. I was better off when Amanda was at home. What about *your* family, Morris? What are they doing these days?"

"Well, the twins will be going to college in the fall. Of course *I* shall have to pay for their tuition, even though Désirée is rich as Croesus from her royalties. It makes me mad, but her lawyers have me over a barrel, which is where she always wanted me."

"What's Désirée doing?"

"Trying to finish her second book, I guess. It's been five years since the first one, so I figure she must be badly blocked. Serves her right for trying to screw every last cent out of me."

"I read her novel, what was it called?"

"*Difficult Days*. Nice title, huh? Marriage as one long period pain. Sold a million and a half in paperback. What did you think of it?"

"What did *you* think of it, Morris?"

"You mean because the husband is such a monster? I

kind of liked it. You wouldn't believe the number of women who propositioned me after that book came out. I guess they wanted to experience a real male chauvinist pig before the species became extinct.''

"Did you oblige?"

"Nuh, I gave up screwing around a long time ago. I came to the conclusion that sex is a sublimation of the work instinct." Hilary tittered. Thus encouraged, Morris elaborated: "The nineteenth century has its priorities right. What we really lust for is power, which we achieve by work. When I look around at my colleagues these days, what do I see? They're all screwing their students, or each other, like crazy, marriages are breaking up faster than you can count, and yet nobody seems to be happy. Obviously they would rather be working, but they're ashamed to admit it.''

"Maybe that's Philip's problem," said Hilary, "but somehow I don't think so.''

"Philip? You don't mean to tell me that he's been cheating on you?"

"Nothing serious—or not that I know of. But he has a weakness for pretty students. For some reason they seem to have a weakness for him. I can't think why."

"Power, Hilary. They wet their pants at the thought of his power. I bet this started when he got the chairmanship, right?''

"I suppose it did," she admitted.

"How did you find out?"

"A girl tried to blackmail the Department over it. I'll show you."

She unlocked a leather writing case, and took from it what appeared to be the Xerox copy of an examination script. She passed it to Morris, who began to read.

Question 5. By what means did Milton try to "justify the ways of God to man" in "Paradise Lost?"

"You can always tell a weak examinee," Morris observed. "First they waste time copying out the question. Then they take out their little rulers and rule *lines* under it.''

I think Milton succeeded very well in justifying the ways of God to man by making Satan such a horrible person, though Shelley said that Milton was of the Devil's party without knowing it. On the other hand it is probably impossible to justify the ways of God to man because if you believe in God then he can do anything he likes anyway, and if you don't there's no point trying to justify Him. "Paradise Lost" is an epic poem in blank verse, which is another clever way of justifying the ways of God to man because if it rhymed it would seem too pat. My tutor Professor Swallow seduced me in his office last February, if I don't pass this exam I will tell everybody. John Milton was the greatest English poet after Shakespeare. He knew many languages and nearly wrote "Paradise Lost" in Latin in which case nobody would be able to read it today. He locked the door and made me lie on the floor so nobody could see us through the window. I banged my head on the wastepaper bin. He also considered writing his epic poem about King Arthur and the knights of the Round Table, which is a pity he didn't as it would have made a more exciting story.

"How did you get hold of this?" Morris asked, as he skimmed through the script.

"Someone in the Department sent it to me, anonymously. I suspect it was Rupert Sutcliffe. He was first marker on the paper. It was a resit, in September, a couple of years ago. The girl had failed in June. Sutcliffe and some of the other senior members of staff confronted Philip with it."

"And?"

"Oh, he admitted he'd had the girl, on his office carpet, like she said—that rather nice Indian you burned a hole in with your cigar, do you remember?" Hilary's tone was casual, even flippant, but it seemed to Morris that it concealed a deep hurt. "*He* claimed that she seduced him—started unbuttoning her blouse in the middle of a consultation. As if he couldn't have just told her to do it up again. The girl didn't take it any further, fortunately. She left shortly afterwards—her family went abroad.''

''Is that all?''

''What do you mean?''

''I mean, is that the only time Philip has cheated on you?''

''How do I know? It's the only time he's been caught. But nobody I discussed it with seemed particularly surprised. And when I go to Department do's I get a look that I can only describe as pitying.''

They were both silent for a few moments. Then Morris said: ''Hilary, are you trying to tell me that you're unhappy?''

''I suppose I am.''

After another pause, Morris said: ''If Désirée were sitting here now, she'd tell you to forget Philip, make your own life. Get yourself a job, find another guy.''

''It's too late.''

''It's never too late.''

''I took a postgraduate certificate of education course a few years ago,'' said Hilary, ''and as soon as I finished it, they started closing down schools in the city because of the falling birthrate. So there are no jobs. I do a little tutoring for the Open University, but it's not a career. As to lovers, it's definitely too late. You were my first and last, Morris.''

''Hey,'' he said softly.

''Don't be nervous, I'm not going to drag you upstairs for a trip down memory lane . . .''

''Too bad,'' said Morris gallantly, but with a certain relief.

''For one thing, Philip will be back soon . . . No, I made my bed ten years ago, and I must lie in it, cold and lumpy as it often seems.''

''How d'you mean?''

''Well, you know, when the four of us were . . . carrying on. Philip wanted a separation, but I begged him to come back home, give our marriage another chance, go back to being where we were before, a reasonably contented married couple. I was weak. If I'd said, to hell with you, do what you like, I daresay he would have come crawling back with his tail between his legs inside a year. But because I *asked* him to come back, with no conditions, he, well, has me over a barrel, as you would say.''

"Do you still, ah, make it together?''

"Occasionally. But presumably he's not satisfied. There was a story in the paper the other day, about a man who'd had a heart attack and asked his doctor if it was safe to have sexual intercourse, and the doctor said, 'Yes, it's good exercise, but nothing too exciting, just with your wife.' ''

Morris laughed.

"I thought it was funny, too,'' said Hilary. "But when I read it out to Philip he scarcely cracked a smile. He obviously thought it was a deeply poignant story.''

Morris shook his head, and cut himself another slice of Brie. "I'm amazed, Hilary. Frankly, I always thought of you as the dominant partner in this marriage. Now Philip seems to be calling all the shots.''

"Yes, well, things have gone rather well for him lately. He's started to make a bit of name for himself at last. He's even started to look more handsome than he ever did before in his life.''

"I noticed,'' said Morris. "The beard is a knockout.''

"It conceals his weak chin.''

"That silver-grey effect is very distinguished.''

"He has it touched up at the barber's,'' said Hilary. "But middle-age becomes him. It's often the way with men. Whereas women find themselves hit simultaneously by the menopause and the long-term effects of childbearing. It doesn't seem quite fair . . . Anyway, Philip managed to get his Hazlitt book finished at last.''

"I never knew about that,'' Morris said.

"It's had very little attention—rather a sore point with Philip. But it *was* a book, and he had it accepted by Lecky, Windrush and Bernstein just when the chair here became vacant, which was a bit of luck. He'd been effectively running the Department for years, anyway, so they appointed him. His horizons began to expand immediately. You've no idea of the *mana* the title of Professor carries in this country.''

"Oh, I have, I have!'' said Morris Zapp.

"He started to get invited to conferences, to be external

examiner at other universities, he got himself on the British Council's list for overseas lecture tours. He's always off travelling somewhere these days. He's going to Turkey in a few weeks time. Last month it was Norway."

"That's how it is in the academic world these days," said Morris Zapp. "I was telling a young guy at the conference just this morning. The day of the single, static campus is over."

"And the single, static campus novel with it, I suppose?"

"Exactly! Even two campuses wouldn't be enough. Scholars these days are like the errant knights of old, wandering the ways of the world in search of adventure and glory."

"Leaving their wives locked up at home?"

"Well, a lot of the knights are women, these days. There's positive discrimination at the Round Table."

"Bully for them," said Hilary gloomily. "I belong to the generation that sacrificed their careers for their husbands. I never did finish my MA, so now I sit at home growing fat while my silver-haired spouse zooms round the world, no doubt pursued by academic groupies like that Angelica Thingummy he brought here the other night."

"Al Pabst? She's a nice girl. Smart, too."

"But she needs a job, and Philip might be in a position to give her one some day. I could see that in her eyes as she hung on his every word."

"Most of the conference she's been going around with our old friend Dempsey."

"Robin Dempsey? That's a laugh. No wonder Philip was making snide comments about him at breakfast, he's probably jealous. Perhaps Dempsey has a job to fill at Darlington. Shall I make some coffee?"

Morris helped her stack the dishwasher, and then they took their coffee into the lounge. While they were drinking it, Philip returned.

"How was the banquet?" Morris asked.

"Awful, awful," Philip groaned. He sank into a chair and covered his face with his hands. "I don't want to talk about it. Busby deserves to be taken out and shot. Or hung in chains from the walls of Martineau Hall—that would be more appropriate."

"I could have told you it would be awful," said Hilary.

"Why didn't you, then?" said Philip irritably.

"I didn't want to interfere. It's your conference."

"*Was* my conference. Thank God it's over. It's been a total disaster from start to finish."

"Don't say that, Philip," said Morris. "After all, there was my paper."

"It's all very well for you, Morris. You've had a nice quiet evening at home. I've been listening to two degenerate oafs shrieking obscene songs into a microphone for the last two hours, and trying to look as if I was enjoying myself. Then they put me in some stocks and encouraged the others to throw bread rolls at me, and I had to look as if I was enjoying that too."

Hilary crowed with laughter, and clapped her hands. "Oh, now I wish I'd gone," she said. "Did they really throw rolls at you?"

"Yes, and I thought one or two of them did it in a distinctly vindictive fashion," said Phillip sulkily. "But I don't want to talk about it anymore. Let's have a drink."

He produced a bottle of whisky and three glasses, but Hilary yawned and announced her intention of retiring. Morris said he would have to leave early the next morning to catch his plane to London, and perhaps he had better say goodbye to her now.

"Where are you off to, then?" Hilary asked.

"The Rockefeller villa at Bellagio," he said. "It's a kind of scholar's retreat. But I also have a number of conferences lined up for the summer: Zürich, Vienna, maybe Amsterdam. Jerusalem."

"Goodness," said Hilary. "I see what you mean about errant knights."

"Some are more errant than others," said Morris.

"I know," said Hilary meaningfully.

They shook hands and Morris pecked her awkwardly on the cheek. "Take care," he said.

"Why should I?" she said. "*I'm* not doing anything adventurous. Incidentally, I thought you were against foreign travel, Morris. You used to say that travel narrows the mind."

"There comes a moment when the individual has to yield to the *Zeitgeist* or drop out of the ball game," said Morris. "For me it came in '75, when I kept getting invitations to Jane Austen centenary conferences in the most improbable places—Poznan, Delhi, Lagos, Honolulu—and half the speakers turned out to be guys I knew in graduate school. The world is a global campus, Hilary, you'd better believe it. The American Express card has replaced the library pass."

"I expect Philip would agree with you," said Hilary; but Philip, pouring out the whisky, ignored the cue. "Goodnight, then," she said.

"Goodnight, dear," said Philip, without looking up from the glasses. "We'll just have a nightcap." When Hilary had closed the door behind her, Philip handed Morris his drink. "What are all these conferences you're going to this summer?" he asked, with a certain covetousness.

"Zürich is Joyce. Amsterdam is Semiotics. Vienna is Narrative. Or is it Narrative in Amsterdam and Semiotics in Vienna. . . ? Anyway. Jerusalem I *do* know is about the Future of Criticism, because I'm one of the organizers. It's sponsored by a journal called *Metacriticism*, I'm on the editorial board."

"Why Jerusalem?"

"Why not? It's a draw, a novelty. It's a place people want to see, but it's not on the regular tourist circuit. Also the Jerusalem Hilton offers very competitive rates in the summer because it's so goddam hot."

"The Hilton, eh? A bit different from Lucas Hall and Martineau Hall," Philip mused ruefully.

"Right. Look, Philip, I know you were disappointed by the turnout for your conference, but frankly, what can you expect if you're asking people to live in those tacky dormitories and eat canteen meals? Food and accommodation are the most important things about any conference. If the people are happy with *those*, they'll generate intellectual excitement. If they're not, they'll sulk, and sneer, and cut lectures."

Philip shrugged. "I see your point, but people here just can't afford that sort of luxury. Or their universities won't pay for it."

"Not in the UK, they won't. But when I worked here I

discovered an interesting anomaly. You could only have up to fifty pounds a year or some such paltry sum to attend conferences in this country, but there was no limit on grants to attend conferences overseas. The solution is obvious: you should hold your next conference abroad. Somewhere nice and warm, like Monte Carlo, maybe. Meanwhile, why don't you come to Jerusalem this summer?''

"Who, me? To your conference?"

"Sure. You could knock off a paper on the future of criticism, couldn't you?"

"I don't think it *has* much of a future," said Philip.

"Great! It will be controversial. Bring Hilary along for the ride."

"Hilary?" Philip looked disconcerted. "Oh, no, I don't think she could stand the heat. Besides, I doubt if we could afford her fare. Two children at university is a bit of a drain, you know."

"Don't tell me, I'm bracing myself for it next fall."

"Did Hilary put you up to suggesting this, Morris" said Philip, looking slightly ashamed of his own question.

"Certainly not. What makes you think so?"

Philip squirmed uncomfortably in his seat. "It's just that she's been complaining lately that I'm away too much, neglecting the family, neglecting her."

"And are you?"

"I suppose I am, yes. It's the only thing that keeps me going these days, travelling. Changes of scene, changes of faces. It would defeat the whole object to take Hilary along with me on my academic trips."

"What *is* the object?"

Philip sighed. "Who knows? It's hard to put it into words. What are we all looking for? Happiness? One knows that doesn't last. Distraction, perhaps—distraction from the ugly facts: that there is death, there is disease, there is impotence and senility ahead."

"Jesus," said Morris, "are you always like this after a medieval banquet?"

Philip smiled wanly and refilled their glasses. "Intensity," he said. "Intensity of experience is what we're looking for, I think. We know we won't find it at home anymore, but there's always the hope that we'll find it abroad. I found it in America in '69.''

"With Désirée?"

"Not just Désirée, though she was an important part of it. It was the excitement, the richness of the whole experience, the mixture of pleasure and danger and freedom—and the sun. You know, when we came back here, for a long while I still went on living in Euphoria inside my head. Outwardly I returned to my old routine. I got up in the morning, put on a tweed suit, read the *Guardian* over breakfast, walked into the University, gave the same old tutorials on the same old texts . . . and all the while I was leading a completely different life inside my head. Inside my head, I had decided not to come back to England, so I was waking up in Plotinus, sitting in the sun in my happi-coat, looking out over the Bay, putting on Levis and a sports shirt, reading the *Euphoric Times* over breakfast, and wondering what would happen today, would there be a protest, a demonstration, would my class have to fight their way through teargas and picket lines or should we meet off-campus in somebody's apartment, sitting on the floor surrounded by posters and leaflets and paperbacks about encounter groups and avant garde theatre and Viet Nam.''

"That's all over now," said Morris. "You wouldn't recognize the place. The kids are all into fraternities and preppy clothes and working hard to get into law school."

"So I've heard," said Philip. "How depressing."

"But this intensity of experience, did you never find it again since you were in America?"

Philip stared into the bottom of his glass. "Once I did," he said. "Shall I tell you the story?"

"Just let me get myself a cigar. Is this a cigarillo story or a panatella story?"

"I don't know, I've never told it to anyone before."

"I'm honoured," said Morris. "This calls for something special."

Morris left the room to fetch one of his favourite Romeo y Julietas. When he returned, he was conscious that the furniture and lighting had been rearranged in his absence.

Two highbacked armchairs were inclined towards each other across the width of the hearth, where a gas-fire burned low. The only other light in the room came from a standard lamp behind the chair in which Philip sat, his face in shadow. Between the two chairs was a long, low coffee table bearing the whisky bottle, water jug, glasses and an ashtray. Morris's glass had been refilled with a generous measure.

"Is this where the narratee sits?" he enquired, taking the vacant chair. Philip, gazing absently into the fire, smiled vaguely, but made no reply. Morris rolled the cigar next to his ear and listened approvingly to the crackle of the leaves. He pierced one end of the cigar, clipped the other, and lit it, puffing vigorously. "OK," he said, examining the tip to see that it was burning evenly. "I'm listening."

"It happened some years ago, in Italy," Philip began. "It was the very first lecture tour I did for the British Council. I flew out to Naples, and then worked my way up the country by train: Rome, Florence, Bologna, Padua, ending up at Genoa. It was a bit of a rush on the last day. I gave my lecture in the afternoon, and I was booked to fly home the same evening. The Council chap in Genoa, who'd been shepherding me about the place, gave me an early dinner in a restaurant, and then drove me out to the airport. There was a delay in the flight departure—a technical problem, they said, so I told him not to wait. I knew he had to get up early the next morning to drive to Milan for a meeting. That comes into the story."

"I should hope so," said Morris. "There should be nothing irrelevant in a good story."

"Anyway, the British Council man, J. K. Simpson, I can't remember his first name, a nice young chap, very friendly, enthusiastic about his job, he said, 'OK, I'll leave you then, but if the flight's cancelled, give me a ring and I'll get you into a hotel for the night.'

"Well, the delay went on and on, but eventually we took off, at about midnight. It was a British plane. I was sitting next to an English businessman, a salesman in woollen textiles I think he was . . ."

"Is that relevant?"

"Not really."

"Never mind. Solidity of specification," said Morris with a tolerant wave of his cigar. "It contributes to the reality effect."

"We were sitting towards the rear of the aircraft, just behind the wing. He had the window set, and I was next to him. About ten minutes out of Genoa, they were just getting ready to serve drinks, you could hear the clink of bottles from the back of the plane, when this salesman chap turned away from the window, and tapped me on the arm and said, 'Excuse me, but would you mind having a look out there. Is it my imagination or is that engine on fire?' So I leaned across him and looked out of the window. It was dark of course, but I could see flames sort of licking round the engine. Well, I'd never looked closely at a jet engine at night before, for all I knew that was always the effect they gave. I mean you might expect to see a kind of fiery glow coming out of the engine at night. On the other hand, these were definitely flames, and they weren't just coming out of the hole at the back. 'I don't know what to think,' I said. 'It certainly doesn't look quite right.' 'Do you think we should tell somebody?' he said. 'Well, they must have seen it for themselves, mustn't they?' I said. The fact was, neither of us wanted to look a fool by suggesting that something was wrong, and then being told that it wasn't. Fortunately a chap on the other side of the aisle noticed that we were exercised about something, and came across to have a look for himself. 'Christ!' he said, and pushed the button to call the stewardess. I think he was probably some sort of engineer. The stewardess came by with the drinks trolley at that moment. 'If it's a drink you want, you'll have to wait your turn,' she said. The cabin staff were a bit snappish because of the long delay. 'Does the captain know that his starboard engine is on fire?' said the engineer. She gaped at him, squinted out of the window, then ran up the aisle, pushing her trolley in front of her, like a nursemaid running with a pram. A minute later and a man in uniform, the second pilot I suppose, came down the aisle, looking worried and carrying a big torch, which he shone out the window at the engine. It was on fire all right. He ran back to the cockpit. Very soon the plane banked and headed back to Genoa. The

Captain came on the PA to say that we would be making an emergency landing because of a technical problem, and that we should be prepared to leave the aircraft by the emergency exits. Then somebody else told us exactly what to do. I must say he sounded remarkably cool, calm and collected."

"It was a cassette," said Morris. "They have these prerecorded cassettes for all contingencies. I was in a Jumbo, once, going over the Rockies, and a stewardess put on the emergency ditching tape by mistake. We were having lunch at the time, I remember, a perfect sunny day at 30,000 feet, when this voice suddenly said, *'We are obliged to make an emergency landing on water. Do not panic if you are unable to swim. The rescue services have been advised of our intentions.'* People froze with their forks halfway to their mouths. Then all hell let loose until they sorted it out."

"There was a fair amount of wailing and gnashing of teeth in our plane—quite a lot of the passengers were Italian, and you know what they're like—they don't hide their feelings. Then the pilot put the plane into a terrifying dive to put the fire out."

"Jesus!" said Morris Zapp.

"He was thoughtful enough to explain first what he was going to do, but only in English, so all the Italians thought we were going to crash into the sea and started to scream and weep and cross themselves. But the dive worked—it put the fire out. Then we had to circle over the sea for about twenty minutes, jettisoning fuel, before we tried to land back at Genoa. It was a very long twenty minutes."

"I'll bet."

"Frankly, I thought they were going to be my last twenty minutes."

"What did you think about?"

"I thought, how stupid. I thought, how unfair. I suppose I prayed. I imagined Hilary and the children hearing about the crash on the radio when they woke up the next morning, and I felt bad about that. I thought about surviving but being terribly crippled. I tried to remember the terms of the British Council's insurance policy for lecturers on Specialist Tours— so much for an arm, so much for a leg below the knee, so much for a leg above the knee. I tried not to think about being burned to death.

"Landing at Genoa is a pretty hairy experience at the best of times. I don't know if you know it, but there's this great high promontory that sticks out into the sea. Planes approaching from the north have to make a U-turn round it, and then come in between it and the mountains, over the city and the docks. And we were doing it at night with one engine kaput. The airport was on full emergency alert, of course, but being a small airport, in Italy, that didn't amount to much. As we hit the ground, I could see the fire trucks with their lights flashing, racing towards us. As soon as the plane stopped, the cabin crew opened the emergency exits and we all slid out down those inflatable chute things. The trouble was they couldn't open the emergency exit nearest to us, me and the wool man, because it gave on to the wing with the duff engine. So we were the last out of the plane. I remember thinking it was rather unfair, because if it hadn't been for us the whole thing might have blown up in mid-air.

"Anyway, we got out all right, ran like hell to a bus they had waiting, and were taken to the terminal. The fire engines smothered the plane in foam. While they were getting our baggage out of the plane I telephoned the British Council chap. I suppose I wanted to express my relief at having survived by telling somebody. It was queer to think that Hilary and the children were asleep in England, not knowing that I'd had a narrow escape from death. I didn't want to wake Hilary up with a call and give her a pointless retrospective fright. But I felt I had to tell *someone* . Also, I wanted to get out of the airport. A lot of the Italian passengers were in hysterics, kissing the ground and weeping and crossing themselves and so on. It was obvious that we shouldn't be flying out till the next morning and that it was going to take hours to sort out our accommodation for the night. And Simpson had told me to phone him if there was any problem, so although it was now well past one o'clock, I did. As soon as he grasped what had happened, he said he'd come straight out to the airport. So about half an hour later, he picked me up and drove me into the city to find a hotel. We tried a few, but no luck—either they were shut up for the night or they were full, there was a trade fair on in Genoa that week. So he said, look, why don't you come home with me, we haven't got a guest bedroom, I'm afraid, but there's a kind of put-u-up in the living-room. So he took me home to his apartment, in a modern block, halfway up the mountain that overlooks the city and the sea. I felt extraordinarily calm and wide-awake, I was rather impressed by my own sangfroid, as a matter of fact. But when he offered me some brandy I didn't say no. I looked around the living-room, and felt a sudden pang of homesickness. I'd been living in hotel rooms for the past twelve days, and eating meals in restaurants. I rather enjoy that nowadays, but then I was still a bit of a novice at the foreign lecture tour, and I'd found it quite a strain. And here was a little oasis of English domesticity, where I could relax and feel completely at home. There were toys scattered about the living-room, and English newspapers, and in the bathroom St Michaels's underwear hanging up to dry. While we were drinking the brandy, and I was telling Simpson the whole story of the plane, his wife came into the room, in her dressing-gown, yawning and rubbing the sleep out of her eyes. I hadn't met her before. Her name was Joy."

"Ah," murmured Morris. "You remember *her* first name."

"I apologized for disturbing her. She said it didn't matter, but she didn't look particularly pleased. She asked me if I would like something to eat, and I suddenly realized that I was ravenously hungry. So she brought some Parma ham from the kitchen, and some cake, and a pot of tea, and we ended up having a sort of impromptu meal. I was sitting opposite Joy. She was wearing a soft blue velour dressing-gown, with a hood, and a zip that went from hem to throat. Hilary had one just like it once, and looking at Joy out of the corner of my eye was like looking at some younger, prettier version of Hilary—I mean, Hilary when she was young and pretty herself, when we were first married. Joy was, I guessed, in her early thirties, with fair wavy hair and blue eyes. A rather heavy chin, but with a wide, generous mouth, full lips. She had a trace of a northern accent, Yorkshire I thought. She did a little English teaching, conversation classes at the university, but basically saw her rôle as supporting her husband's career. I daresay she made the effort to get up and be hospitable to me for his sake. Well, as we talked, and ate, and drank, I suddenly felt myself overcome with the most powerful desire for Joy.''

"I knew it," said Morris

"It was as if, having passed through the shadow of death, I had suddenly recovered an appetite for life that I thought I had lost for ever, since returning from America to England. In a way it was keener than anything I had ever known before. The food pierced me with its exquisite flavours, the tea was fragrant as ambrosia, and the woman sitting opposite to me seemed unbearably beautiful, all the more because she was totally unconscious of her attractions for me. Her hair was tousled and her face was pale and puffy from sleep, and she had no make-up or lipstick on, of course. She sat quietly, cradling her mug of tea in both hands, not saying much, smiling faintly at her husband's jokes, as if she'd heard them before. I honestly think that I would have felt just the same about any woman, in that situation, at that moment, who wasn't downright ugly. Joy just represented woman for me then. She was like Milton's Eve, Adam's dream—he woke and found it true, as Keats says. I suddenly thought how nice women were. How soft and kind. How lovely it would be, now *natural*, to go across and put my arms round her, to bury my head in her lap. All this while Simpson was telling me about the appalling standards of English-language teaching in Italian secondary schools. Eventually he glanced at his watch and said that it had gone four, and instead of going back to bed he thought he would drive to Milan while he was wide awake and rest when he got there. He was taking the Council car, he told me, so Joy would run me to the airport in theirs.''

"I know what's coming," said Morris, "yet I can hardly believe it."

"He had his bag already packed, so it was only a few minutes before he was gone. We shooks hands, and he wished me better luck with my flight the next day. Joy went with him to the front door of the apartment, and I heard them kiss goodbye. She came back into the living-room, looking a little shy. The blue dressing-gown was a couple of inches too long for her, and she had to hold up the skirt in front of her—it gave her a courtly, vaguely medieval air as she came back into the room. I noticed that her feet were bare. 'I'm sure you'd like to get some sleep now,' she said. 'There is a second bed in Gerard's room, but if I put you in there he might be scared when he wakes up in the morning.' I said the sofa would be fine. 'But Gerard gets up frightfully early, I'm afraid he'll disturb you,' she said. 'If you don't mind taking our bed, I could quite easily go into his room myself.' I said no, no; she pressed me, and said would I just give her a few moments to change the sheets, and I said I wouldn't dream of putting her to such trouble. The thought of that bed, still warm from her body, was too much for me. I started to shake all over with the effort to stop myself from taking an irrevocable leap into moral space, pulling on the zip-tab at her throat like a parachute ripcord, and falling with her to the floor.''

"That's a very fancy metaphor, Philip," said Morris. "I can hardly believe you've never told this story before."

"Well, actually, I did write it down," said Philip, "for my own satisfaction. But I've never shown it to anybody." He refilled their glasses. "Anyway, there we were, looking at each other. We heard a car accelerate away outside, down the hill, Simpson presumably. 'What's the matter?' she said, 'You're trembling all over.' She was trembling herself a little. I said I supposed it was shock. Delayed reaction. She gave me some more brandy, and swallowed some herself. I could tell that she knew it wasn't really shock that was making me tremble, that it was herself, her proximity, but she couldn't quite credit her own intuition. 'You'd better lie down,' she said, 'I'll show you the bedroom.'

"I followed her into the main bedroom. It was lit by a single bedside lamp with a purple shade. There was a large double bed, with a duvet half thrown back. She straightened it out, and plumped the pillows. I was still shaking all over. She asked me if I would like a hot water bottle. I said: 'There's only one thing that would stop me shaking like this. If you would put your arms round me . . .'

"Although it was a dim light in the room, I could see that she went very red. 'I can't do that,' she said. 'You shouldn't ask me.' 'Please,' I said, and took a step towards her.

"Ninety-nine women out of a hundred would have walked straight out of the room, perhaps slapped my face. But Joy just stood there. I stepped up close to her and put my arms round her. God, it was wonderful. I could feel the warmth of her breasts coming through the velour dressing-gown, and my shirt. She put her arms round me and gently clasped my back. I stopped shaking as if by magic. I had my chin on her shoulder and I was moaning and raving into her ear about how wonderful and generous and beautiful she was, and what ecstasy it was to hold her in my arms, and how I felt reconnected to the earth and the life force and all kinds of romantic nonsense. And all the time I was looking at myself reflected in the dressing-table mirror, in this weird purple light, my chin on her shoulder, my hands moving over her back, as if I were watching a film, or looking into a crystal ball. It didn't seem possible that it was really happening. I saw my hands slide down the small of her back and cup her buttocks, bunching the skirt of her dressing-gown, and I said to the man in the mirror, silently, in my head, you're crazy, now she'll break away, slap your face, scream for help. But she didn't. I saw her back arch and felt her press against me. I swayed, and staggered slightly, and as I recovered my balance I altered my position a little, and now in the mirror I could see her face, reflected in another mirror on the other side of the room, and, my God, there was an expression of total abandonment on it, her eyes were half shut and her lips were parted and she was smiling. Smiling! So I pulled back my head and kissed her, full on the lips. Her tongue went straight into my mouth like a warm eel. I pulled gently at the zip on the front of her dressing-gown and slid my hand inside. She was naked underneath it."

Philip paused and stared into the fire. Morris discovered that he was sitting forward on the edge of his seat and that his cigar had gone out. "Yeah?" he said, fumbling for his lighter. "Then what happened?"

"I slipped the dressing-gown from her shoulders, and it crackled with static electricity as it slid off and settled at her feet. I fell on my knees and buried my face in her belly. She ran her fingers through my hair, and dug her nails into my shoulders. I lay her down on the bed and began to tear off my clothes with one hand while I kept stroking her with the other, afraid that if I once let go of her I would lose her. I had just enough presence of mind to ask if she was protected, and she nodded, without opening her eyes. Then we made love. There was nothing particularly subtle or prolonged about it, but I've never had an orgasm like it, before or since. I felt I was defying death, fucking my way out of the grave. She had to put her hand over my mouth, to stop me from shouting her name aloud: Joy, Joy, Joy.

"Then, almost instantly, I fell asleep. When I woke up I was alone in the bed, naked, covered with the duvet. Sunlight was coming through the cracks in the window shutters, and I could hear a vacuum cleaner going in another room. I looked at my watch. It was 10.30. I wondered if I had just dreamed of making love to Joy, but the physical memory was too keen and specific, and my clothes were scattered round the floor where I had thrown them off the night before. I put on my shirt and trousers and went out of the bedroom, into the living-room. A little Italian woman with a scarf round her head was hoovering the carpet. She grinned at me, turned off the Hoover and said something unintelligible. Joy came into the room from the kitchen, with a little boy at her side, holding a Dinky car, who stared at me. Joy looked quite different from the night before— smarter and more poised. She seemed to have cut her hand and was wearing an Elastoplast, but otherwise she was immaculately turned out, in some kind of linen dress, and her hair was smooth and bouncy as if she had just washed it. She gave me a bright, slightly artificial smile, but avoided eye contact. 'Oh, hallo,' she said, 'I was just going to wake you.' She had phoned the airport and my plane left at 12.30. She would run me down there as soon as I was ready. Would I like some breakfast, or would I like to take a shower first? She was the complete British Council hostess— polite, patient, detached. She actually asked me if I'd slept well. I wondered again whether the episode with her the night before had been a wet dream, but when I saw the blue dressing-gown hanging on the back of the bathroom door, it brought the whole thing back with a sensuous detail that just couldn't have been imaginary. The exact shape of her nipples,

blunt and cylindrical, was imprinted on the nerve-endings of
my finger-tips. I remembered the unusual luxuriance of her
pubic hair, and its pale gold colour, tinged with purple from
the bedside lamp, and the line across her belly where her
sun-tan stopped. I couldn't have dreamed all that. But it was
impossible to have any kind of intimate conversation with
her, what with the cleaning woman hoovering away, and the
little boy round her feet all the time. And it was obvious that
she didn't want to anyway. She bustled about the flat and
chattered to the cleaning woman and the boy. Even when
she drove me to the airport she brought the kid along with
her, and he was a sharp little bugger, who didn't miss much.
Although he was sitting in the back, he kept leaning forward
and poking his head between the two of us, as if to stop us
getting intimate. It began to look as if we would part
without a single reference to what had happened the night
before. It was absurd. I just couldn't make her out. I felt I
had to discover what had prompted her extraordinary action.
Was she some kind of nymphomaniac, who would give
herself to any man who was available—was I the most
recent of a long succession of British Council lecturers who
had passed through that purple-lit bedroom? It even crossed
my mind that Simpson was in collusion with her, that I had
been a pawn in some kinky erotic game between them, that
perhaps he had returned silently to the flat and hidden
himself behind one of those mirrors in the bedroom. A
glance at her profile at the wheel of the car was enough to
make such speculations seem fantastic—she looked so normal, so wholesome, so English. What had motivated her,
then? I was desperate to know.

"When we got to the airport, she said, 'You won't mind
if I just drop you, will you?' But she had to get out of the
car to open the boot for me, and I realized that this was my
only chance to say anything to her privately. 'Aren't we
going to talk about last night?' I said, as I lifted my bag out
of the boot. 'Oh,' she said, with her bright hostess's smile,
'you mustn't worry about disturbing our sleep. We're used
to it in this job, people arriving at all sorts of odd hours.
Not usually, of course, in burning aeroplanes. I do hope you
have a less eventful flight today. Goodbye, Mr Swallow.'

" 'Mr Swallow!' This was the women who just a few hours before had had her legs wrapped somewhere round the back of my neck! Well, it was very clear that, whatever her motives, she wanted to pretend that nothing had happened between us the night before—that she wanted to excise the whole episode from history, cancel it, unweave it. And that the best way I could convey my own gratitude was to play along with her. So, with great reluctance, I didn't press for an inquest. I just allowed myself one indulgence. She'd extended her hand, and, instead of just shaking it, I pressed it to my lips. I reckoned it wouldn't seem a particularly showy gesture in an Italian airport. She blushed, as deeply as she had blushed the night before when I asked her to put her arms round me, and the whole unbelievable tenderness of that embrace flooded back into my consciousness, and hers too, I could see. Then she went back to the front of the car, got into the driver's seat, gave me one last look through the window, and drove away. I never saw her again."

"Maybe you will one day," said Morris.

Philip shook his head. "No, she's dead."

"Dead?"

"All three of them were killed in an air-crash the following year, in India. I saw their names in the list of passengers. There were no survivors. 'Simpson, J. K., wife Joy and son Gerard.' "

Morris expelled his breath in a low whistle. "Hey, that's really sad! I didn't think this story was going to have an unhappy ending."

"Ironic, too, isn't it, when you think of how we met? At first I felt horribly guilty, as if I had somehow passed on to her a death which I had narrowly escaped myself. I convinced myself that it was just superstition. But I shall always keep a little shrine to Joy in my heart."

"A little what?"

"A shrine," Philip said solemnly. Morris coughed cigar smoke and let it pass. "She gave me back an appetite for life I thought I had lost for ever. It was the total unexpectedness, the gratuitousness of that giving of herself. It convinced me that life was still worth living, that I should make the most of what I had left."

"And have you had any more adventures like that one?" Morris enquired, feeling slightly piqued at the extent to which he had been affected, first by the eroticism of Philip's tale, then by its sad epilogue.

Philip blushed slightly. "One thing I learned from it, was never to say no to someone who asks for your body, never reject someone who freely offers you theirs."

"I see," said Morris drily. "Have you agreed this code with Hilary?"

"Hilary and I don't see eye to eye on a lot of things. Some more whisky?"

"Positively the last one. I have to get up at five tomorrow."

"And what about you, Morris?" said Philip, pouring out the whisky. "How's your sex life these days?"

"Well, after Désirée and I split up I tried to get married again. I had various women living in, graduate students mostly, but none of them would marry me—girls these days have no principles—and I gradually lost interest in the idea. I'm living on my own right now. I jog. I watch TV. I write my books. Sometimes I go to a massage parlour in Esseph."

"A massage parlour?" Philip looked shocked.

"They have a very nice class of girl in those places, you know. They're not hookers. College-educated. Clean, well-groomed, articulate. When I was a teenager I spent many exhausting hours trying to persuade girls like that to jerk me off in the back seat of my old man's Chevvy. Now it's as easy as going to the supermarket. It saves a lot of time and nervous energy."

"But there's no relationship!"

"Relationships kill sex, haven't you learned that yet? The longer a relationship goes on, the less sexual excitement there is. Don't kid yourself, Philip—do you think it would have been as great with Joy the second time, if there'd been one?"

"Yes," said Philip. "Yes."

"And the twenty-second time? The two hundredth time?"

"I suppose not," Philip admitted. "Habit ruins everything in the end, doesn't it? Perhaps *that's* what we're all looking for—desire undiluted by habit."

"The Russian Formalists had a word for it," said Morris.

"I'm sure they did," said Philip. "But it's no use telling me what it was, because I'm sure to forget it."

"*Ostranenie,*" said Morris. "Defamiliarization. It was what they thought literature was all about. *'Habit devours objects, clothes, furniture, one's wife and the fear of war . . . Art exists to help us recover the sensation of life.'* Viktor Shklovsky."

"Books used to satisfy me," said Philip. "But as I get older I find they aren't enough."

"But you're hitting the trail again soon, eh? Hilary tells me Turkey. What are you doing there?"

"Another British Council tour. I'm lecturing on Hazlitt."

"Are they very interested in Hazlitt in Turkey?"

"I shouldn't think so, but it's the bicentenary of his birth. Or rather, it was, last year, when this trip was first mooted. It's taken rather a long time to get off the ground . . . By the way, did you receive a copy of my Hazlitt book?"

"No—I was just saying to Hilary, I hadn't even heard about it."

Philip uttered an exclamation of annoyance. "Isn't that typical of publishers? I specifically asked them to send you a complimentary copy. Let me give you one now." He took from the bookcase a volume in a pale blue wrapper, scribbled a dedication inside, and handed it to Morris. It was entitled *Hazlitt and the Amateur Reader.* "I don't expect you to agree with it, Morris, but if you think it has any merit at all, I'd be very greatful if you could do anything to get it reviewed somewhere. It hasn't had a single notice, so far."

"It doesn't look like the sort of thing *Metacriticism* is interested in," said Morris. "But I'll see what I can do." He riffled through the pages. "Hazlitt is kind of an unfashionable subject, isn't he?"

"Unjustly neglected, in my view," said Philip. "A very interesting man. Have you read *Liber Amoris*?"

"I don't think so."

"It's a lightly fictionalized account of his obsession with his landlady's daughter. He was estranged from his wife at the time, hoping rather vainly to get a divorce. She was the archetypal pricktease. Would sit on his knee and let him feel her up, but not sleep with him or promise to marry him when he was free. It nearly drove him insane. He was totally obsessed. Then one day he saw her out with another man. End of illusion. Hazlitt shattered. I can feel for him. That girl must have—''

Philip's voice faltered, and Morris saw him turn pale, staring at the living-room door. Following the direction of his gaze, Morris saw Hilary standing at the threshold, wearing a faded blue velour dressing-gown, with a hood and a zip that ran from throat to hem.

''I couldn't sleep,'' she said. ''Then I realized I'd forgotten to tell you not to lock the front door. Matthew isn't in yet. Are you feeling all right, Philip? You look as if you'd seen a ghost.''

''That dressing-gown . . .''

''What about it? I dug it out because my other one's at the cleaners.''

''Oh, nothing, I thought you'd got rid of it years ago,'' said Philip. He drained his glass. ''Time for bed, I think.''

PART II

AT 5 a.m., precisely, Morris Zapp is woken by the bleeping of his digital wristwatch, a sophisticated piece of miniaturized technology which can inform him, at the touch of a button, of the exact time anywhere in the world. In Cooktown, Queensland, Australia, for instance, it is 3 p.m., a fact of no interest to Morris Zapp, as he yawns and gropes for the bedside lamp switch—though as it happens, at this very moment in Cooktown, Queensland, Rodney Wainwright, of the University of North Queensland, is labouring over a paper for Morris Zapp's Jerusalem conference on the Future of Criticism.

It is hot, very hot, this afternoon, in North Queensland; sweat makes the ballpen in Rodney Wainwright's fingers slippery to hold, and dampens the page where the cushion of his palm rests upon it. From his desk in the study of his one-storey house here on the steamy outskirts of Cooktown, Rodney Wainwright can hear the sounds of the waves breaking on the nearby beach. There, he knows, are most of his students in English 351, ''Theories of Literature from Coleridge to Barthes'', cleaving the blue and white water or lying prone on the dazzling sand, the girls with their bikini bra straps trailing, untied for an even tan. Rodney Wainwright knows they are there because this morning, after the class broke up, they invited him to join them, grinning and nudging each other, a friendly but challenging gesture which, being decoded, meant: *"OK, we've played your cultural game this morning—are you willing to play ours this afternoon?"* "Sorry," he had said, "there's nothing I'd like more, but I have this paper to write." Now they are on the beach and he is at his desk. Later, as the sun sinks behind their backs, they will break out cans of beer and light a barbecue fire and someone will pick out a tune on a guitar. When it is quite dark there may be a proposal to go swimming in the nude—Rodney Wainwright has heard rumours that this is the usual climax to a beach party. He imagines the participation in such exercise of Sandra Dix, the buxom blonde from England who always sits in the front row of English 351 with her mouth and blouse-front perpetually agape. Then, with a sigh, he focuses his vision on the ruled foolscap before him, and re-reads what he wrote ten minutes ago.

> *The question is, therefore, how can literary criticism maintain its Arnoldian function of identifying the best which has been thought and said, when literary discourse itself has been decentred by deconstructing the traditional concept of the author, of authority?*

Rodney Wainwright inserts a pair of inverted commas around *"authority"* and wills his mind to think of the next sentence. The paper must be finished soon, for Morris Zapp has asked to see a draft before accepting it for the conference, and on acceptance depends the travel grant which will enable Rodney Wainwright to fly to Europe this summer (or rather winter), to refresh his mind at the fountainhead of modern critical thought, making useful and influential contacts, adding to the little pile of scholarly honours, distinctions, achievements, that may eventually earn him a chair at Sydney or Melbourne. He does not want to grow old in Cooktown, Queensland. It is no country for old men. Even now, at thirty-eight, he stands no chance with the likes of Sandra Dix beside the bronzed and bulging heroes of the beach. The effects of twenty years' dedication to the life of the mind are all too evident when he puts on a pair of swimming trunks, however loosely cut: beneath the large, balding, bespectacled head is a pale, pear-shaped torso, with skinny limbs attached like afterthoughts in a child's drawing. And even if by some miracle Sandra Dix should be inclined to overlook these imperfections of the flesh in the dazzled contemplation of his mind, his wife Beverley would soon put a stop to any attempt at friendship beyond the call of tutorial duty.

As if to reinforce his thought, Bev's broad bum, inadequately disguised by an ethnic print frock, now intrudes into the frame of Rodney Wainwright's abstracted vision. Bent nearly double, and sweating profusely under her floppy sunhat, she is shuffling backwards across the rank lawn, dragging something—what? A hosepipe? A rope? Some animal on a lead? Eventually it proves to be a child's toy, some brightly coloured wheeled object that wags and oscillates obscenely as it moves along, followed by a gurgling toddler, a child of some visiting neighbour. A strong-minded woman, Bev. Rodney Wainwright regards her bottom with respect, but without desire. He imagines Sandra Dix executing the same movement in her blue jeans, and sighs. He forces his eyes back on to the ruled foolscap before him.

"One possible solution," he writes, and then pauses, gnawing the end of his ballpen.

> *One possible solution would be to run to the beach,*
> *seize Sandra Dix by the hand, drag her behind a*
> *sand dune, pull down her bikini pants and*

"Cuppa tea, Rod? I'm just going to make one for Meg and me."

Bev's red perspiring face peers in at the open window. Rodney stops writing and guiltily covers his pad. After she has gone, he rips out the page, tears it up into small pieces, and tosses it into the wastepaper basket, where it joins several other torn and screwed-up pieces of paper. He starts again on a clean sheet.

The question is, therefore, how can literary criticism...

Morris Zapp, who has nodded off these last few minutes, suddenly wakes again in a flurry of panic, but, examining the illuminated face of his digital watch, is relieved to discover that it is only 5.15. He gets out of bed, scratching himself and shivering slightly (the Swallows, with typical British parsimony, switch off the central heating at night), pulls on a bathrobe and pads softly across the landing to the bathroom. He tugs at the lightcord just inside the door and flinches as blinding fluorescent light pings and ricochets off white and yellow tiles. He micturates, washes his hands, and puts out his tongue at the mirror above the handbasin. It resembles, this tongue, the dried-out bed of a badly polluted river. Too much alcohol and too many cigars last night. And every night.

This is a low-point in the day of the globe-trotting academic, when he must wrench himself from sleep, and rise alone in the dark to catch his early plane; staring at his coated tongue in the mirror, rubbing red-rimmed eyes, fingering the stubble on his jowls, he wonders momentarily why he is doing it, whether the game is worth the candle. To shake off these depressing thoughts, Morris Zapp decides to take a quick shower, and too bad if the whining and shuddering of the water pipes wakes his hosts. He whines and shudders himself in some degree, since the water is barely tepid, but the effect of the shower is invigorating. His world-wide traveller's razor, designed to operate on all known electric currents, and if need be on its own batteries, hums, and Morris Zapp's brain begins to hum too. He glances at his watch again: 5.30. The taxi has been ordered for six, time enough for him to fix himself a cup of coffee in the kitchen downstairs. He will breakfast at Heathrow while he waits for his connection to Milan.

Three thousand miles to the west, at Helicon, New Hampshire, a writers' colony hidden deep in a pine forest, Morris Zapp's ex-wife, Désirée, tosses restlessly in bed. It is 12.30, and she has been awake since retiring an hour earlier. This is, she knows, because she is anxious about the previous day's work. A thousand words she managed to write in

one of the little cabins in the woods to which, each morning, the resident writers repair with their lunch pails and
thermos flasks, to lock themselves away with their respec-
tive muses; and she came back to the main house in the late
afternoon exhilarated by this exceptional achievement. But
as she chatted with the other writers and artists in the course
of the evening, over dinner, in front of the TV, across the
ping-pong table, tiny doubts began to assail her about those
thousand words. Were they the right, the only possible
words? She resisted the urge to rush upstairs to her room to
read them through again. The routine at Helicon is strict,
almost monastic: the days are for silent, solitary wrestling
with the creative act; the evenings for sociability, conversation, relaxation. Désirée promised herself she would not
look at her manuscript before she went to bed, but let it lie
till morning, let the first minutes of the next day be reserved
for the purpose—the longer she left it the more likely she
was to forget what she had written, the more likely therefore
that she would be able to *read herself* with something like
an objective eye, to feel, without anticipating it, the shock
of recognition she hoped to evoke in her readers.

She went to bed at 11.30, with her eyes consciously
averted from the orange folder, lying on top of the pine
chest, which contained the precious thousand words. But it
seemed to glow in the dark—even now, with her eyes
closed, she can feel its presence, like a pulsing source of
radioactivity. It is part of a book that Désirée has been
trying to write for the past four years, a book combining
fiction and non-fiction—fantasy, criticism, confession and
speculation; a book entitled, simply, *Men*. Each section has
at its head a well-known proverb or aphorism about women
in which the key-word had been replaced by "man" or
"men". She has already written, "Frailty Thy Name Is
Man", "No Fury Like A Man Scorned" and "Wicked Men
Bother One. Good Men Bore One. That Is The Only
Difference Between Them." Presently she is working on the
inversion of Freud's celebrated cry of bafflement: "What
Does A Man Want?" The answer, according to Désirée is,
"Everything—and then some."

Désirée turns on to her stomach and kicks impatiently at

the skirt of her nightdress, which has gotten entangled round
her legs with all her twisting and turning. She wonders
whether to try and relax with the help of her vibrator, but it
is an instrument she uses, as a nun her discipline, more out
of principle than real enthusiasm, and besides, the battery is
nearly flat, it might run out of juice before she reached her
climax, just like a man—hey, that's quite good! She switches
on the lamp on the night-table and scrawls in the little notebook she keeps always within reach: *"Vibrator with flat
battery just like a man."* Out of the corner of her eye she
can see the orange folder burning into the varnished wood
of the chest. She turns out the light, but now she is wide
awake, it is hopeless, there is nothing to be done but to take
a sleeping pill, though it will make her sluggish for the first
couple of hours in the morning. She turns on the night-table
lamp again. Now where are the pills? Oh yes, on the chest,
next to the manuscript. Perhaps if she allows herself one
tiny peep, just one sentence to go to sleep on . . .

Standing at the chest in her bare feet, with a sleeping
tablet in one hand, arrested halfway to her mouth, Désirée
opens the folder and begins to read. Before she knows it,
she has come to the end of the three typed pages, swallowed
them in three greedy gulps. She can hardly believe that the
words which it cost her so many hours and so much effort to
find and weld together could be consumed so quickly; or
that they could seem so vague, so tentative, so uncertain of
themselves. It will all have to be rewritten tomorrow. She
swallows a pill, then a second, wanting only oblivion now.
Waiting for the pills to do their work, she stands at the
window and looks out at the tree-covered hills which surround the writers' colony, a monotonous, monochrome landscape in the cold light of the moon. Trees as far as the eye
can see. Enough trees to make a million and a half paperback copies of *Men*. Two million. "Grow, trees, grow!"
Désirée whispers. She refuses to admit the possibility of
defeat. She returns to the bed and lies stiffly on her back,
her eyes closed, her arms at her side, waiting for sleep.

Morris Zapp returns to the guest bedroom, dresses himself
comfortably for travelling—corduroy pants, white cotton

polo-neck sports jacket—closes and locks the suitcase he had packed the night before, checks the closet and drawers for any stray belongings, pats various pockets to confirm the presence of his life-support system: billfold, passport, tickets, pens, spectacles, cigars. He tiptoes, as far as it is possible for a man carrying a heavy suitcase to tiptoe, across the landing, and carefully descends the stairs, each tread of which creaks under his weight. He puts the case down beside the front door and glances at his watch again. 5.45.

Far out above the cold North Atlantic ocean, aboard TWA Flight 072 from Chicago to London, time suddenly jumps from 2.45 to 3.45, as the Lockheed Tristar slips through the invisible interface between two time-zones. Few of the three hundred and twenty-three souls aboard are aware of the change. Most of them still have their watches adjusted to Chicago local time, where it is 11.45 p.m. on the previous day, and anyway most of them are asleep or trying to sleep. Aperitifs and dinner have been served, the movie has been shown, duty-free liquor and cigarettes dispensed to those desirous of purchasing them. The cabin crew, weary from the performance of these tasks, are clustered round the galleys, quietly gossiping as they check their stocks and takings. The refrigerated cabinets, the microwave ovens and electric urns, which were full when the aircraft took off from O'Hare airport, are now empty. Most of the food and drink they contained is now in the passengers' bellies, and before they land at Heathrow much of it will be in the septic tanks in the aircraft's belly.

The main lights in the passenger section, doused for the showing of the film, have not been switched on again. The passengers, replete, and in many cases sozzled, sleep uneasily. They slump and twist in their seats, trying vainly to arrange their bodies in a horizontal position, their heads loll on their shoulders as if they have been garroted, their mouths gape in foolish smiles or ugly sneers. A few passengers, unable to sleep, are listening to recorded music on stereophonic headphones, or even reading, in the narrow beams of the tiny spotlights artfully angled in the cabin ceiling for that purpose; reading books about sex and adven-

ture by Jacqueline Susann and Harold Robbins and Jack
Higgins, thick paperbacks with gaudy covers bought from
the bookstalls at O'Hare. Only one reader has a hardback
book on her lap, and actually seems to be making notes as
she reads. She sits erect, alert, in a window seat in row 16
in the Ambassador class. Her face is in shadow, but looks
handsome, aristocratic, in profile, like a face on an old
medallion, with a high, noble brow, a haughty Roman nose,
and a determined mouth and chin. In the pool of light shed
onto her lap, an exquisitely manicured hand guides a slender
gold-plated propelling pencil across the lines of print, occasionally pausing to underline a sentence or make a marginal
note. The long, spear-shaped finger-nails on the hand are
lacquered with terracotta varnish. The hand itself, long and
white and slender, looks almost weighed down with three
antique rings in which are set ruby, sapphire and emerald
stones. At the wrist there is a chunky gold bracelet and the
hint of a cream silk shirt-cuff nestling inside the sleeve of a
brown velvet jacket. The reader's legs are clothed in generously
cut knickerbockers of the same soft material, terminating
just below the knee. Her calves are sheathed in cream-
coloured textured hose and her feet in kidskin slippers
which have replaced, for the duration of the flight, a pair of
high-heeled fashion boots made of cream leather, engraved,
under the instep, with the name of an exclusive Milanese
maker of custom footwear. The lacquered nails flash in the
beam of the reading lamp as a page is crisply turned,
flattened and smoothed, and the slender gold pencil continues its steady traversing of the page. The heading at the top
of the page is "Ideology and Ideological State Apparatus-
es" and the title on the spine is *Lenin and Philosophy and
Other Essays,* an English translation of a book by the
French political philosopher, Louis Althusser. The marginal
notes are in Italian. Fulvia Morgana, Professor of Cultural
Studies at the University of Padua, is at work. She cannot
sleep in airplanes, and does not believe in wasting time.

In the same airplane, some forty metres to the rear of Fulvia
Morgana, Howard Ringbaum is trying to persuade his wife
Thelma to have sexual intercourse with him, there and then,

in the back row of the economy section. The circumstances
are ideal, he points out in an urgent whisper: the lights are
dim, everybody within sight is asleep, and there is an empty
seat on either side of them. By pushing back the arm-rests
dividing these four places they could create enough room to
stretch out horizontally and screw.

"Ssh, someone will hear you," says Thelma, who does
not realize that her spouse is perfectly serious.

Howard presses the call-button for cabin service, and
when a stewardess appears, requests two blankets and two
pillows. Nobody, he assures Thelma, will know what they
are doing under the blankets.

"All I'm going to do under mine is sleep," Thelma says.
"As soon as I've finished this chapter." She is reading a
novel entitled *Could Try Harder*, by a British author, Ronald
Frobisher. She yawns and turns a page. The book is rather
dull. She bought it years ago on their last visit to England,
took it home to Canada unopened, packed it again when
they moved back to the States; then, looking yesterday for
something to read on the plane, plucked it down from a high
shelf and blew the dust off it, thinking this would be a good
way to re-attune herself to English speech and manners. But
the novel is set in the Industrial Midlands, and the dialogue is
thick with a dialect that they are unlikely to encounter in the
vicinity of Bloomsbury. Howard has a grant from the National Endowment for the Humanities, to work at the British
Museum for six months. They have arranged to rent a small
apartment over a shop just off Russell Square. Thelma is
going to enrol in a lot of those wonderfully cheap adult
education classes they have in England on everything from
foreign languages to flower arranging, and really *do* all the
museums and galleries in the capital.

The stewardess brings blankets and pillows in polythene
bags. Howard spreads the blankets over their knees and puts
his hand up Thelma's skirt. She pushes away.

"Howard! *Stop* it! What's gotten into you anyway?"
Though flustered, she is not altogether displeased by this
unwonted display of ardour.

What has gotten into Howard Ringbaum is, in fact, the
Mile High club, an exclusive confraternity of men who have

achieved sexual congress while airborne. Howard read about this club in a magazine, while waiting his turn in a barbershop about a year ago, and ever since has been consumed with an ambition to belong. A colleague at Southern Illinois, where Howard now teaches English pastoral poetry, to whom Howard confessed this unfulfilled ambition one night, revealed himself to be a member of the club, and offered to put Howard's name forward if he fulfilled the single condition of membership. Howard asked if wives counted. The colleague said that it wasn't customary, but he thought the membership committee might stretch a point. Howard asked that proof was required, and the colleague said a semen-stained paper napkin bearing the logo of a recognized commercial airline and countersigned by the partner in congress. It is a measure of Howard Ringbaum's humourless determination to succeed in every form of human competition that he succumbed to this crude hoax without a moment's hesitation. The same characteristic trait, displayed in a party game called Humiliation devised by Philip Swallow many years before, cost Howard Ringbaum dear—cost him his job, in fact, led to his exile to Canada, from which he has only recently been able to return by dint of writing a long succession of boring articles on English pastoral poetry amid the windswept prairies of Alberta—but he has not learned from the experience. "What about the toilet?" he whispers. "We could do it in the toilet."

"Are you crazy?" Thelma hisses. "There's hardly room to pee in there, let alone . . . For heaven's sake, honey, control yourself. Wait till we get to our little apartment in London." She smiles at him indulgently.

"Take off your panties and sit on my prick," says Howard Ringbaum unsmilingly.

Thelma hits Howard in the crotch with her book and he doubles up in pain. "Howard?" she says anxiously. "Are you all right, honey? I didn't mean to hurt you."

Morriz Zapp goes into the Swallows' kitchen, boils a kettle, and fixes himself a cup of strong, black, instant coffee. Outside the sky is growing lighter, and a few birds are chirping hesitantly in the trees. It is 6 a.m. by the kitchen

clock. Morris drains his cup and stations himself in the front
hall to forestall the cab-driver's ring on the doorbell, which
might waken the household.

But someone is already awake. There is a creak on the
stairs, and Philip comes into view in the order of: leather
slippers, bare bony ankles, striped pyjama trousers, mud-
coloured dressing-gown, and silver beard.

"Just off, then?" he says, stifling a yawn.

"I hope I didn't waken you," says Morris.

"Oh, no. Anyway, can't let you go off without a word of
goodbye."

An awkward silence ensues. Both men are perhaps a little
embarrassed by the memory of confidences exchanged the
night before under the influence of whisky.

"You might let me know what you think about my book,
some time," says Philip.

"Wilco. I have it with me to read on the plane. By the
way, I have a new book coming out soon myself."

"Another one?"

"It's called *Beyond Criticism*. Neat huh? I'll send you a
copy."

Both men jump at the shrill noise of the doorbell.

"Ah, there's your taxi!" says Philip. "Plenty of time, it
only takes half an hour to get to the airport at this time of
day. Well, goodbye then, old man. Thanks for coming."

"Thanks for everything, Philip," says Morris, grasping
the other's hand. "See you in the new Jerusalem."

"Pardon?"

"The conference. The Jerusalem Hilton is in the new part
of the city."

"Oh, I'm with you. Well, we'll see. I'll think about it."

The cab driver picks up Morris's suitcase and carries it to
the car, a courtesy that never ceases to amaze Morris Zapp,
coming as he does from a country where cab drivers are
locked into their driving seats and snarl at their customers
through bars, like caged animals. As the taxi turns the
corner, Morris looks back to see Philip waving from the
front porch, clutching the flaps of his dressing-gown together
with his other hand. Above his head a curtain is drawn back

from a bedroom window and a face—Hilary's?—hovers palely behind the glass.

In Chicago it is midnight; yesterday hesitates for a second before turning into today. A cold wind blows off the lake, sends litter blowing across the pavement like tumbleweed, chills the bums and whores and drug addicts who huddle for shelter beneath the arches of the elevated railway. Inside the city's newest and most luxurious hotel, however, it is almost tropically warm. The distinctive feature of this building is that everything you would expect to find outside it is inside, and vice versa, except for the weather. The rooms are stacked around a central enclosed space, and their balconies project inwards, into a warm air-conditioned atmosphere, overlooking a fountain and a lily pond filled with multi-coloured fish. There are palm-trees growing in here, and flowering vines that climb up the walls and cling to balconies. Outside, transparent elevators like tiny glass bubbles creep up and down the sheer curtain walling of the building, giving the occupants vertigo. It is the architecture of inside-out.

In a penthouse suite from whose exterior windows the bums and whores and drug addicts are quite invisible, and even the biggest automobiles on the Loop look like crawling bugs, a man lies, naked, on his back, at the centre of a large circular bed. His arms and legs are stretched out in the form of an X, so that he resembles a famous drawing by Leonardo, except that his body is thin and scraggy, an old man's body, tanned but blotchy, the chest hair grizzled, the legs bony and slightly bowed, the feet calloused and horny. The man's head, however, is still handsome: long and narrow, with a hooked nose and a mane of white hair. The eyes, if they were open, would be seen to be dark brown, almost black. On the bedside table is a pile of magazines, academic quarterlies, some of which have fallen or been thrown, to the floor. They have titles like *Diacritics, Critical Inquiry, New Literary History, Poetics and Theory of Literature, Metacriticism*. They are packed with articles set in close lines of small print, and long lists of references. They contain no pictures. But who needs pictures when he has a living breathing centrefold all his own?

Kneeling on the bed beside the man, in the space between his left arm and his left leg, is a shapely young Oriental woman, with long, straight, shining black hair falling down over her golden-hued body. Her only garment is a tiny *cache-sexe* of black silk. She is massaging the man's scrawny limbs and torso with a lightly perfumed mineral oil, paying particular attention to his long, thin, circumcised penis. It does not respond to this treatment, flopping about in the young woman's nimble fingers like an uncooked chippolata.

This is Arthur Kingfisher, doyen of the international community of literary theorists, Emeritus Professor of Columbia and Zürich Universities, the only man in academic history to have occupied two chairs simultaneously in different continents (commuting by jet twice a week to spend Mondays to Wednesdays in Switzerland and Thursdays to Sundays in New York), now retired but still active in the world of scholarship, as attender of conferences, advisory editor to academic journals, consultant to university presses. A man whose life is a concise history of modern criticism: born (as Arthur Klingelfischer) into the intellectual ferment of Vienna at the turn of the century, he studied with Shkolvsky in Moscow in the Revolutionary period, and with I. A. Richards in Cambridge in the late twenties, collaborated with Jakobson in Prague in the thirties, and emigrated to the United States in 1939 to become a leading figure in the New Criticism in the forties and fifties, then had his early work translated from the German by the Parisian critics of the sixties, and was hailed as a pioneer of structuralism. A man who has received more honorary degrees than he can remember, and who has at home, at his house on Long Island, a whole room full of the (largely unread) books and offprints sent to him by disciples and admirers in the world of scholarship. And this is Song-Mi Lee, who came ten years ago from Korea on a Ford Foundation fellowship to sit at Arthur Kingfisher's feet as a research student, and stayed to become his secretary, companion, amenuensis, masseuse and bedfellow, her life wholly dedicated to protecting the great man against the importunities of the academic world and soothing his despair at no longer being able to achieve an erection or an original thought. Most men of his age would have resigned themselves to at least the first of these impotencies, but Arthur Kingfisher had always led a very active sex life and regarded it as vitally connected, in some deep and mysterious way, with his intellectual creativity.

The telephone beside the bed emits a discreet electronic cheep. Song-Mi Lee wipes her oily fingers on a tissue and stretches across the prone body of Arthur Kingfisher, her rosy nipples just grazing his grizzled chest, to pick up the receiver. She squats back on her heels, listens, and says into the instrument, "One moment please, I will see if he is available." Then, holding her hand over the mouthpiece, she says to Arthur Kingfisher: "A call from Berlin—will you take it?"

"Why not? It's not as though it's interrupting anything," says Arthur Kingfisher gloomily. "Who do I know in Berlin?"

The taxi jolts and rumbles through the outer suburbs of Rummidge, throwing Morris Zapp from side to side on the back seat, as the driver negotiates the many twists and turns in the route to the airport. An endless ribbon of nearly identical three-bedroomed semi-detached houses unwinds beside the moving cab. The curtains are still drawn across the windows of most of these houses. Behind them people dream and doze, fart and snore, as dawn creeps over the roofs and chimneys and television aerials. For most of these people, today will be much like yesterday or tomorrow: the same office, the same factory, the same shopping precinct. Their lives are closed and circular, they tread a wheel of habit, their horizons are near and unchanging. To Morris Zapp such lives are unimaginable, he does not even try to imagine them; but their stasis gives zest to his mobility—it creates, as his cab speeds through the maze of streets and crescents and dual carriageways and roundabouts, a kind of psychic friction that warms him in some deep core of himself, makes him feel envied and enviable, a man for whom the curvature of the earth beckons invitingly to ever new experiences just over the horizon.

Back in the master bedroom of the Victorian villa in St

John's Road, Philip and Hilary Swallow are copulating as quietly, and almost as furtively, as if they were stretched out on the rear seats of a jumbo jet.

Returning to bed after seeing off Morris Zapp, Philip, slightly chilled from standing at the front door in his dressing gown and pyjamas, found the warmth of Hilary's ample body irresistible. He snuggled up to it spoonwise, curving himself around the soft cushion of her buttocks, passing his arm round her waist and cupping one heavy breast in his hand. Unable to sleep, he became sexually excited, lifted Hilary's nightdress and began to caress her belly and crotch. She seemed moist and compliant, though he was not sure if she was fully awake. He entered her slowly, from behind, holding his breath like a thief, in case she should suddenly come to her senses and push him away (it had happened before).

Hilary is, in fact, fully awake, though her eyes are closed. Philip's eyes are also shut. He is thinking of Joy, a purple-lit bedroom on a warm Italian night. She is thinking of Morris Zapp, in this same bed, in this same room, curtains drawn against the afternoon sun, ten years ago. The bed creaks rhythmically; the headboard bangs once, twice, against the wall; there is a grunt, a sigh, then silence. Philip falls asleep. Hilary opens her eyes. Neither has seen the other's face. No word has passed between them.

Meanwhile the telephone conversation between Berlin and Chicago is coming to its conclusion. A voice whose English is impeccable, and only slightly tinged with a German accent, is speaking.

"So, Arthur, we cannot tempt you to speak at our conference in Heidelberg? I am most disappointed, your thoughts on *Rezeptionsästhetik* would have been most deeply appreciated, I am sure."

"I'm sorry Siegfried, I just have nothing to say."

"You are excessively modest, as usual, Arthur."

"Believe me, it's not false modesty. I wish it was."

"But I quite understand. You have many demands upon your time ... By the way, what do you think of this new UNESCO chair of literary criticism?"

After a prolonged pause, Arthur Kingfisher says: "News travels fast. It's not even official yet."

"But it is true?"

Choosing his words with evident care, Arthur Kingfisher says, "I have reason to think so."

"I understand you will be one of the chief assessors for the chair, Arthur, is that so?"

"Is this what you really called me about, Siegfried?"

Hearty, mirthless laughter from Berlin. "How could you imagine such a thing, my dear fellow? I assure you that our desire for your presence at Heidelberg is perfectly sincere."

"I thought you had the chair at Baden-Baden?"

"I do, but we are collaborating with Heidelberg for the conference."

"And what are you doing in Berlin?"

"The same as you are doing in Chicago, I presume. Attending another conference—what else? 'Postmodernism and the Ontological Quest.' Some interesting papers. But our Heidelberg conference will be better organized . . . Arthur, since you raise the question of the UNESCO chair—"

"I didn't raise it, Siegfried. You did."

"It would be hypocritical of me to pretend that I would not be interested."

"I'm not surprised, Siegfried."

"We have always been good friends, Arthur, have we not? Ever since I reviewed the fourth volume of your *Collected Papers* in the *New York Review of Books*."

"Yes, Siegfried, it was a nice review. And nice talking to you."

The hand that replaces the telephone receiver in its cradle in a sleekly functional hotel room on the Kurfürstendamm is sheathed in a black kid glove, in spite of the fact that its owner is sitting up in bed, wearing silk pyjamas and eating a Continental breakfast from a tray. Siegfried von Turpitz has never been known to remove this glove in the presence of another person. No one knows what hideous injury or deformity it conceals, though there have been many speculations: a repulsive birthmark, a suppurating wound, some *unheimlich* mutation such as talons instead of fingers, or an artificial hand made of stainless steel and plastic—the original, it is alleged by those who favour this theory, having been crushed and mangled in the machinery of the Panzer tank which Siegfried von Turpitz commanded in the later stages of World War II. He allows the black hand to rest for a moment on the telephone receiver, as if to seal the instrument against any leakage of information left in the cable that connected him, a few moments before, to Chicago, while with his ungloved hand he meditatively crumbles a croissant. Then he removes the receiver and with a black leathern index finger dials the operator. Consulting a black leather-bound notebook, he places a long-distance call to Paris. His face is pale and expressionless beneath a skullcap of flat blond hair.

Morris Zapp's taxi throbs impatiently at red traffic-lights on a broad shopping street, deserted at this hour except for a milk float and a newspaper delivery van. A large billboard advertising British Airways Poundstretcher fares suggests that the airport is not far away. Another, smaller advertisement urging the passer-by to *"Have a Fling with Faggots Tonight"* is not, Morris knows from his previous sojourn in the region, a manifesto issued by Rummidge Gay Liberation, but an allusion to some local delicacy based on offal. With any luck he himself will be tucking in, tonight, to a steaming dish of tender, fragrant *tagliatelli*, before passing on to, say, *costoletta alla milanese*, and perhaps a slice or two of *panettone* for dessert. Morris's mouth floods with saliva. The taxi lurches forward. A clock above a jeweller's shop says that the time is 6.30.

In Paris, as in Berlin, it is 7.30, because of the different arrangements on the Continent for daylight saving. In the high-ceilinged bedroom of an elegant apartment on the Boulevard Huysmans, the telephone rings beside the double bed. Without opening his eyes, hooded like a lizard's in the brown, leathery face, Michel Tardieu, Professor of Narratology at the Sorbonne, extends a bare arm from beneath his duvet to lift the telephone from its cradle. *"Oui?"* he murmurs, without opening his eyes.

"Jacques?" inquires a Germanic voice.

"*Non*. Michel."

"Michel *qui*?"

"Michel Tardieu."

There is a Germanic grunt of annoyance. "Please accept my profound apologies," says the caller in correct but heavily accented French. "I dialled the wrong number."

"But don't I know you?" says Michel Tardieu, yawning. "I seem to recognize your voice."

"Siegfried von Turpitz. We were on the same panel at Ann Arbor last autumn."

"Oh yes, I remember. 'Author-Reader Relations in Narrative.' "

"I was trying to call a friend called Textel. His name is next to yours in my little book, and both are Paris numbers, so I mixed them up. It was excessively stupid of me. I hope I did not disturb you too much."

"Not too much," says Michel, yawning again. *'Au revoir.'* He turns back to embrace the naked body beside him in the bed, curving himself spoonwise around the soft cushion of the buttocks, brushing with his fingers the suave, silky skin of belly and inner thigh, nuzzling the slender nape beneath the perfumed locks of golden hair. *Chéri*," he whispers soothingly, as the other stirs in his sleep.

In his oak-panelled bedroom at All Saints' College, Oxford, the Regius Professor of Belles-Lettres sleeps chastely alone. No other person, man or woman, has shared that high, old-fashioned single bed—or, indeed, any other bed—with Rudyard Parkinson. He is a bachelor, a celibate, a virgin. Not that you would guess that from the evidence of his innumerable books, articles and reviews, which are full of knowing and sometimes risqué references to the variations and vagaries of human sexual behaviour. But it is all sex in the head—or on the page. Rudyard Parkinson was never in love, nor wished to be, observing with amused disdain the disastrous effects of that condition on the work-rate of his peers and rivals. When he was thirty-five, already secure and successful in his academic career, he considered the desirability of marrying—coolly, in the abstract, weighing the conveniences and drawbacks of the married state—and decided against it. Occasionally he would respond to the beauty of a young undergraduate to the extent of laying a timid hand on the young man's shoulder, but no further.

From an early age, reading and writing have entirely occupied Rudyard Parkinson's waking life, including those parts allocated by normal people to love and sex. Indeed, it could be said that reading is his love and writing his sex. He is in love with literature, with the English poets in particular—Spenser, Milton, Wordsworth, and the rest. Reading their verse is pure, selfless pleasure, a privileged communion with great minds, a rapt enjoyment of truth and beauty. Writing, his own writing, is more like sex: an assertion of will, an exercise of power, a release of tension. If he doesn't write something at least once a day he becomes irritable and depressed—and it has to be for publication, for to Rudyard Parkinson unpublished writing is like masturbation or *coitus interruptus*, something shameful and unsatisfying.

The highest form of writing is of course a book of one's own, something that has to be prepared with tact, subtlety, and cunning, and sustained over many months, like an affair. But one cannot always be writing books, and even while thus engaged there are pauses and lulls when one is merely reading secondary sources, and the need for some release of pent-up ego on to the printed page, however trivial and ephemeral the occasion, becomes urgent. Hence Rudyard Parkinson never refuses an invitation to write a book review; and as he is a witty, elegant reviewer, he receives many such invitations. The literary editors of London's daily and weekly newspapers are constantly on the telephone to him, parcels of books arrive at the porter's lodge by every post, and he always has at least three assignments going at the same time—one in proof, one in draft and one at the note-taking stage. The book on which he is taking notes at this time lies, spreadeagled, open and face-down, on the bedside cabinet, next to his alarm clock, his spectacles and his dental plate. It is a work of literary theory by Morris Zapp, entitled *Beyond Criticism*, which Rudyard Parkinson is reviewing for the *Times Literary Supplement*. His denture seems to menace the volume with a fiendish grin, as though daring it to move while Rudyard Parkinson takes his rest.

The alarm rings. It is 6.45. Rudyard Parkinson stretches out a hand to silence the clock, blinks and yawns. He opens the door of his bedside cabinet and pulls out a heavy ceramic chamber pot emblazoned with the College arms. Sitting on the edge of the bed with his legs apart, he empties his bladder of the vestiges of last night's sherry, claret and port. There is a bathroom with toilet in his suite of rooms, but Rudyard Parkinson, a South African who came to Oxford at the age of twenty-one and perfected an impersonation of Englishness that is now indistinguishable from authentic specimens, believes in keeping up old traditions. He replaces the chamber pot in its cupboard, and closes the door. Later a college servant, handsomely tipped for the service, will empty it. Rudyard Parkinson gets back into bed, turns on the bedside lamp, puts on his spectacles, inserts his teeth, and begins to read Morris Zapp's book at the page where he abandoned it last night.

From time to time he underlines a phrase or makes a marginal note. A faint sneer plays over his lips, which are hedged by grey muttonchop whiskers. It is not going to be a favourable review. Rudyard Parkinson does not care for American scholars on the whole. His own work is sometimes treated by them with less respect than is its due. Or, as in the case of Morris Zapp, not treated at all, but totally ignored (he had of course checked the Index under P for his own name—always the first action to be taken with a new book). Besides, Rudyard Parkinson has written three favourable reviews in succession in the last ten days—for the *Sunday Times*, the *Listener*, and the *New York Review of Books*, and he is feeling a little bored with praise. A touch of venom would not come amiss this time, and what better target than a brash, braggart American Jew, pathetically anxious to demonstrate his familiarity with the latest pretentious critical jargon?

In Central Turkey it is 8.45. Dr Akbil Borak, BA (Ankara) PhD (Hull), is having breakfast in his little house on a new estate just outside the capital. He sips black tea from a glass, for there is no coffee to be found in Turkey these days. He warms his hands on the glass because the air is cool inside the house, there being no oil for the central heating either. His plump, pretty wife, Oya, puts before him bread, goat cheese and rose-hip jam. He eats abstractedly, reading a book propped up on the dining-room table. It is *The Collected Works of William Hazlitt,* Vol. XIV. At the other side of the table his three-year-old son knocks over a glass of milk. Akbil Borak turns a page obliviously.

"I do not think you should read at breakfast," Oya complains, as she mops up the milk. "It is a bad example for Ahmed, and it is not nice for me. All day I am on my own here with no one to talk to. The least you can do is be sociable before you leave for work."

Akbil grunts, wipes his moustache, closes the book, and rises from the table. "It will not be for much longer. There are only seven more volumes, and Professor Swallow arrives next week."

The news, abruptly announced a few weeks earlier, of Philip Swallow's imminent arrival in Turkey to lecture on William Hazlitt has struck dismay into the English faculty at Ankara, since the only member of the teaching staff who knows anything about the Romantic essayists (the man, in fact, who had originally mooted, two years earlier, the idea of making Hazlitt's bicentenary with a visiting lecturer from Britain, but, hearing no more about the proposal gradually forgot all about it) is absent on sabbatical leave in the United States; and nobody else in the Department, at the time of receiving the message, had knowingly read a single word of Hazlitt's writings. Akbil, who was delegated, because of the acknowledged excellence of his spoken English, to meet Philip Swallow at the airport and escort him around Ankara, felt obliged to make good this deficiency and defend the honour of the Department. He has, accordingly, withdrawn the *Complete Works* of William Hazlitt in twenty-one volumes from the University Library, and is working his way through them at the rate of one volume every two or three days, his own research on Elizabethan sonnet sequences being temporarily sacrificed to this end.

Volume XIV is *The Spirit of the Age*. Akbil pops it into his briefcase, buttons up his topcoat, kisses the still pouting Oya, pinches Ahmed's cheek, and leaves the house. It is the end unit of a row of new terraced houses, built of grey breeze-blocks. Each house has a small garden of identical size and shape, their boundaries neatly demarcated by low breeze-block walls. These gardens have a rather forlorn aspect. Nothing appears to grow inside the walls except the same coarse grass and spiky weeds that grow outside. They seem purely symbolic gardens, weak gestures towards some cosy suburban lifestyle glimpsed by an itinerant Turkish town-planner on a quick tour of Coventry or Cologne; or perhaps feeble attempts to ward off the psychic terror of the wilderness. For beyond the boundary walls at the bottom of each garden the central Anatolian plain abruptly begins. There is nothing for thousands of miles but barren, dusty, windswept steppes. Akbil shivers in a blast of air that comes straight out of central Asia, and climbs into his battered Citroën Deux Chevaux. He wonders, not for the first time, whether they did right to move out of the city, to this bleak and desolate spot, for the sake of a house of their own, a garden, and clean air for Ahmed to breathe. It had reminded him and Oya, when they first saw pictures of the estate in the brochure, of the little terraced house in which they had lived during his three years' doctoral research as a British Council scholar. But in Hull there had been a pub and a fish-and-chip shop on the corner, a little park two streets away with swings and a see-saw, cranes and ships' masts visible over the roofs, a general sense of nature well under the thumb of culture. This past winter—it had been a harsh one, made all the worse by the shortages of oil, food and electricity—he and Oya had huddled together round a small wood-burning stove and warmed themselves with the shared memories of Hull, murmuring the enchanted names of streets and shops, "George Street", "Hedden Road", "Marks and Spencer's", "British Home Stores". It never seemed odd to Akbil and Oya Borak that the city's main railway terminus was called Hull Paragon.

Inside the Rummidge airport terminal, in contrast to the sleepy suburb beyond the perimeter fence, the day has already well and truly begun. Morris Zapp is not, after all, the only man in Rummidge who is on the move. Beefy businessmen in striped suits, striped shirts and striped ties, carrying sleek executive briefcases and ingenious overnight wardrobe bags, all zips, buttons, straps and pouches, are checking in for their flights to London, Glasgow, Belfast, and Brussels. A group of early vacationers, bound for a package tour in Majorca, and dressed in garish holiday gear, wait patiently for a delayed plane: fat, comfortable folk, who sit in the departure lounge with their legs apart and their hands on their knees, yawning and smoking and eating sweets. A small line of people standing by for seats on the flight to Heathrow looks anxiously at Morris Zapp as he marches up to the British Midland desk and dumps his suitcase on the scales. He checks it through to Milan, and is directed to Gate Five. He goes to the newsstand and buys a copy of *The Times*. He joins a long line of people shuffling through the security checkpoint. His handbaggage is opened and searched. Practised fingers turn over the jumble of toiletries, medicines, cigars, spare socks, and a copy of *Hazlitt and the Amateur Reader* by Philip Swallow. The lady making the search opens a cardboard box, and small, hard, cylindrical objects, wrapped in silver foil, roll into the palm of her hand. *"Bullets?"* her eyes seem to enquire. "Suppositories," Morris Zapp volunteers. Few privacies are vouchsafed to the modern traveller. Strangers rifling through your luggage can tell at a glance the state of your digestive system, what method of contraception you favour, whether you have a denture that requires a fixative, whether you suffer from haemorrhoids, corns, headaches, eye fatigue, flatulence, dry lips, allergic rhinitis and premenstrual tension. Morris Zapp travels with remedies for all these ailments except the last.

He passes through the electronic metal detector, first handing over his spectacle case, which he knows from experience will activate the device, collects his shoulderbag and proceeds to the waiting lounge by Gate 5. After a few minutes the flight to Heathrow is called, and Morris follows the ground hostess and the other passengers out on to the tarmac apron. He frowns at the sight of the plane they are to board. It is a long time since he has flown in a plane with *propellers*.

In Tokyo, it is already late afternoon. Akira Sakazaki has come home from his day's work at the University, where he teaches English, just in time to miss the worst of the rush hour, and avoid the indignity of being manhandled into the carriages of the subway trains by burly officials specially employed for this purpose so that the automatic doors may close. A bachelor, whose family home is in a small resort far away in the mountains, he lives alone in a tall modern apartment block. He is able to afford this accommodation because, though well appointed, it is extremely restricted in space. In fact he cannot actually stand up in it, and on unlocking the door, and having taken off his shoes, is obliged to crawl, rather than step, inside.

The apartment, or living unit, is like a very luxurious padded cell. About four metres long, three metres wide and one and a half metres high, its walls, floor and ceiling are lined with a seamless carpet of soft, synthetic fibre. A low recessed shelf along one wall acts as a sofa by day, a bed by night. Shelves and cupboards are mounted above it. Recessed or fitted flush into the opposite wall are a stainless steel sink, refrigerator, microwave oven, electric kettle, colour television, hi-fi system and telephone. A low table sits on the floor before the window, a large, double-glazed porthole which looks out on to a blank, hazy sky; though if one goes up close and squints downwards one can see people and cars streaming along the street below, converging, meeting and dividing, like symbols on a video game. The window cannot be opened. The room is air-conditioned, temperature-controlled and soundproof. Four hundred identical cells are stacked and interlocked in this building, like a tower of eggboxes. It is a new development, an upmarket version of the "capsule" hotels situated near the main railway termini that have proved so popular with Japanese workers in recent years. There is a small hatch in one wall that gives access to a tiny windowless bathroom, with a small chair-shaped tub just big enough to sit in, and a toilet that can be used only in a squatting position, which is customary for Japanese men in any case. In the basement of the building there is a traditional Japanese bathhouse with showers and big communal baths, but Akira Sakazaki rarely makes use of it. He is well satisfied with his accommodation, which provides all modern amenities in a compact and convenient form, and leaves him the maximum amount of time free for his work. How much time people waste in walking from one room to another—especially in the West! Space is time. Akira was particularly shocked by the waste of both in Californian homes he visited during his graduate studies in the United States: separate rooms not just for sleeping, eating and excreting, but also for cooking, studying, entertaining, watching television, playing games, washing clothes and practising hobbies—all spread out profligately over acres of land, so that it could take a whole minute to walk from say, one's bedroom to one's study.

Akira now takes off his suit and shirt, and stows them carefully away in the fitted cupboard above the sofa/bed. He crawls through the hatch into his tiny bathroom, soaps and rinses himself all over, then fills the armchair-shaped tub with very hot water. Silent fans extract the steam from the bathroom as he simmers gently, opening his pores to cleanse them of the city's pollution. He splashes himself with clean, lukewarm water, and crawls back into the main room. He dons a cotton *yukata* and sits cross-legged on the floor before the low table, on which there is a portable electric typewriter. To one side of the typewriter there is a neat stack of sheets of paper whose surface is divided into two hundred ruled squares, in each of which a Japanese character has been carefully inscribed by hand; on the other side of the typewriter is a neat pile of blank sheets of the same squared paper, and a hardcover edition of a novel, with a well-thumbed dustjacket: *Could Try Harder,* by Ronald Frobisher. Akira inserts a blue aerogramme, carbon paper and flimsy into the typewriter, and begins a letter in English.

Dear Mr Frobisher,
            I am now nearly halfway through my translating of ''Could Try Harder''. I am sorry to

> *bother you so soon with further questions, but I
> would be very grateful if you would help me with the
> following points. Page references are to the second
> impression of 1970, as before.*

Akira Sakazaki takes up the book to find the page reference
to his first query, and pauses to scrutinize the photograph of
the author on the back flap of the jacket. He often pauses
thus, as if by contemplating the author's countenance he
may be able to enter more sympathetically into the mind
behind it, and intuitively solve the problems of tone and
stylistic nuance which are giving him so much trouble. The
photograph, however, dark and grainy, gives away few
secrets. Ronald Frobisher is pictured against a door with
frosted glass on which is engraved in florid lettering the
word "PUBLIC". This itself is a puzzle to Akira. Is it a public
lavatory, or a public library? The symbolism would be quite
different in each case. The face of the author is round,
fleshy, pockmarked, and peppered with tiny black specks,
like grains of gunpowder. The hair is thin, dishevelled.
Frobisher wears thick, horn-rimmed spectacles and a grub-
by raincoat. He glares somewhat truculently at the camera.
The note under the photograph reads:

> Ronald Frobisher was born and brought up in the
> Black Country. He was educated at a local grammar
> school, and at All Saints' College, Oxford. After
> graduating, he returned to his old school as a
> teacher of English until 1957, when the publication
> of his first novel, *Any Road,* immediately established
> him as a leading figure in the new generation of
> "Angry Young Men". Since 1958 he has been a
> full-time writer, and now lives with his wife and two
> children in Greenwich, London. *Could Try Harder* is
> his fifth novel.

And still his most recent, though it was published nine years
ago. Akira has often wondered why Ronald Frobisher published
no new novel in the last decade, but it does not seem polite
to enquire.

Akira finds the page he is looking for, and lays the book
open on the table. He touchtypes:

p. 107, 3 down. "Bugger me, but I feel like some faggots tonight."

Does Ernie mean that he feels a sudden desire for homosexual intercourse? If so, why does he mention this to his wife?

Morris Zapp should have been in Heathrow by now, but there has been a delay in leaving Rummidge. The plane is still parked on the apron outside the terminal building.

"What do you think they're doing—winding up the elastic?" he quips to the man sitting in the aisle seat next to him.

The man stiffens and pales. "Is there something wrong?" he says in the accents of the American Deep South.

"It could be visibility. Looks kinda foggy out there in the middle of the airfield. You from the South?"

"Fog?" says the man in alarm, peering across Morris out of the window. He is wearing faintly tinted rimless glasses.

At that moment the four engines of the plane cough into life, one by one, just like an old war movie, and the propellers carve circles in the damp morning air. The plane taxis to the end of the runway, and goes on taxiing, wheels bumping over the cracks in the concrete, with no perceptible increase in speed. Morris cannot see much beyond the plane's wingtip. The man in the tinted spectacles has his eyes closed, and grips the arms of his seat with white knuckles. Morris has never seen anyone look so frightened. The plane turns again and carries on taxiing.

"Have we taken off yet?" says the man, after some minutes have passed in this fashion.

"No, I think the pilot is lost in the fog," says Morris.

The man hurriedly undoes his safety belt, muttering, "I'm getting out of this crazy plane." He shouts towards the pilot's cabin, "Stop the plane, I'm getting off."

A hostess hurries down the aisle towards him. "You can't do that, sir, please sit down and fasten your safety belt."

Protesting, the man is persuaded back into his seat. "I have one of these extended travel tickets," he remarks to Morris, "so I thought I would go from London to Stratford-on-Avon by air. Never again."

At that moment the captain comes on the intercom to explain that he has been taxiing up and down the runway to try and disperse the ground mist with his propellers.

"I don't believe it," says Morris.

The manoeuvre is, however, evidently successful. They are given permission to take off. The plane halts at the end of the runway, and the engine note rises to a higher pitch. The cabin shudders and rattles. The Southerner's teeth are chattering, whether from fear or vibration it is impossible to tell. Then the plane lurches forward, gathers speed and, surprisingly quickly, rises into the air. Soon they are through the cloud cover, and bright sunlight floods the cabin. The Southerner's spectacles are the photosensitive sort and turn into two opaque black discs, so it is difficult to tell whether his fear has abated. Morris wonders whether to strike up a conversation with the man, but there is so much noise from the engines that he shrinks from the effort, and there is something slightly spooky about the opaque glasses that does not inspire friendly overtures. Instead, Morris takes out his newspaper and pricks his ears at the welcome sound of the coffee trolley coming up the aisle.

Morris Zapp basks in the sun, a cup of coffee steaming on the tray before him, and reads in his copy of *The Times* of clashes between police and protesters against the National Front in Southall; of earthquakes in Yugoslavia, fighting in Lebanon, political murders in Turkey, meat shortages in Poland, car bombs in Belfast, and of many other tragedies, afflictions, outrages, at various points of the globe. But up here, in the sun, above the clouds, all is calm, if not quiet. The plane is not as smooth and fast as a jet, but there is more legroom than usual, and the coffee is good and hot. As the newspaper informs him, there are many worse places to be.

"Bugger me," grunts Ronald Frobisher, stooping to pick up the morning's mail from the doormat, "If there isn't another letter from that Jap translator of mine."

It is eight-thirty-five a.m. in Greenwich—Greenwich Mean Time, indeed, the zero point from which all the world's time zones are calculated. The blue aerogramme that Ronald

Frobisher turns over in his fingers is not, of course, the one that Akira Sakazaki typed a few minutes ago, but one he mailed last week. Another is at this moment in the cargo section of a jumbo jet somewhere over the Persian Gulf, *en route* to London, and yet another is hurtling through the computerized machinery of the Tokyo Central Post Office, racing along the conveyor belts, veering left, veering right, submerging and resurfacing like a kayak shooting rapids.

"That must be at least the fifth or sixth one in the last month," Ronald Frobisher grumbles, as he returns to the breakfast-room.

"Eh?" says his wife, Irma, without looking up from the *Guardian*.

"That bloke who's translating *Could Try Harder* into Japanese. I must have answered about two hundred questions already."

"I don't know why you bother," says Irma.

"Because it's interesting, to tell you the truth," says Ronald Frobisher, sitting down at the table and slitting open the aerogramme with a knife.

"An excuse to postpone work, you mean," says Irma. "Don't forget that script for Granada is due next Friday." She has not taken her eyes off the *Guardian*'s Woman's page. Conversations with Ronald are predictable enough for her to read and talk to him simultaneously. She can even pour herself a cup of tea at the same time, and does so now.

"No, really, it's fascinating. Listen. *"Page 86, 7 up. 'And a bit of spare on the back seat.' Is it a spare tyre that Enoch keeps on the back seat of his car?"*

Irma sniggers, not at his query from Akira Sakazaki, but at something on the *Guardian*'s Woman's page.

"I mean, you can see the problem," says Ronald. "It's a perfectly natural mistake. I mean, why *does* 'a bit of spare' mean sex?"

"I don't know," says Irma, turning the page. "You tell me. You're the writer."

"Page 93, 2 down. 'Enoch, 'e went spare.' Does this mean Encoh went to get a spare part for his car? You've got to feel sorry for the bloke. He's never been to England, which makes it all the more difficult."

"Why does he bother? I can't see the Japanese being
interested in reading about sex life in the back streets of
Dudley."

"Because I'm an important figure in postwar British
fiction, that's why. You never did grasp that fact, did you?
You never could believe that I could be considered *literature*. You just think I'm a hack that turns out TV scripts."

Irma, used to Ronald Frobisher's little tantrums, reads
blithely on. Frobisher crunches angrily on toast and marma-
lade and opens another letter. "Listen to this," he says.
"*Dear Mr Frobisher, We are holding a conference in
Heidelberg in September on the subject of the Reception of
the Literary Text, and we are anxious to have the participation of some distinguished contemporary writers such as
yourself*... You see what I mean? It could be quite interesting, actually. I've never been to Heidelberg. Some kraut
called von Turpitz."

"Aren't you going to rather a lot of these conferences?"

"It's all experience. You could come as well, if you
like."

"No thanks, I've had enough of traipsing around churches
and museums while you chew the fat with the local syco-
phants. Why are all your fans foreigners, these days? Don't
they know that the Angry Young Man thing is all over?"

"It's got nothing to do with the Angry Young Man
thing!" says Ronald Frobisher, angrily. He opens another
envelope. "D'you want to come to the Royal Academy of
Literature do? It's on a boat this year. I'm supposed to be
giving away one of the prizes."

"No, thanks." Irma turns another page of the *Guardian*.
A jet drones overhead, on the flightpath to Heathrow.

Fog at Heathrow, which caused TWA Flight 072 from
Chicago to be diverted to Stanstead, has suddenly cleared,
so the plane has turned back and is making its approach to
Heathrow from the east. Three thousand feet above the
heads of Ronald and Irma Frobisher, Fulvia Morgana snaps
shut her copy of *Lenin and Philosophy* and puts it away,
along with her kidskin slippers, in her capacious burnt-
orange suede shoulder-bag by Fendi. She eases her feet into

the cream-coloured Armani boots, and fastens them snugly round her calves, taking care not to snag her tights in the zips. She gazes haughtily down at the winding Thames, St Paul's, the Tower of London, Tower Bridge. She picks out the dome of the British Museum, beneath which Marx forged the concepts that would enable man not only to interpret the world, but also to change it: dialectical materialism, the surplus theory of value, the dictatorship of the proletariat. But the pseudo-gothic fantasy of the Houses of Parliament, propping up the top-heavy bulk of Big Ben, reminds the airborne Marxist how slow the rate of change has been. The Mother of Parliaments, and therefore the Mother of Repression. All parliaments must be abolished.

"Ooh, look, Howard! Big Ben!" exclaims Thelma Ringbaum, nudging her husband in the back row of the economy class.

"I've seen it before," he says sulkily.

"We'll be landing in a minute. Don't forget the duty-free liquor."

Howard gropes under his seat for the plastic bag in which there are two fifths of scotch, purchased at O'Hare airport, which have travelled approximately eight thousand miles since they were distilled, and are now within a few hundred of their place of origin. A muffled thud announces that the undercarriage has been lowered. The Tristar begins its descent to Heathrow.

Morris has already landed at Heathrow, and is gobbling ham and eggs and toast, sitting on a high stool at the counter of the Terminal One Restaurant, with Philip Swallow's *Hazlitt and the Amateur Reader* propped up against the sugar bowl. It is greed, not urgency, that makes him eat so fast, for he has two hours to wait before his flight to Milan is due to depart. Licking the butter from his fingers, he opens the book, which has, unsurprisingly, an epigraph from William Hazlitt:

I stand merely upon the defensive. I have no positive inferences to make, nor any novelties to bring for-

ward, and I have only to defend a common sense feeling against the refinement of a false philosophy.

Morris Zapp sighs, shakes his head, and butters another slice of toast.

In Cooktown, Queensland, Rodney Wainwright is chewing his dinner with more deliberation, partly because he has a loose molar and the chops are overdone, partly because he has no appetite. "Jesus Christ, it's hot," he mutters, dabbing at his forehead with his serviette. "Language, Rod," Bev murmurs reprovingly, glancing at their two children, Kevin aged fourteen, Cindy aged twelve, who are gnawing their bones zestfully out of greasy fingers. Rodney Wainwright's paper on the future of criticism has not gone well in the past three or four hours. He covered two sheets of foolscap, then tore them up. The argument remains blocked at, "The question is therefore, how can criticism . . ." Shadows are long on the rank lawn. The boom of the waves carries through the open casement. On the beach, no doubt, at this very moment Sandra Dix, her wet bikini exchanged for faded sawn-off jeans and clinging tee-shirt, is turning over freshly caught fish on a hot gridiron.

In Helicon, New Hampshire, Désirée Zapp sleeps, breathing heavily, and dreams of flying—swooping and soaring in her nightgown in a clear blue sky above the multitudinous pine trees.

Philip Swallow wakes for the second time this morning, and touches his genitals lightly, swiftly, a gesture of self-reassurance performed every morning since he was five years old and his mother told him that if he didn't stop playing with his willie it would drop off. He stretches out beneath the sheets. Where Hilary was, there is a cooling hollow in the mattress. He looks at the clock on the bedside table, rubs his eyes, stares, blasphemes and jumps out of bed. Hurrying downstairs, he passes his son, Matthew, on his way up. " 'Ullo, our Dad," says Matthew, whose current humour it is to pretend to be a working-class youth from the North of England. "Shouldn't you be at school?" Philip coldly enquires. "Trooble at t'pit," says Matthew. "Industrial action by the Association of Schoolmasters." "Disgraceful," says Philip, over his shoulder, "University teachers would never strike." "Only because no one would notice," Matthew calls down the stairs.

Arthur Kingfisher sleeps, curled spoonwise around the shapely back and buttocks of Song-Mi Lee, who, before they retired, prepared for him a pipe of opium. So his dreams are psychedelic: deserts of purple sand with dunes that move like an oily sea, a forest of trees with little golden fingers instead of leaves that caress the wayfarer as he brushes against them, a vast pyramid with a tiny glass elevator that goes up one side, down the other, a chapel at the bottom of a lake, and on the altar, where the crucifix should be, a black hand, cut off at the wrist, its fingers splayed.

Siegfried von Turpitz now has black gloves on both of his hands. They grip the steering wheel of his black BMW 635CSi coupé, with 3453 cc Bosch L-jetronic fuel-injection engine and five speed Getrag all-synchromesh gearbox. He holds the car to a steady one hundred and eighty kilometres per hour in the fast lane of the autobahn between Berlin and Hanover, compelling slower vehicles to move over not by flashing his headlights (which is forbidden by law) but by moving up behind them swiftly, silently and very close; so that when a driver glances into a rear-view mirror which only moments ago was empty save for a small black dot on the horizon, he finds it, to his astonishment and terror, entirely filled by the dark mass of the BMW's bonnet and tinted windscreen, behind which, under a skullcap of flat, colourless hair, floats the pale impassive visage of Siegfried von Turpitz—and, as fast as the shock to his nerves permits, such a driver swerves aside to let the BMW pass.

In the rather old-fashioned kitchen of the high-ceilinged apartment on the Boulevard Huysmans, Michel Tardieu grinds coffee beans by hand (for he cannot bear the shriek of a Moulinex) and wonders idly why Siegfried von Turpitz should have wanted so urgently to speak to Jacques Textel that he tried to phone him at 7.30 in the morning. Michel Tardieu is himself acquainted with Textel, a Swiss anthropologist who once occupied the chair at Berne, but moved into international cultural administration and is now somebody quite important in UNESCO. It is time, Michel reflects, that he and Textel had lunch together.

As he finishes the grinding, he hears the front door of the apartment slam. Albert, ravishing in dark blue woollen blouson and tight white Levis that Michel brought him back after his last visit to the States, comes in and dumps on the kitchen table, with a distinctly sulky air, a paper bag of croissants and rolls, and a copy of *Le Matin*. Albert resents this regular early morning errand, and complains about it frequently. He complains now. Michel urges him to look upon the chore in the light of modern narrative theory. "It is a quest, *chéri*, a story of departure and return: you venture out, and you come back, loaded with treasure. You are a hero." Albert's response is brief and obscene. Michel smiles good-humouredly, pouring boiling water into the coffee-filter. He intends to keep Albert to this matutinal duty, just to remind him who pays for the coffee and croissants, not to mention the clothes and shoes and coiffures and records and ice-skating lessons.

In Ankara, Akbil Borak has at last arrived at the precincts of the University, some ninety minutes after leaving home, thirty of which were spent queuing for petrol. Crowds are converging on the campus, walking indifferently in the roadway and on the pavements. Sounding his horn at frequent intervals, Akbil nudges his way through this stream of humanity that parts in front of the Deux Chevaux and meets again behind. He spots a vacant space on the pavement and mounts the kerb to park. The stream of pedestrians breaks and scatters momentarily, then swirls again around the stationary vehicle. Akbil locks his car and walks briskly across the central square. Two rival political groups of students, one of the left, the other of the right, are engaged in heated argument. Voices are raised, there is pushing and scuffling, someone falls to the ground and a girl screams. Suddenly two armed soldiers come running in their heavy boots, firearms levelled at the trouble-makers, shouting at them orders to disperse, which they do, some retreating backwards with their arms raised in surrender or supplication. It was not like this at Hull, Akbil reflects, as he takes cover behind a massive statue of black iron representing Kemal Ataturk inviting the youth of Turkey to partake of the benefits of learning.

Akira Sakazaki has typed his last question, for the time being, to Ronald Frobisher (a tricky one concerning the literal and metaphorical meanings of *crumpet* and its relation to *pikelet*), addressed, sealed and stamped the letter ready for mailing tomorrow morning, popped a TV dinner into the microwave oven, and, while waiting for it to cook, reads his airmail edition of the *Times Literary Supplement* and listens to Mendelssohn's Violin Concerto on his stereo headphones.

Big Ben strikes nine o'clock. Other clocks, in other parts of the world, strike ten, eleven, four, seven, two.

Morris Zapp belches, Rodney Wainwright sighs, Désirée Zapp snores. Fulvia Morgana yawns—a quick, surprisingly wide yawn, like a cat's—and resumes her customary repose. Arthur Kingfisher mutters German in his sleep. Siegfried von Turpitz, caught in a traffic jam on the autobahn, drums on the steering-wheel impatiently with the fingers of one hand. Howard Ringbaum chews gum to ease the pressure on his eardrums and Thelma Ringbaum struggles to squeeze her swollen feet back into her shoes. Michel Tardieu sits at his desk and resumes work on a complex equation representing in algebraic terms the plot of *War and Peace*. Rudyard Parkinson helps himself to kedgeree from the hotplate on the sideboard in the Fellows' breakfast-room and takes his place at the table in a silence broken only by the rustle of newspapers and the clinking and scraping of crockery and cutlery. Akbil Borak sips black tea from a glass in a small office which he shares with six others and grimly concentrates on *The Spirit of the Age*. Akira Sakazaki strips the foil from his TV dinner and tunes his radio to receive the BBC

World Service. Ronald Frobisher looks up *"spare"* in the *Oxford English Dictionary.* Philip Swallow bustles into the kitchen of his house in St John's Road, Rummidge, avoiding the eye of his wife. And Joy Simpson, who Philip thinks is dead, but who is alive, somewhere on this spinning globe, stands at an open window, and draws the air deep into her lungs, and shades her eyes against the sun, and smiles.

Two

THE job of check-in clerk at Heathrow, or any airport, is not a glamorous or particularly satisfying one. The work is mechanical and repetitive: inspect the ticket, check it against the passenger list on the computer terminal, tear out the ticket from its folder, check the baggage weight, tag the baggage, ask Smoking or Non-smoking, allocate a seat, issue a boarding pass. The only variation in this routine occurs when things go wrong—when flights are delayed or cancelled because of bad weather or strikes or technical hitches. Then the checker bears the full brunt of the customers' fury without being able to do anything to alleviate it. For the most part the job is a dull and monotonous one, processing people who are impatient to conclude their brief business with you, and whom you will probably never see again.

Cheryl Summerbee, a checker for British Airways in Terminal One at Heathrow, did not, however, complain of boredom. Though the passengers who passed through her hands took little notice of her, she took a lot of notice of them. She injected interest into her job by making quick assessments of their characters and treating them accordingly. Those who were rude or arrogant or otherwise unpleasant she put in uncomfortable or inconvenient seats, next to the toilets, or beside mothers with crying babies. Those who made a favourable impression she rewarded with the best seats, and whenever possible placed them next to some attractive member of the opposite sex. In Cheryl Summerbee's hands, seat allocation was a fine art, as delicate and complex an operation as arranging blind dates between clients of a lonelyhearts agency. It gave her a glow of satisfaction, a pleasant sense of doing good by stealth, to reflect on how many love affairs, and even marriages, she must have instigated between people who imagined they had met by pure chance.

Cheryl Summerbee was very much in favour of love. She firmly believed that it made the world go round, and did her bit to keep the globe spinning on its axis by her discreet management of the seating on British Airways Tridents. On the shelf under her counter she kept a Bills and Moon romance to read in those slack periods when there were no passengers to deal with. The one she was reading at the moment was called *Love Scene*. It was about a girl called Sandra who went to work as a nanny for a film director whose wife had died tragically in a car accident, leaving him with two young children to look after. Of course Sandra fell in love with the film director, though unfortunately he was in love with the actress taking the leading role in the film he was making—or was he just pretending to be in love with her to keep her sweet? Of course he was! Cheryl Summerbee had read enough Bills and Moon romances to know that—indeed she hardly needed to read any further to predict exactly how the story would end. With half her mind she despised these love-stories, but she devoured them with greedy haste, like cheap sweets. Her own life was, so far, devoid of romance—not for lack of propositions, but because she was a girl of old-fashioned moral principle, who intended to go to the altar a virgin. She had met several men who were very eager to relieve her of her virginity, but not to marry her first. So she was still waiting for Mr Right to appear. She had no very clear image of what he would look like except that he would have a hard chest and firm thighs.

All the heroes of Bills and Moon romances seemed to have hard chests and firm thighs.

The man wearing the tweed deerstalker didn't look as if he had these attributes—quite the contrary—but Cheryl took an instant liking to him. He was a little larger than life, every line in his figure slightly exaggerated, like a cartoon character; but he seemed to know it himself, and not to give a damn. It made you smile just to look at him, swagering across the floor of the crowded terminal, with his absurd hat tilted forward, and a fat cigar clenched in his teeth, his double-breasted trench-coat flapping open on a loud check sports jacket. Cheryl smiled at him as he hesitated in front of the two desks servicing the Milan flight, and, catching this smile, he joined the line in front of her.

"Hi," he said when his turn came to be attended to. "Have we met before?"

"I don't think so, sir," said Cheryl. "I was just admiring your hat." She took his ticket and read the name on it: *Zapp M., Prof.*

Professor Zapp took off his deerstalker and held it at arm's length. "I bought it right here in Heathrow just a few days ago," he said. "I don't suppose I'll need it in Italy." Then his expression changed from complacency to annoyance. "Goddammit, I promised to give it to young McGarrigle before I left." He slapped the hat against his thigh, confirming this limb's lack of firmness. "Is there anywhere I can mail a parcel from here?"

"Our Post Office is closed for alterations, but there's another one in Terminal Two," said Cheryl. "I presume you would like a seat in the smoking section, Professor Zapp? Window or aisle?"

"I'm easy. The question is, how am I going to wrap this hat in a parcel?"

"Leave it with me. I'll post it for you."

"Really? That's very sweet of you, Cheryl."

"All part of the service, Professor Zapp," she smiled. He was one of those rare passengers who noticed the name badge pinned to her uniform, or, having noticed it, used it. "Just write your friend's name and address on this label, and I'll see to it when I go off duty." While he was occupied with this task, she scanned the seating plan in front of her, and ran through on the computer display the list of passengers who had already checked in. About a quarter of an hour ago she had dealt with an extremely elegant Italian lady professor, of about the right age—younger, but not too young—and who spoke very good English, apart from a little trouble with her aspirates. Ah yes, here she was: MORGANA F. PROF. She had been very particular, requesting a window-seat of the plane. Cheryl didn't mind this; she respected people who knew what they wanted, as long as they didn't kick up a fuss if it wasn't available. Professor Morgana had looked as if she was capable of kicking up a royal fuss, but the occasion had not arisen. Cheryl had been able to accommodate her exactly as requested, in row 10, window seat A. She now removed the sticker from seat 10B on the seat-plan in front of her, and affixed it to Professor Zapp's boarding pass. He gave her his hat, with the label and two pound notes tucked into one of the flaps.

"I don't think it will cost that much to send," she said, reading the label: *"Percy McGarrigle, Department of English, University College, LIMERICK, Ireland."*

"Well, if there's any change, have a drink on me."

As he spoke they both heard a small, muffled explosion— the sound, distinctive and unmistakable, of a bottle of duty-free liquor hitting the stone composition floor of an airport concourse and shattering inside its plastic carrier bag; also a cry of "Shit!" and a dismayed, antiphonal "Oh, *Howard!*" A few yards away, a man and a woman were glaring accusingly at each other across a loaded baggage trolley from which the plastic carrier bag had evidently fallen. Professor Zapp, who had turned his head to locate the origin of the fatal sound, now turned back to face Cheryl, hunching his shoulders and turning up the collar of his raincoat.

"Don't do anything to attract that man's attention," he hissed.

"Why? Who is he?"

"His name is Howard Ringbaum and he is a well-known fink. Also, although he doesn't know it yet, I have rejected a paper he submitted for a conference I'm organizing."

"What is a fink?"

"A fink is a generally despicable person, like Howard Ringbaum."

"What's so awful about him? He doesn't look so bad."

"He's very self-centred. He's very mean. He's very calculating. Like, for instance, when Thelma Ringbaum says it's time they gave a party, Howard doesn't just send out invitations—he calls you up and asks you whether, if he were to give a party, you would come.'

"That must be his wife with him now," said Cheryl.

"Thelma's all right, she's just fink-blind," said Professor Zapp. "No one can figure out how she can stand being married to Howard."

Over Professor Zapp's shoulder, Cheryl watched Howard Ringbaum gingerly pick up the plastic carrier bag by its handles. It bulged ominously at the bottom with the weight of spilled liquor. "Maybe I could filter it," Howard Ringbaum said to his wife. As he spoke, a piece of jagged glass pierced the plastic and a spout of neat scotch poured on to his suede shoe. "Shit!" he said again.

"Oh, *Howard*!"

"What are we doing in this place, anyway?" he snarled. "You said it was the way out."

"No, Howard, *you* said it was the way out, I just agreed."

"Have they gone yet?" Professor Zapp muttered.

"They're going," said Cheryl. Observing that the passengers waiting in line behind Professor Zapp were getting restive, she brought their business to a rapid conclusion. "Here's your boarding card, Professor Zapp. Be in the Departure Lounge half an hour before your flight time. Your baggage has been checked through to Milan. Have a pleasant journey."

Thus it was that about one hour later Morris Zapp found himself sitting next to Fulvia Morgana in a British Airways Trident bound for Milan. It didn't take them long to discover that they were both academics. While the plane was still taxiing to the runway, Morris had Philip Swallow's book on Hazlitt out on his lap, and Fulvia Morgana her copy of

Althusser's essays. Each glanced surreptitiously at the other's reading matter. It was as good as a masonic handshake. They met each other's eyes.

"Morris Zapp, Euphoric State." He extended his hand.

"Ah, yes, I 'ave 'eard you spick. Last December, in New York."

"At the MLA? You're not a philosopher, then?" He nodded at *Lenin and Philosophy*.

"No, cultural studies is my field. Fulvia Morgana, Padua. In Europe critics are much interested in Marxism. In America not so much."

"I guess in America we've always been more attracted by Freud than Marx, Fulvia." Fulvia Morgana. Morris flicked rapidly through his mental card index. It was a name he vaguely remembered having seen on the title-pages of various prestigious journals of literary theory.

"And now Derrida," said Fulvia Morgana. "Everybody in Chicago—I 'ave just been to Chicago—was reading Derrida. America is crazy about deconstruction. Why is that?"

"Well, I'm a bit of a deconstructionist myself. It's kind of exciting—the last intellectual thrill left. Like sawing through the branch you're sitting on."

"Exactly! It is so narcissistic. So 'opeless."

"What was your conference about?"

"It was called, 'The Crisis of the Sign'."

"Oh, yeah. I was invited but I couldn't make it. How was it?"

Fulvia Morgana shrugged her shoulders inside her brown velvet jacket. "As usual. Many boring papers. Some interesting parties."

"Who was there?"

"Oh, everyone you would expect. The Yale hermeneutic gang. The Johns Hopkins reader-response people. The local Chicago Aristotelians, naturally. And Arthur Kingfisher was there."

"Really? He must be pretty old now."

"He gave the—what do you call it—keynote address. On the first evening."

"Any good?"

"Terrible. Everybody was waiting to see what line he would take on deconstruction. Would 'e be for it or against it? Would 'e follow the premises of 'is own early structuralist work to its logical conclusion, or would 'e recoil into a defence of traditional humanist scholarship?" Fulvia Morgana spoke as though she were quoting from some report of the conference that she had already drafted.

"Let me try and guess," said Morris.

"You would be wasting your time," said Fulvia Morgana, unfastening her seat belt and smoothing her velvet knicker-bockers over her knees. The plane had taken off in the course of this conversation, though Morris had hardly noticed. "'E said, on the one hand this, on the other hand that. 'E talked all around the subject. 'E waffled and wandered. 'E repeated things 'e said twenty, thirty years ago, and said better. It was embarrassing, I am telling you. In spite of all, they gave 'im a standing ovation."

"Well, he's a great man. *Was* a great man, anyway. A king among literary theorists. I think that to many people he kind of personified the whole profession of academic literary studies."

"Then I must say that the profession is in a very un'ealthy condition," said Fulvia. "What are you reading—a book on 'Azlitt?"

"It's by a British friend of mine," said Morris. "He gave it to me just yesterday. It's not the sort of thing I usually go for." He felt anxious to dissociate himself from Phillip's quaintly old-fashioned subject, and equally archaic approach to it.

Fulvia Morgana leaned over and peered at the name on the dust jacket. "Philip Swallow. I know 'im. 'E came to Padua to give a lecture some years before."

"Right! He was telling me about his trip to Italy last night. It was very eventful."

"'Ow was that?"

"Oh, his plane caught fire on the way home—had to turn back and make an emergency landing. But he was OK."

"'Is lecture was not very eventful, I must say. It was very boring."

"Yeah, well, that doesn't surprise me. He's a nice guy,

Philip, but he doesn't exactly set your pulse racing with intellectual excitement.''

"What is the book like?"

"Well, listen to this, it will give you the flavour." Morris read aloud a passage he had marked in Philip's book: *"He is the most learned man who knows the most of what is farthest removed from common life and actual observation, that is of the least practical utility, and least liable to be brought to the test of experience, and that, having been handed down through the greatest number of intermediate stages, is the most full of uncertainty, difficulties and contradictions."*

"Very interesting," said Fulvia Morgana. "Is that Philip Swallow?"

"No, that's Hazlitt."

"You surprise me. It sounds very modern. 'Uncertainties, difficulties, contradictions.' 'Azlitt was obviously a man ahead of his time. That is a remarkable attack on bourgeois empiricism.''

"I think it was meant to be ironic," said Morris gently. "It comes from an essay called 'The Ignorance of the Learned'."

Fulvia Morgana pouted. "Ooh, the English and their ironies! You never know where you are with them."

The arrival of the drinks trolley at this point was a happy distraction. Morris requested scotch on the rocks and Fulvia a Bloody Mary. Their conversation turned back to the topic of the Chicago conference.

"Everybody was talking about this UNESCO chair," said Fulvia. "Be'ind their 'ands, naturally."

"What chair is that?" Morris felt a sudden stab of anxiety, cutting through the warm glow imparted by the whisky and the agreeable happenstance of striking up acquaintance with this glamorous colleague. "I haven't heard anything about a UNESCO chair."

"Don't worry, it's not been advertised yet," said Fulvia, with a smile. Morris attempted a light dismissive laugh, but it sounded forced to his own ears. "It's supposed to be a chair of Literary Criticism, endowed by UNESCO. It's just a rumour, actually. I expect Arthur Kingfisher started it. They say 'e is the chief assessor.''

"And what else," said Morris, with studied casualness, "do they say about this chair?"

He did not really have to wait for her reply to know that here, at last, was a prize worthy of his ambition. The UNESCO Chair of Literary Criticism! That *had* to carry the highest salary in the profession. Fulvia confirmed his intuition: $100,000 a year was being talked about. "Tax-free, of course, like all UNESCO salaries." Duties? Virtually nonexistent. The chair was not to be connected with any particular institution, to avoid favouring any particular country. It was a purely conceptual chair (except for the stipend) to be occupied wherever the successful candidate wished to reside. He would have an office and secretarial staff at the Paris headquarters, but no obligation to use it. He would be encouraged to fly around the world at UNESCO's expense, attending conferences and meeting the international community of scholars, but entirely at his own discretion. He would have no students to teach, no papers to grade, no committees to chair. He would be paid simply to think—to think and, if the mood took him, to write. A roomful of secretaries at the Place Fontenoy would wait patiently beside their word-processors, ready to type, duplicate, collate, staple and distribute to every point of the compass his latest reflections on the ontology of the literary text, the therapeutic value of poetry, the nature of metaphor, or the relationship between synchronic and diachronic literary studies. Morris Zapp felt dizzy at the thought, not merely of the wealth and privilege the chair would confer on the man who occupied it, but also of the envy it would arouse in the breasts of those who did not.

"Will he have the job for life, or for a limited tenure?" Morris asked.

"I think she will be appointed for three years, on secondment from 'er own university.''

"She?" Morris repeated, alarmed. Had Julia Kristeva or Christine Brooke-Rose already been lined up for the job? "Why do you say, 'she'?"

"Why do you say ''e'?"

Morris relaxed and raised his hands in a gesture of surrender. "*Touché*! Someone who was once married to a best-selling feminist novelist shouldn't walk into that kind of trap."

"'Oo is that?"

"She writes under the name of Désirée Byrd."

"Oh yes, *Giorni Difficili*. I 'ave read it." She looked at Morris with new interest. "It is autobiographical?"

"In part," said Morris. "This UNESCO chair—would you be tempted by it yourself?"

"No," said Fulvia emphatically.

Morris didn't believe her.

As Morris Zapp and Fulvia Morgana addressed themselves to a light lunch served 30,000 feet above south-eastern France, Persse McGarrigle arrived at Heathrow by the Underground railway. With Angelica gone, there had been nothing to detain him at Rummidge, so he had skipped the Business Meeting which constituted the last formal session of the Conference and taken the train to London. He was hoping to get a cheap standby seat on the afternoon flight to Shannon, since his conference grant had been based on rail/sea travel and would not cover the normal economy air fare. The Aer Lingus desk in Terminal Two took his name and asked him to come back at 2.30. While he was hesitating about what to do in the intervening couple of hours, the concourse was temporarily immobilized by a hundred or more Muslim pilgrims, with "Saracen Tours" on their luggage, who turned to face Mecca and prostrated themselves in prayers. Two cleaners leaning on their brooms within earshot of Persse viewed this spectacle with disgust.

"Bloody Pakis," said one. "If they *must* say their bloody prayers, why don't they go and do it in the bloody chapel?"

"No use to them, is it?" said his companion, who seemed a shade less bigotted. "Need a mosque, don't they?"

"Oh *yerse*!" said the first man sarcastically. "That's all we need in 'Eathrow, a bloody mosque."

"I'm not sayin' we ought to 'ave one," said the second man patiently, "I'm just sayin' that a Christian chapel wouldn't be no use to 'em. Them bein' in-fid-els." He seemed to derive great satisfaction from the pronunciation of this word.

"I s'pose you think we ought to 'ave a synagogue an' a 'Indoo temple too, an' a totam pole for Red Indians to dance around? What they doin' 'ere, anyway? They should be in Terminal Free if they're goin' to bloody Mecca."

"Did I hear you say there was a chapel in this airport?" Persse cut in.

"Well, I know there *is* one," said the more indignant of the two men. "Near Lorst Property, innit, Fred?"

"Nah, near the Control Tower," said Fred. "Go dahn the subway towards Terminal Free, then follow the signs to the Bus Station. Go right to the end of the bus station and then sorter bear left, then right. Yer can't miss it."

Persse did, however, miss it, more than once. He traipsed up and down stairs and escalators, along moving walkways, through tunnels, over bridges. Like the city centre of Rummidge, Heathrow discouraged direct, horizontal movement. Pedestrians about and about must go, by devious and labyrinthine ways. Once he saw a sign "To St George's Chapel," and eagerly followed its direction, but it led him to the airport laundry. He asked several officials the way, and received confusing and contradictory advice. He was tempted to give up the quest, for his feet were aching, and his grip dragged ever more heavily on his arm, but he persevered. The spectacle of the Muslim pilgrims at prayer had reminded him of the sorry state of his own soul, and though he did not expect to find a Catholic priest in attendance at the chapel to hear his confession, he felt an urge to make an act of contrition in some consecrated place before entrusting himself to the air.

When he found himself outside Terminal Two for the third time he almost despaired, but seeing a young woman in the livery of British Airways ground staff approaching, he accosted her, promising himself that this would be his last attempt.

"St George's Chapel? It's near the Control Tower," she said.

"That's what they all tell me, but I've been searching

high and low this last half hour, and the devil take me if I can find it.''

"I'll show you, if you like," said the young woman cheerfully. A small plastic badge on her lapel identified her as "Cheryl Summerbee."

"That's wonderfully kind of you," said Persse. "If you're quite sure I'm not interfering with your work."

"It's my lunch break," said Cheryl, who walked with a curious high-stepping gait, lifting her knees high and planting her feet down daintily and deliberately, like a circus pony. She gave an impression of energetic movement without actually covering much ground, but her style of walking made her shoulder-length blonde hair and other parts of her anatomy bounce about in a pleasing manner. She had a slight squint which gave her blue eyes a starry, unfocused look that was attractive rather than otherwise. She was carrying a shopping bag of bright plastic-coated canvas, from the top of which protruded a romantic novelette entitled *Love Scene,* and a deerstalker of yellowish brown tweed with a bold red check which looked familiar to Persse. "It's not my hat," Cheryl explained, when he remarked upon it. "A passenger left it with me this morning, to mail to a friend of his."

"It wasn't a Professor Zapp, by any chance?"

Cheryl stopped in mid-stride, one foot poised above the pavement. "How did you know?" she said wonderingly.

"He's a friend of mine. Who were you to send the hat to?"

"Percy McGarrigle, Limerick."

"Then I can save you the trouble," said Persse. "For I'm the very man." He took from his jacket pocket the white cardboard identification disc issued to him at the Rummidge Conference, and presented it for Cheryl's inspection.

"Well," she said. "There's a concidence." She took the hat from her bag and, holding it by the flaps, placed it with a certain ceremony on his head. "A perfect fit," she smiled. "Like Cinderella's slipper." She tucked the label addressed in Morris Zapp's hand in Persse's breast pocket, and it seemed to him, inexplicably, that she gave a quick poulterer's pinch to his pectoral muscles as she did so. She held up two pound notes. "Your American professor friend told me to buy a drink with the change. Now there's enough for two drinks and a couple of sandwiches."

Persse hesitated. "I'd love to join you, Cheryl," he said, "but I must find that chapel." This was only part of the reason. A sense of loyalty to Angelica, in spite of the trick she had played on him the night before, also restrained him from accepting Cheryl's invitation.

"Oh, yes," said Cheryl, "I was forgetting the chapel." She conducted him another fifty yards, then pointed out the shape of a large wooden crucifix in the middle distance. "There you are."

"Thanks a million," he said, and watched with admiration and regret as she pranced away.

Apart from the plain wooden cross, the chapel resembled, from outside, an air raid shelter rather than a place of worship. Behind a low wall of liver-coloured brick, all that was visible was a domed roof build of the same material, and an entrance with steps leading underground. At the bottom of the stairs there was a small vestibule with a table displaying devotional literature, and an office door leading off. On the wall was a small green baize noticeboard on which visitors to the chapel had pinned various prayers and petitions written on scraps of paper. *"May our son have a safe journey and return home soon." "God save the Russian Orthodox Church." "Lord, look with favour on Thy servants Mark and Marianne, as they go to sow Thy seed in the mission fields." "Lord, please let me get my luggage back (lost in Nairobi)."* The chapel itself had been scooped out of the earth in a fan-shape, with the altar at the narrowest point, and a low ceiling, studded with recessed lights, that curved to meet the floor; so that to sit in one of the front pews was rather like taking one's place in the forward passenger cabin of a wide-bodied jet, and one would not have been surprised to see a *No Smoking—Fasten Safety Belts* sign light up above the altar, and a stewardess rather than an usher patrolling the aisle.

There was a small side chapel, where, much to Persse's surprise and pleasure, a red sanctuary lamp was flickering beside a tabernacle fixed to the wall, indicating that the

Blessed Sacrament was reserved. Here he said a simple but sincere prayer, for the recovery of Angelica and of his own purity of heart (for he interpreted her flight as a punishment for his lust). Feeling calmed and fortified, he rose to his feet. It occurred to him that he might leave a written petition of his own on the noticeboard. He wrote, on a page torn from a small notebook, *"Dear God, let me find Angelica."* He wrote her name on a separate line, in the trailing continuous script he had used to inscribe it in the snow at Rummidge. If it was God's will, she might pass this way, recognize his hand, relent, and get in touch with him.

Persse did not immediately approach the noticeboard with his petition, since a young woman was standing before it in the act of pinning one of her own to the green baize. Even with her back to him she presented an incongruous figure in this setting: jet-black hair elaborately curled and coiffed, a short white imitation-fur jacket, the tightest of tight red needlecord trousers, and high-heeled gold sandals. Having fixed her prayer to the noticeboard, she stood immobile before it for a moment, then took from her handbag a silk scarf decorated with dice and roulette wheels, which she drew over her head. As she turned and tottered past him on her high heels into the chapel, Persse glimpsed a pale, pretty face which he vaguely felt he had seen before, perhaps in the course of his peregrinations around Heathrow that morning. As he pinned his petition to the noticeboard, he could not resist glancing at the rectangle of pink card he had seen the girl place there:

> *Please God, don't let my father or my mother worry themselves to death about me and don't let them find out what I am doing now or any of the workpeople on the farm or the other girls at the hotel God please.*

Persse levered the card from the noticeboard with his thumbnail, turned it over and read what was printed on the other side:

GIRLS UNLIMITED

Hostesses Escorts Masseuses Artistes
An International Agency. Headquarters: Soho Sq.,
LONDON, W.I. Tel: 012 4268 Telegrams CLIMAX London.

Persse replaced the card on the noticeboard as he had found
it, and went back into the chapel. The girl was kneeling in
the back row, her face bowed, her heavily mascaraed eyelids
lowered. Persse sat down in the corresponding pew on the
other side of the central aisle, and studied her profile. After
few minutes the girl crossed herself, stood up and stepped
into the aisle. Persse followed suit and accosted her:

"Is it Bernadette McGarrigle?"

He caught her in his arms as she fainted away.

As Morris Zapp and Fulvia Morgana flew over the Alps,
dissecting the later work of Roland Barthes and enjoying a
second cup of coffee, the municipal employees of Milan
called a lightning strike in support of two clerks in the tax
department dismissed for alleged corruption (according to
the senior management they had been exempting their families from property taxes, according to the union they were
being victimized for not exempting the senior management
from property taxes). The British Airways Trident landed,
therefore, in the midst of civic chaos. Most of the airport
staff were refusing to work, and the passengers had to
recover their baggage from a heap underneath the aircraft's
belly, and carry it themselves across the tarmac to the
terminal building. The queues for customs and passport
control were long and unruly.

"'Ow are you travelling to Bellagio?" Fulvia asked
Morris, as they stood in line.

"The villa said they would send a car to meet me. Is it
far?"

"Not so far. You must visit us in Milano during your
stay."

"That would be very nice, Fulvia. Is your husband an
academic too?"

"Yes, 'e is Professor of Italian Renaissance Literature at
Rome."

Morris pondered this for a moment or two. "He works in Rome. You work in Padua. Yet you live in Milan?"

"The communications are good. You can fly several times a day between Milan and Rome, and there is an *autostrada* to Padua. Besides, Milan is the true capital of Italy. Rome is sleepy, lazy, provincial."

"What about Padua?"

Fulvia Morgana looked at him as if suspecting irony. "Nobody lives in Padua," she said simply.

They got through customs with surprising speed. Something about Fulvia's elegant, authoritative mien, or maybe her velvet knickerbockers, attracted an official as though by magnetism, and soon they were free of the sweating, milling, impatient throng. On the other side of passport control, however, was another sweating, milling impatient throng, of meeters and greeters. Some held up cards with names printed on them, but none of the names was Zapp.

"Don't let me keep you, Fulvia," said Morris, unhappily. "If nobody shows I guess I can take a bus."

"The buses will be on strike," said Fulvia. "Do you have a phone number for the villa?"

Morris gave her the letter confirming that he would be met. "But this says you are arriving last Saturday, at Melpensa—the other airport," she observed.

"Yeah, well I changed my plans, to take in Rummidge. I wrote them about it."

"I don't suppose they received your letter," she said. "The postal service here is a national disgrace. If I have a really urgent letter for the States I drive to Switzerland to mail it. Look after the bags." She had spied an empty phone booth, and swooped down on it, snatching the prize from under the nose of an infuriated businessman. Moments later she returned to confirm her guess. "As I thought, they 'ave not received your letter."

"Oh, shit," said Morris. "What shall I do?"

"It is all arranged," said Fulvia. "You will spend tonight with us, and tomorrow the villa will send a car to our 'ouse."

"Well, that's very kind of you," said Morris.

"Wait outside the doors with the luggage," said Fulvia, "and I will bring the car."

Morris stood guard over their bags, basking in the warm spring sunshine, and casting a connoisseur's eye over the more interesting automobiles that drew up outside the terminal to collect or deposit passengers. A bronze-coloured Maserati coupé which until now he had seen only in magazines, priced at something over $50,000, drew his attention, but it was some moments before he realized that Fulvia was seated at the wheel behind its tinted glass and beckoning him urgently to get in. As they swept through the airport gates, she appeared to shake her fist at the pickets, but when they smiled broadly and responded with the same gesture, Morris realized that it was one of solidarity with the workers' cause.

"There's something I must ask you, Fulvia," said Morris Zapp, as he sipped Scotch on the rocks poured from a crystal decanter brought on a silver tray by a black-uniformed, white-aproned maid to the first-floor drawing-room of the magnificent eighteenth-century house just off the Villa Napoleone, which they had reached after a drive so terrifyingly fast that the streets and boulevards of Milan were just a pale grey blur in his memory. "It may sound naive, and even rude, but I can't suppress it any longer."

Fulvia arched her eyebrows above her formidable nose. They had both rested, showered, and changed, she into a long, loose flowing robe of fine white wool, which made her look more than ever like a Roman empress. They faced each other, sunk deep in soft, yielding, hide-covered armchairs, across a Persian rug laid on the honey-coloured waxed wooden floor. Morris looked around the spacious room, in which a few choice items of antique furniture had been tastefully integrated with the finest specimens of modern Italian design, and whose off-white walls bore, he had ascertained by close-range inspection, original paintings by Chagall, Mark Rothko and Francis Bacon. "I just want to know," said Morris Zapp, "how you manage to reconcile living like a millionaire with being a Marxist."

Fulvia, who was smoking a cigarette in an ivory holder, waved it dismissively in the air. "A very American question, if I may say so, Morris. Of course I recognize the contradictions in our way of life, but those are the very contradictions characteristic of the last phase of bourgeois capitalism, which will eventually cause it to collapse. By renouncing our own little bit of privilege"—here Fulvia spread her hands in a modest proprietorial gesture which implied that she and her husband enjoyed a standard of living only a notch or two higher than that of, say, a Puerto Rican family living on welfare in the Bowery—"we should not accelerate by one minute the consummation of the process, which has its own inexorable rhythm and momentum, and is determined by the pressure of mass movements, not by the puny actions of individuals. Since in terms of dialectical materialism it makes no difference to the 'istorical process whether Ernesto and I, as individuals, are rich or poor, we might as well be rich, because it is a role that we know 'ow to perform with a certain dignity. Whereas to be poor with dignity, poor as our Italian peasants are poor, is something not easily learned, something bred in the bone, through generations." Fulvia spoke rapidly and fluently, as though quoting something she and her husband had had occasion to say more than once. "Besides," she added, "by being rich we are able to 'elp those 'oo are taking more positive action."

"Who are they?"

"Oh, various groups," Fulvia said vaguely, as the telephone began to ring. She swept across the room, her white robe billowing out behind her, to answer it; and conducted a conversation in rapid Italian of which Morris understood nothing except an occasional *caro* and, once, the mention of his own name. Fulvia replaced the receiver and returned more deliberately to her seat. "My 'usband," she said, "'E is delayed in Rome because of the strike. Milan airport is closed. 'E will not return tonight."

"Oh, I'm sorry," said Morris.

"Why?" said Fulvia Morgana, with a smile as faint and enigmatic as the Mona Lisa's.

"Won't you go back home, Bernadette? Your Mammy is destroyed with worrying about you, and your Daddy too."

Bernadette shook her head vigorously, and lit a cigarette, fumbling nervously with the lighter and chipping her scarlet nail polish in the process. "I cannot go home," she said in a voice which, though hoarse from too many cigarettes and, no doubt, strong drinks, still retained the lilting accent of County Sligo. "I can never go home again." She did not raise her eyes, under their long, mascara-clogged lashes, to meet Persse's, but shaped the tip of her cigarette in the green moulded plastic ashtray on the white moulded plastic table in the Terminal Two snackbar. A ham salad, of which she had eaten barely two mouthfuls, was on a plate before her. Cutting up his own food, Persse studied her face and figure, and wondered that he had traced in them, as she passed him in the chapel, the lineaments of Bernadette as he had last seen her: on a family outing to the strand at Ross's Point, one summer when they were both thirteen or fourteen, shy and tongue-tied with each other. He remembered her as a slim, wild tomboy, with tangled black hair and a gap-toothed smile, running into the surf with her best frock tucked up, and being scolded by her mother for getting it soaked with spray. "Why can you not?" he gently pressed her.

"Because I have a child and no husband, is why."

"Ah," said Persse. He knew the mores of the West of Ireland well enough not to discount the gravity of this obstacle. "So you did have the baby?"

"Is that what they think, then?" Bernadette flashed at him, looking up to meet his eye. "That I had it brought off?"

Persse blushed. "Well, your uncle Milo . . ."

"Uncle Milo? That auld scheymer!" The memory of Dr O'Shea seemed to bring the brogue flooding back into her speech, like saliva into the mouth or adrenalin into the bloodstream. "What the divil does he have to do with it?"

"Well, it was through him that I found out about your trouble, just the day before yesterday. In Rummidge."

"Been up there, have you? I haven't been near the place in years. God, but that was a terrible gloomy old house in, what was it, Gittings Road, that you had to lug the vacuum up three flights of stairs and you could break your neck it was so dark on the landings because himself was too mean to put proper bulbs into the lights . . ." Bernadette shook her head and snorted cigarette smoke through her nostrils. "A slave I was there—working in the hotel in Sligo was a rest cure in comparison. The only mortal creature who was kind to me was a lodger they had on the top floor, an American professor. He used to let me watch his colour telly and read his dirty books." Bernadette chuckled reminiscently, displaying teeth that were white, even, and presumably false. "*Playboy* and *Penthouse* and that sort of stuff. Pictures of girls naked as God made them, bold as brass and letting their names be printed underneath. It was a real eye-opener to an innocent young girl from County Sligo, I can tell you." Bernadette glanced slyly at Persse to see if she was embarrassing him. "One day my Uncle Milo caught me lookin' at them, and beat the livin' daylights out of me."

"Where is your child now?" Persse asked.

"He's with foster parents," said Bernadette. "In London."

"Then you could go back home on your own?"

"And abandon Fergus?"

"Well, for a short visit."

"No thank you. I know too well what it would be like. The looks from behind the curtains in the windows. The starin' and whisperin' after mass on a Sunday morning."

"So what are your plans for the future?"

"To save enough money to retire, buy a little business—a boutique maybe—and have Fergus back to bring him up myself."

"Retire from what, Bernadette?"

"I'm in the entertainment business," she said vaguely. She glanced at her wristwatch. "I must go soon."

"First, give me your address."

She shook her head. "I don't have one. I travel about a lot in my work."

"I suppose Girls Unlimited would forward a letter?"

She paled under makeup. "How do you know about that?" Then the penny dropped. "You shouldn't read other people's private prayers," she said indignantly. "Or what's written on the other side of them."

"You're right, Bernadette, I shouldn't have. But then I'd

never have recognized you. Now I'll be able to tell your Mammy and Daddy that you're safe and well."

"Don't tell them about Girls Unlimited, whatever you do," she begged.

"What is it that you do, then, Bernadette? You're not one of those hostesses, are you?"

"I certainly am not!" she said indignantly. "There's no money in that unless you sleep with the customers afterwards, and I've had enough of sleepin' with." She lit another cigarette and looked at Persse appraisingly through the smoke. "I'm a stripper, if you must know," she said at length.

"Bernadette! You're not!"

"I am, so," she said, brazening it out. "I do a little dance, and I take off my belongings one by one. My best act is called The Chambermaid. Marlene the Chambermaid— that's my professional name, Marlene. I'm better rewarded for takin' that uniform off than I ever was puttin' it on, I can tell you."

"But how can you bear to . . ."

"The first time was hard, but you get used to it quick enough."

"Used to those men staring at you?"

"You needn't act so superior, Persse McGarrigle," said Bernadette, tossing her head. "What about that day in the cowshed at your people's farm, when you begged me to let down my drawers and show you all my secrets?"

Persse blushed furiously. "We must have been mere children then. I can hardly remember it."

"I remember you wouldn't show me your own little gadget, anyhow," said Bernadette drily. "Wasn't that just typical? Honest to God, when I see the men starin' at me in the clubs, when I'm doin' my act, and I'm down to my G-string, they look just like a bunch of dirty-minded little boys. What do they keep comin' for, I ask myself. Are they expectin' to see somethin' different one day? Sure, every woman is made much the same in that portion of her anatomy. What's the fascination?"

Persse evaded the question by asking one of his own.

"What about the father of your child?" he said. "Shouldn't he be helping you with money?"

"I don't know where he is."

"Wasn't he a guest at you hotel? It should be possible to trace him from the register."

"I wrote him a letter once. It came back with 'Not Known At This Address' on it."

"Who was he? What was his name?"

"I'm not telling," said Bernadette. "I've no wish to get involved with him again. He might try and get Fergus off me. He was a queer gloomy sort of fellow." She looked again at her watch. "I really must go now. Thanks for the salad." She looked at it apologetically. "Sorry I had no appetite."

"Never mind that," said Persse. "Look, Bernadette, if you ever change your mind about going back to Ireland, there's a priest in Rummidge who will help you. He has a fund for repatriating young Irish people. The Our Lady of Knock Fund."

"Our Lady of the Knocked-Up would be more like it," said Bernadette, sardonically.

"Knocked-up?"

"Haven't you heard that expression before?"

"Indeed I have. Anyway, this priest is call Father Finbar O'Malley—"

"O'Malley, is it? Sure his people have the farm three miles up the road from ours," said Bernadette. "His mother is the biggest gossip in the parish. He's the last person in the world I'd go to. Remember now—don't tell Mammy and Daddy what I'm doing. You can give them my love."

"I will," he said.

She leaned across the table and brushed his cheek with her lips. He inhaled a heady waft of perfume. "You're a good fellow, Persse."

"And you're a better girl than you pretend," he said.

"Goodbye," she said huskily, and hobbled away without a backward glance, unsteady on her gold high-heels.

Soon she was lost to his sight in the restless ebb and flow of humanity on the concourse floor. Persse meditatively consumed her uneaten ham salad. Then he went to the Aer

Lingus desk, where they told him apologetically that the flight to Shannon was full. There was, however, a British Airways flight to Dublin leaving shortly, with plenty of spare seats, if that was any use to him. Persse decided to fly to Dublin and hitch from there to Limerick. He accordingly hurried to Terminal One, and presented himself at the check-in desk for the Dublin flight.

"Hallo again," said Cheryl Summerbee. "Did you find the chapel all right?"

"Yes thank you."

"Do you know, I've never been inside, all the time I've been working here. What's it like?"

"Rather like an airplane," said Persse, glancing anxiously at his watch.

"Nice and quiet, I expect," said Cheryl, leaning forward on her elbows and bringing her blue, slightly askew eyes quite close to his.

"Yes, it is very peaceful," said Persse. "Er, excuse me, Cheryl, but doesn't the plane leave quite soon?"

"Don't worry, you'll catch it," Said Cheryl. "Now let's find you a really nice seat. Smoking or non-smoking?"

"Non-smoking."

Cheryl tapped on her computer keyboard, and frowned at the screen. Then her brow cleared. "16B," she said. "A lovely seat."

Persse was the last to board the plane. He couldn't see anything special about seat 16B, which was the middle one in a row of three. The window and aisle seats were both occupied by nuns.

The dinner—*gaspacho*, roast guinea fowl and stuffed peppers, fresh sliced oranges in a caramel sauce, and a *dolcelatte* cheese—was superb, as was the wine, made and bottled, Fulvia informed Morris, on the estate of her father-in-law, the count. They ate by candlelight in a panelled dining-room, shadows and highlights flickering over the dark wooden surfaces of walls and table, discreetly waited on by a maid and a manservant. At the conclusion of the meal, Fulvia regally dismissed this pair to their own quarters, and informed Morris that coffee and liqueurs awaited them in the drawing-room.

"This lavish hospitality overwhelms me, Fulvia," said Morris, leaning up against the white marble mantelpiece and sipping his coffee, a thimbleful of sweet, scalding liquid the colour and consistency of pitch, with a caffeine kick like a thousand volts. "I don't know how to thank you."

Fulvia Morgana looked up at him from the sofa where she was half reclined, the slit skirt of her white robe falling away from one shapely leg. Her red lips curled back over two rows of sharp, white, even teeth. "Soon I show you 'ow," she said; and the possibility, which Morris Zapp had been mentally assessing all evening with a mixture of alarm and incredulity, that Fulvia Morgana meant to seduce him, now became a certainty. "Sit 'ere," she said, patting the sofa cushions, as though addressing a pet dog.

"I'm OK here for a minute," said Morris, setting down his cup and saucer on the mantelpiece with a nervous rattle, and busying himself with the lighting of a cigar. "Tell me, Fulvia, who d'you think will be in the running for this UNESCO chair?"

She shrugged. "I don't know. Tardieu, perhaps."

"The narratologist? Hasn't his moment passed? I mean, ten years ago everybody was into that stuff, actants and functions and mythemes and all that jazz. But now . . ."

"Only ten years! Does fashion in scholarship 'ave such a short life?"

"It's getting shorter all the time. There are people coming back into fashion who never even knew they were out of it. Who else?"

"Oh, I don't know. Von Turpitz is surely to apply."

"That Nazi?"

"'E was not a Nazi, I believe, just a conscripted soldier."

"Well, he looks like a Nazi. Like all the ones I've seen, anyway, which is admittedly only in movies."

Fulvia abandoned her pose on the sofa and went to the drinks trolley. "Cognac or liqueur?"

"Cognac would be great. What about Turpitz's last book— did you read it? It was just a rehash of Iser and Jauss."

"Don't let us talk any more about books," she said,

floating across the dimly lit room with a brandy glass like a huge bubble in her hand. "Or about chairs and conferences." She stood very close to him and rubbed the back of her free hand over his crotch. "Is it really twenty-five centimetres?" she murmured.

"What gives you that idea?" he said hoarsely.

"Your wife's book . . ."

"You don't want to believe everything you read in books, Fulvia," said Morris, grabbing the glass of cognac and draining it in a single gulp. He coughed and his eyes filled with tears. "A professional critic like you should know better than that. Novelists exaggerate."

"But 'ow much do they exaggerate, Morris?" she said. "I would like to see for myself."

"Like practical criticism?" he quipped.

Fulvia did not laugh. "Didn't you make you wife measure it with her tape measure?" she persisted.

"Of course I didn't! That's just feminist propaganda. Like the whole book."

He lurched towards one of the deep armchairs, puffing clouds of cigar smoke like a retreating battleship, but Fulvia steered him firmly towards the sofa, and sat down beside him, pressing her thigh against his. She undid a button of his shirt and slid a cool hand inside. He flinched as the gems on one of her rings snagged in his chest hair.

"Lots of 'air," Fulvia purred. "*That* is in the book."

"I'm not saying the book is entirely fictitious," said Morris. "Some of the minor details are taken from life—"

"'Airy as a beast . . . You were a beast to your wife, I think."

"Ow!" exclaimed Morris, for Fulvia had dug her long lacquered nails into his flesh for emphasis.

"'Ow? Well, for example, tying 'er up with leather straps and doing all those degrading things to 'er."

"Lies, all lies!" said Morris desperately.

"You can do those things to me, if you like, *caro*," Fulvia whispered into his ear, pinching his nipple painfully at the same time.

"I don't want to do anything to anybody, I never did,"

Morris groaned. "The only time we ever fooled around with that S/M stuff, it was Désirée's idea, not mine."

"I don't believe you, Morris."

"It's true. Novelists are terrible liars. They make things up. They change things around. Black becomes white, white black. They are totally unethical beings. Ouch!" Fulvia had nibbled his earlobe hard enough to draw blood.

"Come," she said, rising abruptly to her feet.

"Where are we going?"

"To bed."

"Already?" Morris consulted his digital watch. "It's only ten after ten. Can't I finish my cigar?"

"No, there isn't time."

"What's the hurry?"

Fulvia sat down beside him again. "Don't you find me desirable, Morris?" she said. She pressed herself seductively against him, but there was a faintly menacing glint in her eyes which suggested that her patience was running out.

"Of course I do, Fulvia, you're one of the most attractive women I've ever met," he hastened to assure her. "That's the trouble. You're bound to be disappointed, especially after Désirée's write-up. I mean, I retired from this sort of thing years ago."

Fulvia drew away and stared at him, dismayed. "You mean, you're . . ."

"No, not impotent. But out of practice. I live on my own. I jog. I write my books. I watch TV."

"No love affairs?"

"Not in a long while."

Fulvia looked at him with compassion. "You poor man."

"You know, I don't miss it as much as I thought I would. It's a relief to be free of all the hassle."

"'Assle?"

"Yeah, you know—all the undressing and dressing again in the middle of the day, and showering before and after, and making sure your undershorts are clean and brushing your teeth all the time and gargling with mouthwash."

Fulvia threw back her head and laughed loud and long. "You funny man," she gasped.

Morris Zapp grinned uncertainly, for he had not intended to be *that* funny.

Fulvia stood up again, tugging Morris to his feet. "Come on, you funny man, I will remind you of what you are missing."

"Well, if you insist," he sighed, stubbing out his cigar. In this more relaxed mood Fulvia seemed less intimidating. "Give me a kiss," he said.

"A kiss?"

"Yeah, you remember kissing. It used to come between saying '*Hi*' and fucking. I'm an old fashioned guy."

Fulvia smiled and pressed the length of her body against him long and fiercely. Morris ran his hands down her back and over her hips. She appeared to be wearing nothing underneath the white robe. He felt desire stirring in him like dull roots after spring rain.

Fulvia's bedroom was a deeply carpeted octagon, lined, walls and ceiling, with rose-tinted mirrors that multiplied every gesture like a kaleidoscope. A bevy of Fulvias stepped, naked as Botticelli's Venus, from the white foam of their discarded dresses and converged upon him with a hundred outstretched arms. A whole football team of Morris Zapps stripped to their undershorts with clumsy haste and clamped hairy paws on ranks of peach-shaped buttocks receding into infinity.

"How do you like it?" murmured Fulvia, as they stroked and grappled on the crimson sheets of the huge circular bed.

"Amazing!" Morris said. "It's like being at an orgy choreographed by Busby Berkeley."

"No more jokes, Morris," said Fulvia. "It isn't erotic."

"Sorry. What would you like me to do?"

Fulvia had her answer ready. "Tie me up, gag me, then do whatever you desire." She pulled from a bedside cabinet a pair of handcuffs, leather thongs, sticky tape and bandages.

"How do these work?" said Morris, fumbling with the handcuffs. "Like so." Fulvia slipped the cuffs over his wrists and fastened them with a snap. "Ha, ha! Now you are my prisoner." She pushed him down on to the bed.

"Hey, what are you doing?"

What she was doing was pulling off his undershorts. "I

think your wife exaggerated just a *leetle*, Morris," she said, kneeling over him, her long cool fingers busy.

"*Ars longa*, in life shorter," Morris murmured. But it was like the last despairing witticism of a drowning man. He closed his eyes and surrendered himself to sensation.

Then Morris heard a thud from below stairs, as of a door closing, and a male voice called out Fulvia's name. Morris opened his eyes, his body rigid with apprehension, apart from one zone which was limp with it. "Who's that?" he hissed.

"My 'usband," said Fulvia.

"*What*?" A score of naked, handcuffed Morris Zapps leapt from the bed and exchanged looks of alarm and consternation. "I thought you said he was stuck in Rome?"

"'E must 'ave decided to drive," said Fulvia calmly. She raised her head, and her voice, to call out something in Italian.

"What are you doing? What did you say?" demanded Morris, struggling with his undershorts. It wasn't easy, he discovered, to put them on while wearing handcuffs.

"I told 'im to come up."

"*Are you crazy*? How am I supposed to get out of here?" He hopped around the room with his undershorts half on and half off, opening closet doors, looking for a second exit or somewhere to hide, and tripped over his own shoes. Fulvia laughed. He shook the handcuffs an inch from her Roman nose. "Will you kindly take these fucking things off my wrists," he said, in a whisper that was like a suppressed scream. Fulvia searched lackadaisically for the key in a drawer of the bedside cabinet. "Quick, quick!" Morris urged frantically. He could hear someone mounting the stairs, humming a popular song.

"Relax, Morris, Ernesto is a man of the world," said Fulvia. She inserted a key into the handcuffs and with a click he was free. But with another click the bedroom door opened, and a man in a pale, elegant suit, grey-haired and deeply tanned, came in. "Ernesto, this is Morris," said Fulvia, kissing her husband on both cheeks and leading him across the room where Morris was hastily pulling up his undershorts.

"Felice di conoscerla, signore," Ernesto's face crinkled in a broad smile and he extended a hand which Morris shook limply.

"Ernesto does not speak English," said Fulvia. "But 'e understands."

"I wish I did," said Morris.

Ernesto opened one of the mirrored closet doors, hung up his suit, kicked off his shoes, and walked towards the *en suite* bathroom, pulling his shirt over his head. A stream of muffled Italian came from inside the shirt.

"What did he say?" Morris gaped, as the bathroom door closed behind Ernesto.

"'E's going to take a shower," said Fulvia, plumping the pillows on the bed. "Then 'e will join us."

"Join us? Where?"

"'Ere, of course," said Fulvia, getting into the bed, and arranging herself in the centre of it.

Morris stared. "Hey!" he accused her "I believe you planned this all along!"

Fulvia smiled her Mona Lisa smile.

In the tiny bathroom of their apartment in Fitzroy Square, Thelma Ringbaum was preparing for bed with more than usual care. It had been a long and tiring day: the agency through which they were renting the apartment had lost the key and kept them waiting several hours while a duplicate was obtained. Then, when they finally got into it they found that the water had been turned off in some inscrutable fashion and they had to phone the agency to send a man to turn it on—and to do *that* they had to go out and search the neighbourhood for an unvandalized phone booth because the telephone in the apartment had been disconnected. The kitchen stove was so filthy that Thelma decided she would have to clean it before they even made themselves a cup of coffee, and the inside of the icebox was like a small working model of a glacier and had to be defrosted before they could use it. Having had no proper sleep the previous night, Thelma was, by the time she had completed these tasks, and gone marketing for basic foods at the local stores, and fixed their supper (because Howard wouldn't go out to a restaurant), ready to drop. But there was a tryst pending between herself and Howard, and Thelma's life was not so full of romance that she could afford to break it. Also, Howard needed cheering up after finding that disappointing letter from Morris Zapp on the doormat.

In spite of her weariness, and the discouraging décor of the bathroom, all cobwebs and peeling paint, Thelma felt a quickening of erotic excitement as she prepared herself for Howard's pleasure. She softened her bathwater with fragrant foam, massaged herself afterwards with scented skin cream, dabbed perfume behind her ears and in other intimate hollows and crevices of her anatomy, and put on her sexiest nightgown, a frivolous garment of sheer black nylon. She brushed her hair for one hundred strokes, and bit her lips to make them red. Then she tip-toed to the living-room, threw open the door and posed on the threshold. "Howard!" she cooed.

Howard was crouched in front of the ancient black-and-white TV, fiddling with the controls while the picture buzzed and flickered. "Yes?" he said, without turning round.

Thelma giggled. "*Now* you can have me, honey."

Howard Ringbaum turned round in his seat and looked at her stonily. "Now I don't want you," he said, and resumed his fiddling with the controls of the television.

At that moment, Thelma Ringbaum determined that she would be unfaithful to her husband at the earliest possible opportunity.

All around the world people are in different states of dress and undress, alone or in couples, waking or sleeping, working or resting. As Persse McGarrigle walks along an Irish country road in the middle of the night, with Morris Zapp's deerstalker tipped back on his head, the same sunbeam that, reflected off the moon, now illuminates his way, and shows him the shapes of darkened farms and cottages where men and beasts slumber and snore, has just a few seconds ago woken up the pavement dwellers of Bombay and the factory workers of Omsk, shining directly into their wincing faces or stealing through the gaps in tattered curtains and broken blinds.

Further east, it is already midmorning. In Cooktown, Queensland, in his office a the University of North Queensland, Rodney Wainwright is working at his paper on the Future of Criticism. To try and recover the impetus of his argument, he is copying out what he has already written, from the beginning, as a pole vaulter lengthens his run-up to achieve a particularly daunting jump. His hope is that the sheer momentum of discourse will carry him over that stubborn obstacle which has delayed him for so long. So far it is going well. His hand is moving fluently across the foolscap. He is introducing many new gracenotes and making various subtle revisions of the original text as he proceeds. He tries to suppress his own knowledge of what comes next, tries not to see the crucial passage looming ahead. He is trying to trick his own brain. Don't look, don't look! Keep going, keep going! Gather all your strength up into one ball, ready to spring, NOW!

> *The question is, therefore, how can literary criticism maintain its Arnoldian function of identifying the best which has been thought and said, when literary discourse itself had been decentred by deconstructing the traditional concept of the author, of 'authority'.*
> *Clearly*

Yes, clearly . . . ?

> *Clearly*

Clearly what?

The vaulter hangs suspended in the air for a moment, his face red with effort, eyes bulging, tendons knotted, the pole bent almost to breaking point under his weight, the crossbar only inches from his nose. Then it all collapses: the pole breaks, the bar is dislodged, the athlete falls back to earth, limbs flailing. Rodney Wainwright slumps forward onto his desk and buries his face in his hands. Beaten again.

There is a timid knock on the door. "Come in," Rodney

Wainwright moans, looking up through latticed fingers. A blonde, girlish head peers round the door, eyes wide.

"Are you all right, Dr Wainright?" says Sandra Dix. "I came to see you about my assignment."

On a different latitude, but much the same longitude, Akira Sakazaki, seated crosslegged in his carpeted cubicle in the sky, is grading papers—English-language exercises by his first year students at the university. *"Having rescued girl drowning, lifeguard raped in blanket her,"* he reads. Sighing, shaking his head, Akira inserts articles, rearranges word order, and corrects the spelling of *"wrapped"*. Such work is small beer to the translator of Ronald Frobisher. "Small beer," says Akira aloud, and smiles toothily to himself. It is an English phrase whose meaning he has learned only this morning, from one of the novelist's letters.

Akira is dressed in his Arnold Palmer sports shirt this morning, and his Jack Nicklaus golf shoes stand beside the door ready to be slipped on when it is time to leave for the University. For today is his day for golf. This evening he will break his journey home to play for an hour at one of Tokyo's many driving ranges. Already his fingers itch to curl themselves round the shaft of his club. Standing on the upper gallery of the floodlit, netted range, erected like a gigantic birdcage in the isosceles triangle made by three criss-crossing railway lines, he will lash a hundred yellow-painted golfballs into space, see them rise, soar above the million roofs and TV aerials, only to hit the net and fall anticlimactically to earth, like stricken birds.

In this sport, Akira sees an allegory of the elations and frustrations of his work as translator. Language is the net that holds thought trapped within a particular culture. But if one could only strike the ball with sufficient force with perfect timing, it would perhaps break through the netting, continue on its course, never fall to earth, but go into orbit around the world.

In London, Ronald Frobisher is asleep in his study, wearing dressing-gown and pyjamas, slumped in front of the television set on which he was watching, some hours earlier, the repeat of an episode from a police thriller series for which he wrote the script. Bored by his own dialogue, he dropped off to sleep in his chair; and the late news, weather forecast, and an epilogue by an earnest Evangelical clergyman on the reality of sin, have all washed over him unheeded. Now the television set emits only a high-pitched whine and a faint bluish light which imparts to the novelist's stubbly, pock-marked jowels a deathlike hue. Neglected at his feet lies a blue aerogramme with questions neatly typed: *"p. 152, 'jam-butty'. What is it? p. 182, 'Y-fronts'. What are they? p. 191 'sweet fanny adams'. Who is she?"*

Arthur Kingfisher is also seated in front of a television set, though he is not asleep, since it is still early evening in Chicago (where he is staying on for a few days after the conclusion of the conference on "The Crisis of the Sign" in order to repeat his keynote address in the form of a lecture at Northwestern University for a one-thousand-dollar fee). He is watching, intermittently, a pornographic movie ordered by telephone and piped to his room on one of the hotel's video channels—intermittently, because he is at the same time reading a book on hermeneutics which he has agreed to review for a learned journal, an assignment which is now long overdue, and he glances up from the page only when the aridity of the discourse becomes too much for even his dry old brain to bear, or when the film's sound track, shifting from banal dialogue to panting and moaning, warns him that its feeble pretence of telling a story has been abandoned in favour of its real point and purpose. At the same time, Song-Mi Lee, stooping over his shoulder in a charming silk kimono, is excavating the wax from Arthur Kingfisher's ear, using a small curved bamboo implement specially designed for the purpose and widely used in Korean bathhouses.

Suddenly, Arthur Kingfisher becomes excited—whether it is the images of copulation on the small screen or the subtle stimulation of his inner ear, or the mental glimpse of some new horizon of conceptual thought prompted by the writer on hermeneutics, it would be difficult to say; but he feels a distinct sensation of life between his legs, drops the book, and hurries Song-Mi Lee towards the bed, pulling off his bathrobe and urging her to do likewise.

She obeys; but the kimono is delicate and valuable, its sash is wound around Song-Mi Lee's tiny waist in a complex knot, and it is at least half a minute before she has disrobed, by which time Arthur Kingfisher's excitement has subsided—or perhaps it was always an illusion, a phantom, wishful thinking. He returns despondently to his book and his seat in front of the TV. But he has forgotten what new theoretical leap he had begun to see the possibilities of a few moments ago, and the naked bodies writhing and clutching and quivering on the screen now seem merely to mock his impotence. He slaps the book shut, snaps off the TV and closes his eyes in despair. Song-Mi Lee silently recommences the removal of wax from his ear.

In Helicon, New Hampshire, it is evening, dinner is over, and Désirée Zapp is crouched conspiratorially over the payphone in the lobby of the writers' colony, talking to her agent in New York in an urgent whisper, anxious not to be overheard by any of the other residents. For what she is confessing to her agent is that she is "blocked", and this word, like "cancer" in a surgical ward, is never under any circumstances to be uttered aloud, though it is in the minds of all. "It's not working out for me, this place, Alice," she whispers into the telephone.

"What? I can't hear you, this must be a bad line," says Alice Kauffman, from her apartment on 48th Street.

"I'm no further forward than when I came here six weeks ago," says Désirée, risking a slight increase of volume. "The first thing I do every morning is to tear up what I wrote the day before. It's driving me crazy."

A great sigh, like a bellows emptying, comes down the line from New York to New Hampshire. Alice Kauffman weighs two hundred and thirty pounds and runs her agency from her apartment because she is too heavy to travel comfortably even by taxi to another part of Manhattan. If Désirée knows her, and she does know Alice very well, her agent will at this moment be sprawled on a divan with a pile of manuscripts on one side of her massive hips and an open box of Swiss cherry-liqueur chocolates on the other. "Then quit, honey," says Alice. "Check out tomorrow. Run."

Désirée looks nervously over her shoulders, fearful that this heretical advice might be overheard. "Where to?"

"Give yourself a treat, a change of scene," says Alice. "Take a trip someplace. Go to Europe."

"Hmm," says Désirée thoughtfully. "I did get an invitation to a conference in Germany, just this morning."

"Accept," says Alice. "Your expenses will be tax-deductible."

"They were offering to pay my expenses."

"There'll be extras," said Alice. "There always are. Did I tell you by the way, that *Difficult Days* is going to be translated into Portugese? That's the seventeenth language, not counting Korea which pirated it."

Far away in Germany, Siegfried von Turpitz, who sent the conference invitation to Désirée, is asleep in the bedroom of his house on the edge of the Black Forest. Tired from his long drive, he lies to attention, on his back, his black hand outside the sheets. His wife, Bertha, asleep in the other twin bed, has never seen her husband without the glove. When he is taking a bath, his right hand dangles over the side of the tub to keep dry; when he takes a shower it projects horizontally from between the curtains like a traffic policeman's signal. When he comes to her bed she is not always sure, in the dark, whether it is a penis or a leather-sheathed finger that probes the folds and orifices of her body. On their wedding night she begged him to remove the glove, but he refused. "But if the lights are out, Siegfried?" she pleaded. "My first wife asked me to do that once," said Siegfried von Turpitz cryptically, "but I forgot to put the glove back on before I fell asleep." Von Turpitz's first wife was known to have died of a heart attack, found one morning by her husband lying dead in the bed beside him. Bertha never asked Siegfried again to remove his glove.

Most people in Europe are asleep now, though Michel Tardieu is awake behind his reptilian eyelids, troubled by a faint aroma of perfume emanating from the body of Albert, asleep beside him, which is not the familiar fragrance of his own favourite toilet water, *Tristes Tropiques,* which Albert customarily borrows in liberal quantities, but something sickly and cloying, vulgarly synthetic, something (his nose twitches as he strives to translate olfactory sensations into verbal concepts) such as (his lizard eyelids flick open in horror at the thought) a *woman* might use! Akbil Borak, however, is not awake, having fallen asleep sitting up in bed, fifty pages from the end of *The Spirit of the Age,* and is bowed forward as if poleaxed, his nose flattened against the open book reposing on his knees, while Oya, her head turned away from the light of the reading lamp, slumbers obliviously beside him. And Philip and Hilary Swallow are asleep back to back in their double bed which, being as old as their marriage, sags in the middle like a shallow trench, so that they tend to roll towards each other in their sleep; but whenever Philip's bony haunches touch Hilary's fleshy ones, their bodies spring apart like opposed magnets and, without waking, each shifts back to the margins of the mattress.

Persse McGarrigle stops in the middle of the road to transfer his bag from one aching arm to another. The hitching had gone well enough as far as Mullingar, but there he was picked up by a man on his way home from a wedding and far gone in his cups, who drove past the same signpost three times, finally confessed that he was lost, and fell abruptly asleep over the wheel of his car. Persse rather regrets, now, that he didn't doss down himself in the back seat of the car, for his chances of getting another lift this night seem remote.

He stops again, and looks speculatively about him. It is warm and dry enough to sleep out. Spying a haystack in a field to his right, Persse climbs over the gate and makes towards it. A startled donkey rises to its feet and canters away. He throws down his grip, kicks off his shoes and stretches out in the fragrant hay, staring up at the immense sky arching above his head, studded with a million stars. They pulse with a brilliance that city-dwellers could never imagine. One of them seems to be moving across the sky in relation to other stars, and at first Persse thinks he has discovered a new comet. Then he realizes from its slow and steady progress that it is a communications satellite in geostable orbit, a tiny artificial moon that faithfully keeps its station above the Atlantic, moving in pace with the earth's rotation, receiving and sending back messages, images and secrets, to and from countless human beings far below. "Bright satellite!" he murmurs, "Would I were steadfast as thou art." And he recites the whole sonnet aloud, willing it to rebound from space into Angelica's thoughts, or dreams, wherever she is, that she might feel the strength of his longing to be with her.

> *Pillowed upon my fair love's ripening breast*
> *To feel for ever its soft fall and swell*
> *Awake for ever in a sweet unrest,*
> *Still, still to hear her tender taken breath*
> *And so live ever—or else swoon to death.*

But no, cancel that last bit about dying. Poor old Keats was at his last gasp when he wrote that—he knew he had no chance of getting his head down on Fanny Brawne's ripening breast, having hardly any lungs left in his own. But he, Persse McGarrigle, has no intention of dying yet awhile. Living for ever is more the ticket, especially if he can find Angelica.

So musing, Persse fell peacefully asleep.

PART III

One

WHEN Persse finally got back to his Department at University College Limerick, there were two letters from London waiting for him. He could tell at a glance that neither was from Angelica—the envelopes were too official-looking, the typing of his name and address too professional—but their contents were not without interest. One was from Felix Skinner, reminding him that Lecky, Windrush and Bernstein would be very interested to see Persse's thesis on the influence of T. S. Eliot on Shakespeare. The other was from the Royal Academy of Literature, informing him that he had been awarded a prize of £1000 under the Maud Fitzsimmons Bequest for the Encouragement of Anglo-Irish Poetry. Persse had sent in a sheaf of manuscript poems for this prize six months before, and had forgotten all about it. He whooped and threw the letter into the air. Catching it as it floated to the ground, he read the second paragraph, which stated that the prize, together with a number of other awards administered by the Academy, would be presented at a reception, which it was hoped Mr McGarrigle would be able to attend, to be held in three weeks' time on the *Annabel Lee*, Charing Cross Embankment.

Persse went to see his Head of Department, Professor Liam McCreedy, and asked if he could take a sabbatical in the coming term.

"A sabbatical? This is a rather sudden request, Persse," said McCreedy, peering at him from behind his usual battlements of books. Instead of using a desk, the Professor sat at an immense table, almost entirely covered with tottering piles of scholarly tomes—dictionaries, concordances and Old English texts—with just a small area in front of him cleared for writing. The visitor seated on the other side of these fortifications was placed at a considerable disadvantage in any discussion by not always being able to see his interlocutor. "I don't think you've been here long enough to qualify for a sabbatical," McCreedy said doubtfully.

"Well, leave of absence, then. I don't need any pay. I've just won a thousand-pound prize for my poetry," said Persse, in the general direction of a variorum edition of *The Battle of Maldon;* but Professor McCreedy's head bobbed up at the other end of the table, above Skeat's *Dialect Dictionary.*

"Have you, now?" he exclaimed. "Well, hearty congratulations. That puts a rather different complexion on the matter. Er, what would you be wanting to be doing during this leave, exactly?"

"I want to study structuralism, sir," said Persse.

This announcement sent the Professor diving for cover again, into some slit trench deep in the publications of the Early English Text Society, from which his voice emerged muffled and plaintive. "Well, I don't know that we can manage the modern literature course without you, Mr McGarrigle."

"There are no lectures in the summer term," Persse pointed out, "because all the students are swotting for their examinations."

"Ah, but that's just it!" said McCreedy triumphantly, taking aim from behind Klaeber's *Beowulf.* "Who will mark the Modern Literature papers?"

"I'll come back and do that for you," Persse offered. It was not a very onerous commitment, since there were only five students in the course.

"Well, all right, I'll see what I can do," sighed McCreedy.

Persse went back to his digs near the Limerick gasworks and drafted a two-thousand word outline of a book about the influence of T. S. Eliot on modern readings of Shakespeare and other Elizabethan writers, which he typed up and sent off to Felix Skinner with a covering note saying that he would prefer not to submit the original thesis at this stage, since it needed a lot of revision before it would be suitable for publication.

Morris Zapp took his departure from Milan as soon as he decently could, if "decent" was a word that could be applied to the Morgana ménage, which he ventured to doubt. The troilism party had not been a success. As soon as it became evident that he was expected to fool around with Ernesto as well as Fulvia, Morris had made his excuses and left the mirrored bedchamber. He also took the precaution of locking the door of the guest bedroom behind him. When he rose the next morning, Ernesto, evidently an *autostrada* addict, had already left to drive back to Rome, and Fulvia, coolly polite across the coffee and croissants, made no allusion to the events of the previous night, so that Morris began to wonder whether he had dreamed the whole episode; but the sting of the various superficial flesh wounds Fulvia's long nails had inflicted on his chest and shoulders convinced him otherwise.

A uniformed driver from the Villa Serbelloni called soon after breakfast, and Morris exhaled a sigh of relief as the big Mercedes pulled away from Fulvia's front porch: he couldn't help thinking of her as a kind of sorceress within whose sphere of influence it would be dangerous to linger. Milan was socked in by cloud, but as the car approached its destination the sun came out and Alpine peaks became visible on the horizon. They skirted a lake for some miles, driving in and out of tunnels that had windows cut at intervals in the rock to give lantern-slide glimpses of blue water and green shoreline. The Villa Serbelloni proved to be a noble and luxurious house built on the sheltered slope of a promontory that divided two lakes, Como and Lecco, with magnificent views to east, south and west from its balconies and extensive gardens.

Morris was shown into a well-appointed suite on the second floor, and stepped out on to his balcony to inhale the air, scented with the perfume of various spring blossoms, and to enjoy the prospect. Down on the terrace, the other resident scholars were gathering for the prelunch aperitif—he had glimpsed the table laid for lunch in the dining-room on his way up: starched white napery, crystal glass, menu cards. He surveyed the scene with complacency. He felt sure he was going to enjoy his stay here. Not the least of its attractions was that it was entirely free. All you had to do, to come and stay in this idyllic retreat, pampered by servants and lavishly provided with food and drink, given every facility for reflection and creation, was to apply.

Of course, you had to be distinguished—by, for instance, having applied successfully for other, similar handouts, grants, fellowships and so on, in the past. That was the beauty of the academic life, as Morris saw it. To them that had had, more would be given. All you needed to do to get started was to write one really damned good book—which admittedly wasn't easy when you were a young college teacher just beginning your career, struggling with a heavy teaching load on unfamiliar material, and probably with the demands of a wife and young growing family as well. But on the strength of that one damned good book you could get a grant to write a second book in more favourable circumstances; with two books you got promotion, a lighter teaching load, and courses of your own devising; you could then use your teaching as a way of doing research for your next book, which you were thus able to produce all the more quickly. This productivity made you eligible for tenure, further promotion, more generous and prestigious research grants, more relief from routine teaching and administration. In theory, it was possible to wind up being full professor while doing nothing except to be permanently absent on some kind of sabbatical grant or fellowship. Morris hadn't quite reached that omega point, but he was working on it.

He stepped back into the cool, restful shade of his

spacious room, and discovered an adjoining study. On the broad, leather-topped desk was a neat stack of mail that had been forwarded to Bellagio by arrangement. It included a cable from someone called Rodney Wainwright in Australia, whom Morris had forgotten all about, apologizing for the delay in submitting his paper for the Jerusalem conference, an enquiry from Howard Ringbaum about the same conference which had crossed with Morris's rejection of Ringbaum's paper, and a letter from Désirée's lawyers about college tuition fees for the twins. Morris dropped these communications in the waste basket and, taking a sheet of the villa's crested notepaper from the desk drawer, typed, on the electric typewriter provided, a letter to Arthur Kingfisher, reminding him that they had been co-participants in an English institute seminar on Symbolism some years before; saying that he had heard that he, Arthur Kingfisher, had given a brilliant keynote address to the recent Chicago conference on "The Crisis of the Sign", and begging him, in the most flattering of terms, for the favour of an offprint or Xerox of the text of this address. Morris read through the letter. Was it a shade too fulsome? No, that was another law of academic life: *it is impossible to be excessive in flattery of one's peers*. Should he mention his interest in the UNESCO Chair? No, that would be premature. The time would come for the hard sell. This was just a gentle, preliminary nudge of the great man's memory. Morris Zapp licked the envelope and sealed it with a thump of his hairy-knuckled fist. On his way to the terrace for aperitifs he dropped it into the mail box thoughtfully provided in the hall.

Robin Dempsey went back to Darlington in a thoroughly demoralized state of mind. After the humiliation of Angelica's practical joke (his cheeks still burned, all four of them, whenever he thought of that Irish bumpkin observing his preparations for bed from inside the wardrobe) another day of frustration and aggravation had followed. The conference business meeting, chaired by Philip Swallow, somewhat flustered and breathless from a late arrival, had rejected his own offer to hold next year's conference at Darlington, and voted in favour of Cambridge instead. Then, when he called later in the morning at his former home to take his two younger children out for the day, he overheard them complaining that they didn't want to go. Janet had ensured that they accompanied him in the end, but only, she made clear to Robin, so that she and her boyfriend, Scott, an ageing flowerchild who still affected denim and long hair at the age of thirty-five, could go to bed together in the afternoon. Scott was a freelance photographer, seldom in employment, and one of Robin Dempsey's many grudges against his ex-wife was that she was spending part of the maintenance money he paid her on keeping this good-for-nothing layabout in cigarettes and lenses.

Jennifer, sixteen, and Alex, fourteen, sulkily escorted him to the City Centre, where they declined the offer of a visit to the Art Gallery or Science Museum in favour of looking through endless racks of records and clothing in the Shopping Centre boutiques. They cheered up somewhat when Robin bought them a pair of jeans and an LP each, and even condescended to talk to him over the hamburgers and chips which they demanded for lunch. This conversation did not, however, improve his spirits, consisting as it did mainly of allusions to musicians he had never heard of, and enthusiastic tributes to Scott, who evidently had.

So the day wore on. The hamburgers, coming on top of the medieval banquet, made him flatulent, and the drive back to Darlington uncomfortable. He arrived home at dusk. His small modern town house, newspapers and junk mail drifted up behind the front door, seemed chilly and unwelcoming. He walked from room to room, turning on radio, TV, electric fires, to try and dispel his loneliness and depression, but to no avail. Instead of unpacking, he got back into his Golf and drove down to the University's Computer Centre.

As he had expected, Josh Collins, the Senior Lecturer in Computing, was still there, alone in the brightly-lit prefabricated building, working on a program. Some people claimed that Josh Collins never went home, that he had no home, but dossed down at night on the floor between his humming, blinking, clicking machines.

"Hallo, Josh, what's new?" said Robin with forced joviality.

Josh looked up from a long scroll of data printout. "Eliza's arrived," he said.

"Really? That's great!" said Robin Dempsey. It was just the diversion he needed.

ELIZA, so named after the heroine of *Pygmalion*, was a program designed to enable computers to talk, that is, to conduct coherent conversations in standard English with human users, by means of a visual display. The conversations had to be a contextually specific type, with well-defined rules and goals, in which the computer could take an essentially prompting and questioning role, programmed with a repertoire of possible responses to cues likely to appear in the context. The psychiatrist-patient interview was considered ideal for this purpose, being one of the most regulated discourse situations, and had accordingly been adopted as the model for ELIZA. The experiment was of considerable interest to linguisticians researching into the systematic aspects of verbal interaction.

"Let me try it out," said Robin.

"OK," said Josh. "Use the terminal in the corner. When I give you the nod, write in 'Hallo'."

Robin Dempsey seated himself at a console consisting of a typewriter keyboard and visual display screen. Josh took a large spool of tape into the glass-partitioned section of the room where the mainframe computer was situated, and soon nodded to Robin to indicate that ELIZA was on line.

"HALLO," Robin typed on the keyboard.

"HALLO, HOW ARE YOU FEELING?" replied ELIZA, the printed words appearing instantly on the VDU.

"I'M FEELING TERRIBLE," Robin replied.

"WHAT DO YOU MEAN BY THAT PRECISELY?"

"I'M FEELING DEPRESSED."

"WHY DO YOU THINK YOU ARE DEPRESSED?"

"BECAUSE I'M LONELY."

"DO YOU LIVE WITH YOUR FAMILY?"

"NO."

"DO YOU HAVE ANY FRIENDS?"

"NOT REALLY."

"WHY IS THAT?"

Robin Dempsey paused for some considerable time before he typed in his reply: "I DON'T KNOW."

"DO YOU REALLY NOT KNOW OR ARE YOU JUST AVOIDING THE QUESTION?"

Robin Dempsey flushed and typed rapidly: "I USED TO HAVE FRIENDS ONCE."

"WHEN WAS THAT?"

"BEFORE I WAS MARRIED."

"YOU DIDN'T TELL ME YOU WERE MARRIED."

"I'M DIVORCED."

"TELL ME ABOUT YOUR DIVORCE."

Robin Dempsey typed rapidly for fifteen minutes without stopping, until he became aware of Josh Collins, hovering at his shoulder. "Yes?" he said coldly, screening the VDU from Josh's view.

"You OK, Robin?"

"Yes, thank you."

"Interesting?"

"Very."

"Can I read the printout?"

"No," said Robin Dempsey, "you can't."

Felix Skinner skimmed through Persse's outline and thought it distinctly promising. "But before we give him a contract, we need a reader's report," he said. "Who shall we send it to?"

"I don't know, Mr Skinner, I'm sure," said Gloria, his secretary, crossing her legs and patting her wavy, honey-coloured hair. She waited patiently with her pencil poised above her notepad. She had only been Felix Skinner's personal secretary for a couple of months, but already she was used to her boss's habit of thinking aloud by asking her questions that she hadn't a clue how to answer.

Felix Skinner bared his yellow fangs, noting, not for the first time, what a very shapely pair of legs Gloria possessed. "What about Philip Swallow?" he proposed.

"All right," said Gloria. "Is his address on file?"

"On second thoughts," said Felix, holding up a caution-ary finger, "perhaps not. I have a feeling he was a teeny weeny bit jealous of my interest in young McGarrigle, the other day. He might be prejudiced."

Gloria yawned daintily, and picked a speck of fluff from the front of her jumper. Felix lit a fresh Gauloise from the stub smouldering between his fingers and admired the contours of the jumper. "I tell you what!" he exclaimed triumphantly, "Rudyard Parkinson."

"I know the name," said Gloria gamely. "Isn't he at Cambridge?"

"Oxford. My old tutor, actually. Shall we phone him first?"

"Well, perhaps you'd better, Mr Skinner."

"Wise counsel," said Felix Skinner, reaching for the telephone. When he had dialled he leaned back in his swivel chair and treated Gloria to another canine grin. "You know, Gloria, I think it's time you called me Felix."

"Oh, Mr Skinner..." Gloria blushed with pleasure. "Thank you."

Felix got through to Rudyard Parkinson quite quickly. (He was supervising a postgraduate, but the porter at All Saints had instructions to put all long-distance calls straight through to the Professor's room even if he was engaged. Long-distance calls usually meant books to review.) Parkinson declined, however, to take on the assessment of Persse McGarrigle's proposal. "Sorry, old man, got rather a lot on my plate at the moment," he said. "They're giving me an honorary degree in Vancouver next week. It didn't really sink in, when I accepted, that I'd actually have to *go* there to collect it."

"I say, what a bore," said Felix Skinner sympathetically. "Could you suggest anyone else? It's sort of about the modern reception of Shakespeare and Co. being influenced by T. S. Eliot."

"Reception? That rings a bell. Oh yes, I had a letter yesterday about a conference on something like that. A hun called von Turpitz. Know him?"

"Yes, we published a translation of his last book, actually."

"I should try him."

"Good idea," said Felix Skinner. "I should have thought of him myself."

He rang off and dictated a letter to Siegfried von Turpitz asking for his opinion of Persse McGarrigle's outline and offering him a fee of £25 or £50 worth of books from Lecky, Windrush and Bernstein's current list. "Enclose a copy of our catalogue with that, will you Gloria, and of course a Xerox of McGarrigle's typescript." He stubbed out his cigarette and glanced at his watch. "I feel quite fagged after all that effort. Am I having lunch with anybody today?"

"I don't think so," said Gloria, consulting his diary. "No."

"Then would you care to join me for a little Italian nosh and a glass or two of *vino* at a *trattoria* I know in Covent Garden?"

"That would be very nice . . . Felix," said Gloria complacently.

"Cheek!" Rudyard Parkinson exclaimed, putting down the telephone receiver. The postgraduate he was supervising, not sure whether he was being addressed or not, made no comment. "Why should he think I would want to read some totally unknown bog-Irishman's ramblings? Some of one's former students do rather presume on the relationship." The postgraduate, who had taken his first degree at Newcastle and whose initial awe of Parkinson was rapidly turning into disillusionment, tried to arrange his features in some appropriate expression of sympathy and concern. "Now, where were we?" said Rudyard Parkinson, "Yeats's death wish . . ."

"Keats's death wish."

"Ah, yes. I beg your pardon." Rudyard Parkinson stroked his muttonchop whiskers and gazed out of his window at the cupola on top of the Sheldonian and, further off, the spire of St Mary's Church. "Tell me, if you were flying to Vancouver would you go by British Airways or Air Canada?"

"I'm not much of an expert on air travel," said the young man. "A charter flight to Majorca is about the limit of my experience."

"Majorca? Ah yes, I remember visiting Robert Graves there once. Did you happen to meet him?"

"No," said the postgraduate. "It was a package holiday. Robert Graves wasn't included."

Rudyard Parkinson glanced at the young man with momentary suspicion. Was it possible that callow Newcastle could be capable of irony—and at *his* expense? The youth's impassive countenance reassured him. Parkinson turned back to face the window. "I thought I'd be patriotic and go British Airways," he said. "I hope I've done the wise thing."

Oxford was still in vacation as far as the undergraduates were concerned, but at Rummidge it was the first day of the summer term, and a fine one. The sun blazed down from a cloudless sky on the Library steps and the grass quadrangle. Philip Swallow stood at the window of his office and surveyed the scene with a mixture of pleasure, envy and unfocused lust. A warm afternoon always brought out the girls in their summer dresses, like bulbs forcing their way through the turf and abruptly flowering in a blaze of colour. All over the lawns they were strewn, in attitudes of abandonment, straps down and skirts hitched up to tan their winter-pale limbs. The boys lounged in clusters, eyeing the girls, or pranced between them, stripped to their jeans, skimming frisbees with an ostentatious display of muscle and skill. Here and there pair-bonding had already occurred, and youthful couples sunned themselves clasped in each other's arms, or wrestled playfully in a thinly disguised mime of copulation. Books and ringbinders lay neglected on the greensward. The compulsion of spring had laid its irresistible spell upon these young bodies. The musk of their mutual attraction was almost visible, like pollen, in the atmosphere.

Right under Philip's window, a girl of great beauty, dressed simply but ravishingly in a sleeveless cotton shift, clasped the hands of a tall, athletic young man in tee-shirt and jeans. They held hands at arm's length and gazed raptly into each other's eyes, unable, it seemed, to tear themselves apart to attend whatever lecture or lab session called. Philip couldn't blame them. They made a handsome couple, glowing with health and the consciousness of their own good looks, trembling on the threshold of erotic bliss. "More happy love," Philip murmured behind his dusty windowpane.

> *"More happy, happy love!*
> *For ever warm and still to be enjoyed,*
> *For ever panting and for ever young."*

Unlike the lovers on the Grecian Urn, however, these ones did eventually kiss: a long and passionate embrace that lifted the girl on to the tips of her toes, and that Philip felt vicariously down to the very roots of his being.

He turned away from the window, disturbed and slightly ashamed. There was no point in getting all worked up by the Rummidge rites of spring. He had forsworn sexual interest in students ever since the unfortunate affair of Sandra Dix—Rummidge students, anyway. He had to rely on his trips abroad for amorous adventure. He didn't know quite what to expect of Turkey, straddling the line between Europe and Asia. Would the women be liberated and available, or locked up in purdah? The telephone rang.

"Digby Soames here, British Council. It's about your lectures in Turkey."

"Oh yes. Didn't I give you the titles? There's 'The Legacy of Hazlitt' and 'Jane Austen's Little Bit of Ivory' —that's a quotation from—"

"Yes, I know," Soames interrupted. "The trouble is, the Turks don't want it."

"Don't want it?" Philip felt slightly winded.

"I've just had a telex from Ankara. It says, *'No mileage in Jane Austen here, can Swallow lecture on Literature and History and Society and Philosophy and Psychology instead'*."

"That's a tall order," said Philip.

"Yes, it is, rather."

"I mean, there isn't much time for preparation."

"I could telex back 'No', if you like."

"No, don't do that," said Philip. He was always cravenly eager to please his hosts on these trips abroad; eager to please the British Council, too, in case they stopped inviting him to go on them. "I expect I can cobble something together."

"Jolly good, I'll telex to that effect, then," said Soames. "Everything else all right?"

"I think so," said Philip. "I don't know quite what to

expect of Turkey. I mean, is it a reasonably ... modern country?"

"The Turks like to think it is. But they've had a hard time lately. A lot of terrorism, political murders and so on, from both left and right."

"Yes, I've read about it in the papers," said Philip.

"Rather plucky of you to go, really," said Soames, with a jovial laugh. "The country is on the rocks, no imports allowed, so there's no coffee, no sugar. No bumpaper, either, I understand, so I should take some with you. Petrol shortages won't affect you, but power cuts might."

"Doesn't sound too cheerful," said Philip.

"Oh, you'll find the Turks very hospitable. If you don't get shot by accident and you take your tea without sugar you should have a very enjoyable trip," said Soames with another merry chuckle, and rang off.

Philip Swallow resisted the temptation to return to the window and resume his covert observation of student mating behaviour. Instead, he ran his eyes along his bookshelves in search of inspiration for a lecture on Literature and History and Society and Philosophy and Psychology. What, as always, caught his attention was a row of mint copies of *Hazlitt and the Amateur Reader* in their pale blue wrappers, which he had bought from Lecky, Windrush and Bernstein at trade discount to give away to visitors, having despaired of commercial distribution of the book. A little spasm of resentment against his publishers prompted him to pick up the phone and make a call to Felix Skinner.

"Sorry," said the girl who answered, "Mr Skinner's at a meeting."

"I suppose you mean lunch," said Philip sarcastically, glancing at his watch. It was a quarter to three.

"Well, yes."

"Can I speak to his secretary?"

"She's at lunch too. Can I take a message?"

Philip sighed. "Just tell Mr Skinner that Professor Zapp never received the complimentary copy of my book, which I specifically requested should be sent to him on publication."

"OK, Professor Zapp."

"No, no, my name's Swallow, Philip Swallow."

"OK, Mr Swallow. I'll tell Mr Skinner as soon as he gets back."

Felix Skinner was in fact already back from lunch at the time of Philip Swallow's phone call. He was, to be precise, in a basement storeroom on the premises of Lecky, Windrush and Bernstein. He was also, to be even more precise, in Gloria, who was bent forwards over a pile of cardboard boxes, divested of her skirt and knickers, while Felix, with his pinstripe trousers round his ankles, and knees flexed in a simian crouch, copulated with her vigorously from behind. Their relationship had ripened rapidly since the morning, warmed by several gin and tonics and a large carafe of Valpolicella over lunch. In the taxi afterwards, Felix's exploring hands encountered no defence—quite the contrary, for Gloria was a warm-blooded young woman, whose husband, an engineer with the London Electricity Board, was working the night shift. Accordingly, when they got into the lift of the Lecky, Windrush and Bernstein building, Felix pressed the button to go down rather than up. The storeroom in the basement had served him on similar occasions before, as Gloria guessed but did not remark upon. It was hardly a romantic bower of bliss, the concrete floor being too cold and dirty to lie down on, but their present posture suited them both, since Gloria did not have to look at Felix's horrible teeth or inhale his breath, which now reeked of garlic as well as Gauloises, while he could admire, as he held her hips, the way her plump white cheeks bulged between the constriction of suspender belt and stockings.

"Stockings!" he groaned. "How did you know I adored stockings and suspenders?"

"I didn't knowwwww!" she gasped. "Oh! oh! oh!" Gloria felt the boxes shift and slide underneath her as Felix thrust harder and faster. "Look out!" she cried.

"What?" Felix, his eyes shut tight, was concentrating on his orgasm.

"I'm falling!"

"I'm coming!"

"OH!"

"AH!"

They came and fell together in a heap of crushed cardboard and spilled books. Dust filled the air. Felix rolled on to his back and sighed with satisfaction. "That was bloody marvellous, Gloria. The earth moved, as they say."

Gloria sneezed. "It wasn't the earth, it was all these parcels." She rubbed her knee. "I've laddered my stocking," she complained. "What are they going to think upstairs?"

She looked at Felix for some response, but his attention had been distracted by the books that had fallen out of the broken boxes. He was on all fours, his trousers still fettering his ankles, staring at the books with astonishment. They were identical copies, in pale blue jackets. Felix opened one and extracted a small printed slip.

"My God," he said. "No wonder poor old Swallow never got a single review."

The day before he left for Vancouver, Rudyard Parkinson received a letter from Felix Skinner and a copy of *Hazlitt and the Amateur Reader*. "*Dear Rudyard,*" said the letter, "*We published this book last year, but it was largely ignored by the press—unjustly in my view. Accordingly, we are sending out a fresh batch of review copies this week. If you yourself could possible arrange to review it somewhere, that would be marvellous. I know how busy you are, but I have a hunch that the book might take your fancy. Yours ever, Felix.*"

Rudyard Parkinson curled his lip over this missive and glanced at the book with lukewarm interest. He had never heard of Philip Swallow, and a first book by a redbrick professor did not promise much. As he riffled the pages, however, his attention was caught by a quotation from an essay of Hazlitt's entitled "On Criticism": "*A critic does nothing nowadays who does not try to torture the most obvious expression into a thousand meanings . . . His object indeed is not to do justice to his author, whom he treats with very little ceremony, but to do himself homage, and to show his acquaintance with all the topics and resources of criticism.*" Hmmm, though Rudyard Parkinson, there might be some ammunition here to use against Morris Zapp. He slipped the book into his briefcase, along with his passport and his red, white and blue airticket.

The journey to Vancouver was not a comfortable one. To make a little profit on the trip, he was travelling economy class, for the host University was paying his expenses based on first-class fares. This proved to be a mistake. First he had an altercation at Heathrow with a pert girl at the check-in desk who refused to accept his overnight case as cabin baggage. Then, when he boarded the aircraft he found that he was most unluckily seated next to a mother with a small child on her lap, which cried and wriggled and spat half-masticated food all over Rudyard Parkinson for most of the long and wearisome flight. He began bitterly to repent of the vanity which had prompted him to accept this perfectly useless degree, flying ten thousand miles in three days just for the pleasure of dressing up in unfamiliar robes, hearing a short and probably inaccurate panegyric in his honour, and exchanging small talk afterwards with a crowd of boring Canadian nonentities at some ghastly reception or banquet where they would all no doubt drink iced rye whisky throughout the meal.

In the event, there was wine at the dinner following the degree ceremony and, Rudyard Parkinson had to admit, rather good wine—Pouilly Fuissé '74 with the fish, and a really remarkable Gevrey Chambertin '73 with the filet steak. The conversation at table was as banal as he had feared, but he did have an interesting exchange at the reception beforehand with another of the honorary graduands, Jacques Textel, the Swiss anthropologist and UNESCO bureaucrat, who genially toasted him with a dry martini.

"Congratulations," he said. "I know I'm only here because the University is hoping to squeeze some money out of UNESCO, but you're being honoured for your own work."

"Nonsense, your degree was thoroughly deserved," anyone else would have replied; but Rudyard Parkinson, being Rudyard Parkinson, merely smirked and fluffed out his whiskers.

"You've no idea how many honorary degrees I've collected since I became ADG," said Textel.

"ADG?"

"Assistant Director General."

"Do you find it interesting work?"

"As an anthropologist, yes. The Paris HQ is like a tribe. Has its own rituals, taboos, order of precedence . . . Fascinating. As an administrator, it drives me crazy." Textel deftly placed his empty glass on the tray of a passing waiter with one hand and took a full glass with the other. "Take this chair of literary criticism, for instance . . ."

"What's that?"

"You haven't heard about it? I'm surprised. Siegfried von Turpitz has—he rang me up at seven-thirty in the morning to ask me about it. I'd just dropped off to sleep, too, being jet-lagged after a flight from Tokyo . . ."

"What is this chair?" Rudyard Parkinson persisted.

Textel told him. "Interested?" he concluded.

"Oh, no," said Rudyard Parkinson, smiling and shaking his head. "I'm quite content."

"That's nice to hear," said Jacques Textel. "In my experience top academics are the least contented people in the world. They always think the grass is greener in the next field."

"I don't think the grass anywhere is greener than in the Fellows' Garden at All Saints," said Rudyard Parkinson smugly.

"I can believe that," said Jacques Textel. "Of course, whoever gets this UNESCO chair won't have to move anywhere."

"Won't he?"

"No, it's a purely conceptual chair. Apart from the salary, which is likely to be in the region of a hundred thousand dollars."

At that juncture a servant announced that dinner was served. Rudyard Parkinson was seated at some distance from Jacques Textel, and the latter was hustled away immediately after the meal to catch a plane to Peru, where he was due to open a conference on the preservation of Inca sites the following day. This separation was a cause of some concern to Rudyard Parkinson, who would have liked an opportunity to correct the impression he might have given

that he was wholly lacking in personal interest in the
UNESCO chair. The more he thought about it—and he
thought about it for almost the entire duration of the flight
back to London—the more attractive it seemed. He was so
used to receiving invitations to apply for lavishly endowed
chairs in North America that refusing them was by now a
reflex action. They always tried to tempt him with the
promise of teams of research assistants, for whom he would
have no use at all (could research assistants write his
reviews for him?) and generous travel grants that would
allow him to fly to Europe as often as he wanted. ("But I
already *am* in Europe," he would point out, if he took the
trouble to reply at all.) This chair, however, was decidedly
different. Perhaps he had dismissed it too hastily, even if
UNESCO was an institution routinely sneered at in Oxford
Common Rooms. Nobody was going to sneer at one hundred thousand dollars a year, tax-free, to be picked up
without the trouble of moving one's books. The problem
was, how to intimate these second thoughts without crawling
too obviously to Textel. No doubt the post would be
advertised in due course, but Rudyard Parkinson was experi-
enced enough in such matters to know that the people who
were appointed to top academic posts never actually applied
for them before they were approached. That, of course, was
what Textel had been doing—it was clear as daylight in
retrospect—and he had muffed the opportunity. Rudyard
Parkinson clenched his grip on the armrest of his seat with
chagrin. Well, a discreet note to Textel could hint at a
change of heart. But something more was needed, something like a campaign, a broadside, a manifesto—but subtle,
indirect. What could be done?

Opening his briefcase to find a notepad on which to draft
a letter to Textel, Rudyard Parkinson's eye fell upon the
book by Philip Swallow. He took it out, and began to
browse. Soon he began to read with close attention. A plan
was forming itself in his mind. A long middle for the *TLS*.
The English School of Criticism. How gratifying to encounter, in the dreary desert of contemporary criticism, an
exponent of that noble tradition of humane learning, of
robust common sense and simple enjoyment of great

books . . . Professor Swallow's timely and instructive study . . .
In contrast, the jargon-ridden lucubrations of Professor Zapp,
in which the perverse paradoxes of fashionable Continental
savants are, if possible, rendered even more pretentious and
sterile . . . The time has come for those who believe in
literature as the expression of universal and timeless human
values to stand up and be counted . . . Professor Swallow has
sounded a clarion call to action. Who will respond?

Something like that should do the trick, Rudyard Parkinson
mused, gazing out of the window at the sun rising or setting
somewhere or other over a horizon of corrugated cloud.
Vancouver, of which he had in any case seen little except
rainswept roads between the airport and the University, had
already faded from his memory.

Philip Swallow set off for his Turkish lecture tour in a more
than usually flustered state. He had been working up to the
last minute on his lecture about Literature and History,
Society, Philosophy, and Psychology, to the neglect of more
mundane preparations, such as packing his suitcase. Hilary
was sullen and uncooperative as, late on the eve of his
departure, he hunted for clean underwear and socks. "You
should have thought of this earlier," she said. "You know I
do my big wash tomorrow." "You knew I was leaving
tomorrow," he said bitterly, "you might have deduced that
I'd need some clean clothes to take with me." "Why should
I give any thought to your needs? Do you give any thought
to mine?" "What needs?" said Philip. "You can't imagine
that I would have any, can you?" said Hilary. "I don't want
to have a big argument," said Philip wearily. "I'd just like
some clean socks and pants and vests. If that isn't too much
to ask."

He was standing on the threshold of the drawing-room,
holding a tangled bundle of soiled underwear which he had
just excavated from the laundry basket. Hilary put down her
novel with a thump, and snatched the bundle from his arms.
She stomped out to the kitchen, leaving a trail of odd socks
in her wake. "They'll have to be dried in the tumble-
drier," she threw over her shoulder.

Philip went to his study to gather together the books and

papers he would need. As usual, he wasted a great deal of time wondering which books to take on his journey. He had a neurotic fear of finding himself stranded in some foreign hotel or railway station with nothing to read, and in consequence always travelled with far too many books, most of which he brought home unread. Tonight, unable to decide between two late Trollope novels, he packed both, along with some poems by Seamus Heaney, a new biography of Keats and a translation of the *Divine Comedy* which he had been carrying around with him on almost every trip for the last thirty years without ever having made much progress in it. By the time he had completed this task, Hilary had retired to bed. He lay beside her, wakeful and restless, listening to the noise of the tumble-drier crunching in the kitchen, like the engine of a ship. His mind anxiously reviewed a checklist of the things he should have packed: passport, money, tickets, traveller's cheques, lecture notes, sunglasses, Turkish phrasebook. They were all in his brief-case, but he had a feeling something was missing. He was catching the same early morning plane to Heathrow as Morris Zapp had taken, and wouldn't have much time to spare in the morning.

Philip seldom slept well before leaving on one of his trips abroad, but tonight he was particularly wakeful. Usually he and Hilary would make love on such occasions. There was an unspoken agreement between them to sink their differences in a valedictory embrace which, however perfunctory, at least had the effect of relaxing them sufficiently to send them both off to sleep for a few hours. But when Philip tried an exploratory caress or two on Hilary's humped form, she shook off his hand with a sleepy grunt of irritation. Philip tossed and turned, filled with resentment and self-pity. He postulated his death in an air crash on the way to Turkey, and imagined with grim satisfaction Hilary's guilt and self-reproach on hearing the news. The only drawback to this scenario was that it entailed his own extinction, a high price to pay to punish her for not washing his socks in good time. He essayed, instead, a compensatory amorous adventure in Turkey, but found this difficult, having no idea what Turkey, or Turkish women, looked like. Eventually he settled for a chance meeting with Angelica Pabst, who, since nobody seemed to know where she had come from, or departed to, might as well be encountered in Turkey as anywhere else. One of the many disappointments of the Rummidge conference had been his failure to follow up the friendly relations he had established with that very attractive young woman on the first evening. With the help of a fantasy in which he rescued Angelica from the clutches of political terrorists on a Turkish railway train, and was rewarded with rapturous sexual intercourse, Angelica being conveniently clad in nothing more than a diaphanous nightie at the time of this crisis, Philip dozed off, though he woke at frequent intervals in the course of the night, and felt more fatigued than rested when his alarm clock finally roused him at 5.30.

Five-thirty isn't really early enough, considering that the taxi has been ordered for six, as Philip quickly realizes, washing, dressing, and shaving himself with ill-coordinated limbs, groping in the drawers and wardrobes of the darkened bedroom for his travelling clothes, fumbling with the locks on his suitcase. Hilary makes no move to get up and assist him, or to make him a cup of coffee. He cannot really blame her, in view of the hour, but he does, nevertheless, blame her. At three minutes to six he is, in a manner of speaking, ready—unevenly shaven, with hair uncombed and shoes unpolished, but ready. Then he remembers the item missing from his mental checklist—lavatory paper. He searches in the kitchen cupboard for a fresh roll without success and with increasing panic, throwing aside packets of detergent, soap powder, paper napkins, washing-up liquid, Brillo pads, in the urgency of his quest. He bounds up the stairs, bursts into the bedroom, hits the light switch, and peremptorily questions Hilary's shrouded back.

"Where's the toilet paper?"

Hilary raises and twists her head, stupid with sleep. "Eh?"

"Toilet paper. I need to take some with me."

"We're out of it."

"*What?*"

"I was going to get some today."

Philip throws his arms into the air. "Marvellous? Bloody marvellous!"

"You could buy some yourself."

"At six o'clock in the morning?"

"The airport might—"

"And the airport might not. Or I might not have time."

"You can take what's left in the downstairs loo, if you like."

"Thanks very much," says Philip sarcastically. He thumps down the stairs, two steps at a time. There is a half a roll of pink toilet tissue in the downstairs cloakroom, suspended from a cylindrical roller attached by a spring-loaded axle to a ceramic holder screwed to the wall. Philip fumbles with this apparatus, seeking to remove the toilet roll from the roller. The front doorbell shrills. Philip starts, the toilet roll falls off the roller and unwinds itself across the floor of the cloakroom with amazing rapidity. Philip swears, tries to roll the paper up again, abandons the attempt, opens the front door to the taxi-driver, indicates his suitcase, runs to his study, stuffs a wad of A4 Bank typing paper into his briefcase, runs back to the hall, shouts an angry, "Goodbye, then," up the stairs, snatches his raincoat from its hook and leaves the house, slamming the front door behind him.

"All right, sir?" says the taxi-driver, as Philip collapses in the back seat.

Philip nods. The driver lets in the clutch and engages bottom gear. The taxi begins to move—then stops abruptly, obedient to a cry from the direction of the house. For here comes Hilary, trotting down the garden path, in her nightie, just an old coat thrown over her shoulders, scarcely decent, clasping to her bosom an untidy bundle of socks and underclothing. Philip lowers the window of the taxi.

"You forgot to take them out of the drier," Hilary says breathlessly, bundling socks, singlets and Y-fronts through the window and on to his lap. The taxi-driver looks on with amusement.

"Thanks," says Philip grudgingly, as he clutches the clothes.

Hilary is grinning at him. "Goodbye, then. Have a safe journey." She bends forward and offers her face at the window for a kiss, lips pursed and eyes closed. Philip can hardly refuse to respond, and leans forward to administer a perfunctory peck.

But then an extraordinary thing happens. Hilary's old coat falls open, the neckline of her nightgown gapes, and Philip glimpses the curve of her right breast. It is an object he knows well. He made his first tactile acquaintance with it twenty-five years ago, tentatively fondling it, through the impeding upholstery of a Marks and Spencer's fisherman's knit jumper and a stoutly constructed Maidenform brassière, as he kissed its young postgraduate owner goodnight on the porch of her digs one night after a Film Society showing of *Battleship Potemkin*. He first set entranced eyes upon its naked flesh on his wedding night. Since then he must have seen and touched it (and its twin) several thousand times—stroked it and kneaded it and licked it and nuzzled it, watched it suckling his children and sucked its nipple himself on occasion—during which time it lost its pristine firmness and satin texture, grew fuller and heavier and less elastic, and became as familiar to him as an old cushion, comfortable but unremarkable. But such is the mystery of desire—the fickleness and unpredictability of its springs and motions—that this unexpected glimpse of the breast, swinging free inside the loose folds of the nightgown, in a shadowy gap from which rises to his nostrils a pleasant smell of warm bed and body, makes Philip suddenly faint with the longing to touch, suck, lick, nuzzle, etc. it again. He does not want to go to Turkey. He does not want to go anywhere at this moment, except back to bed with Hilary. But of course, he cannot. Is it only because he cannot that he wants to so much? All he can do is to press his lips on Hilary's more enthusiastically than he had intended—or than she expected, for she looks at him with a quizzical, affectionate, even tender regard as the taxi, at last, inexorably moves away. Philip looks back through the rear window. Hilary stoops to pluck from the gutter a stray sock, and waves it forlornly after him, like a makeshift favour.

Not many hours after Philip Swallow flew out of Heathrow on a Turkish Airlines DC10 bound for Ankara, Persse

McGarrigle flew in on an Aer Lingus Boeing 737 from Shannon, for it was the day of the Royal Academy of Literature's prizegiving party.

The *Annabel Lee* was an old pleasure steamer that had once plied up and down the Thames estuary. Now repainted and refurbished, her paddles stilled and her smokestack unsullied, she was moored beside the Thames at Charing Cross Embankment, accommodating a restaurant, bars and reception rooms that could be hired for functions like this one. The London literati cooed their delight at the novelty of the venue as they alighted from their taxis or debouched from the Tube station and strolled along the Embankment. It was a fine May evening, with the river almost at flood, and a brisk breeze flapping the flags and pennants on the *Annabel Lee*'s rigging. When they got on board, some were not so sure it was a good idea. There was a distinct sensation of movement under one's feet, and whenever a biggish craft passed on the river, its wash heaved the *Annabel Lee* up and down sharply enough to make the guests stagger on the plush red carpet of the main saloon. Soon, however, it was difficult to distinguish between the effect of the river and the effect of the booze. Persse had never been to a literary party before, but the main object seemed to be to drink as much as possible as fast as possible, while talking at the top of your voice and at the same time looking over the shoulder of the person you were talking to and smiling and waving at other people who were also drinking and talking and smiling and waving. As for Persse, he just drank, since he didn't know a soul. He stood on the fringe of the party, feeling throttled in an uncustomary collar and tie, shifting his weight from one foot to another, until it was time to push his way back to the bar for another drink. There were waiters circulating with red and white wine, but Persse preferred Guinness.

"Hallo, is that Guinness you're drinking?" said a voice at his shoulder. "Where did you get it?"

Persse turned to find a large, fleshy, pockmarked face peering covetously at his drink through horn-rimmed glasses.

"I just asked for it at the bar," said Persse.

"This wine is like horsepiss," said the man, emptying

his glass into a potted plant. He disappeared into the crowd, and came back a few moments later, dragging a case of Guinness. "I don't usually like bottled beer," he said. "But Guinness, in my experience, is better bottled than draught in England. Different matter in Dublin."

"I'm much of your opinion," said Persse, as the man topped up his glass. "Would it be something to do with the water, I wonder."

They had a learned technical conversation about the brewing of stout ale, illustrated by frequent sampling, for some time before they got round to introducing themselves. "Ronald Frobisher!" Persse exclaimed. "I've read some of your books. Are you getting a prize this evening?"

"No, I'm presenting one—Most Promising First Novel. When I started writing fiction there didn't seem to be more than a couple of literary prizes, and they were only worth about a hundred quid each. Nowadays there are so many that it's difficult to avoid winning one if you manage to publish anything at all. Sorry, didn't mean to cast aspersions on your—"

"That's all right," said Persse. "I understand your feelings. As a matter of fact I haven't even published my poems yet."

"That's what I mean, see?" said Frobisher, opening another bottle of Guinness. He had an ingenious knack of using the top of one bottle to lever off the cap from another. "I mean, I don't begrudge you your money—good luck to you—but the situation is getting daft. There are people here tonight who make a *living* out of prizes, bursaries and what have you. I can see the day coming when there'll be a separate prize for every book that's published. Best First Novel about a graduate housewife living in Camden Town with two young children and a cat and an unfaithful husband who works in advertising. Best travel book by a man under twenty-nine who has been round the world using only scheduled bus services and one pair of jeans. Best—"

As Frobisher was warming to this theme, a young woman came up and told him that he would soon be making the presentation of the Most Promising First Novel prize. He put down his glass. "Look after the Guinness," he exhorted Persse, as he moved off.

Persse resumed drinking and shifting his weight from one foot to the other. But soon he saw a face that he recognized, and waved to it in the manner he had observed other guests using. Felix Skinner came over, trailing a buxom young woman with honey-coloured hair, and another couple. "Hallo, old man, what brings you here?" he said.

"I've come to collect a prize for my poetry."

"I say, have you really?" Skinner exposed his fangs in a yellow smile. "Many congratulations. Sorry about the Shakespeare–Eliot book, by the way. This is my secretary, Gloria." He pushed forward the buxom young woman who shook Persse's hand listlessly. Her face was pale. "When are we going, Felix?" she said. "I'm feeling seasick." "We can't leave yet, my dear, the prizes haven't been given out," said Felix, and turned to introduce the other couple. "Professor and Mrs Ringbaum, from Illinois. Howard is one of our authors."

Howard Ringbaum nodded dourly at Persse. His wife smiled and hiccupped. "Thelma, cut it out," he said, apparently without moving his lips. "I can't help it," she said, winking at Persse. "You could try drinking less," said Ringbaum.

At the other end of the room someone banged on the table and began making a speech. "Frightful man, Ringbaum," Skinner whispered into Persse's ear. "We published one of his books about four years ago, I say published, we took the sheets for five hundred copies, had to remainder most of them, and on the strength of that he conned me into giving him and wife lunch today and I haven't been able to get rid of them since. *He* bores the pants off you and *she* seems to be some kind of nymphomaniac—kept playing footsie with me in the restaurant. Damned embarrassing with Gloria there, I can tell you."

At precisely that moment, Persse became aware of the presence of another's leg against his own. He turned to find Mrs Ringbaum standing very close to him. "Are you really a poet?" she said breathily. The breath was heavily scented with gin.

"Yes, I am," said Persse.

"Would you write a poem to me," said Mrs Ringbaum, "if I made it worth your while?"

"One can't produce poems to order, I'm afraid," he said. He took a step backwards, but Mrs Ringbaum followed, glued to him like a ballroom-dancing partner.

"I don't mean money," she said.

"Thelma," said Howard Ringbaum querulously from behind her back, "am I allergic to anchovies?" He was holding up a small sandwich with a bite-shaped hole in it. Persse took advantage of this distraction to put Skinner between himself and Mrs Ringbaum. "What was that you said about my book?" he asked Skinner.

"Oh, haven't you had my letter? No? That's Gloria, she's been getting a little bit slack, lately. Well, I'm afraid we had a very negative report on your proposal. Ah, I see Rudyard Parkinson is making the biography award."

A man with muttonchop whiskers and a plump, self-pleased countenance had mounted the platform and was addressing the assembled guests. It was a speech in praise of somebody's book, though the smirk hovering round his lips seemed somehow to twist and devalue the sentiments they uttered, and to solicit knowing titters from his audience.

"Rudyard Parkinson . . . You've read his books, haven't you, Howard?" said Thelma Ringbaum.

"Absolute crap," said Howard Ringbaum.

Persse opened himself another bottle of Guinness, using Ronald Frobisher's technique. "So you don't want to publish my book after all?" he said to Felix Skinner.

"'Fraid not, old man."

"What did your reader say about it, then?"

"Well, that it wouldn't do. Wasn't on. Didn't stand up. In a word."

"Who is he?"

"I'm afraid I can't tell you that," said Felix Skinner. "It's confidential."

There was a burst of applause, and flashlights blinked, as the biographer went up to receive his prize from Rudyard Parkinson. "He isn't here tonight, by any chance?" said Persse wistfully. "Because if he is, I'd like to fight him."

Felix Skinner laughed uncertainly. "No, no, he's a long way from London. But a very eminent authority, I assure you. Ah, Rudyard, how very good to see you. Marvellous speech!"

Rudyard Parkinson, who had yielded the platform to Ronald Frobisher, smirked and brushed his whiskers upwards with the back of his hand. "Oh, hallo Skinner. Yes, I thought it went down pretty well."

Felix Skinner performed introductions.

"This is a real privilege, Professor Parkinson," said Howard Ringbaum, holding on to Parkinson's hand and gazing raptly into his eyes. "I'm a great admirer of your work."

"Kind of you," Parkinson murmured.

"Howard! Howard, that's Ronald Frobisher," cried Thelma Ringbaum excitedly, pointing to the platform. "You remember, I was reading one of his books on the plane on the way over."

"I recommend your book on James Thomson to all my students," said Howard Ringbaum to Rudyard Parkinson, ignoring his wife. "I've written a few articles on the subject myself, and it would be a real pleasure to—"

"Ah yes, poor Forbisher," said Parkinson, who seemed to prefer this topic of conversation. "He was up at Oxford when I was a young Fellow, you know. I'm afraid he's burned himself out. Hasn't published a new novel for years."

"They're doing one of his books on the telly," said Gloria from somewhere behind and beneath them. All turned and looked at her with surprise. She was stretched out on a bench seat that followed the curve of the ship's side, with her shoes off and her eyes closed.

"Yes," said Parkinson, with a curl of his lip, "I daresay they are. I don't possess a television receiver myself."

A woman in the crowd in front of them turned and frowned, and someone else hissed, "Ssh!" Ronald Frobisher was giving a speech in a low undertone, his hands thrust deep into the pockets of his corduroy jacket, his spectacles owlishly opaque under the lights.

"I can't imagine that he has much to say that is worth

straining one's ears for," murmured Parkinson. "As a matter of fact he looks distinctly squiffy to me."

"By the way," said Felix Skinner to him. "Did you, er, by any chance, get a book by, er, Philip Swallow, which I er..."

"Yes, I did. Not at all bad. I've arranged to do it for the *TLS*, along with another book. Should be in tomorrow's issue. I think you'll be pleased."

"Oh, jolly good! I'm tremendously grateful."

"I think it has important implications," said Parkinson solemnly. "More than the author himself is aware of."

There was another burst of applause as Ronald Frobisher handed an envelope to a smiling young woman in a fringe and homespun smock. The chairman who had opened the proceedings returned to the platform. "Now a number of awards and bursaries for young poets," he announced. "That must be you," said Thelma Ringbaum to Persse. "Hurry up." Persse began to push his way towards the front.

"First, the Maud Fitzsimmons bequest for the Encouragement of Anglo-Irish poetry," said the chairman. "Is Persse McGarrigle...?"

"Here!" cried Persse from the floor. "Hold on, I'm coming." A gust of laughter greeted his appearance on the platform, which Persse belatedly attributed to the fact that he was still holding a bottle of Guinness in his hand.

"Congratulations," said the chairman, handing him a cheque. "I see you have brought your inspiration with you."

"My inspiration," said Persse emotionally, "is a girl called Angelica."

"And very nice too," said the chairman, giving him a gentle push towards the steps. "And the next award..."

When Persse got back to his point of origin, he found Ronald Frobisher in angry confrontation with Rudyard Parkinson. "What would you know about literary creation anyway, Parkinson?" Frobisher was demanding. "You're just a ponce for the Sunday papers. Once a ponce, always a ponce. I remember you poncing about the quad at All Saints—"

"Now, now, that's enough," said Felix Skinner, trying to interpose himself between the two men.

"Are they going to fight?" said Thelma Ringbaum excitedly.

"Shut up, Thelma," said Howard Ringbaum.

"Really Frobisher," said Parkinson, "this sort of behaviour is bad enough in one of your novels. In real life it's quite intolerable." He spoke disdainfully, but backed away at the same time. "Anyway, I wasn't the only reviewer who didn't care for the last novel you wrote, when was it, ten years ago?"

"Eight. But you were the only one who made that crack about my old Dad, Parkinson. I've never forgiven you for that." Holding an empty Guinness bottle by the neck, Frobisher made a lunge in Parkinson's direction. Someone screamed. Felix Skinner pinned Frobisher's arms to his sides, and Howard Ringbaum grabbed the back of his collar and pulled, throttling the novelist. Thinking that this was an unfair as well as excessive use of force, Persse laid a restraining hand upon Ringbaum. Thelma threw herself into the scuffle and kicked her husband enthusiastically on the ankle. He released Frobisher with a howl of pain, and turned indignantly upon Persse. The upshot of all this was that a few minutes later, Persse and Frobisher found themselves alone together on the Embankment, having been requested in pressing terms by the management of the *Annabel Lee* to leave the reception forthwith.

"Silly buggers," said Frobisher, straightening his tie. "Did they really think I was going to bottle that ponce? I just wanted to give him a fright."

"I think you succeeded," said Persse.

"Well, I'll just make sure," said Frobisher, "I'll scare the shit out of the lot of them." He disappeared down some dank steps to a lower level of the Embankment.

It was dark now, and Persse could not see what his companion was doing. Supporting his chin on his elbows, and his elbows on the Embankment wall, he gazed across the river at the floodlit concrete slabs of the Festival Hall and the National Theatre. Empty bottles, sandwich papers, handkerchiefs, cardboard boxes, cigarette ends and other testimony of the summer night drifted downstream, for the tide had turned. The lights of the *Annabel Lee* glanced and darted in golden reflections on the dark water. At her stern a female figure was leaning over the rail, being sick. Frobisher reappeared at Persse's side, breathing heavily and wiping his hands on a rag.

Inside the saloon there was a buzz of excitement over the incident. "It's like the fifties all over again," said someone. "There was always a chance of some writer taking a poke at a critic in those days. The pub next to the Royal Court was a good place to watch."

Rudyard Parkinson was not disposed to take the matter so lightly. "I'll see that Frobisher is expelled from the Academy for this outrage," he said, trembling a little. "If not, I shall resign myself."

"Quite right," said Felix Skinner. "Did anyone see where Gloria got to?"

"That Irish punk nearly broke my ankle," said Howard Ringbaum. "I'm going to sue somebody for this."

"Howard," said Thelma, "I think the boat's moving."

"Shut up, Thelma."

Very slowly the *Annabel Lee* began to drift away from the Embankment. The rope attaching the ship to the gangplank creaked with the strain, then snapped. Space appeared between the end of the gangplank and the side of the ship.

"I don't think you should have done that," said Persse.

"When I graduated at Oxford," said Ronald Frobisher, in a tone of fireside reminiscence, "my Mam and Dad came up for the ceremony. Parkinson was a Research Fellow at the same college. He'd tutored me for a term—a pompous bastard I thought he was even then, though admittedly he'd read a lot. Anyway, we bumped into him in the quad that day, so I introduced him to Mam and Dad. My Dad was a skilled worker, sand-moulder in a foundry, he had a wonderful touch, the management grovelled to him whenever they had a tricky job to be done. Of course, Parkinson knew fuck-all about that, and cared less. To him Dad was just a stupid prole in a cloth cap and best suit, to be patronized like mad. He twittered away and Dad got more and more nervous and kept coughing to hide his nervousness. Now it so happened that he'd not long ago had all his teeth out, common enough in a middle-aged working man, have 'em all out and be done with 'em, was the form of preventive dentistry favoured in our neighbourhood, and his false set didn't fit too well. To cut a long story short, he coughed the top set right out of his mouth. Caught them, too, and shoved them in his pocket. It was funny really, but Parkinson looked as if he was going to faint. Anyway, many years later I wrote a novel about a character based on my Dad—he was dead by then—and Parkinson reviewed it for one of the Sundays. He said, I remember the exact words, *'It's difficult to share the author's sentimental regard for the main character. That your dentures fit badly doesn't automatically guarantee that you are the salt of the earth.'* Now there was nothing about false teeth in the book. That was a completely private piece of spite. I've never forgiven Parkinson for that.''

The ship had now moved some distance downstream from its original position. Gloria lifted her white face from the rail and stared across the water as if dimly recognizing them. Frobisher waved to her and, in a puzzled, hesitant fashion, she waved back.

''I still don't think you should have done it,'' said Persse. ''They might hit a bridge.''

''It's all right,'' said Frobisher, ''I left one long ripe tied that should hold her. I know a thing or two about boats. I used to work on narrowboats in my vacations when I was a student. The Staffordshire and Worcestershire Canal. Those were the days.''

Faint cries and shrieks of alarm were audible from the ship. A door burst open and light flooded onto the deck. A man shouted across the water.

''I think we should move on,'' said Persse.

''Good idea,'' said Frobisher. ''I'll buy you a drink. It's only''—he checked his watch—''five to nine.'' Then he clapped a hand to his brow. ''Christ, I'm supposed to be doing a radio interview at nine!'' He stepped into the road and waved down a passing taxi. ''Bush House,'' he told the driver, and bundled Persse into the vehicle. They rolled together from one side of the back seat to the other as the cab made a rapid U-turn.

"Who is interviewing you?" Persse asked.

"Somebody in Australia."

"*In* Australia?"

"They can do amazing things these days, with satellites. Australian telly is going to show the serial of *Any Road Further* soon, so they want to do a tie-in radio interview for some arts programme."

"I don't think I've read *Any Road Further,*" said Persse.

"That's not surprising. It only exists as a telly serial. What happens to Aaron Stonehouse when he becomes rich and famous and fed up, like me." He looked at his watch again. "The Aussies have booked some studio time at the BBC. They won't be pleased if I'm late."

Fortunately for Ronald Frobisher, there had been some delay in getting the line open from Australia, and he was safely ensconced in the studio by the time the voice of the producer in Sydney came through, surprisingly loud and clear. Persse sat in the control room with the sound engineer, listening and watching the proceedings with some fascination. The engineer explained the set-up to him. The producer was in Sydney, the interviewer in Cooktown, Queensland. The questions went from Cooktown to Sydney by wire, and from Sydney to London by the Indian Ocean and European satellites, and Ronald Frobisher's replies went back to Australia via the Atlantic and Pacific Ocean satellites. A short question-and-answer exchange girdled the world in about ten seconds.

Watching the head-phoned Ronald Frobisher through the big glass pane that sealed off the studio from the control room, Persse admired the ease with which the writer handled this unusual discourse situation, chatting to his interlocutor, a rather dim-sounding man called Rodney Wainwright, as if he were on the other side of the table instead of on the other side of the world. Wainwright asked him if Aaron Stonehouse was still an Angry Young Man. "Still angry, not so young," said Ronald. Was the novel dying? "Like all of us, it has been dying since the day it was born." When did he do most of his writing? "In the ten minutes after my first morning coffee break."

When the interview was over, Persse went out of the control room to meet him. "Well done," he said.

"Did it seem all right?" Frobisher looked pleased with himself.

The sound engineer called them back into the control room. "This is rather amusing," he said. "Listen."

The voices of Rodney Wainwright and his producer in Sydney, a man called Greg, were still coming from the speakers. They seemed to be old buddies.

"When are you coming to Sydney, then, Rod?"

"I don't know, Greg. I'm pretty tied up here. Got a conference paper to write."

"Time we had some beers together, sport, and checked out the talent on Bondi beach."

"Well, to tell you the truth, Greg, the talent is not so bad up here in Queensland."

"I bet the girls don't go topless."

There was a pause. "Well, only by private arrangement."

Greg chortled. "You should see Bondi these days, on a fine Sunday. It'd make your eyes pop out of your head."

The sound engineer smiled at Persse and Ronald. "Sydney have forgotten to close down the line," he said. "They don't realize that we can still hear them."

"Can they hear us?" said Persse.

"No, not unless I switch this mike on."

"You mean we're eavesdropping from twelve thousand miles away?" said Persse. "That's a queer thought."

"Ssh!" hissed Ronald Frobisher, holding up a finger. The conversation in Australia had turned to another topic—himself.

"I didn't like his last one," Rodney Wainwright was saying. "And that was, what, eight years ago?"

"More than eight," Greg agreed. "You think he's washed up?"

"I'm sure he is," said Rodney Wainwright. "He had absolutely nothing to say about postmodernism. He didn't seem to even understand the question."

Ronald Frobisher bent to switch on the sound engineer's

mike, "You can stick your question about postmodernism up your arse, Wainwright," he said.

There was a stunned silence from the antipodes. Then, "Who said that?" Rodney Wainwright quavered.

"Jesus," said Greg.

"Jesus?"

"I mean, Jesus, the fucking line is still open," said Greg.

Two thousand miles away, in Turkey, it has been dark for some hours. The little row of terraced houses outside Ankara looks to Akbil Borak, as he bumps towards it in his Deux Chevaux along the service road from the main highway, rather like a ship, with lights shining from its cabin windows, moored on the edge of the dark immensity that is the central Anatolian plain. He stops the car, kills the engine, and climbs stiffly out. It has been a long day.

In the kitchen Oya has left him a little snack and black tea in a thermos. Having eaten well that evening, at the University's expense, he leaves the snack, but drinks the tea. Then he goes upstairs, treading softly on the narrow stairs so as not to wake Ahmed. "Is that you, Akbil?" Oya sleepily enquires from the bedroom. Akbil murmurs a reassuring reply, and goes into Ahmed's room, to gaze fondly at his sleeping son, and tuck a dangling arm under the blankets. Then he goes to the bathroom. Then he gets into bed and makes love to Oya.

Akbil Borak has sex with his wife almost every night, ordinarily (that is, when he is not having to sit up over the collected works of William Hazlitt). In Turkey, this past winter, there have been few other pleasures to indulge in. It is also, he believes, good for the health. Tonight, since he is tired, their congress is brief and straightforward. Akbil soon rolls off Oya with a sigh of satisfaction, and pulls the quilt up over his shoulders.

"Don't go to sleep, Akbil," Oya complains. "I want to hear about your day. Did Professor Swallow arrive safely?"

"Yes, the plane was only a little late. I went with Mr Custer in the British Council car to meet him."

"What is he like?"

"Tall, thin, stooping. He has a fine silver beard."

"Is he a nice man?"

"I think so. A little nervous. Eccentric, you might say. He had a vest hanging out of his raincoat pocket."

"A vest?"

"A white undervest. Perhaps he took it off in the plane because he was too hot, I don't know. He fell down outside the airport."

"Oh dear! Had he been drinking on the airplane?"

"No, he put his foot in a pothole. You know how bad the roads are since the winter. This hole must have been half a metre deep, right outside the terminal building. I felt ashamed. We really have no idea how to make roads in this country."

"Is Professor Swallow married?"

"Yes, he has three children. But he did not seem interested in talking about them," said Akbil sleepily.

Oya pinched him. "Then what happened? After he fell down?"

"We picked him up, Mr Custer and I, and dusted him down and drove him into Ankara. He was rather nervous on the drive, he kept ducking down behind the back of the driver's seat. You know that the highway to the airport is only paved on one side for certain stretches, so traffic moving in both directions uses the same side of the road. I suppose it is a bit alarming if you are not used to it."

"Then what happened?"

"Then we went to Anitkabir to lay a wreath on Ataturk's tomb."

"Whatever for?"

"Mr Custer thought it would be a nice gesture. And a funny thing happened. I will tell you." Akbil suddenly shed his drowsiness at the memory, and propped himself up one elbow to tell Oya the story. "You know it is quite an awe-inspiring experience, the first time you go to Anitkabir. To walk down that long, long concourse, with the Hittite lions and the other statues, and the soldiers standing guard on the parapets, so still and silent they look like statues themselves, but all armed. Perhaps I should not have told Professor Swallow that it was a capital offence to show disrespect to the memory of Ataturk."

"Well, so it is."

"I said it as a kind of joke. However he seemed to be very worried by the information. He kept saying, 'Is it all right if I blow my nose?' and 'Will the soldiers be suspicious of my limp?' "

"Does he have a limp?"

"Since he fell down at the airport he has a slight limp, yes. Anyway, Mr Custer told him, 'Don't worry, just do exactly as I do.' So we march down the concourse, Mr Custer in front carrying the wreath, and Professor Swallow and I following in step, under the eyes of the soldiers. We swung left into the Great Meeting Place, very smartly, just like soldiers ourselves, and approached the Hall of Honour. And then Mr Custer had the misfortune to trip over a paving stone that was sticking up and, being impeded by the wreath, fell on to his hands and knees. Before I could stop him, Professor Swallow flung himself to the ground and lay prostrate like a Muslim at prayer."

Oya gasped and giggled. "And what happened next?"

"We picked him up and dusted him down again. Then we laid the wreath and visited the museum. Then we went back to the British Council office to discuss Professor Swallow's programme. He must be a man of immense learning."

"Why do you say that?"

"Well, you know that he has come here to lecture on Hazlitt because it was the centenary last year. The other lecture he offered was on Jane Austen, and only our fourth-year students have read her books. So we asked the British Council if he could possibly offer a lecture on some broader topic, such as Literature and History, or Literature and Society, or Literature and Philosophy . . ." Akbil Borak yawned and closed his eyes. He seemed to have lost the thread of his story.

"Well?" said Oya, poking him impatiently in the ribs with her elbow.

"Well, apparently the message was somewhat garbled in the telex transmission. It said, please would he give a lecture on Literature *and* History *and* Society *and* Philosophy *and* Psychology. And, do you know, he agreed. He has prepared a lecture on Literature and Everything. We had a good laugh about it."

"Professor Swallow laughed?"

"Well, Mr Custer laughed the most," Akbil conceded.

"Poor Professor Swallow," Oya sighed. "I do not think he had a very nice day."

"In the evening it was better," said Akbil. "I took him to a kebab restaurant and we had a good meal and some raki. We talked about Hull."

"He knows Hull?"

"Strangely, he has never been there," said Akbil. "So I was able to tell him all about it."

He turned onto his side, with his back to Oya, and pulled the quilt over his shoulders. Accepting that he would not talk any more, Oya settled herself to sleep. She stretched out a hand to switch off the bedside lamp, but, an instant before her fingers reached the switch, the light went out of its own accord.

"Another power cut," she remarked to her husband. But he was already breathing deeply in sleep.

"The trouble is," said Ronald Frobisher, "that twat Wainwright and that ponce Parkinson are right about one thing. I've dried up. Been blocked on a novel for six years now. Haven't published one for eight." He gazed mournfully into his tankard of real ale. Persse was still on Guinness. They were in the saloon bar of a pub off the Strand. "So I earn a living from the telly. Adapting my own novels or other people's. The odd episode of *Z-Cars* or *The Sweeney*. The occasional 'Play for Today'."

"It's strange that you can still write drama, but not fiction."

"Ah well, you see, I can do dialogue all right," said Frobisher. "And somebody else does the pictures. But with fiction it's the narrative bits that give the writing its individuality. Descriptions of people, places, weather, stuff like that. It's like ale that's been kept in the wood: the flavour of the wood permeates the beer. Telly drama's like keg in comparison: all gas and no flavour. It's style I'm talking about, the special, unique way a writer has of using language. Well, you're a poet, you know what I'm talking about."

"I do," said Persse.

"I had a style once," said Frobisher wistfully. "But I lost it. Or rather I lost faith in it. Same thing, really. Have another?"

"It's my round," said Persse, getting to his feet. But he was obliged to return from the bar emptyhanded. "This is very embarrassing," he said, "but I'm going to have to ask you for a loan. All I have is some Irish punts and a cheque for one thousand pounds. The barman refused to cash it."

"It's all right. Have another drink on me," said Frobisher, proffering a ten pound note.

"I'll borrow this off you if I may," said Persse.

"What are you going to spend it on, the thousand pounds?" Frobisher asked him when he returned with the drinks, gripping a pocket of potato crisps between his teeth.

"Looking for a girl," said Persse indistinctly.

"Looking for the Grail?"

"A girl. Her name is Angelica. Have some crisps."

"No thanks. Nice name. Where does she live?"

"That's the problem. I don't know."

"Good-looking?"

"Beautiful."

"You know that American Professor's wife back at the party? She made a pass at me."

"She made a pass at me too," said Persse. Frobisher looked mildly disappointed by this information. He began to eat crisps in an abstracted sort of way. In no time at all there was nothing left in the bag except a few crumbs and grains of salt. "How did you come to lose faith in your style?" Persse enquired.

"I'll tell you. I can date it precisely from a trip I made to Darlington six years ago. There's a new university there, you know, one of those plateglass and poured-concrete affairs on the edge of the town. They wanted to give me an honorary degree. Not the most prestigious university in the world, but nobody else had offered to give me a degree. The idea was, Darlington's a working-class, industrial town, so they'd honour a writer who wrote about working-class, industrial life. I bought that. I was sort of flattered, to tell you the truth. So I went up there to receive this degree. The

usual flummery of robes and bowing and lifting your cap to
the vice-chancellor and so on. Bloody awful lunch. But it
was all right, I didn't mind. But then, when the official part
was over, I was nobbled by a man in the English Department. Name of Dempsey.''

''Robin Dempsey,'' said Persse.

''Oh, you know him? Not a friend of yours, I hope?''

''Definitely not.''

''Good. Well, as you probably know, this Dempsey
character is gaga about computers. I gathered this over
lunch, because he was sitting opposite me. 'I'd like to take
you over to our Computer Centre this afternoon,' he said.
'We've got something set up for you that I think you'll find
interesting.' He was sort of twitching in his seat with
excitement as he said it, like a kid who can't wait to unwrap
his Christmas presents. So when the degree business was
finished, I went with him to this Computer Centre. Rather
grand name, actually, it was just a prefabricated hut, with a
couple of sheep cropping the grass outside. There was
another chap there, sort of running the place, called Josh.
But Dempsey did all the talking. '' 'You've probably heard,'
he said, 'of our Centre for Computational Stylistics.' 'No,' I
said, 'Where is it?' 'Where? Well, it's here, I suppose,' he
said. 'I mean, I'm it, so it's wherever I am. That is,
wherever I am when I'm doing computational stylistics,
which is only one of my research interests. It's not so much
a place,' he said, 'as a headed notepaper. Anyway,' he went
on, 'when we heard that the University was going to give
you an honorary degree, we decided to make yours the first
complete corpus in our tape archive.' 'What does that
mean?' I said. 'It means,' he said, holding up a flat metal
canister rather like the sort you keep film spools in, 'It
means that every word you've ever published is in here.'
His eyes gleamed with a kind of manic glee, like he was
Frankenstein, or some kind of wizard, as if he had me
locked up in that flat metal box. Which, in a way, he had.
'What's the use of that?' I asked. 'What's the use of it?' he
said, laughing hysterically. 'What's the *use*? Let's show
him, Josh.' And he passed the canister to the other guy, who
takes out a spool of tape and fits it on to one of the

machines. 'Come over here,' says Dempsey, and sits me down in front of a kind of typewriter with a TV screen attached. 'With that tape,' he said, 'we can request the computer to supply us with any information we like about your ideolect.' 'Come again?' I said. 'Your own special, distinctive, unique way of using the English language. What's your favourite word?' 'My favourite word? I don't have one.' 'Oh yes you do!' he said. 'The word you use most frequently.' 'That's probably *the* or *a* or *and*,' I said. He shook his head impatiently. 'We instruct the computer to ignore what we call grammatical words—articles, prepositions, pronouns, modal verbs, which have a high frequency rating in all discourse. Then we get to the real nitty-gritty, what we call the lexical words, the words that carry a distinctive semantic content. Words like *love* or *dark* or *heart* or *God*. Let's see.' So he taps away on the keyboard and instantly my favourite word appears on the screen. What do you think it was?''

"Beer?" Persse ventured.

Frobisher looked at him a shade suspiciously through his owlish spectacles, and shook his head. "Try again."

"I don't know, I'm sure," said Persse.

Frobisher paused to drink and swallow, then looked solemnly at Persse. "Grease," he said, at length.

"Grease?" Persse repeated blankly.

"*Grease. Greasy. Greased.* Various forms and applications of the root, literal and metaphorical. I didn't believe him at first, I laughed in his face. Then he pressed a button and the machine began listing all the phrases in my works in which the word *grease* appears in one form or another. There they were, streaming across the screen in front of me, faster than I could read them, with page references and line numbers. *The greasy floor, the roads greasy with rain, the grease-stained cuff, the greasy jam butty, his greasy smile, the grease-smeared table, the greasy small change of their conversation,* even, would you believe it, *his body moved in hers like a well-greased piston.* I was flabbergasted, I can tell you. My entire *oeuvre* seemed to be saturated in grease. I'd never realized I was so obsessed with the stuff. Dempsey was chortling with glee, pressing buttons to show what my other favourite words were. *Grey* and *grime* were high on the list, I seem to remember. I seemed to have a penchant for depressing words beginning with a hard 'g'. Also *sink, smoke, feel, struggle, run* and *sensual*. Then he started to refine the categories. The parts of the body I mentioned most often were *hand* and *breast,* usually one on the other. The direct speech of male characters was invariably introduced by the simple tag *he said,* but the speech of women by a variety of expressive verbal groups, *she gasped, she sighed, she whispered urgently, she cried passionately.* All my heroes have brown eyes, like me. Their favourite expletive is *bugger.* The women they fall in love with tend to have Biblical names, especially ones beginning with 'R'—*Ruth, Rachel, Rebecca,* and so on. I like to end chapters with a short moodless sentence.''

''You remember all this from six years ago?'' Persse marvelled.

''Just in case I might forget, Robin Dempsey gave me a printout of the whole thing, popped it into a folder and gave it to me to take home. 'A little souvenir of the day,' he was pleased to call it. Well, I took it home, read it on the train, and the next morning, when I sat down at my desk and tried to get on with my novel, I found I couldn't. Every time I wanted an adjective, *greasy* would spring into my mind. Every time I wrote *he said,* I would scratch it out and write *he groaned* or *he laughed,* but it didn't seem right—but when I went back to *he said,* that didn't seem right either, it seemed predictable and mechanical. Robin and John had really fucked me up between them. I'm never been able to write fiction since.''

He ended, and emptied his tankard in a single draught.

''That's the saddest story I ever heard,'' said Persse.

The lights in the pub dimmed and brightened. ''Time, ladies and gents!!'' called the barman.

''Come on,'' said Frobisher. ''I know a place where we can get a drink. In Soho.''

At Darlington's Computer Centre, the strip-lighting burns late. The student users of the facility have gone home long ago, back to their digs and halls of residence, back to the distractions of the Union bar and the Union disco, leaving behind them the paper excreta of the day's labours: punched data cards in various colours, swathes of printout, dogends, and crumpled paper cups. The air has a stale, slightly singed odour, as if the electronic machinery has burned up all its natural sweetness. There are only two men left in the building. One, sitting in a glass-partitioned booth, peels the polyfilm wrapping from a cheese sandwich and eats it, thoughtfully observing the other man, who is hunched over a console in a corner of the main room.

"NOBODY SEEMS TO LIKE ME," Robin Dempsey types.

"WHAT MAKES YOU SAY THAT?" replies ELIZA.

"IN THE STAFF CANTEEN I WATCH MY COLLEAGUES COMING TOWARDS MY TABLE WITH THEIR TRAYS AND THEN VEERING AWAY WHEN THEY RECOGNIZE ME."

"WHY DO YOU THINK THEY DO THAT?"

"BECAUSE THEY DON'T WANT TO TALK TO ME."

"WHY DO YOU THINK THEY DON'T WANT TO TALK TO YOU?"

"BECAUSE THEY'RE AFRAID I WILL TALK TO THEM ABOUT MY RESEARCH AND THEY CAN'T STAND THAT BECAUSE I DO MORE RESEARCH THAN THE REST OF THEM PUT TOGETHER."

"TELL ME ABOUT YOUR RESEARCH"

Robin Dempsey types for an hour without stopping.

Persse had never been in Soho before. He was shocked, but also excited, by the blatant attempts to arouse lust made from every quarter, appealing to every sense. Striptease, peepshows, massage parlours, pornographic films, videos, books and magazines. The rhythmic beat of jungle rock throbbing from the bottom of cellar stairs. Odours of fish and garlic steaming from ventilators. Tarts and touts lounging in doorways. The work *Sex* blazoned everywhere—on shopfronts, bookcovers, tee-shirts, in capitals and lower case, in print, in neon, in bulbs, red, yellow, blue, vertically, horizontally, diagonally.

"Soho's been ruined," Ronald Frobisher was complaining. "Just one big pornographic wasteland, it is now. All the nice little Italian groceries and wine shops are getting pushed out." He stopped on the corner of an intersection, hesitating. "You can get lost, it changes so fast. This used to be a shop selling coffee beans, I seem to remember." Now it was a shop selling pornographic literature. Persse peered inside. Men stood facing the wall-racks, silent and thoughtful, as if they were urinating, or at prayer. "They don't seem to be having much fun in there," he remarked, as they moved on.

"No, well, it's not surprising, is it? I believe they throw them out if they start wanking in the shop." Frobisher turned down a narrow side street and stopped outside a doorway over which there was an illuminated sign: *"Club Exotica."*

"Well I'm buggered," said Frobisher. "What's happened to the old 'Lights Out'?"

"It seems to have been turned into a striptease place," said Persse, looking at the photographs of the artistes displayed in a glass case on the wall outside: Lola, Charmaine, Mandy.

"Coming in, boys?" said a squat, swarthy man from just inside the door. "These girls will put some lead in your pencil."

"Ribbon in my typewriter is more what I need," said Frobisher. "What happened to the 'Lights Out' club which used to be here?"

"I dunno," said the man with a shrug. "Come inside, see the show, you won't regret it."

"No thanks. Come on, Persse."

"Just a minute." Persse leaned against the wall with both hands, feeling faint. One of the pictures was unmistakably a photograph of Angelica. She was naked, swathed in chains, with her arms pinioned behind her back. Her hair streamed out behind her. Her expression was one of simulated distress and fear. A red paper disc over her pubis bore the legend, *"Censored,"* and a red strip across her breasts identified her as "Lily". A. L. Pabst. Angelica Lily Pabst.

"What's the matter, Persse?" said Frobisher. "Are you all right?"

"I want to go in here," said Persse.

"What?"

"That's right," said the doorkeeper, "the young man has the right idea."

"You don't want to go in there, it's just a rip-off," said Frobisher.

"Don't listen to him," said the doorkeeper. "It's only three pounds, and that includes your first drink."

"Look, if you really want to see a strip show, let me take you somewhere with a bit of class," said Frobisher. "I know a place in Brewer Street."

"No," said Persse. "It has to be this place."

"You know something?" said the doorman. "You got good taste. Not like this old man here."

"Who are you calling old?" Frobisher said truculently. Grumbling, he followed Persse down the steps just inside the doorway. Persse paid for them both with the change left from Frobisher's ten pound note. "I resent paying for this sort of thing," the writer said as they stumbled and groped their way to a vacant table. The Club Exotica was as dark as the sex cinema in Rummidge, except for a small stage where, bathed in pink light, and to the accompaniment of recorded disco music, a young woman, not Angelica, wearing only high boots with spurs, was vigorously riding a rocking horse. They sat down and ordered whisky. "I mean, if I want to see a bit of tit and bum, I only have to write it into a telly script," said Frobisher. " *With a tantalizing smile, she slowly unbuttons her blouse.' 'Her robe slides to the floor; she is wearing nothing underneath.'* That sort of thing. Then a few weeks later, I sit back in the comfort of my own home and enjoy it. This looks like the kind of corny strip show where the girls are always pretending to be doing something else."

Ronald Frobisher's judgment appeared to be correct. A succession of "turns" followed the rocking-horse rider, in which nudity was displayed in various incongruous contexts—a fire station, an airliner, an igloo. Sometimes there would be more than one artiste involved, and there was a young man, muscular but clearly homosexual, who occasionally combined with the girls to mime some trite story of situation, usually wielding a whip or instrument of torture. There was no sign of Angelica.

The tables were arranged in arcs facing the stage. When anyone rose to leave the front row, someone moved forward from behind to take his place.

"You want to move up?" Frobisher asked.

Persse shook his head.

"Had enough?" Frobisher enquired hopefuly.

"I want to wait till the end."

"The *end*? We'll be here all night. They just keep the acts going in rotation till closing time, you know."

"Well, we haven't seen them all, yet," said Persse.

The stage lights faded on the spectacle of a naked girl thrashing about like a fish in a net suspended from the flies. There was lukewarm applause from the audience. The curtains closed and from behind a faint clinking of chains carried to Persse's ears. He sat up and leaned forward, hardly able to draw a breath.

The recorded music this time was less bland, more symphonic rock than disco, with a lot of distorted electric guitar. The curtain rose to reveal a naked girl in exactly the posture of "Lily" in the photograph outside: naked, chained to a pasteboard rock, writhing and twisting in her bonds, mouth and eyes wide with fear, long hair streaming in a current of air blowing from a wind machine in the wings. But it was not Angelica. It was the girl on the rocking horse. Persse slumped back in his seat, not sure whether he was relieved or disappointed.

"Let's go," he said.

"Well, we might as well wait till this act is finished," said Frobisher. "As a matter of fact, it's the first one that has come within a mile of turning me on. Something to do with the way those chains dig into the flesh, I think."

Persse had to admit that the spectacle had an impact that the previous entertainment had lacked. The nudity, for once, was thematically appropriate. The lighting and sound were expressive: wave effects were projected on to the backcloth, and the sound of surf had been mixed with the guitar chords. Whoever had produced this item knew something about the Andromeda archetype, though in the end it was travestied. The young homosexual, dressed up as Perseus, or possibly St George, arrived to rescue the sacrificial virgin, but was chased off the stage by another naked girl in a dragon mask, who proved to have amorous rather than violent designs upon the captive. The lights faded on a scene of lesbian lovemaking.

"Rather neat, that," said Frobisher, as they climbed the stairs to street level.

"Enjoy the show, boys?" said the doorkeeper.

"What happened to Lily?" Persse demanded.

"Who?"

Persse pointed at the photograph.

"Oh, you mean Lily Papps."

Frobisher guffawed. "Good name for a stripper."

"Is that what she calls herself?" Persse asked.

"Yeah, Lily Papps, with two pees. She left a few weeks back. We haven't got round to doing a photo of the new girl."

"What happened to Lily? Where can I find her?" said Persse.

The man shrugged. "Don't ask me. These girls—they come, they go. Mind you, Lily was special. Not just a nice body—she had a brain too. You know that dragon number? Good, eh? That was her own idea."

"Someone you know?" Frobisher enquired, as they walked away from the Club Exotica.

"It's the girl I told you about. The one I'm looking for."

Frobisher raised an eyebrow. "You didn't tell me she was a stripper."

"She's not really. I don't know why she's doing it. Money, I suppose. She's an educated girl. She's doing a PhD. She shouldn't be doing that sort of thing at all."

"Ah," said Frobisher. "I understand. You're going to track down this damsel and rescue her from the sordid life to which poverty has condemned her?"

"I'd like to do that," said Persse, "for her own sake."

"Not for your own?"

Persse hesitated. "Well, yes I suppose so . . . Only it was a shock, seeing her picture in that place back there. I didn't know, you see." It was still hard for him to imagine the girl he remembered from the Rummidge conference, eagerly discussing structuralism, romance, the poetry of Keats,

performing in a nude cabaret in some sordid Soho cellar.
His soul recoiled from the idea, but after all it was not an
irredeemable degradation. No doubt for Angelica, as for
Bernadette, it was simply a job, a way of earning money—
though why she should have to choose *that* way was a
mystery. One day he would discover the answer. Meanwhile, he must trust Angelica, and his first impressions of
her. "Yes," he said, lengthening his stride, "I want to find
her for my own sake."

Philip Swallow woke suddenly in his hotel room in Ankara
with all the symptoms of incipient diarrhoea. It was pitch
dark. He groped for the lightswitch on the wall above his
head and pressed it, with no result. Bulb gone, or power
cut? Sweating, feverish, he tried to recall the geography of
the room. His briefcase was on a dressing-table facing the
end of the bed. About three yards to the right of that was the
door to the bathroom. Carefully he got out of bed and,
tightening his sphincter muscle, felt his way along the edge
of the bed until he reached the foot of it. With his arms
extended in front of him like a blind man, he searched for
the dressing-table, but it was his big toe that located this
piece of furniture first. Whimpering with pain, he delved in
his briefcase for his makeshift toilet paper, and shuffled
along the wall like a rock-climber until he came to the
bathroom door. He tried the lightswitch inside without
effect. A power cut, then. Sink to the left, toilet beyond it.
Ah, there, thank God. He lowered himself on to the toilet
seat and voided his liquefied bowels. A foul smell filled the
darkness. It must have been the kebab, or, more likely, the
salad that accompanied it. Still, at least he had managed to
get to the loo in time, in spite of the power cut.
    Philip began to wipe himself. When the lights came on of
their own accord he found he was up to page five of his
lecture on "The Legacy of Hazlitt."

Two

PERSSE woke late the next morning, after a night of troubled dreams, with a dry mouth and a moderate headache. He lay on his back for some time, staring at the sprinkler nozzle, a metallic omphalos in the ceiling of his room at the YMCA, wondering what to do next. He decided to go back to the Club Exotica and make further enquiries about the whereabouts of "Lily".

Soho seemed distinctly less sinful in the late morning sunshine. Admittedly the pornshops and the sex cinemas were already open, and had a few devout customers, but their façades and illuminated signs had a faded, shamefaced aspect. The streets and pavements were busy with people with jobs to do: dustmen collecting garbage, messengers on scooters delivering parcels, suited executives with briefcases, and young men pushing wheeled racks of ladies' dresses. There were wholesome smells in the air, of vegetables, fresh bread and coffee. At a newsagents, Persse bought a copy of the *Guardian* and the *Times Literary Supplement*. "LONDON LITERATI ADRIFT" said a headline on the front page of the former. "RUDYARD PARKINSON ON THE ENGLISH SCHOOL OF CRITICISM" announced the cover of the latter.

217

By retracing the route he had taken with Ronald Frobisher the night before, Persse found the Club Exotica—only it wasn't the Club Exotica any more. That name, in tubular glass script, lay discarded on the pavement, trailing flex. Over the door two workmen were erecting another, larger sign, "PUSSYVILLE".

"What happened to the Exotica?" Persse asked them. One looked down at him and shrugged. The other, without looking, said, "Changed its name, dinnit?"

"Under new management?"

"I should fink so. The gaffer's inside now."

Persse descended the stairs and pushed through the quilted swing doors at the bottom. Inside, unshaded bulbs hanging from the ceiling cast a bleak light on stained carpet and shabby furniture. A vacuum cleaner whined among the tables. In the middle of the floor, a man in a striped suit was inspecting a young woman who was wearing only briefs and high-heeled shoes. The man carried a clipboard in his hand, and circled the girl in the manner of a used-car dealer scrutinizing a possible purchase for signs of rust. Along one wall other girls lolled in négligés, evidently awaiting the same appraisal.

"Yes?" said the man, catching sight of Persse. "Have you brought the new lights?"

"No," said Persse, modestly averting his eyes from the half-naked young woman. "I'm looking for a girl called Lily."

"Anybody here called Lily?" said the man.

After a moment's silence, a girl stood up at the end of the row. "I'm Lily," she said, with one hand on her hip, shooting a languorous glance at Persse from beneath a frizzy blonde hairdo.

"I'm afraid I don't know you," stammered Persse.

"You were never Lily," said the girl next to the blonde, tugging her back into her seat. "You just fancy 'im." Laughter rippled along the row of seats.

"She used to perform here." said Persse, "when it was the Club Exotica."

"Yeah, well, this isn't the Club Exotica any more. It's Pussyville, and I have to find twelve topless waitresses by

Monday, so if you don't mind . . .'' The man frowned at his clipboard.

"Who owned the Club Exotica?" Persse asked.

"Girls Unlimited," said the man, without looking up.

"It's in Soho Square," said the frizzy blonde.

"I know," said Persse, "but thank you."

Five minutes' walk took him to Soho Square. Girls Unlimited was on the fourth floor of a building on the west side. After stating his business, he was admitted to the office of a lady called Mrs Gasgoine. The room was carpeted in red, and furnished with white filing cabinets and tubular steel chairs and tables. There was a large map of the world on the wall. Mrs Gasgoine was elegantly dressed in black, and smoking a cigarette in a holder.

"What can I do for you, Mr McGarrigle?"

"I'm looking for a girl called Lily Papps. I believe she worked for you at the Club Exotica."

"We've sold our interest in the Club Exotica."

"So I understand."

"Are you a client of ours?"

"Client?"

"Have you hired our girls in the past?"

"Good Lord, no! I'm just a friend of Lily's."

Mrs Gasgoine blew angry smoke through her nostrils. "You mean she was moonlighting with you."

"I suppose you could say that," replied Persse, remembering the glassy corridor in the sky at Rummidge, the snowscape under the moon, the quotations from Keats.

Mrs Gasgoine extinguished her cigarette and twisted the holder to expel the stub. It fell into her ashtray like a spent bullet case. "This isn't a Missing Persons Bureau, Mr McGarrigle, it's a business organization. Lily is one of our most versatile employees. She's been transferred to another job—something that came up at short notice."

"Where?"

"I'm not at liberty to tell you. It's part of our contract with our girls that we don't divulge their whereabouts to family or friends. Quite often, you see, they're running away from some complication at home."

"I don't even know where her home is!" Persse protested.

"And I don't know you from Adam, Mr McGarrigle. You could be a private investigator, for all I know. I'll tell you what I'll do. If you would like to leave me your name and address, I'll forward it to Lily, and if she wants to, she can get in touch with you."

Persse hesitated, doubtful whether Angelica would respond if she knew he had discovered her secret. "Thanks, but I won't put you to that trouble," he said at length.

Mrs Gasgoine looked as if all her suspicions were confirmed.

He left the premises of Girls Unlimited and looked for a bank at which to cash his cheque. On his way, he passed a window at the side of Foyle's bookshop in which an assistant was arranging some rather dusty-looking copies of *Hazlitt and the Amateur Reader* by Philip Swallow, flanking a blown-up photocopy of Rudyard Parkinson's review in the *TLS*. At the bank Persse took out most of his money in traveller's cheques. Then he went to a branch of Thomas Cook and booked himself a flight to Amsterdam. The only thing he could think of doing now was to look for Angelica's adoptive father.

He hadn't been in Amsterdam three hours before he met Morris Zapp. Persse was standing on one of the curved canal bridges in the old town, puzzling over his tourist map, when the American came up and slapped him on the back.

"Percy! I didn't know you were at the conference."

"What conference?"

Morris Zapp indicated the large plastic disc dangling from his lapel, which had his name printed inside a circular inscription, "VIIth International Congress of Literary Semioticians". On his other lapel was a bright enamel button which declared, "*Every Decoding Is Another Encoding*". "I had it made at a customized button shop back home," he explained. "Everybody here is crazy about it. If I'd brought a gross with me I could have made a fortune. A Jap professor offered me ten dollars for this one. But if you're not at the Conference, what are you doing in Amsterdam?"

"A sort of holiday," said Persse. "I won a poetry prize."

He found that he didn't want to confide in Morris about Angelica.

"No kidding! Congratulations!"

A thought struck Persse. "Angelica isn't at the conference by any chance?"

"Haven't seen her, but that doesn't mean she isn't here. The conference only opened yesterday, and there are hundreds of people. We're all in the Sonesta—great hotel. Where are you staying?"

"At a little pension near here."

"It wasn't such a big prize, then?"

"I'm trying to make it go a long way," said Persse. "Perhaps I'll drop in on your conference."

"Why not? I thought I might go to this afternoon's session myself. Meanwhile, how about some lunch? They have great Indonesian food here."

"Good idea," said Persse. The diversion was welcome, for he had had a discouraging morning. The Head Office of KLM had been courteous but discreet. They confirmed that a Hermann Pabst had been an executive director of the airline in the nineteen-fifties, but he had resigned in 1961 to take up a post in America. He wondered how long his £1000 would last at this rate.

Morris Zapp seemed to have already mastered the spider's-web layout of the Amsterdam canals and streets. He led Persse confidently past a quayside flowermarket, over bridges, down narrow alleys, along busy shopping streets. "You know something?" he said, "I really like this place. It's flat, which means I can walk without getting pooped, it has good cigars that are very cheap, and wait till you see the nightlife."

"I was in Soho the other night," said Persse.

"Soho, schmoho," said Morris Zapp. "That's kindergarten compared with what goes on in the *rosse buurt*."

They emerged from a narrow street into a broad square where tables and chairs were spread in the sun outside the cafés. Morris Zapp suggested an aperitif.

"Have we time? What about the conference?" said Persse.

Morris shrugged. "It doesn't matter if we miss a few papers. The only one I want to hear is von Turpitz's"

"Who is he?"

Morris Zapp beckoned to a waiter. "Gin OK? It's the *vin du pays.*" Persse nodded. "Two Bols," Morris ordered, forking the air with his fingers. "Turpitz is a kraut who's into reception theory. Years ago he wrote a book called *The Romantic Reader*—why people killed themselves after reading *Werther* or made pilgrimages to the *Nouvelle Héloise* country . . . Not bad, but basically trad. literary history. Then Jauss and Iser at Konstanz started to make a splash with reception theory, and von Turpitz jumped on the bandwagon."

"Why do you want to hear him, then?"

"Just to reassure myself. He's sort of a rival."

"For a woman?"

"God, no. For a job."

"I thought you were satisfied where you are."

"Every man has his price," said Morris Zapp. "Mine is one hundred grand a year and no duties. Have you heard of something new called the UNESCO Chair of Literary Criticism?"

While Morris was telling Persse about it, the waiter brought them two glasses of neat, chilled gin. "You're supposed to drink it in one gulp," said Morris, sniffing his glass.

"I'm your man," said Persse, raising his own.

"Here's to us, then," said Morris. "May we both achieve everything we desire."

"Amen," said Persse.

They lunched well at an Indonesian restaurant where dark-skinned waiters in white turbans brought to their table a seemingly endless supply of spicy aromatic dishes of chicken, prawn, pork and vegetables. Morris Zapp had dined there the previous evening and appeared to have taken tuition in the menu. "This is peanut sauce," he said, eating greedily. "This is meat stewed in coconut milk, these are pieces of barbecued sucking pig. Have a prawn cracker."

"Will you be able to stay awake this afternoon?" Persse asked, as they heavily descended the stairs of the restaurant and made their way towards the Sonesta. The sky had clouded over, and the atmosphere had become sultry and oppressive, as if a storm was brewing.

"I aim to sleep through the first paper," said Morris. "Just wake me up when von Turpitz appears on the rostrum. You can't mistake him, he wears a black glove on one hand. Nobody knows why and nobody dares to ask him."

The Sonesta was a huge modern hotel grafted on to some old buildings in the Kattengat, including a Lutheran church, in the shape of a rotunda, which had been converted into a conference hall. "I hope it's been deconsecrated," Persse remarked, as they came in under the huge domed ceiling. A mighty organ, built of dark wood and decorated with gilt, and a carved pulpit projecting from the wall, were the only reminders of the building's original function.

"Reconsecrated, you mean," said Morris Zapp. "Information is the religion of the modern world, didn't you know that?"

Persse surveyed the rapidly filling concentric rows of seats, hoping against hope that he might see Angelica there, cool and self-possessed behind her heavy spectacles, with her stainless steel pen poised over her notebook. A man with a brown leathery face and hooded eyes bowed just perceptibly to Morris Zapp as he passed, accompanied by a sulky-looking youth in tight black trousers. "That's Michel Tardieu," Morris murmured. "He's another likely contender for the UNESCO chair. The kid is supposed to be his research assistant. You can tell how good he is at research by the way he wriggles his ass."

"Hallo, young man." Persse felt a light tap on his shoulder, and turned to find Miss Sybil Maiden standing behind him in a Paisley pattern frock, holding a folded fan in her hand.

"Why, hallo, Miss Maiden," he greeted her. "I didn't know you were interested in semiotics."

"I thought I should find out what it is all about," she replied. "One should never dismiss what one does not understand."

"And what do you think of it so far?"

Miss Maiden fluttered her fan. "I think it's a lot of tosh," she declared. "However, Amsterdam is a very charming city. Have you been to the Van Gogh museum? Those

late landscapes from Arles! The cypresses are so wonderful
ly phallic, the cornfields positively brimming with fertility.''

"I think we'd better sit down," said Persse. "They seem
to be starting."

On every seat was a handout which looked at first sight
like the blueprint for an electric power station, all arrows,
lines and boxes, except that the boxes were labelled *tragedy,
comedy, pastoral, lyric, epic* and *romance*. "A Semiotic
Theory of Genre" was the title of the paper, delivered by a
sweating Slav in stumbling English—with French, the official
language of the conference. It was warm in the rotunda.
From behind Persse came the regular swish of Miss Maiden's
fan, punctuated by an occasional snort of incredulity or
contempt. Persse's head felt as heavy as a cannonball.
Every now and again, as he dozed off, it would loll forward
and wake him up by a painful jerk on his neck ligaments.
Eventually, he allowed his chin to sink on to his breast, and
fell into a deep sleep.

Persse woke with a start from a dream in which he was
delivering a paper about the influence of T. S. Eliot on
Shakespeare from a pulpit in a chapel shaped like the inside
of a jumbo jet. What had woken him was a thunderclap.
The sky was dark behind the high windows of the rotunda,
and the lights had been switched on. Rain drummed on the
roof. He yawned and rubbed his eyes. On the rostrum, a
man with a pale face and a skullcap of blond hair was
speaking into the microphone in Germanically accented
English, biting off the consonants and spitting them out as if
they were pips, gestering occasionally with a black-gloved
hand. Persse shook his head in the manner of a swimmer
clearing his ears of water. Although visually he had woken
up, his dream seemed to be continuing on the audio channel. He pinched himself, and felt the sensation. He pinched
Morris Zapp, snoozing beside him.

"Lay off, Fulvia," Morris Zapp mumbled. Then, opening his eyes, he sat up. "Ah, yeah, that's von Trupitz. How
long's he been speaking?"

"I'm not sure. I've been asleep myself."

"Is his stuff any good?"

"I think it's very good," said Persse. Morris Zapp looked glum. "But then," Persse continued, "I'm biased. I wrote it."

"Huh?" Morris Zapp gaped.

Lightning flickered outside the windows and the lights inside the auditorium went out. There was a gasp of surprise and consternation from the audience, immediately drowned by a tremendous thunderclap overhead which made them all jump with fright. The lights came on again. Von Turpitz continued to read his paper in the same relentlessly precise accent, without pause or hesitation. He had evidently been speaking for some time, because he reached the end of his discourse about ten minutes later. He squared off the pages of his script, bowed stiffly to the chairman, and sat down to polite applause. The chairman invited questions. Persse stood up. The chairman smiled and nodded.

"I'd like to ask the speaker," said Persse, "if he recently read a draft outline of a book about the influence of T. S. Eliot on the modern reading of Shakespeare, submitted by me to the publishers Lecky, Windrush and Bernstein, of London."

The chairman looked puzzled. Von Turpitz looked stunned.

"Would you repeat the question, please?" the chairman asked.

Persse repeated it. A sussuration of whispered comment and speculation passed like a breeze around the auditorium. Von Turpitz leaned across to the chairman and said something into his ear. The chairman nodded, and bent forward to address Persse through the microphone. His identification disc dangled from his lapel like a medal. "May I ask, sir, whether you are an officially registered member of the Conference?"

"Well, no, I'm not . . ." said Persse.

"Then I'm afraid your question is out of order," said the chairman. Von Turpitz busied himself with his papers, as though this procedural wrangle had nothing to do with him.

"That's not fair!" Persse protested. "I have reason to think that Professor von Turpitz has plagiarized part of his paper from an unpublished manuscript of my own."

"I'm sorry," said the chairman. "I cannot accept a

question from someone who is not a member of the Conference.''

"Well *I'm* a member," said Morris Zapp, rising to his feet beside Persse, "so let me ask it: did Professor von Turpitz read McGarrigle's manuscript for Lecky, Windrush and Bernstein, or did he not?''

There was mild uproar in the auditorium. Cries of "Shame!" "Point of order, Mr Chairman!" "Answer!" and "Let him speak!" with equivalent ejaculations in various other languages, could be distinguished in a general babble of conversation. The chairman looked helplessly at von Turpitz, who seized the microphone, delivered an angry speech in German, pointing a black finger menacingly at Persse and Morris Zapp, and then stalked off the platform.

"What did he say?" Morris demanded.

Persse shrugged. "I don't speak German.''

"He said he wasn't going to stay here and be insulted,'' said Miss Maiden from behind them, "but he looked distinctly guilty to me. You were quite right to stand up for yourself against the Black Hand, young man.''

"Yeah, this is going to get around," said Morris Zapp, rubbing his hands together. "This is not going to help von Turpitz's reputation one little bit. Come on, Percy, I'll buy you another Bols.''

Morris's jubilation did not, however, last for long. In the bar he spotted a folded copy of the *Times Literary Supplement* sticking out of Persse's jacket pocket. "Is that the latest issue?" he asked. "Mind if I take a look at it?''

"I shouldn't if I were you," said Persse, who had read it on the plane to Amsterdam.

"Why not?''

"Well, it contains a rather unfriendly review of a book of yours. By Rudyard Parkinson.''

"That asshole? The day I get a good review from him, I'll know I'm washed up. Let me see." Morris almost snatched the journal from Persse and, with trembling fingers, flicked through the pages until he located Parkinson's review. "But this is all about Philip Swallow's book," he said, frowning, as he ran his eyes up and down the columns of print.

"The bit about you is at the end," Persse said. "You're not going to like it."

Morris Zapp didn't like it. When he had finished reading the review, he was silent for a few moments, pale and breathing heavily. "It's a limey plot," he said at length. "Parkinson is pushing his own claim to the UNESCO chair under cover of praising Philip Swallow's pathetic little book on Hazlitt."

"Do you think so?" said Persse.

"Of course—look at the title: 'The English School of Criticism.' He should have called it 'The English School of Genteel Crap.' May I borrow this?" he concluded, standing up and stuffing the *TLS* into his pocket.

"Sure—but where are you going?"

"I'm gonna look over my paper for tomorrow morning—see if I can work in some cracks against Parkinson."

"I didn't know you were giving a paper."

"How else could I claim my conference expenses? It's the same paper that I gave at Rummidge, slightly adapted. It's a wonderfully adaptable paper. I aim to give it all over Europe this summer. You want to take a stroll round the town tonight?"

"All right," Persse said. They made arrangements to meet. As soon as Morris Zapp had disappeared, the lean leathery figure of Michel Tardieu slid into the vacant space beside Persse in the curved, upholstered bar alcove.

"A most dramatic intervention," he said, after introducing himself. "Do I infer that you are a specialist in the work of T. S. Eliot?"

"That's right," said Persse. "I did my Master's dissertation on him."

"You may be interested, then, in a conference some Swiss friends of mine are organizing this summer."

"I'm not sure what my movements will be this summer," said Persse.

"I expect to attend this conference myself," said Michel Tardieu, putting his hand on Persse's knee beneath the table.

"I'm looking for a girl, you see," said Persse.

"Ah," shrugged Tardieu, removing his hand. "*C'est la vie, c'est la narration.* Each of us is a subject in search of an object. Have you by any chance seen a young man in a black velvet suit?''

"No, I'm afraid I haven't," said Persse. "If you will excuse me, I have to go now."

Outside the Sonesta the sky was blue again, and the late-afternoon sun shone on a rinsed and gleaming city. Persse took a canal ride in one of the sleek Plexiglass-covered tourist launches that slid through the narrow waterways and threaded the bridges at what seemed reckless speed, almost grazing each other as they passed in opposite directions, crackling commentaries in four languages from their loudspeakers. Once he glimpsed a girl walking across a bridge a hundred yards ahead who, from that distance, looked like Angelica, but this, he knew, was a mirage produced by his own desire. When the boat reached the bridge, the girl had disappeared.

Later that evening, when the canals were long black mirrors laid flat between the trees and the streetlamps, Morris conducted Persse on a stroll around the red light district, a maze of little streets near the Nieuwemarkt. It was, as Morris had promised, a far more extraordinary and shocking spectacle than anything Soho offered, and almost too much for an innocent young man from County Mayo to comprehend. In each brightly lit window sat a prostitute, dressed for her trade in some slinky gown or filmy négligé, boldly eyeing the passersby for possible custom. These were veritably streets of sin, the objects of men's lust being frankly displayed like goods in a shop window. You had only to step inside and settle the price, and the woman would draw thick heavy curtains across the casement and satisfy your desire. Two things prevented this traffic in female flesh from seeming simply sordid. The first was that the interiors of the houses were spotlessly clean, and furnished in a cosy petit-bourgeois style, with upholstered chairs, embroidered antimacassars, potted plants, and immaculate linen turned down on the bed that could usually be glimpsed at the rear. The second thing was that all the women were young and attractive, and in many cases were passing the time in the homely occupation of knitting.

"Why do they do it?" Persse wondered aloud to Morris Zapp. "They look such nice girls. They could be married and raising families instead of selling themselves like this." He did not like to catch the women's eyes, not so much because he feared falling under the spell of their allure as because he felt slightly ashamed to be observing their self-exposure while remaining safely wrapped in his own virtue.

Morris shrugged. "Maybe they're planning to settle down later. When they've made their pile."

"But who would marry a . . . girl who had done that for a living?"

Morris moved ahead of Persse on the narrow, crowded pavement, and tossed his reply back over his shoulder. "Perhaps he wouldn't know."

The streets were becoming increasingly crowded by pedestrians, most of whom seemed to be window-shopping tourists like themselves, rather than serious customers. There were even couples, courting or married, to be seen amid the throng, walking arm-in-arm, grinning and nudging each other, deriving a cheap erotic thrill from the ambience of sexual licence. For some reason this depressed Persse more than any other component of the scene, and made him feel sorrier for the girls in the windows.

And then he saw her, in a house with a low red door and the number 13 painted on it. Angelica. There was no question that it was Angelica. She was sitting in the little parlour, not at the window, but on a chaise-longue beside a standard lamp with a rose-coloured shade, and she was painting her nails with nail-varnish, concentrating so intently on the task that she did not look up as he stood on the pavement and stared in through the window, thunderstruck. Her long dark hair was loose about her shoulders and she wore a black dress of some shiny material cut low across her bosom. The nail varnish was scarlet. When she extended her hand to examine the effect under the lamp it looked as though she had dipped her fingers in fresh blood.

Persse walked on in a daze. He felt as though he were drowning, fighting for breath. He cannoned blindly into other, protesting pedestrians, stumbled over a kerb, heard a squeal of brakes, and found himself sprawled over the bonnet of a car whose driver, leaning out of the window, was shouting angrily at him in Dutch or German.

"'Tis pity she's a whore," Persse said to the driver.

"Percy, what the hell are you doing?" said Morris Zapp, materializing out of the crowd that was observing this incident with mild interest. "I've been looking all over for you." He took Persse's arm and steered him back to the pavement. "Are you OK? What d'you want to do?"

"I'd rather be on my own for a while, if you don't mind," Persse said.

"Ah ha! You saw something that took your fancy in one of those windows back there, huh? Well, I don't blame you, Percy, you're only young once. Just do me a favour, if the girl offers you a condom, forget the Pope, wear it for my sake, OK? I'd hate to be the occasion of your getting the clap. I think I'll go back to the hotel. *Ciao.*"

Morris Zapp squeezed Persse's bicep and waddled away. Persse retraced his steps, rapidly, purposefully. Morris had put an idea into his head, a way of relieving his feelings of bitterness, betrayal, disgust. He would burst into the cosy, rose-tinted little parlour and demand *"How much?"* How much did the elusive maiden he had wooed and pursued along the paths and corridors of Rummidge, without winning so much as a kiss, how much did she charge for opening her legs to a paying customer? Was there a discount for an old friend, for a poet, for a paid-up member of the Association of University Teachers? Rehearsing these sarcasms in his head, imagining Angelica starting up from the chaise-longue, white-faced, aghast, clutching at her heart, he pushed his way through the shuffling crowds of voyeurs until he found himself outside the house with the red door. Its curtains were drawn.

Persse felt physically sick. He leaned against the wall and dug his nails into the hard gritty surface. A group of British youths passed, four abreast, yelling a football song, dribbling an empty beer can before them. One caught Persse a glancing blow with his shoulder, but Persse made no protest. He felt numb, blank, not even anger was left.

The chanting of the English yobbos faded as they turned a

corner and the street became momentarily quiet and empty. After a few minutes the red door opened and closed again behind a young man who stood for a moment, adjusting his tight black trousers. Persse recognized him as the companion of Michel Tardieu. He looked furtively to left and right, then sauntered off. Light fell across the pavement as the curtains were drawn back inside the front room. Persse moved out of the shadows and looked in. A pretty Eurasian girl in a white petticoat smiled at him encouragingly. Persse gaped at her. He examined the door of the house: red, and with number 13 painted on it. He had made no mistake. He returned to the window. The same girl smiled again, and with a sweep of her eyes and a tilt of her head invited him to enter. When he did so, she greeted him with a smile and some unintelligible words of Dutch.

"Excuse me," he said.

"You American?" she enquired. "You like to spend some time with me? Forty dollar."

"There was another girl in here just now," said Persse.

"She gone. She babysitter. Don't worry, I give you good time."

"Babysitter?" Hope, relief, self-reproach surged in Persse's breast.

"Yeah, I got kid upstairs. Don't worry, he sleeps, don't hear a thing."

"Angelica is your babysitter?"

"You mean Lily? She's a friend, helps me out sometimes. I told her to draw the curtain, but she don't bother."

"Where has she gone? Where can I find her?"

The girl shrugged, sulky. "I dunno. You want to spend some time with me or not? Thirty dollar."

Persse took a hundred-guilder note out of his wallet and put it down on the table. "Where can I find Lily?"

With the speed and dexterity of a prestidigitator, the girl picked up the note, folded it with the fingers of one hand, and tucked it into her décolletage. "She works at a cabaret, Blue Heaven, on the Achterburg Wal."

"Where's that?"

"Turn right at the end of the street, then over the bridge. You will see the sign."

"Thanks," said Persse.

He raced along the street like a hurley player, jinking through the crowds and the traffic, juggling the ball of his confused emotions. For one dizzy moment he thought he had discovered Angelica in some totally innocent, totally benevolent occupation, a secular sister of mercy ministering to the prostitutes of Amsterdam. That had been wishful thinking, of course. But if Angelica wasn't just a babysitter, she wasn't a whore either—how could he ever have dreamed that she was? His shame at having entertained such an idea, however plausible the circumstantial evidence, made him readier to accept the fact that she performed in nude revues. He couldn't approve of it, he hoped to persuade her to give it up, but it didn't fundamentally affect his feelings for her.

He swerved round the corner of the street and raced across the bridge; saw blue neon letters trembling in the black water, and leapt three steps at a time down to the canalside cobbles. Some people queuing for admission to the Blue Heaven turned their heads and stared as Persse came thudding up to the entrance and skidded to a halt, panting, in front of the foyer. It had an illuminated façade, rather like a small cinema, on which the programme was advertised in moveable letters. "LIVE SEX SHOW,"it stated, in English. "SEE SEX ACTS PERFORMED ON STAGE. THE REAL FUCKY FUCKY." On the pillars supporting the entrance canopy there were photographic stills of the performance. In one of them Angelica, naked, kneeling, was being mounted from behind by a hairy young man, also naked, and grinning. She looked exactly as she had done in what he had thought, till now, was a hallucination in the Rummidge cinema. He turned on his heel and walked slowly away.

What did Persse do next? He got drunk, of course, like any other disillusioned lover. He bought a half-litre of Bols in a stone bottle at a liquor store and went back to his pension and lay on the bed and drank himself into insensibility. He woke next morning under a burning electric light bulb, uncertain which was worse, the pain in his head or the taste in his mouth, though neither was a patch on the ache in his heart. He had an open return ticket to Heathrow. Without bothering to enquire into the availability of flights, he checked out of the pension and took a bus to Schiphol airport, staring vacantly out through the window at the depressing environs of Amsterdam; factories, service stations and greenhouses scattered over the flat and featureless landscape like jetsam on a beach from which the tide had gone out and never returned.

He secured a seat on the next plane to London, and sat for an hour in the lounge next to the departure gate, not reading, not thinking, just sitting; the vacancy and anonymity of the place, with its rows of plastic moulded seats facing a huge tinted window framing blank sky, suited the zero state of his mind and heart. The flight was called, he shuffled aboard, past mechanically nodding and smiling cabin staff, the plane rose into the air like a lift, he stared through a porthole at a cloudscape as flat and featureless as the landscape below. A tray of food wrapped in polyfilm was placed before him and he consumed its contents stolidly, without any sensation of taste or aroma. The plane dumped him on the ground again, and he walked through the endless covered ways of Heathrow, so long their lines seemed to meet at the horizon.

Only Club class seats were available on the next flight to Shannon, but he cashed another traveller's cheque and paid the extra without demur. What did he need to husband his money for now? His life was laid waste, his occupation gone. The summer stretched before him barren as a desert. He had two hours to wait before his flight was called. He dragged his feet to St George's chapel. His petition was still pinned to the green baize board, curling slightly at the edges: *"Dear God, let me find Angelica."* He ripped the paper from its securing thumbtack, and crumpled it in his fist. He went inside the chapel, and sat for an hour in the back pew, staring blankly at the altar. On his way out he left another petition on the noticeboard: *"Dear God, let me forget Angelica. Lead her from the life that degrades her."*

He sat for another half an hour in another anonymous waiting area, and shuffled in line aboard another airplane, past mechanically nodding and smiling cabin crew, and took his seat. The airplane rose like a lift into the air and he stared through the porthole at another featureless prairie of cloud. Another tray of tasteless, odourless food was placed on his lap, with a complimentary half bottle of chilled claret, because he was travelling Club class. But this time there appeared to be some deviation from the monotonous routine of flight. Persse, sitting in the forward section of the plane, observed much coming and going of the cabin crew through the curtain that screened the door to the flight deck. It gradually penetrated his dulled and apathetic sensibility that the three hostesses were alarmed about something.

Sure enough, the captain came on the intercom to inform the passengers that the plane had burst a nosewheel tyre on takeoff, and they would therefore be making an emergency landing at Shannon, where fire and rescue services were standing by. A murmur of apprehension passed through the cabins at this announcement. As if he had heard it, the captain tried to reassure the passengers, explaining that he did not doubt that he would be able to land safely, but emergency procedures were obligatory following a tyre burst—in case, he added, there should be a further burst (which was perhaps explaining too much). Shortly before landing, the passengers would be instructed to take off their shoes and adopt the recommended posture for emergency landing. The cabin crew would demonstrate, and give advice and help where needed.

In fact the cabin crew themselves looked in need of advice and help. Seldom had Persse seen three young women who looked more frightened, and gradually their fear communicated itself to the passengers. The terror of the latter was intensified by some violent turbulence which the aircraft encountered as it began its descent. Though this had absolutely nothing to do with the burst tyre, some unmechanically-minded passengers drew the opposite conclusion and emitted small screams of fear or pious ejaculations as the aircraft bucked and staggered in the air. Some pored over the plastic cards giving safety instructions tucked into the back of every seat, with coloured diagrams of the plane's emergency exits, and unconvincing pictures of passengers gaily sliding down the inflatable chutes, like children on a playground slide. Others, operating on the belt-and-braces principle, rooted out life-jackets from beneath their seats and practised putting them on. The air hostesses ran distractedly up and down the aisle, dissuading people from inflating their life jackets and fending off urgent orders for strong drink.

Indifferent to life himself, Persse observed the conduct of those around him with detached curiosity. His seat gave him a ringside view of the cabin crew. He saw the chief stewardess take a handmike from its recess near the galley and clear her throat preparatory to making an announcement. Her expression was solemn. "Ladies and gentlemen," she said, in a Kerry accent, "we have received a request from a passenger for a public recitation of the Act of Contrition. Is there a priest on board who would be willing to lead us in prayer?" She waited anxiously for a few moments, looking down the length of the plane (the curtain between the Club- and economy-class sections had been drawn back) for signs of a volunteer. Another hostess came forward from the economy section, shaking her head. "No luck, Moira," she murmured to the chief stewardess. "Wouldn't you know it, just when you need a priest, there isn't one. Not even a nun."

"What shall I do?" said Moira distractedly, her hand over the mike.

"You'll have to say the Act of Contrition yourself."

Moira looked frantic. "I've forgotten it," she whimpered. "I haven't been to confession since I went on the pill."

"Oh, Moira, you never told me you were on the pill."

"You do it, Brigid."

"Oh, I couldn't."

"Yes, you could. Didn't you tell me you were a Child of Mary?" The chief stewardess said into the microphone: "Since there doesn't appear to be a priest on board, stewardess Brigid O'Toole will lead us all in the Act of Contrition." She thrust the mike into the hands of the dismayed Brigid, who looked at it as if it was a snake that might bite her at any moment. The plane reared and dropped sickeningly. The two girls, thrown off-balance, clung together for support.

"In the name of the Father . . ." Moira prompted in a whisper.

"In the name of the Father and of the Son and of the Holy Ghost," Brigid croaked into the microphone. She clapped her hand over it and hissed: "My mind's gone blank. I can't remember the Act of Contrition."

"Well, say any prayer you like," Moira urged. "Whatever comes into your head."

Brigid shut her eyes tightly and held the microphone to her lips. "For what we are about to receive," she said, "may the Lord make us truly thankful."

Persse was still laughing when they landed, quite safely, at Shannon airport, ten minutes later. Brigid gave him a sheepish grin as he left the aircraft. "Sorry about the fuss, sir," she murmured.

"Not a bit of it," he said. "You gave me back an appetite for life."

He went to the Irish Tourist Board desk at the airport and enquired about renting a cottage in Connemara. "I want somewhere very quiet and isolated," he said. He had decided what to do with the rest of his study leave. He would buy a second-hand car, fill the back seat with books and writing paper and Guinness and his cassette player and Bob Dylan tapes, and spend the summer in some humble equivalent of Yeats's lonely tower, writing poetry.

While they were telephoning for him, he picked up a leaflet advertising the American Express card, and for want of anything else to do, filled in the application form.

Philip Swallow settled his hotel bill and sat in the foyer with his packed bags beside him, waiting to be picked up by the British Council car—or, rather, Landrover, for such was the vehicle prudently favoured by the Council in Ankara. Philip had never seen such roads in a modern city, pitted and potholed like the surface of the moon. Whenever there was rain the roads flooded because the construction workers who laid them had disposed of all debris by throwing them into the drains, which were therefore permanently blocked.

The hotel manager passed Philip, smiled, stopped and bowed. "You go back to England tonight, Professor?"

"No, no. To Istanbul. By the night train."

"Ah!" The manager's face lit up with envy and pathos. "Istanbul is very beautiful."

"So I've heard."

"Very old. Very beautiful. Not like Ankara."

"Oh, I've enjoyed my stay in Ankara very much," said Philip. Such lies become second nature to the cultural traveller. He had not enjoyed his stay in Ankara at all, and would be glad to shake the dust of the place off his feet—and there was plenty of that, whenever it didn't happen to be raining.

Admittedly, things had improved after his first day: they could hardly have got worse. Akbil Borak had been very kind and attentive, even if his only two topics of conversation did seem to be Hull and Hazlitt. There was no doubt that he really did know an awful lot about Hazlitt—rather more than Philip himself, in fact; though it was a pity that he drew attention to their common familiarity with the Romantic essayist by referring to him as "Bill Hazlitt". Philip had been tying for days to think of a way of correcting this habit without appearing to be rude.

The other Turks he had met had been equally kind and hospitable. Almost every evening there had been a party or dinner or reception for him, at one of the Universities or in someone's cramped, overfurnished apartment. At private parties there would be food and drink somehow scrounged or saved in spite of the endemic shortages—at what cost and domestic sacrifice Philip hated to think. Official receptions were discreetly supplied with booze by the British Council, largesse deeply appreciated by the Turks, who looked upon Philip in consequence as a kind of lucky mascot. Not for a long time had the university teachers of English in Ankara had so many parties in such a short time. They turned up night after night, the same faces beaming with pleasure, shaking Philip's hand enthusiastically as if they had just met him for the first time. There was laughter and chatter and recorded music—sometimes dancing. Philip laughed and chatted and drank, and even on one occasion essayed a clumsy *pas de deux* with a lady professor of mature years who retained a remarkable aptitude for the belly-dance. This performance was greeted with loud applause, and described

by a misty-eyed British Council officer who witnessed it as
a breakthrough in Anglo-Turkish cultural relations. But in
some deep core of himself, where raki and Embassy scotch
could not reach, Philip felt lonely and depressed. He recognized the symptoms of his malaise because he had suffered
from it before on his travels, though never so severely. It
was a feeling that defined itself as a simple, insistent
question: *Why am I here?* Why was he in Ankara, Turkey,
instead of in Rummidge, England? It was a question that
posed itself less sharply at parties than when he sat beside a
lectern at the front of some dusty classroom facing rows of
curious, swarthy young men and dark-eyed young women
and listened to some Turkish professor introducing him at
laborious length, punctiliously enumerating every academic
distinction that could be squeezed from the reference books
(Philip confidently expected one day to hear his O-level
results being recited, if not his brilliant performance in the
eleven-plus) while he himself nervously fingered the hastily
rewritten opening pages of his lecture on Hazlitt; or when he
lay upon his hotel bed in the slack hours between lecturing
and partying and sightseeing (not that there was a great deal
to see in Ankara once you had visited the Anitkabir and the
Hittite museum, but the tireless Akbil Borak had made sure
that he saw it all), picking out previously unread bits of the
crumpled *Guardian* he had brought with him days before,
and listening to the strains of foreign music and the sound of
foreign tongues coming through the walls and the strident
noise of traffic rising from the street. *Why am I here?*
Hundreds, probably thousands of pounds of public money
had been expended on bringing him to Turkey. Secretaries
had typed letters, telex machines had chattered, telephone
wires hummed, files thickened in offices in Ankara, Istanbul,
London. Precious fossil fuel had been burned away in the
stratosphere to propel him like an arrow from Heathrow to
Esenboga. The domestic economies and digestions of the
academic community of Ankara had been taxed to their
limits in the cause of entertaining him. And for what
purpose? So that he could bring the good news about
Hazlitt, or Literature and History and Society and Psychology and Philosophy, to the young Turkish bourgeoisie, whose

chief motive for studying English (so Akbil Borak had confided in a moment of raki-induced candour) was to secure a job as a civil servant or air hostess and to avoid the murderously factious social science faculties? When he was driven through the streets of Ankara, teeming with a vast anonymous impoverished proletariat, dressed in dusty cotton drab, toiling up and down the concrete hills with the dogged inscrutable persistence of ants, under the unsmiling surveillance of the omnipresent, heavily armed military, he could understand the modest pragmatism of the students' ambitions. But how would Hazlitt help them?

"Excuse me, sir." The hotel manager was back. "Will you be requiring dinner? The train to Istanbul does not leave for several hours."

"Oh, no thank you," said Philip. "I'm going out." The manager bowed and withdrew.

Custer, the British Council's cultural affairs officer, had invited Philip to a buffet supper at his apartment. "I won't pretend it's in your honour," he had explained. "We've got a string quartet from Leeds arriving in the afternoon. Got to lay on something for them, so you might as well come along. Nothing elaborate, you know, quite informal. There'll be a few other people there. Tell you what," he added, as if struck by a brilliant idea, "I'll invite Borak."

"I think he may have seen enough of me in the last few days . . ." Philip suggested.

"Oh no, he'd be offended if I didn't invite him. His wife, too. Hassim will collect you from the hotel about seven. Bring your luggage with you, and I'll run you down to the station at about ten to catch your train."

Recognizing the tall figure and melancholy moustache of Hassim, the Council driver, negotiating the revolving door, Philip stood up and carried his bags across the foyer. Hassim, who spoke no English, relieved him of his suitcase and led the way to the Landrover.

Of course, Philip reflected, as he climbed into the seat beside Hassim, and they jolted away, he might have felt quite differently about this trip if it hadn't been for that surprising spasm of desire for Hilary at the very moment of his departure from home. The warm promise of that glimpsed swaying breast had imprinted itself upon his mind, taunting and tormenting him as he lay awake in his narrow hotel bed, reinforcing the question, *Why am I here?* Sex with Hilary wasn't the greatest erotic sensation in the world, but at least it was something. A temporary release from tension. A little pleasant oblivion. Here in Turkey there wasn't a hope of erotic adventure. The friendly women he met were all married, with husbands in genial but watchful attendance. The dimpled, sloe-eyed girl students never seemed to be allowed closer than lecturing distance to him, unless they appeared in the rôle of daughters to one of the academic couples, and Philip had the feeling that to make a pass at one of *them* might provoke a diplomatic incident. Turkey was, on the surface anyway, a country of old-fashioned moral propriety.

The Landrover crawled forward amid congested traffic. There seemed to be a permanent traffic jam in the centre of Ankara—if this was the centre. Philip had acquired no sense of the geography of the city because it all looked the same to him—untreated concrete, cracked pavements, pitted roads, everything the colour of ash, scarcely a tree or blade of grass to be seen, in spite of its being spring. It was getting dark, now, and under their sparse and inadequate street lighting the streets grew deep and sinister shadows, except where kerosene lamps flared amid an improvised street market, with shawled women haggling over vegetables and kitchen-ware, or where bleak fluorescent light bounced through plateglass windows from the Formica tabletops of a smoke-filled working-men's café. Philip had the feeling that if Hassim were suddenly to stop the Landrover and pitch him out into the street, he would never be seen again—he would be dragged into the shadows, stripped and robbed of everything he possessed, murdered and flung into one of the blocked drains. He felt a long way from home. Why was he here? Was it, perhaps, time to call a halt to his travels, abandon the quest for intensity of experience he had burbled on about to Morris Zapp, hang up his lecture notes and cash in his traveller's cheques, settle for routine and domesticity, for safe sex with Hilary and the familiar round of the Rummidge academic year, from Freshers' Conference to Finals Examiners' Meeting, until it was time to retire, retire from both sex and work? Followed in dure course by retirement from life. Was that it?

The Landrover stopped: they had arrived at a modern apartment block on one of the hills that ringed the city. Hassim gestured Philip into the lift and pressed the button for the sixth floor. Custer came to the front door of the apartment, flushed, in shirtsleeves, a glass in his hand. "Ah, there you are, come in, come in! Let me take your case. Go into the drawing-room and I'll bring you a drink. Gin and tonic? Borak's in there. By the way, it isn't a string quartet after all, it's a jazz quartet. London cocked up again."

Custer led him down a hall, opened a door and ushered Philip into the drawing-room, moderately full of people standing in groups with glasses in their hands. The first face that Philip focused on was Joy Simpson's.

Akbil Borak never ceased to be surprised by Philip Swallow's behaviour. On the day of his arrival the Englishman had twice abruptly measured his length upon the ground, and now, on the evening of his departure, he looked as if he was going to do it again, in Mr and Mrs Custer's drawing-room, for he stumbled on the threshold, and only saved himself from falling by grabbing at a chairback for support. Heads turned all across the room, and there was a moment's embarrassed hush; then, seeing that there was nothing seriously amiss, the groups resumed their convivial chatter.

Akbil had been standing next to Oya, talking to the drummer from the jazz quartet and to Mrs Simpson, the British Council librarian at Istanbul, a pleasant, if reserved lady, with shapely buttocks and beautiful blonde hair. Akbil was telling Mrs Simpson about the shops in Hull, and mentally wondering whether the fair women of the north had golden pubic hair to match their heads, when Philip Swallow made his noisy entrance, crashing into the furniture near the door. Akbil hurried forward to offer assistance, but Philip, rising from his knees, shook off his hand and took a few uncertain steps towards Mrs Simpson. His face was white. "*You!*" he whispered hoarsely, staring at Mrs Simpson. She, too, had turned slightly pale, as well she might at this strange greeting. "Hallo," she said, holding her glass tightly with the fingers of both hands. "Alex Custer told me that you might drop in tonight. How are you enjoying Turkey?"

"You have met before, then?" said Akbil, glancing from one to the other.

"Briefly," said Mrs Simpson. "Several years ago, in Genoa, wasn't it, Professor Swallow?"

"I thought you were dead," said Philip Swallow. He had not altered the direction of his gaze, or even blinked.

Oya clutched at Akbil's sleeve with excitement. "Oh, how is that?" she cried.

Mrs Simpson frowned. "Oh dear, I suppose you read that list in the newspapers," she said to Philip Swallow. "It was issued prematurely by the Indian authorities. It caused a great deal of confusion and distress, I'm afraid."

"You mean you survived that crash?"

"I wasn't on the plane. I was supposed to be—this was about three years ago," she explained parenthetically to Akbil and Oya and the jazz drummer. "My husband was posted to India. I was going with him, but at the last moment my doctor said not to go, I was eight months pregnant and he thought it would be too risky, so John went alone, and I stayed behind with Gerard, our little boy, but somehow our names were left on the passenger list, or some passenger list. The plane crashed, landing in the middle of a storm."

"And your husband. . . ?" Oya quavered.

"There were very few survivors," said Mrs Simpson simply, "and he wasn't one of them."

Oya was weeping copiously. "I pity you," she said, snuffling into a handkerchief.

"I thought you were dead," said Philip Swallow again, as if he had not heard this explanation, or, having heard it, had failed to take it in.

"But you see, Professor Swallow, she is not dead after all! She lives!" Oya gave a little clap of her hands and rose on to the tops of her toes, smiling through her tears. Akbil had the sense that his wife was supplying all the emotion that the two English should be exhibiting. The jazz drum-

mer had slipped away unnoticed at some point in Mrs
Simpson's recital. "You should be happy," said Oya to
Philip. "It is like a fairy story."

"I am of course very pleased to see Mrs Simpson alive
and well," he said. He seemed to have recovered his
composure, though his face was still pale.

"And the art of pleasing consists in being pleased, as Bill
Hazlitt says," Akbil struck in, rather neatly, he thought.

"But what are you doing in Ankara?" Philip asked Mrs
Simpson.

"I'm just here for a few days, for some meetings. I run
the Council library in Istanbul."

"I'm going to Istanbul tonight," said Philip Swallow,
with some signs of excitement.

"Oh? How long will you be staying there?"

"Three or four days. I go home on Friday."

"Unfortunately, I'm here till Friday."

Philip Swallow looked as if he couldn't believe this
intelligence. He turned to Akbil. "Akbil, Alex Custer seems
to have forgotten all about my drink, could you possibly . . . ?"

"Of course," said Akbil, "I will seek it."

"I will help you," said Oya. "Mrs Simpson also needs a
refill." She took Mrs Simpson's glass and almost pushed
Akbil towards the door.

"Why did you not stay with them?" Akbil muttered to
Oya in Turkish. "They will think us rude."

"I have a feeling they wish to be alone," said Oya. "I
think there is something between them."

"Do you think so?" Akbil was astonished. He looked
back over his shoulder. Philip Swallow was certainly deep in
conversation with Mrs Simpson, who looked flustered for
once. "That man never ceases to surprise me," he said.

Three hours later, Philip paced anxiously up and down the
broad platform of Ankara's main railway station beside the
tall coaches of the Ankara-Istanbul express. The train had a
period air, vaguely reminiscent of thirties' thrillers, as did
the whole scene. Wisps of smoke and steam drifted out of
deep shadows into the bright glare of arch lights. A family
of peasants had camped out for the night on a bench,

surrounded by their bundles and baskets. The mother, suckling her baby, gazed impassively at the women in chic velvet trouser-suits who led caravans of porters bearing their matched suitcases towards the first class coaches. Uniformed officials clasping millboards strutted up and down, giving orders to menials and kicking beggars out of the way. The second- and third-class compartments were already full, exhaling odours of garlic, tobacco and perspiration from their ventilators; the passengers within, wedged tightly together, hip to hip, knee to knee, prepared themselves stoically for the night's long journey. From time to time a figure would dart from one of these coaches across the platform to a small kiosk that sold tea, fizzy drinks, pretzel-shaped bread and poisonous-looking sweets.

In the first-class compartments, where Philip had a berth, the atmosphere was more relaxed. Bottles clinked against glasses, and card parties were being organized, though the lights were almost too dim to see the cards by. There was an atmosphere of gossip and intrigue, of assignations made and bribes passed. At the end of the corridor there was a red glow from the small solid-fuel furnace which the sleeping-car attendant was vigorously stoking, sweat pouring off his brow.

"It supplies heat and hot water to the sleepers," Custer had explained, when seeing Philip off. "Looks rather primitive, but it's effective. It can get quite cold out on the plains at night, even in spring."

Philip managed to persuade Custer and Akbil Borak not to wait with him until the train departed. "There's no point, really," he assured them. "I'll be quite all right."

"One of the pleasantest things in the world is going on a journey," said Akbil Borak with a smile, "but I prefer to go by myself."

"Do you really?" said Custer. "I prefer company."

"No, no!" Borak laughed. "I was quoting Bill Hazlitt. The essay 'On going on a journey'."

"Please don't wait," said Philip.

"Well," said Custer, "perhaps I should get back and see to the jazz quartet."

"And I must collect my wife from your apartment, Mr Custer," said Borak.

They shook Philip's hand and after exchanging the pleasantries usual on such occasions, took themselves off. Philip watched them go with relief. If Joy decided in the end to join him, she would not want to be seen doing so by Custer and Borak.

But that had been half an hour ago, and still she had not come.

"I can't possibly go back to Istanbul tonight," she had said, when he got her alone for a few minutes at Custer's party. "I've only just arrived in Ankara. My suitcase is still in the hall, unpacked."

"That makes it all the simpler," said Philip. "Just pick it up and leave with me." He ate her with his eyes, wolfing the features he had thought he would never see again, the softly waved blonde hair, the wide generous mouth, the slightly heavy chin.

"I've come here on Council business."

"You could make some excuse."

"Why should I?"

"Because I love you." The words came out without premeditation.

She blushed and lowered her eyes. "Don't be ridiculous."

"I've never forgotten that night," he said.

"For heaven's sake," she murmured. "Not here. Not now."

"When then? I must talk to you."

"Ah, have you two introduced yourselves?" cried Mrs Custer, coming up to them with a plate of canapés.

"We've met before, actually. In Genoa," said Joy.

"Really? Ah, well, that's the way, isn't it when one is in the Council, one is always bumping into old acquaintances in the most unlikely places. And how are you, Joy? How are the children—Gerard, isn't it, and—"

"Mrs Simpson was just telling me that Gerard is not at all well," said Philip. Joy stared at him.

"Oh dear! Nothing serious I hope?" Mrs Custer said to Joy.

Philip's heart thumped as he waited for her reply.

"He had a bit of a temperature when I left," she said at length. "I may phone my girl later to see how he is."

Philip turned his head aside to conceal his triumph.

"Oh, yes, please do," said Mrs Custer. "Use the phone in our bedroom, it's more private." She swept the room with a hostess's regard. "Oh dear, the saxophonist is browsing at our bookshelves—I always think that's a bad sign at a party, don't you? Do come and talk to him, Joy—will you excuse us, Professor Swallow?"

"Of course," said Philip.

He could not contrive to be alone with Joy for the rest of the evening. He watched her movements closely, but did not see her go into the Custers' bedroom. When it was time for him to leave for the station, well before the party was due to end, he was obliged to shake her formally by the hand in the presence of the other guests. "Goodbye, then," he said, trying to hold her gaze. "I hope your little boy is all right. Have you phoned yet?"

"Not yet," she said. "Goodbye, Professor Swallow."

And that was that. He shot her one brief, beseeching look, and left the apartment with Custer and Borak. He could only hope and pray that after he had gone she would have made the call to Istanbul and concocted some story about her child that would require her immediate return home.

Philip took another turn beside the wagon-lit and checked his watch against the station clock. There were only three minutes to go before the train was due to depart. The suspense was agonizing, yet he felt strangely exhilarated. The depression of the past week had lifted, was already forgotten. He was again a man at the centre of his own story—and what a story! He could still hardly believe that Joy was not dead, after all, but alive. Alive! That warm, breathing flesh that he had clasped in the purple-lit bedroom in Genoa was still warm, still breathed. He felt himself transformed by the miraculous reversal of fortune, lifted up as by a wave. He heard himself saying to her in the corner of the Custers' drawing-room, *"Because I love you,"* simply, sincerely, without hesitation, without embarrassment, like a hero in a film. He was not, after all, finished, washed up, ready for retirement. He was still capable of a great romance. Intensity had returned to experience. Where it would lead him to, he did not know, or care. He had a vague premonition of difficulties and pain ahead, to do with Hilary, the children, his career, but pushed them aside. All his mental energy was concentrated on willing Joy to reappear.

Doors slammed along the length of the train. Railway officials, posted at intervals along the platform like sentries, stiffened and looked to each other for signals. The minute hand of the station clock twitched forward. One minute to go.

Philip climbed reluctantly into the train, lowered the window of the door, and hung out of it, looking desperately in the direction of the ticket barrier. A uniformed official standing just beneath him looked to his left and right, then raised a whistle to his lips.

"Stop!" cried Philip, opening the door and jumping down on to the platform. He had seen a woman's figure suddenly appear at the ticket barrier, her fair hair catching the light of the arc lamps. The man with the whistle, protesting in Turkish, tried to push Philip back into the train; then, when this failed, to close the door. As they wrestled, Joy came running across the broad platform, swinging a small suitcase in one hand. Philip pointed, the official stopped struggling and indignantly adjusted his uniform. Philip gave him a large-denomination banknote. The man smiled and held the door open for them to board the train. The door slammed behind them. A whistle shrilled. The train jerked into motion. In the dimly-lit corridor curious faces peered out of doorways, as Philip propelled Joy towards his compartment. He ushered her inside and slid the door shut behind him.

"You came," he said. It was the first word either of them had spoken.

Joy sank on to the made-up bed, and closed her eyes. Her bosom rose and fell as she gulped air. "I have a ticket," she gasped. "But no berth."

"You can share this one," he said.

As the train rocked and rumbled throught the night they made awkward but rapturous love on the narrow bunk bed, their sighs and cries muffled by the creaking and rattling of the rolling-stock. Afterwards they clung together and talked. Or rather Joy talked—jerkily, hesitantly at first, then more fluently—while Philip mostly listened, responding with phatic strokings and squeezing of her soft limbs.

"That was so lovely, it's the first time since John . . . Yes, I've had opportunities, but I've been so racked with guilt . . . I thought John being killed was a sort of punishment, you see. For being unfaithful to him. With you, of course—did you think I was promiscuous, or something? The only time, yes, does that surprise you? Why did I let you, yes, I often wondered about that. I never did anything so insane, before or since, until now, and this is different, anyway, since I know you, in a manner of speaking, and John isn't here to be hurt. But that first time, there I was, a happily-married woman, well fairly happy anyway, as happy as most wives are, and I gave myself to a total stranger who suddenly appeared out of nowhere in the middle of the night, as if you were a god or an angel or something and there was nothing I could do but submit. When I woke up the next morning I thought it had been a dream, but when I saw that John had left and your bags were in the hall, and realized that it had all really happened I nearly went mad. Well I may have seemed calm to you but I can tell you that I was on the verge of hysteria, I had to keep going into the bathroom and jabbing a pair of nail scissors into my hand so that the pain in my hand would stop me thinking about what I had done.

"Do you ever have a feeling when you're driving fairly fast, in heavy traffic, that the whole thing is extraordinarily precarious, though everyone involved seems to take it for granted? All the drivers in their cars and lorries look so bored, so abstracted, just wanting to get from A to B; yet all the time they're just inches, seconds, away from sudden death. It only needs someone to turn their steering-wheel a few inches this way rather than that, for everyone to start crashing into one another. Or you're driving along some twisty coastal road, and you realize that if you were to take your hands off the wheel for just a second you would go shooting off the edge into thin air. It's a frightening feeling, because you realize how easy it would be to do it, how quick, how simple, how irreversible. It seemed to me that I had done something like that, only I had swerved off the road into life, not death.

"I couldn't complain about John as a husband. He was a kind man, faithful as far as I know, doted on Gerard, worked hard at his career. By normal standards it was a successful marriage. The physical side was all right as far as I could tell. I mean, I didn't have any experience to compare it with, and John didn't have much either. We met when we were students at university, and we lived together for several years before we got married, our parents were terribly shocked when they found out, but actually it meant that we were pretty innocent about sex, never having known anybody else that way. I sometimes had an uneasy suspicion that John had decided to, not consciously you know, but well decided to find himself a girl as soon as he could in his first year and settle into a steady relationship, so as not to be distracted from getting on with his studies by sex. I mean, it was just like being married, really, and when we actually *got* married it was a purely social event, an expensive party, there was no difference in our lives before and after. The honeymoon was just a foreign holiday. I remember feeling rather sad on our wedding night that it was all so familiar, that neither of us was nervous or shy, and I had a wicked thought that perhaps we should go out and find another couple in the same situation—the hotel was full of honeymooners—and exchange partners, or all get into bed together. I wasn't serious, it was just a thought, but I suppose it was symptomatic. I didn't mention it to John, he wouldn't have understood, he would have been hurt, thought I was getting at him. He was a conscientious lover, read up books about foreplay and so on, did his best to please me, and he did please me—I mean I never actually wanted to make love with him, not enough to take the initiative, I left that to him, but if he wanted to I usually enjoyed it.

"But somehow there was something missing. I always felt that. Passion perhaps. I never felt that John desired me passionately, or I him. I used to read about people making

love in novels, and they seemed so ecstatic, so carried away.
I never felt that. Then I would read sensible books about sex
and marriage and the correspondence columns in the wom-
en's magazines and decide that the novels were lying, the
writers were making it all up, that I was jolly lucky to be
having sex at all, never mind whether it was ecstatic or not.
And then, that night, you appeared, and for the first time in
my life I knew what it was like to be desired, passionately.''

Here there was a hiatus in Joy's monologue while Philip
once more fervently demonstrated how well-founded this
intuition had been. Some time later she resumed.

''While I was sitting on the sofa with John, opposite you,
and he was chuntering on about phonetics and testing
techniques and language laboratories, I could feel your
desire coming from you like radio-activity, burning through
my dressing-gown. It astonished me that John couldn't
sense it himself, that he was so oblivious to it that he was
going to go off and leave us alone together. I was fascinat-
ed, excited. I had no intention at that point of letting you
make love to me, indeed I didn't think you would have the
nerve to even make a pass. I was so sure of myself that I let
John go off to Milan without a qualm. But when I came
back into the living-room and you started to shake, I started
to shake too—you noticed? And then when we were in the
bedroom and you were shaking more than ever, it seemed to
me that you were like the core of a nuclear reactor that's,
what's the word, gone critical, that you would shake yourself to pieces, or melt a hole in the floor, consume yourself
with you own passion, if I didn't do something.''

''I had come back from the dead,'' Philip groaned,
remembering. ''You were life, beauty. I wanted to be
reconnected to life. You healed me.''

''I took my hands off the wheel,'' said Joy. ''I went over
the edge with you because I had never been wanted like that
before.''

In the early morning, they sat face to face in the restaurant
car, with their fingers entwined beneath the table, sipping
glasses of hot tea from their free hands, as the train trundled
throught the pleasant little towns and villages on the Asian

shore of the Sea of Marmara. There was vegetation here—
trees and shrubs and vines—between the houses. The landscape seemed positively lush after the arid heights of Ankara.
A few early risers were out in their gardens, watering the
plants, or enjoying a quiet smoke in the slanting light of the
rising sun. They waved as the train passed.

"You never wrote to me," said Joy.

"I didn't know how to, without risking compromising
you," said Philip. "I thought you wouldn't want me to,
anyway. You seemed so cold that morning I left Genoa, I
thought you wanted to forget the whole thing had happened."

"I did," said Joy, "but I found that was impossible."

"Then it wasn't long before I read in the newspaper that
you were dead."

"Yes, I never thought of that. The papers did publish a
correction."

"I must have missed it," said Philip. "Anyway, *you*
could have written to me, especially when your husband . . . I
mean, when you were . . . ."

"Free? I didn't want to interfere with your life. I looked
you up. I know all about you. You're married, with three
children, Amanda, Robert and Matthew. Wife Hilary, *née*
Broome, daughter of Commander and Mrs A. J. Broome. I
didn't want to break up your marriage."

"It's not much of a marriage," said Philip. "The children are all grown up, and Hilary's fed up. We nearly
separated ten years ago. I think we should have done." The
image of Hilary's breast had almost faded from his memory,
expunged by the more recent, keener sensation of Joy's
blunt, cylindrical nipples stiffening under his touch. "I've
stood in Hilary's way," he said earnestly. "She'd do better
on her own."

"This is where Asia meets Europe," said Joy, as a battered
taxi rushed them across a vast, new-looking suspension
bridge. Far below, huge tankers and a multitude of smaller
craft churned the waters of the Bosphorus. To their right,
green hills dotted with white houses rose steeply from the
narrowing channel. To their left, domes and minarets punctuated the skyline of an immense city, behind which the

water broadened out into a sea. "Sea of Marmara," Joy explained. "The Black Sea is at the other end of the Bosphorus."

"It's wonderful," said Philip. "This combination of water and sky and hills and architecture reminds me of Euphoria, the view I used to see every morning when I woke up and drew the curtains. It's the Bay Area of the ancient world."

"I tell you what we'll do," said Joy, "We'll take this cab down to the Galata bridge, and take a ferry boat up the Bosphorus to Bogazici, where I live. That's the best way to get your first impressions of Istanbul, from the water."

Philip squeezed her knee. "You are my Euphoria, my Newfoundland," he said.

Half an hour later they stood hand in hand on the deck of a white steamer as it surged up the Bosphorus, away from the teeming quayside. Joy pointed out the landmarks. "That's Santa Sophia, that's the Blue Mosque. I'll take you to see them later. The Golden Horn is behind the bridge. That's the Sea of Marmara, with all the wrecks."

"Why so many?"

"There's far too much traffic on the water here, the ships keep colliding, especially the big tankers. Sometimes they crash into the houses at the edge of the Bosphorus. I took an apartment well up in the hills."

"Am I going to stay with you?" Philip asked.

Joy frowned. "I don't think it would be a good idea. I have a Turkish girl living in, and the children would be inquisitive. There wouldn't be much privacy. I know a nice hotel not far away, I'll come and see you there. But you can eat with us, of course."

"But won't you be able to spend the night with me?" Philip pleaded. "I want to wake up in the morning and find you beside me."

"You can't have everything you want," she said, smiling.

The ferry boat stitched its way up the Bosphorus, stopping frequently at small wooden jetties that were like aquatic bus-stops. The boat would swerve inshore, pull up amid much foaming and rattling as the screws were reversed; passengers carrying shopping bags and briefcases briskly disembarked, new passengers scurried aboard, a bell rang, and in seconds, it seemed, they would be off again. The houses on the shore gradually took on a less antique aspect, the landscape in the background became boskier, as they proceeded. At one of the stops, which had a relaxed, seasidey air to it, Joy led him ashore, and they took a taxi to Joy's apartment, situated on a road that twisted steeply between walled gardens matted with flowering vines. Childish shrieks and cries were heard from the windows as Philip paid the taxi driver the fare for which Joy had bargained at the outset of their ride ("If you don't beat them down by at least half, you've been diddled," she had warned him). "The children are surprised to see me back home so soon," she said.

"What will you tell them?"

"Oh, that my meetings were cancelled, or something."

The children were already running down the garden steps to meet their mother, followed by a plump, smiling girl with small black eyes set in a round brown face like currants in a bun. "Be careful!" she cried. "Gerard! Miranda! Not so fast."

Philip recognized Gerard, who treated him to the same slightly hostile scrutiny that he remembered well from Genoa. Miranda, who looked about three years old, smiled rather sweetly when she was introduced.

"Have you got presents for us, Mummy?" Gerard asked.

Joy looked crestfallen. "Oh, dear, I didn't have time. I came home so unexpectedly."

"I've got something." Philip. "Do you like Turkish Delight?" He opened his briefcase and brought out a cardboard box packed with rose-hip and almond flavoured delight. "This comes from Ankara—I was told it's the best you can get."

"Are you sure you didn't mean to give that to someone else?" said Joy.

"Oh, no," said Philip, who had bought it for Hilary. "Anyway, I can always get some more here."

"Just one piece each for now, then." said Joy. "Give the box to Selina, and say thank you to Professor Swallow."

"Please call me Philip," he said.

"Thank you," said Gerard, rather grudgingly, his mouth full of Turkish delight.

"Thank you Flip," said Miranda.

"Well, show Philip the way, Miranda," said Joy.

The little girl put her sticky hand in Philip's and led him up the steep steps that led to the house. He found himself strangely taken with this child, her trusting eyes and ready smile. Later, as he sat with Joy on the balcony of her first floor apartment, he watched Miranda at play with her dolls in the garden below. They were drinking coffee (a pleasure so rare in Turkey it almost made one faint) and Joy was telling him in condensed form the story of her recent life. "Of course I could have stayed in England and lived on my widow's pension, but I thought that would be just too dreary, so I persuaded the Council to let me train as a librarian and to give me a job. They weren't too keen, but I was able to exert a certain amount of moral pressure. Anyway, I'm a good librarian."

"I'm sure you are," said Philip abstractedly, peering down into the garden. Miranda had seated her dolls in a semicircle and was earnestly talking to them. "I wonder what Miranda's telling her dolls."

"She's probably telling them about you," said Joy. "She's greatly taken with your beard."

"Is that so?" Philip laughed, and stroked his beard self-consciously. He felt ridiculously pleased. "She's a most attractive little girl, isn't she? Reminds me of someone, but I can't think who it is."

"Can't you?" Joy gave him a rather strange look.

"Well, it's not you . . ."

"No, it's not me."

"It must be your husband, I suppose, though I don't remember him very well."

"No, she doesn't take after John."

"Who then?"

"You," said Joy. "She takes after you."

Four days later, gazing down at the snow-crusted Alps from the window of a Turkish Airlines Boeing 727, Philip could still go hot and cold at the memory of that extraordinary moment, as the import of Joy's *"She takes after you"* sank in, and he realized that the little girl playing in the garden beneath him, a fragile assemblage of brown limbs and blonde hair and white cotton smock, scarcely bigger than the dolls she handled, was a child of his loins; that for the past three years, all unknown to him, this little fragment of flesh had been in existence, orbiting his conscious life in silence and obscurity, like an undiscovered star. *"What?"* he breathed. "You mean—Miranda is my . . . our . . . Are you sure?

"Not sure, but you must admit the likeness is striking."

"But, but . . ." he groped for words, gasped for breath. "But you told me, that night, that you were, you know, that it would be all right."

"I lied. I was off the pill, John and I were trying to conceive again. I was afraid that if I told you, it would break the spell, you might stop. Wasn't that wicked of me?"

"No, it was lovely of you, wonderful of you, but, my God, why didn't you tell me?"

"At first I didn't know whether I was pregnant by you or by John. The shock of the crash brought on the birth. As soon as I saw Miranda's eyes, I knew she was yours. But what would have been the point of telling you?"

"I could have divorced Hilary and married you."

"Exactly. I told you this morning, I didn't want that."

"I'm going to anyway, now," said Philip.

Joy said nothing for a few moments. Then she said, not looking at him, but painting rings on the plastic-topped table, dipping her finger in a pool of spilled coffee: "When I heard that you were coming to Turkey, I decided to avoid meeting you, because I was afraid that it would end like this. I arranged to go to Ankara just over the days when you would be in Istanbul—Alex Custer had been on at me for some time to meet the people up there to discuss policy. I got hold of your schedule and worked it all out so that I would arrive in Ankara just as you left. But I miscalculated by just a few hours. When I got to the Custers, they told me that you were coming that evening."

"It was fate," said Philip.

"Yes, I came to that conclusion myself," said Joy. "That's why I joined you on the train."

"You cut it jolly fine," said Philip.

"I wanted to give Fate a chance for second thoughts," said Joy.

Low cloud covered southern England. As the plane dipped through it, the sun disappeared like a light being switched off, and underneath the cloud it was raining. Moisture dribbled down the windows of the aircraft as it taxied on Heathrow's wet tarmac. Waiting in the stuffy, humid baggage hall, Philip felt himself wilting and shrinking as the intensity of the last few days leaked away. He sank onto a seat, allowed his eyelids to droop, and projected upon their inner surface a home movie of Istanbul, its sights, sounds and smells: churches and minarets, water and sky, the acres of slightly damp carpet under their stockinged feet as they gazed up at the dome of the Blue Mosque, the stained glass glowing like gems in the Palace Harem, the prison-like staircases of Istanbul University with an armed soldier on every landing, the labyrinthine alleys of the great covered bazaar, the waterside restaurant where the wash of a passing ship suddenly slopped through a window and drenched a whole table of diners; the hotel where he and Joy made love in the afternoons while huge Russian tankers slid past the windows, so close they momentarily blocked out the light that filtered through the venetian blinds. When the sun shone full upon the window he angled the blinds so that bars of white-hot light striped Joy's body, kindling her blonde pubic hair into flame. He called it the golden fleece, mindful that the Hellespont was not far away. When he kissed her there, his beard brushing her belly, he made a wry joke about the silver among the gold, conscious of the contrast between her beautiful, still youthful body and his scraggy, middle-aged one, but she stroked his head reassuringly. "You make me feel desirable, that's what matters." He nuzzled her, inhaling odours of shore and rockpool; the skin of her inner thighs was as tender as peeled mushrooms; she tasted clean and salty, like some mollusc from the sea. "Ah," he whimpered, "that's divine."

Philip opened his eyes to find his suitcase taking a lonely ride on the carousel. He snatched it up and, somewhat incommoded by the sexual arousal induced by his reverie, ran all the way to Terminal One to catch his connecting flight to Rummidge.

Up, briefly, into the sunshine again, in a noisy Fokker Friendship; then down again through the grey clouds to the sopping fields and gleaming motorways that ringed Rummidge airport. He was surprised and disconcerted to be met by Hilary. Usually he took a taxi home, and he had counted on solitude, during this last stage of his journey, to rehearse what he was going to say to her. But there she was, in her old beige raincoat, waving from the balcony of the terminal building, as he and his fellow passengers decended the steps from the aircraft and picked their way through the oily puddles on the apron.

Inside the terminal Hilary rushed up and kissed him enthusiastically. "Darling, how are you? I'm glad to see you back safe and sound, the most exciting things have been happening—did you see the review?"

"No," he said. "What review?"

"In the *TLS*. Rudyard Parkinson reviewed your Hazlitt book in the most glowing terms, nearly two whole pages."

"Good Lord," said Philip, feeling himself turning pink with pleasure. "That must be Morris's influence. I'll have to write and thank him."

"I don't think so, darling," said Hilary, "because Parkinson was frightfully rude about Morris's book in the same review. He did you together."

"Oh dear," said Philip, feeling an ignoble spasm of *Schadenfreude* at this news.

"And the *Sunday Times* and the *Observer* have asked for a photograph of you, and Felix Skinner—he's ever so excited about it—says that means they're going to review it too. All I could find was an old snap of you at the seaside in shorts, but I expect they'll only use the head."

"Good Lord," said Philip.

"And I've got something else to tell you. About me."

"What?"

"Let me go and get the car first, while you wait for your luggage."

"I've got something to tell you, too."

"Wait till I get the car."

When she brought the car round to the entrance to the terminal, Hilary offered to move over into the passenger seat, but Philip told her not to bother. She drove rather boisterously, revving the engine hard between gear changes, and pulling up sharply at traffic-lights. As the familiar suburban streets slipped past the windows, she told him her big news. "I've found a job, darling. Well, not a job, exactly, but something I really want to do, something really interesting. I've had a preliminary interview and I'm pretty sure they'll accept me for training."

"What is it, then?" said Philip.

Hilary turned and beamed at him. "Marriage Guidance," she said. "I don't know why I didn't think of it before." She returned her attention to the road, not a moment too soon. "I see," said Philip. "That should be very interesting."

"Absolutely fascinating. I can't wait to start the training." She glanced at him again. "You don't seem very enthusiastic."

"It's a surprise," said Philip. "I wasn't prepared for it. I'm sure you'll be very good at it."

"Well," said Hilary, "I feel I do know something about the subject. I mean, we've had our ups and downs, but we're still together after all these years, aren't we?"

"Yes," said Philip. "We are." He gazed out of the car window at the names of shops: Sketchleys, Rumbelows, Radio Rentals, Woolworths. Plateglass windows stacked with refrigerators, music centres, televisions.

"And what was it you wanted to tell me?" said Hilary.

"Oh, nothing," said Philip. "Nothing important."

PART IV

One

_whhhhheeeeeeeeeeeee_ᴇᴇᴇᴇᴇᴇᴇᴇᴇᴇᴇᴇᴇᴇ_EEEEEEEEEEEEE!_

To some people, there is no noise on earth as exciting as the sound of three or four big-jet engines rising in pitch, as the plane they are sitting in swivels at the end of the runway and, straining against its brakes, prepares for takeoff. The very danger in the situation is inseparable from the exhilaration it yields. You are strapped into your seat now, there is no way back, you have delivered yourself into the power of modern technology. You might as well lie back and enjoy it. _Whhheeeeeeeeeeeeeee_! And away we go, the acceleration like a punch in the small of the back, the grass glimpsed through the window flying backwards in a blur, and then falling out of sight suddenly as we soar into the sky. The plane banks to give us one last glimpse of home, flat and banal, before we break through the cloud cover and into the sunshine, the no-smoking sign goes off with a ping, and a faint clink of bottles from the galley heralds the serving of cocktails. _Whheeeeeeeee_! Europe, here we come! Or Asia, or America, or wherever. It's June, and the conference season is well and truly open. In Oxford and Rummidge, to be sure, the students still sit at their desks in the examination halls, like prisoners in the stocks, but their teachers are able to flit off for a few days before the scripts come in for marking; while in North America the second semester of the academic year is already finished, papers have been graded, credits awarded, and the faculty are free to collect their travel grants and head east, or west, or wherever their fancy takes them. *Wheeeeeeeeee!*

The whole academic world seems to be on the move. Half the passengers on transatlantic flights these days are university teachers. Their luggage is heavier than average, weighed down with books and papers—and bulkier, because their wardrobes must embrace both formal wear and leisure-wear, clothes for attending lectures in, and clothes for going to the beach in, or to the Museum, or the Schloss, or the Duomo, or the Folk Village. For that's the attraction of the conference circuit: it's a way of converting work into play, combining professionalism with tourism, and all at someone else's expense. Write a paper and see the world! I'm Jane Austen—fly me! Or Shakespeare, or T. S. Eliot, or Hazlitt. All tickets to ride, to ride the jumbo jets. *Wheeeeeeeeee!*

The air is thick with the babble of these wandering scholars' voices, their questions, complaints, advice, anecdotes. Which airline did you fly? How many stars does the hotel have? Why isn't the conference hall air-conditioned? Don't eat the salad here, they use human manure on the lettuce. Laker is cheap, but their terminal at LA is the pits. Swissair has excellent food. Cathay Pacific give you free drinks in economy. Pan Am are lousy timekeepers, though not as bad as Jugoslavian Airlines (its acronym JAT stands for "joke about time"). Qantas has the best safety record among the international airlines, and Colombia the worst— one flight in three never arrives at its destination (OK, a slight exaggeration). On every El Al flight there are three secret servicemen with guns concealed in their briefcases, trained to shoot hijackers on sight—when taking something from your inside pocket, do it slowly and smile. Did you hear about the Irishman who tried to hijack a plane to Dublin? It was already going there. *Wheeeeeeeeeeeeeee!*

Hijackings are only one of the hazards of modern travel.

Every summer there is some kind of disruption of the international airways—a strike of French air-traffic controllers, a go-slow by British baggage handlers, a war in the Middle East. This year it's the world-wide grounding of the DC-10, following a crash at Chicago's O'Hare Airport on May 25th, when one of these planes shed an engine on take-off and plunged to the ground, killing everyone on board. The captain's last recorded word was "Damn." Stronger expletives are used by travellers fighting at the counters of travel agencies to transfer their tickets to airlines operating Boeing 747s and Lockheed Tristars; or at having to accept a seat on some slow, clapped-out DC-8 with no movies and blocked toilets, flying to Europe via Newfoundland and Reykjavik. Many conferees arrive at their destinations this summer more than usually fatigued, dehydrated and harassed; the dying fall of the engines' *WHHHEEEeeeee-eeeeeeeee*, as the power is finally switched off, is sweet music to their ears, but their chatter is undiminished, their demand for information insatiable.

How much should you tip? What's the best way to get downtown from the airport? Can you understand the menu? Tip taxis ten percent in Bangladesh, five per cent in Italy; in Mexico it is not necessary, and in Japan the driver will be positively insulted if you do. Narita airport is forty kilometres from downtown Tokyo. There is a fast electric train, but it stops short of the city centre—best take the limousine bus. The Greek word for bus stop is *stasis*. The Polish word for scrambled eggs is *jajecznice*, pronounced "yighyehchneetseh", which is sort of onomatopoeic, if you can get your tongue round it. In Israel, breakfast eggs are served soft-boiled and cold—yuk. In Korea, they eat soup at breakfast. Also at lunch and dinner. In Norway they have dinner at four o'clock in the afternoon, in Spain at ten o'clock at night. In Tokyo the nightclubs close at 11.30 p.m., in Berlin they are only just beginning to open by then.

Oh, the amazing variety of *langue* and *parole*, food and custom, in the countries of the world! But almost equally amazing is the way a shared academic interest will overcome these differences. All over the world, in hotels, university residences and conference centres, in châteaux and villas and country houses, in capital cities and resort towns, beside lakes, among mountains, on the shores of seas cold and warm, people of every colour and nation are gathered together to discuss the novels of Thomas Hardy, or the problem plays of Shakespeare, or the postmodernist short story, or the poetics of Imagism. And, of course, not all the conferences that are going on this summer are concerned with English literature, not by any means. There are at the same time conferences in session on French medieval *chansons* and Spanish poetic drama of the sixteenth century and the German *Sturm und Drang* movement and Serbian folksongs; there are conferences on the dynasties of ancient Crete and the social history of the Scottish Highlands and the foreign policy of Bismarck and the sociology of sport and the economic controversy over monetarism; there are conferences on low-temperature physics and microbiology and oral pathology and quasars and catastrophe theory. Sometimes, when two conferences share the same accommodation, confusions occur: it has been known for a bibliographer specializing in the history of punctuation to sit through the first twenty minutes of a medical paper on "Malfunctions of the Colon" before he realized his mistake.

But on the whole, academic subject groups are self-defining, exclusive entities. Each has its own jargon, pecking order, newsletter, professional association. The members probably meet only once a year—at a conference. Then, what a lot of hallos, howareyous, and whatareyouworkingons, over the drinks, over the meals, between lectures. Let's have a drink, let's have dinner, let's have breakfast together. It's this kind of informal contact, of course, that's the real *raison d'être* of a conference, not the programme of papers and lectures which has ostensibly brought the participants together, but which most of them find intolerably tedious.

Each subject, and each conference devoted to it, is a world unto itself, but they cluster together in galaxies, so that an adept traveller in intellectual space (like, say, Morris Zapp) can hop from one to another, and appear in Amsterdam as a semilogist, in Zürich as a Joycean, and in Vienna as a narratologist. Being a native speaker of English helps, of course, because English has become the international language of literary theory, and theory is what unites all these and many other conferences. This summer the topic on everyone's lips at every conference Morris attends is the UNESCO Chair of Literary Criticism, and who will get it. What kind of theory will be favoured—formalist, structuralist, Marxist or deconstructionist? Or will it go to some sloppily eclectic liberal humanist, or even to an antitheorist like Philip Swallow?

"Philip Swallow?" says Sy Gootblatt incredulously to Morris Zapp. It is the 15th of June, the eve of Bloomsday, halfway through the International James Joyce Symposium in Zürich, and they are standing at the bar of the crowded James Joyce Pub on Pelikanstrasse. It is a beautifully preserved, genuine Dublin pub, all dark mahogany, red plush and brass fittings, rescued from demolition at the hands of Irish property developers, transported in numbered parts to Switzerland, and lovingly reconstructed in the city where the author of *Ulysses* sat out the First World War, and died in the Second. Its ambience is totally authentic apart from the hygienic cleanliness of everything, especially the basement toilets where you could, if you were so inclined, eat your dinner off the tiled floors—very different from the foetid, slimy hellholes to be found at the bottom of such staircases in Dublin. "*Philip Swallow*?" says Sy Gootblatt. "You must be joking." Sy is an old friend of Morris's from Euphoric State, which he left some five years ago to go to Penn, switching his scholarly interests at the same time from Hooker to the more buoyant field of literary theory. He is good-looking in his slight, dark way, and a bit of a dandy, but small in stature; he keeps rising restlessly on the balls of his feet as if to see who is to be seen in the crowded room.

"I hope I'm joking," says Morris, "but somebody sent me a cutting from a London paper the other day which says he's being mentioned as an outsider candidate for the job."

"What are the odds—nine million to one?" says Sy, who remembers Philip Swallow chiefly as the author of a parlour game called Humiliation, with which he wrecked one of his and Bella's dinner parties many years ago. "He hasn't published anything worth talking about, has he?"

"He's having a huge success with a totally brainless book about Hazlitt," says Morris, "Rudyard Parkinson gave it a rave review in the *TLS*. The British are on this great antitheory kick at the moment and Philip's book just makes them roll onto their backs and wave their paws in the air."

"But they tell me Arthur Kingfisher is advising UNESCO on this appointment," says Sy Gootblatt. "And he's surely not going to recommend that they appoint someone hostile to theory?"

"That's what I keep telling myself," says Morris. "But these old guys do funny things. Kingfisher doesn't like to think that there is anyone around now who is as good as he used to be in his prime, and he might encourage the appointment of a schmo like Philip Swallow just to prove it."

Sy Gootblatt drains his glass of Guinness and grimaces. "Jesus, I hate this stuff," he says. "Shall we go someplace else? I found a bar on the other side of the river that sells Budweiser."

Pocketing their James Joyce Pub beermats as souvenirs, they push their way to the door—a proceeding which takes some time, as every few paces one or the other of them bumps into someone he knows. Morris! Sy! Great to see you! How's Bella? How's Désirée? Oh, I didn't know. What are you working on these days? Let's have a drink some time, let's have dinner, let's have breakfast. Eventually they are outside, on the sidewalk, in the mild evening. There are not many people about, but the streets have a safe, sedate air. The shop windows are brightly lit, filled with luxury goods to tempt the rich burghers of Zürich. The Swissair window has a coy display of dumpy little airplanes made out of white flower-heads, suspended from wires in the form of a mobile. They remind Morris of fancy wreaths. "A good name for the DC-10," he observes, "The Flying Wreath."

This black humour reflects his sombre mood. Things have not been going well for Morris lately. First there was the attack on his book by Rudyard Parkinson in the *TLS*. Then his paper did not go down at all well in Amsterdam. A claque of feminists, hired, he would't be surprised to learn, by his ex-wife, heckled him as he developed his analogy between interpretation and striptease, shouting "Cunts are beautiful!" when he delivered the line, *"staring into that orifice we find that we have somehow overshot the goal of our quest."* Young McGarrigle, to whom he might have looked for some support, or at least sympathy, in that crisis, had unaccountably disappeared from Amsterdam, leaving no message. Then there was this report that Philip Swallow was being considered for the UNESCO chair—preposterous, but seeing it in print somehow made it seem disturbingly plausible.

"Who sent you the cutting?" Sy asks.

Morris doesn't know. In fact it was Howard Ringbaum, who spotted the item in the London *Sunday Times* and sent it anonymously to Morris Zapp, guessing correctly that it would cause him pain and anxiety. But who inspired the mention of Philip Swallow's name in the newspaper? Very few people know that is was Jacques Textel, who had received from Rudyard Parkinson a copy of his review article, "The English School of Criticism", together with a fawning covering letter, which Textel, irritated by Parkinson's pompous complacency at Vancouver, had chosen to misinterpret as expressing Parkinson's interest in promoting Philip Swallow's candidacy for the UNESCO chair rather than his own. It was Textel who had leaked Philip's name to his British son-in-law, a journalist on the *Sunday Times*, over lunch in the splendid sixth-floor restaurant at the Place Fontenoy; and the son-in-law, who had been ordered to write a special feature on "The Renaissance of the Redbrick University' and was rather short of facts to support this proposition, had devoted a whole paragraph of his article to the Rummidge professor whose recent book had caused such a stir and whose name was being mentioned in connection with the recently mooted UNESCO Chair of Literary Criticism—causing Rudyard Parkinson to choke on his kedgeree when he opened that particular issue of the *Sunday Times* in the Fellows' breakfast-room at All Saints.

Morris and Sy walk across the bridge over the Limmat. The bar that Sy discovered at lunchtime turns out to be in the middle of the red light quarter at night-time. Licensed prostitutes stand on the street corners, one per corner, in the methodical Swiss way. Each is dressed and made up in an almost theatrical fashion, to cater for different tastes. Here you have the classic whore, in short red skirt, black net stockings and high heels; there, a wholesome Tyrolean girl in dirndl skirt and embroidered bodice; and further on, a kinky model in a skin-tight leather jump suit. All look immaculately clean and polished, like the toilets of the James Joyce Pub. Sy Gootblatt, whose wife Bella is visiting her mother in Maine at this time, eyes these women with covert curiosity. "How much do you think they charge?" he murmurs to Morris.

"Are you crazy? Nobody pays to get laid at a conference."

Morris has a point. It's not surprising, when you reflect: men and women with interests in common—more than most of them have with their spouses—thrown together in exotic surroundings, far from home. For a week or two they are off the leash of domesticity, living a life of unwonted self-indulgence, dropping their towels on the bathroom floor for the hotel maid to pick up, eating in restaurants, drinking in outdoor cafés late into the summer nights, inhaling the aromas of coffee and caporals and cognac and bougainvillea. They are tired, overexcited, a little drunk, reluctant to break up the party and retire to solitary sleep. After a life time of repressing and sublimating libido in the interests of intellectual labour, they seem to have stumbled on that paradise envisioned by the poet Yeats:

> Labour is blossoming or dancing where
> The body is not bruised to pleasure soul,
> Nor beauty born out of its own despair,
> Nor blear-eyed wisdom out of midnight oil.

The soul is pleasured in the lecture theatre and seminar room, and the body in restaurants and night clubs. There need be, apparently, no conflict of interests. You can go on talking shop, about phonetics, or deconstruction, or the pastoral elegy or sprung rhythm, while you are eating and drinking and dancing or even swimming. Academics do amazing things under the shock of this discovery, things their spouses and colleagues back home would not believe:

twist the night away in discothèques, sing themselves hoarse in beer cellars, dance on café tables with flowers gripped in their teeth, go midnight bathing in the nude, patronize fairgrounds and ride the giant roller-coasters, shrieking and clutching each other as they swoop down the shining rails, *whheeeeeeeeeeeee*! No wonder they quite often end up in each other's beds. They are recovering the youth they thought they had sacrificed to learning, they are proving to themselves that they are not dryasdust swots after all, but living, breathing, palpitating human beings, with warm flesh and blood, that stirs and secretes and throbs at a lover's touch. Afterwards, when they are back home, and friends and family ask if they enjoyed the conference, they say, oh yes, but not so much for the papers, which were pretty boring, as for the informal contacts one makes on these occasions.

Of course, these conference affairs are not without their incidental embarrassments. You may, for instance, be sexually attracted to someone whose scholarly work you professionaly disapprove of. At the Vienna conference on Narrative, some weeks after the James Joyce Symposium in Zurich, Fulvia Morgana and Sy Gootblatt find themselves in the same crowd in a wine cellar in Michaelerplatz one evening, catching each other's eyes with increasing frequency across the scored and stained trestle table, as the white wine flows. At a convenient opportunity, Sy slides onto the bench beside Fulvia and introduces himself. In the din of the crowded cellar he only catches her first name, but that is all he needs. Their friendship ripens rapidly. Fulvia is staying at the Bristol, Sy at the Kaiserin Elisabeth. The Bristol having the more stars, they spend the night together there. Not till morning, after a very demanding night, which made Sy think wistfully of the Zürich whores (at least with them you could presumably call the plays yourself) does Sy get hold of Fulvia's second name and identify her as the raving Marxist poststructuralist whose essay on the stream-of-consciousness novel as an instrument of bourgeois hegemony (oppressing the working classes with books they couldn't understand) he has rubbished in a review due to appear in the next issue of *Novel*. Sy spends the rest of the conference sheepishly escorting Fulvia around the Ring, dodging into cafés whenever he sees anyone he knows, and nodding solemnly at Fulvia while she holds forth about the necessity of revolution with her mouth full of *Sachertorte*.

At Heidelberg, Désirée Zapp and Ronald Frobisher find adultery virtually thrust upon them by the social dynamics of the conference on *Rezeptionsästhetik*. The only two creative writers, they find themselves constantly together, partly be mutual choice, since they both feel intimidated by the literary critical jargon of their hosts, which they both think is probably nonsense, but cannot be quite sure, since they do not fully understand it, and anyway they can hardly say so to the faces of those who are paying their expenses, so it is a relief to say so to each other; and partly because the academics, privately bored and disappointed by the contributions of Désirée Zapp and Ronald Frobisher to the conference, increasingly leave them to amuse each other. Siegfried von Turpitz, who invited them both, and might have been expected to concern himself with their entertainment, decided early on that the conference was a failure and after a couple of days discovered that he had urgent business in another European city. So Désirée and Ronald find themselves frequently alone together, walking and talking, walking along the Philosophenweg above the Neckar or rambling through the gardens and on the battlements of the ruined castle, and talking, as professional writers will talk to each other, about money and publishers and agents and sales and subsidiary rights and being blocked. And although not irresistibly attracted to each other, they are not exactly unattracted either, and neither wishes to appear in the eyes of the other timidly afraid of sexual adventure. Each has read the other's work in advance of meeting at the conference, and each has been impressed by the forceful and vivid descriptions of sexual intercourse to be found in those texts, and their common assumption that any encounter between a man and a woman not positively repelled by each other will end up sooner or later in bed. In short, each has attributed to the other a degree of libidinous appetite and experience that is in fact greatly exaggerated, and this mutual misapprehension nudges them closer and closer towards intimacy; until one warm night, a little tipsy after a good dinner at the Weinstube Schloss Heidelberg, with its terrace right inside the courtyard of the floodlit castle, as they totter down the cobbled hill together towards the baroque roofs of the old town, Ronald Frobisher stops in the shadow of an ancient wall, enfolds Désirée in his arms and kisses her.

Then of course there is no way of not going to bed together. Both know the inevitable conclusion of a narrative sequence that begins thus—to draw back from it would imply frigidity or impotence. There is only one consideration that cools Ronald Frobisher's ardour as he lies naked under the sheets of Désirée's hotel bed and waits for her to emerge from the bathroom, and it is not loyalty to Irma (Irma went off sex some years ago, following her hysterectomy, and has intimated that she has no objection to Ronald seeking carnal satisfaction elsewhere, providing it is nothing deeply emotional, and she and her friends never hear about it). Unknown to Ronald, an identical thought is troubling Désirée as she disrobes in the bathroom, performs her ablutions and fits her diaphragm (she has ideological and medical objections to the Pill). Getting into bed beside Ronald in the darkened room, she does not immediately turn to him, nor he to her. They lie on their backs, silent and thoughtful. Désirée decides to broach the matter, and Ronald clears his throat preparatory to doing the same.

{ "I was thinking—"
{ "It occurred to me—"
{ "Sorry."
{ "Sorry."

"What were you going to say?"

"No, please—you first."

"I was going to say," says Désirée, in the darkness, "that before we go any further perhaps we ought to come to an understanding."

"Yes!" says Ronald, eagerly, then changes his intonation to the interrogative: "Yes?"

"What I mean is . . ." Désirée stops. "It's difficult to say without sounding as if I don't trust you."

"It's only natural," says Ronald. "I feel just the same."

"You mean, you don't trust me?"

"I mean there's something I might say to you which might imply that I didn't trust you.'

"What is it?''

"It's . . . hard to say.''

"I mean,'' says Désirée. "I've never done it with a writer before.''

"Exactly!''

"And what I'm trying to say is . . .''

"That you don't want to read about it in a novel one of these days? Or see it on television.''

"How did you guess?''

"I had the same thought.''

Désirée claps her hands. "So we can agree that neither of us will use this as material? Whether it's good or bad?''

"Absolutely. Scout's honour.''

"Then let's fuck, Ronald,'' says Désirée, rolling on top of him.

Whheeeeeeeeeeeeeeeeeee! The spin-drier cycle of Hilary Swallow's washing machine makes a sound not unlike a jetplane, especially when she punches the button to stop the motor, and the piercing whine of the rotating drum dies away, falling in pitch, just like the engines of a jumbo jet when the pilot finally cuts them at the end of a long journey. The similarity does not strike Hilary, as she opens the windowed hatch at the front of the appliance, and lifts out a plaited tangle of damp, compacted clothing, for the sound made by a jet engine is less familiar to her than it is to her husband, who is not present to remark upon the likeness, but is in fact in Greece. Philip's absence is a source of understandable grievance in Hilary, as she hangs out his shirts, pants, vests and socks in the garden, for it seems as if he is only at home these days long enough to empty his suitcase of soiled linen, and pack it with freshly laundered shirts and underwear, before he is off on his travels again.

"Look, I'm sorry,'' Philip had said to her this last time, "but Digby Soames is begging me to go to Greece. I think someone else must have dropped out at the last moment.''

"But why does it have to be you? You've only just come back from Turkey.''

"Yes, I know, but I feel I should help the Council out if I can."

The facts of the matter are different. As soon as he got back from Istanbul, Philip was on the phone to Digby Soames begging him to fix him, Philip, up as soon as possible with another lecture tour, conference, or summer school—anything, as long as it was in south-east Europe. He had already arranged with Joy to meet her in Israel during Morris Zapp's conference on the Future of Criticism, but that wasn't till August, and he felt that he couldn't wait that long to see her again.

"Hmm," said Digby Soames. "It's an awkward time for Europe, the academic year is almost over. You wouldn't be interested in Australia by any chance?"

"No, Australia's too far. Greece would be handy."

"Handy for what?" said Digby Soames suspiciously.

"I'm doing some research on the classical background to English poetry," Philip improvised. "I just want to excuse to go to Greece."

"Well, I'll see what I can do," said Digby Soames.

What he was able to do was to arrange a few lectures in Salonika and Athens. "It won't be a proper specialist tour," he warned. "We'll pay your fares but no subsistence. You'll probably get fees for your lectures, though."

Philip flew to Salonika via Munich, gave his lectures, and met Joy by arrangement in Athens. While Hilary is hanging out the washing in her back garden in St John's Road, Rummidge, Philip and Joy are having a late breakfast on the sunny balcony of their hotel room, with a view of the Acropolis.

"Will your wife divorce you, then?" says Joy, buttering a croissant.

"If I choose the right moment," says Philip. "I went home with every intention of telling her about us, but when she announced that she wanted to be a marriage counsellor, it just seemed too cruel. I thought it might destroy her morale before she's even started. Perhaps they wouldn't even have taken her on. You can imagine what people might say—physician heal thyself, and so on."

Joy bites into her croissant and chews meditatively. "What are your plans?"

"I thought," says Philip, squinting in the sun at the Acropolis, already teeming with tourists like a block of cheese being devoured by black ants, "that we might hire a car and drive to Delphi."

"I don't mean this weekend, idiot, I mean long-term plans. About us."

"Ah," says Philip. "Well, I thought I wouldn't say anything to Hilary until she's well settled into her training for marriage guidance. I think that when she feels she's got a purpose in life, she'll be quite happy to agree to a divorce."

"And then what?"

"Then we get married, of course."

"And settle where? Not Rummidge, presumably."

"I haven't thought that far ahead," says Philip. "I think I could probably get a job somewhere else, America perhaps. My stock has gone up rather surprisingly, you know, just lately. One of the Sundays even mentioned my name in connection with this UNESCO Chair of Literary Criticism."

"Would that be in Paris?" says Joy. "I wouldn't mind living in Paris."

"It can be anywhere you like, apparently," says Philip. "But it's wishful thinking, anyway. They'd never appoint me. I can't think how my name got into the paper."

"You never know," says Joy.

Far away in Darlington, Robin Dempsey has also been reading the Sunday papers.

"HALLO, HOW ARE YOU FEELING TODAY?" says ELIZA.

"TERRIBLE," Robin Dempsey types.

"WHAT EXACTLY DO YOU MEAN BY TERRIBLE?"

"ANGRY. INCREDULOUS. JEALOUS."

"WHAT HAS CAUSED YOU TO HAVE THESE FEELINGS?"

"SOMETHING I READ IN THE NEWSPAPER ABOUT PHILIP SWALLOW."

"TELL ME ABOUT PHILIP SWALLOW."

Robin Dempsey types for twenty-five minutes without stopping, until Josh Collins wanders over from his glass-walled cubicle, nibbling a Kit-Kat, upon which Robin stops typing and covers the computer with its plastic hood.

"Want some?" says Josh, offering a piece of the chocolate-covered biscuit.

"No, thank you," says Robin, without looking at him.

"Getting some interesting stuff from ELIZA, are you?"

"Yes."

"You don't think you're overdoing it?"

"Overdoing what?" says Robin coldly.

"No offence, only you're in here morning, noon and night, talking to that thing."

"It doesn't interfere with you, does it?"

"Well, I have to *be* here."

"You'd be here anyway. You're always here."

"I used to like having the place to myself occasionally," says Josh, going rather red. "To work on my own programs in peace. I don't mind telling you," he continues (it is the longest conversation Josh has ever had with anyone), "that it fair gives me the creeps to see you hunched over that VDU, day in and day out. You're becoming dependent upon it."

"I'm simply doing my research."

"It's called transference. I looked it up in a psychology book."

"Rubbish!" shouts Robin Dempsey.

"If you ask me, you need a proper psychiatrist," says John Collins, trembling with anger. "You're off your trolley. That thing"—he points a quivering finger at ELIZA—"can't really talk, you know. It can't actually *think*. It can't answer questions. It's not a bloody *oracle*."

"I know perfectly well how computers work, thank you," says Robin Dempsey, rising to his feet. "I'll be back after lunch.'

He leaves the room in a somewhat flustered state, omitting to switch off the VDU. Josh Colling lifts up the plastic hood and reads what is written on the screen. He frowns and scratches his nose.

Delphi, like the Acropolis, is crawling with tourists, but the site is proof against their intrusion, as Philip and Joy agree, taking a breather halfway up the steep climb from the road, and looking down on the Sacred Plain far below, where the Pleistos winds through multitudinous olive groves to the Gulf of Corinth.

"It's sublime," she says. "I'm so glad we came."

"Apparently the ancients thought this was the centre of the world," says Philip, consulting his guidebook. "There was a stone on this site called the *omphalos*. The navel of the earth. I suppose that great cleft between the mountains was the vagina."

"You've got a one-track mind," says Joy.

"Is that fair?" says Philip. "Last night I sucked your ten toes, individually."

"There's no need to tell everyone in Delphi," says Joy, blushing charmingly.

"Give me a kiss."

"No, not here. The Greeks don't approve of people kissing in public."

"Not many Greeks about," he comments, which is true enough. The coaches that line the road below them have brought tourists of almost every nation except Greeks. Nevertheless Philip is surprised and somewhat disconcerted to be greeted, in the sanctuary of Apollo, by an elderly lady wearing a broad-brimmed straw hat tied under her chin with a chiffon scarf, and carrying a shooting-stick.

"Sybil Maiden," she reminds him. "I attended the conference you organized at Rummidge."

"Oh, yes," says Philip. "How are you?"

"Very well, thank you. The heat is rather trying, but I have just cooled my brow at the Kastalian spring—most refreshing. This is also a great help." She pulls apart the handles of her shooting stick and, planting the point in a crevice between two ancient blocks of stone, seats herself on the little leather hammock at the top of the implement. "They laughed at me at first. Now everybody on the course wants one."

"What course is that?"

"Literature, Life and Thought in Ancient Greece. We have come from Athens for the day by charabanc—or so I call it, to the intense amusement of my fellow students, most of whom are Americans. They are all at the splendidly preserved stadium, further up the hill, running round the race track.''

"Running? In this heat?'' Joy exclaims.

"Jogging, I believe they call it. It seems to be an epidemic psychological illness afflicting Americans these days. A form of masochism, like the *flagellantes* in the Middle Ages. You are Mrs Swallow, I presume?''

"Yes,'' says Philip.

"No,'' says Joy simultaneously.

Miss Maiden glances sharply from one to the other. "There used to be an inscription on the wall of the temple here, '*Know thyself.*' But they did not deem it necessary to add, '*Know thy wife . . .*' ''

"Joy and I hope to marry one day,'' Philip explains, in some confusion. "My personal life is in a transitional state at the moment. I'd be grateful if you would not mention our meeting here to any mutual acquaintance in England.''

"I am no tittle-tattle, Professor Swallow, I assure you. But I suppose you have to protect your reputation, now you are so much in the public eye. I read a very flattering item about you in one of the Sunday newspapers recently.''

"Oh, that . . . I don't know where the journalist got the idea that I was in the running for the UNESCO chair. It was the first I'd heard of it.''

"Ah yes, the Siege Perilous!'' Miss Maiden holds up a hand to command their attention, and begins to recite in a high, vatic chant:

> "*Oh brother,*
> *In our great hall stood a vacant chair*
> *Fashioned by Merlin ere he passed away,*
> *And carven with strange figures; and in and out*
> *The figures, like a serpent, ran a scroll*
> *Of letters in a tongue no man could read.*
> *And Merlin called it, 'The Siege Perilous,'*
> *Perilous for good and ill; 'for there,' he said,*
> *'No man could sit but he should lose himself.'* ''

Miss Maiden drops her hand, and cocks her head interrogatively in Philip's direction. "Well, Professor Swallow?"

"It sounds like Tennyson," he says. "Is it from 'The Holy Grail', in the *Idylls*?"

"Bravo!" exclaims Miss Maiden. "I respect a man who can recognize a quotation. It's a dying art." She dabs her brow with a dainty pocket handkerchief. "Everybody was talking about this UNESCO chair at Amsterdam recently. A most tedious conference in other respects."

"You seem to travel about the world a great deal, Miss Maiden," Joy observes.

"It keeps me young, my dear. I like to know what's going on in the world of scholarship. Who's in, who's out."

"And who," says Joy impulsively, "do *you* think will get the UNESCO Chair?"

Miss Maiden closes her eyes and seems to sway on the fulcrum of her shooting stick as she considers the question. "The most surprising person," she says in a slurred voice. "It always is in these cases."

Fearing that she is about to faint, Philip steps forward to lend his support, but Miss Maiden suddenly opens her eyes and straightens up. "I think I'll go back to the charabanc," she says. "It's airconditioned. So nice to have met you both."

"Are you sure you can manage the steps on your own?" says Philip.

"Perfectly well, thank you," says Miss Maiden. "Goodbye, goodbye!"

They watch her carefully descend the winding steps towards the road where fleets of sightseeing buses are drawn up.

"Strange old girl," says Philip. "But you've got to admire her spirit."

"The most surprising person could be you," says Joy.

In Darlington, it is a fine summer evening. The raw, unfinished campus looks almost attractive in the mellow evening light, though nothing can make the Computer Centre look other than an ugly prefabricated hut. Through its open windows carry the sounds of summer pursuits, the *pock pock* of tennis balls bandied to and fro on the nearby courts, the occasional cry of *Howzat*? from the playing fields, and the sounds of guitars and harmonicas from an impromptu al fresco singalong down by the artificial lake. The two men inside are, however, oblivious to these noises. One watches the other, who watches a screen. The dialogue represented there reads as follows:

R.D.:   I'M NOT FEELING ANY BETTER.

ELIZA: WHY IS THAT?

R.D.:   THIS BUSINESS ABOUT PHILIP SWALLOW.

ELIZA: TELL ME ABOUT PHILIP SWALLOW.

R.D.:   I ALREADY TOLD YOU ABOUT HIM.

ELIZA: IS THERE ANYTHING YOU WOULD LIKE TO ADD
            TO YOUR PREVIOUS REMARKS?

R.D.   SWALLOW EPITOMIZES THE UNFAIRNESS OF LIFE
            TO ME. AT RUMMIDGE HE GOT THE SENIOR LEC-
            TURESHIP I SHOULD HAVE GOT. THEN HE GOT THE
            CHAIR THERE BY A LUCKY FLUKE. NOW HE'S
            HAVING A GREAT SUCCESS WITH THIS PATHETIC
            BOOK ABOUT HAZLITT.

ELIZA: TELL ME ABOUT HAZLITT.

R.D.:   I'M NOT INTERESTED IN HAZLITT. I HAVEN'T
            EVEN READ SWALLOW'S ROTTEN BOOK. I DON'T
            NEED TO. I SAT THROUGH ENOUGH TEDIOUS EX-
            AMINERS MEETINGS WITH HIM TO KNOW WHAT
            IT'S LIKE. THE IDEA OF HIS BEING A SERIOUS
            CANDIDATE FOR THE UNESCO CHAIR IS PREPOS-
            TEROUS.

ELIZA: I WOULDN'T SAY THAT.

It is this last line of the dialogue that Robin Dempsey has been staring at, transfixed, for the last ten minutes. Its appearance made the hairs on the back of his neck bristle, for it is of an entirely different order from anything ELIZA has produced until now: not a question, not a request, not a statement about something already mentioned in the discourse, but an expression of *opinion*. How can ELIZA have opinions? How can she know anything about the UNESCO Chair that Robin doesn't know, or hasn't told her? Robin is almost afraid to ask. At last, slowly and hesitantly, he types:

            WHAT DO YOU KNOW ABOUT IT?

Instantly ELIZA replies:

> MORE THAN YOU THINK.

Robin turns pale, then red. He types:

> ALL RIGHT, IF YOU'RE SO CLEVER, TELL ME WHO
> WILL GET THE UNESCO CHAIR

The screen remains blank. Robin smiles and relaxes. Then he realizes that he has forgotten to indicate the end of his message with a punctuation mark. He presses the period key. On the screen, the letters rippling from left to right faster than thought, appears a name:

> PHILIP SWALLOW.

Robin Dempsey's chair keels over and crashes to the floor as he starts to his feet and staggers backwards, staring aghast at the screen. His face is ashen. Josh Collins comes out of his glass cubicle.

"Anything wrong?"

But Dempsey stumbles past him, out of the building, without a word, his eyes fixed, like a man walking in his sleep. John Collins watches him leave, then goes across to the computer terminal, and reads what is written there. If Josh Collins ever smiled, one might say he was smiling to himself.

After the Joyce Conference in Zürich, Morris returns to his luxurious nest on the shores of Lake Como. The days pass pleasantly. In the mornings he reads and writes; in the afternoons he takes a siesta, and deals with correspondence until the sun has lost some of its heat. Then it is time for a jog through the woods, a shower, a drink before dinner, and a game of poker or backgammon afterwards in the drawing-room. He retires early to bed, where he falls to sleep listening to rock music on his transistor radio. It is a restful, civilized régime. Only his correspondence keeps him conscious of the anxieties, desires and conflicts of the real world.

There is, for instance, a letter from Désirée's lawyers requesting a reply to their previous communication concerning college tuition fees for the twins, and a letter from Désirée herself threatening to visit him at the Rockefeller villa and make a public scene if he doesn't come through with the money pretty damn quick. It seems that she is in Europe for the summer: the letter is postmarked Heidelberg—uncomfortably close. There is another letter from his own lawyer advising him to pay up. Grudgingly, Morris complies. There is a cable, reply paid, from Rodney Wainwright, begging for another extension of the deadline for the submission of his paper for the Jerusalem conference. Morris cables back, "BRING FINISHED PAPER WITH YOU TO CONFERENCE" since it is too late now to strike Rodney Wainwright from the programme.

There is a letter, handwritten on Rummidge English Department notepaper, from Philip Swallow, confirming his acceptance of Morris's invitation to participate in the Jerusalem conference, and asking if he can bring a "friend" with him.

> *"You'll never guess who it is. You remember Joy, the woman I told you about, whom I met in Genoa, and thought was dead? Well, she wasn't killed in that plane crash after all—she wasn't on the plane, though her husband was. I met her by chance in Turkey, and we're madly in love with each other. Hilary doesn't know yet. When the time is right, I'll ask Hilary for a divorce. I think you know our marriage has been a lost cause for quite some time. Meanwhile, Jerusalem would be an ideal opportunity for Joy and I to get together. Naturally I will pay for her accommodation. (Please reserve us a double room at the Hilton.)"*

This missive gives Morris no pleasure at all. "Madly in love," forsooth! Is this language appropriate to a man in his fiftieth year? Hasn't he learned by now that this whole business of being "in love" is not an existential reality, but a form of cultural production, an illusion produced by the mutual reflections of a million rose-tinted mirrors: love poems, pop songs, movie images, agony columns, shampoo ads, romantic novels? Apparently not. The letter reads like the effusion of some infatuated teenager. Morris will not admit to himself that there may be a trace of envy in his harsh assessment. He prefers to identify his response as righteous indignation at being more or less compelled to collude in the deception of Hilary. For a man who claims to believe in the morally improving effects of reading great literature, Philip Swallow (it seems to Morris) takes his marriage vows pretty lightly.

There is a brief letter from Arthur Kingfisher, courteously acknowledging Morris's last and enclosing a xerox copy of his keynote address to the Chicago conference on the Crisis of the Sign. Morris immediately fires back a reply asking if Arthur Kingfisher could by any chance contemplate taking part in the Jerusalem conference on the Future of Criticism. Morris is convinced that if he can only get Arthur Kingfisher to himself for a week or so, he will be able to cajole, wheedle and flatter the old guy into seeing his own irresistible eligibility for the UNESCO chair. He spends a whole day in the composition of this letter, emphasizing the exclusiveness of the conference, a small group of select scholars, not so much a conference as a symposium, setting out the attractions of the Jerusalem Hilton as a venue, alluding delicately to Arthur Kingfisher's half-Jewish ethnic origins, and drawing attention to the many optional sight-seeing expeditions that have been arranged for the participants. Recalling that Fulvia Morgana had mentioned that at Chicago Arthur Kingfisher was inseparable from a beautiful Asian chick, Morris makes it clear that the invitation to Jerusalem includes any companion he cares to bring with him. As a final incentive he hints that the conference might run to a Concorde flight for the transatlantic leg of the journey, having checked this out first by a long-distance phone call to his Israeli friend Sam Singerman, who is co-organizer of the conference, and has raised the financial backing for it from a British supermarket chain whose Zionist chairman has been persuaded that the event will enhance Israel's international cultural prestige. "There'll be no problem about getting Kingfisher's fare," Sam assures Morris. "We can have as much money as we want. The only condition is that we've got to call it the Pricewize International Symposium on the Future of Criticism."

"That's all right," says Morris. "We can live with that. As long as we don't have to give Green Stamps with every

lecture.'' He addresses and seals the letter to Arthur Kingfisher, and goes out on to the balcony of his room to stretch
his limbs. It is late afternoon, and a hazy golden light falls
on the mountains and the lake. Time for his jog.

Morris changes into his red silk running shorts and
Euphoric State sweatshirt and Adidas training shoes, and
drops his letter into the mail box in the hall on his way out
of the villa. Some other residents sunning themselves on the
terrace smile and wave as he trots briskly through the villa
gardens. As soon as he is out of sight, he slows to a more
deliberate pace. Even so, the sweat pours from his brow and
the loudest noise he can hear is the rasp of his own
breathing. His footsteps are muffled by the dead pine nee-
dles that carpet the footpath. He always takes the same
route—a mile-long circuit through the woods, uphill from
the villa, downhill coming back, which usually takes him
about thirty-five minutes. He is determined one day to do
the whole thing without stopping, but this evening, as usual,
he is obliged to stop at the top of the incline about halfway
round, to recover his breath. He leans against a tree, his
chest heaving, looking up through the branches above his
head to the hazy blue of the sky.

Then everything goes black.

Two

whhhhhhhhhhhhhhhhhhhheeeeeeeee!

The wind whistled softly through the reeds at the edge of Lough Gill. Persse McGarrigle squinted anxiously at the sky. Overhead it was as blue as his own eyes, but the horizon looked ominously dark. The students of the Celtic Twilight Summer School, two days out from their base at Limerick on a literary sight-seeing tour, did not, however, look so far. They were in ecstasies at the sunlight glinting on the ruffled waters of the lake, the reeds bowing gracefully in the breeze, the green hills encircling the lough, and the purple, whaleshaped outline of Ben Bulben in the background. Mostly middle-aged Americans, collecting credits for their part-time degree courses back home or combining a European vacation with cultural self-improvement, they jumped down from the bus with cries of delight, and waddled up and down the shore, clicking and whirring with their cameras, watched indulgently by a cluster of Sligo boatmen wearing waders and filthy, tattered Aran sweaters. Rocking gently beside a little wooden jetty were three weathered-looking rowing boats which had been hired to take the students across to the Lake Isle of Innisfree, subject of W. B. Yeats's most frequently anthologized poem.

" '*I will arise and go now, and go to Innisfree,*' " an overweight matron in tartan Bermuda shorts and dayglo pink tee-shirt recited aloud in the accents of Brooklyn, with a knowing smile in Persse's direction. For the past two summers Persse had acted as tutor on this course, directed by Professor McCreedy, and being at a loose end since his disillusioning experience in Amsterdam, had agreed to do so again this summer. "*And a small cabin build there, of clay and wattles made.*' Do we get to see the cabin, Mr McGarrigle?"

"I don't think Yeats actually got around to building it, Mrs Finklepearl," said Persse. "It was more of a dream than a reality. Like most of our dearest ambitions."

"Oh, don't say that, Mr McGarrigle. I believe in looking at the bright side of everything."

"Are we going in those little boats?"

Persse turned to face the addresser of this question with surprise and even pleasure, for it was the first word he had spoken in Persse's hearing since the summer school began.

"It's not far, Mr Maxwell."

"They don't even have motors."

"The men are very strong rowers," Persse assured him. But Mr Maxwell relapsed into gloomy silence. He was dressed more formally than most of the party, in herringbone sports jacket and worsted trousers, and wore the kind of sunglasses that went darker and lighter according to circumstances. In the bright dazzle off the lake, his eyes were two opaque black discs. Maxwell was a bit of a mystery man—a teacher at some small Baptist college in the Deep South, who gave the impression in seminars that the level of discussion was too jejune to tempt his participation, and was consequently feared and disliked by the other students.

'You're not gonna chicken out of the boat-ride, are you, Mr Maxwell?" Mrs Finklepearl taunted him.

"I can't swim," he said shortly.

"Me neither!" cried Mrs Finklepearl. "But nuttin' is gonna stop me going to the Lake Isle of Innisfree. '*Nine bean-rows will I have there, a hive for the honey-bee.*' I think I'll just get my zipper from the bus, though. This breeze is kinda chilly.''

Persse encouraged her to do so, in spite of knowing that this garment was made of scarlet and lime-green nylon, with royal blue piping. He strolled over to the group of boatmen. "Shouldn't there be four boats?" he enquired.

"Paddy Malone's boat is holed," said one of the men. "But sure we'll manage fine with the three. They can all squeeze in."

"What about the weather?" said Persse, surveying the sky again. "It's very dark over to the west."

"The weather will hold for another two hours," he was assured. "As long as you can see Ben Bulben, you've no need to worry." This advice was hardly disinterested, as Persse well knew, for the boatmen stood to lose half their fee, not to mention tips, if the trip were cancelled. But his misgivings were overruled by Professor McCreedy, who was afraid of disappointing the students. "Let us not delay, however," he urged. "Round them up and get them into the boats."

So into the boats they got, amid much laughter and shouted advice and badinage, the ungainly American matrons in their gaudy windcheaters and plastic peeptoe sandals clambering into the rowboats held steady by the grinning boatmen standing in the shallow water. Persse found himself in the prow of his boat with knees pressed against Maxwell's, sitting opposite. There were thirty-six people in the party—twelve to a boat, plus two oarsmen. It was too many. The boats were low in the water—Persse could touch its surface without stretching.

At first, all went well. The oarsmen pulled strongly, and a kind of race developed between the boats, each group urging on its crew. The wavelets dashing against the bows caused only a slight, rather agreeable spray to sprinkle the passengers. But then, as the shore receded and flattened behind them, and the low outline of the Isle of Innisfree rose in front of them, the light seemed to thicken and the wind grew stronger. Persse anxiously surveyed the horizon, which was much nearer than it had been earlier. He could no longer see Ben Bulben. The sun disappeared behind a dark cloud and the colour of the water changed instantly from blue to black, flecked with whitecaps. The boats began to pitch and toss, and to ship large dollops of cold water, causing the passengers to utter shrill cries of alarm and distress. Persse, sitting at the prow, was soon soaked to his skin.

"Better turn back!" he shouted to the two oarsmen in his boat.

One of them shook his head. "Can't risk turning in this squall," he cried. "We're over halfway there, anyhow."

The island, however, still looked dismally distant, shrouded by a shower of rain that swept rapidly towards them across the intervening water, and passed over the boats like a whiplash, stinging the faces of the passengers. They were all so wet now that they no longer bothered to complain when a wave slopped over the side. Their silence was an indication of how frightened they all were, gripping the gunwales, up to their ankles in water, watching the faces of the two oarsmen for reassurance. These two rowed grimly on in the teeth of the wind, their task made harder by the weight of water in the boat. There was no bailing implement aboard, though one or two passengers made feeble efforts to improvise with their shoes and sunhats.

Whether it was because their craft was leakier than the others, or its load heavier, or the oarsmen weaker, Persse observed that their boat was falling behind the other two. Mrs Finklepearl, her eyes closed, was crooning the words of "The Lake Isle of Innisfree" to herself, like a prayer or mantra:

> *'And I shall have some peace there, for peace comes dropping slow,*
> *Dropping from the veils of morning to where the cricket sings . . .'*

A particularly big wave broke over the bow and the recitation ended abruptly in a gurgle and a sob. Maxwell's lenses had turned transparent in the murky light and his pale grey eyes were eloquent of pure terror. He clutched at Persse's arm with a grip as tight as the Ancient Mariner's. "Are we sinking?" he screeched.

"No, no," said Persse. "We're fine. Safe as houses."

But his voice lacked conviction. The boat was dangerously low in the water—indeed it was beginning to look more like a bath than a boat. The veins stood out on the foreheads of the rowers, and their oars seemed almost to bend under the strain of keeping the waterlogged vessel in motion. The island was still more than a hundred yards away. The oarsmen looked at each other meaningfully and rested their oars. One called out to Persse, "I fear she's taken too much water, sir."

"I told you—we're sinking!" screamed Maxwell, clutching Persse still more tightly. "Save me!"

"For God's sake, control yourself man," protested Persse, struggling to free himself from the other's frantic grip.

"But I can't swim! I'll drown! Where are the other boats? Help! Help!"

"Can you only think of saving your own skin?" Persse exclaimed indignantly. "What about the ladies here?"

"You mustn't let me drown. I have a great sin on my conscience." Maxwell's face was contorted with fear and guilt. "This storm is God's judgment upon me."

"He's being very unfair to the rest of us, then," Persse snapped, peering through the rain at the shore of the island, which the other two boats seemed to have reached safely. "Let's shout 'Help' all together, ladies and gentlemen," he urged, to keep their spirits up. "One-two-three . . ."

"*Help!*" they all shouted in ragged chorus, all except Maxwell, who seemed to have abandoned hope. "Yes, it's God's judgment," he moaned. "To drown me in a lake in Sligo, the very place where I deceived the poor girl. I didn't know we'd be coming here when I signed up for the course."

"What girl was that?" said Persse.

"She was a chambermaid," sniffed Maxwell, tears or rain or lakewater running down his face and dripping from his nose. "In a hotel I was staying at, years ago, for the Yeats Summer School. My doctoral dissertation was on Celtic mythology in the early poems."

"The devil take your doctoral dissertation!" cried Persse. "What was the girl's name?"

":She was called Bernadette. I don't remember her second name."

"McGarrigle," said Persse. "The same as mine."

Maxwell's grip on Persse suddenly relaxed. He stared incredulously. "That's right. It *was* McGarrigle. How did you know?"

At that moment the boat slowly sank beneath them to the accompaniment of piteous cries from the rest of the passengers, who soon, however, found that they were floundering in only two feet of water, their vessel having fortunately drifted over a sandbank. The other boatmen waded out from the shore to carry the more elderly and infirm survivors of this shipwreck to dry land. Persse was obliged to carry Maxwell, who had flung his arms round Persse's neck as the boat went down, and refused to unclasp them.

"I've a good mind to hold your head under the water and drown you after all," Persse growled. "But drowning's too good for you. You ruined my cousin's life. Getting her with child and then deserting her."

"I'll make it up to her," whimpered Maxwell. "I'll marry her if you like."

"Huh, she wouldn't want to marry a spalpeen like yourself," said Persse.

"I'll make restitution. I'll make a settlement on her and the child."

"That's more like it," said Persse. "We'll have that put in writing by a Sligo solicitor tomorrow morning. Signed and sealed. I'll undertake to deliver it."

Two days later, Persse flew from Dublin to Heathrow, carrying in his pocket a copy of the legal document, now lodged with a Sligo solicitor, in which Professor Sidney Maxwell, of Covenant College, Atlanta, Georgia, admitted paternity of Bernadette McGarrigle's son, Fergus, and guaranteed her an annual allowance that would be sufficient to permit her to retire from her present employment. Professor McCreedy had granted Persse twenty-four hours' leave from the summer school, and it was his intention to seek another interview with Mrs Gasgoine, to ask her for Bernadette's address, or to forward his message. But when he got to the building in Soho Square, he found the office he had visited before occupied by a travel agency. "Girls Unlimited?" said the receptionist. "No, I never heard of it, but then I've only been here a couple of weeks. Gentlemen looking for Girls Unlimited, Doreen, know anything about it? No, she don't either. You could try the video place on the ground floor." Persse tried the video place on the ground floor but they seemed to suspect him of being a policeman: first they offered him a bribe, and when he asked what it was for, they told him to get lost. Nobody in the entire building would admit to having known that Girls Unlimited ever existed, let alone its present whereabouts. Persse could think of nothing to do but return to Ireland and try advertising in newspapers, or perhaps show-business trade magazines.

He travelled back to Heathrow on the tube in a despondent mood, not only on account of his frustration over Bernadette, but because the journey had revived memories of Angelica. Not that she had been out of his mind for more than five minutes at a time all summer. The petition he had left in St George's chapel on his last visit had not been answered—not the part that pertained to himself anyhow. "Dear God, let me forget Angelica." Would he ever forget that exquisite face and form? The dark hair falling in shining waves about her neck and shoulders at the Rummidge sherry party, or streaming on the wind as she spurned the footpath under her running shoes; her peat-dark eyes gravely attentive in the lecture-room, or dreamily enchanted by his snow poem under the moon? Or glazed and vacant in the obscene photograph outside the Blue Heaven? Persse shook his head irritably at that last image, angry that he had allowed it to rise into his consciousness, as he stepped off the train at Heathrow.

He discovered that he had a two-hour wait till the next plane to Dublin. A sign "To St George's Chapel" caught his eye, and for want of anything better to do, he followed it. This time it led him not to the airport laundry, but the bunker of liver-coloured brick beneath the black wooden cross. He pushed through the swing doors and descended the stairs to the hushed chapel below the ground.

His petition was still there, pinned to the green baize

noticeboard: *"Dear God, let me forget Angelica. Lead her from the life that degrades her."* But it had been annotated in a minute italic hand that Persse knew well—so well that his heart stopped beating for a moment, his lungs bulged with trapped breath, his vision blurred and he almost swooned.

"Appearances can be misleading. Vide F.Q. II. xii. 66."

Persse recovered his balance, snatched the paper from the noticeboard, and ran with it to the nearest terminal building. He knocked aside protesting travellers in his eagerness to get to the bookstall. Did they have a copy of *The Faerie Queene* by Sir Edmund Spenser? No, they did not. Not even the Penguin edition? Not in any edition. Did they not realize that *The Faerie Queene* was one of the jewels in the crown of English poetry? There was not much call for poetry at Heathrow. Sir could, if sir wished, try the other bookstalls in the airport, but his chances of success were slim. Persse ran from terminal to terminal, from bookstall to bookstall, loudly demanding a copy of *The Faerie Queene*. One assistant offered him Enid Blyton, another the latest issue of *Gay News*. He thrust his fingers through his curly hair in frustration. Obviously there was only one thing to do: go back to central London, where the bookshops would still, with any luck, be open.

As he hurried towards the exit of Terminal One with this intention, he was accosted by an eager female voice.

"Hallo there!"

Persse recognized Cheryl Summerbee, sitting on a stool behind a British Airways Information desk. He stopped and retraced his steps. "Hallo. How are you?" he said.

"Bored. I prefer working on check-in, especially when it's Terminal Three—that's long-haul flights. There's more . . . scope. You're not wearing that lovely hat."

"Hat? Oh, you mean Professor Zapp's deerstalker. It's too warm for that."

"Are you over here for long?"

"No, just for the day. I'm going straight back to Ireland tonight. There's a summer school I've got to meet up with in Galway tomorrow."

Cheryl sighed wistfully. "I'd love to go to the west of Ireland. Is it very beautiful?"

"It is. Especially Connemara. I rented a cottage there these last few months ... Look, Cheryl, I'd love to chat with you, but the fact is that I'm in a tearing hurry. I have to get back to London before the bookshops close."

"What book was it you wanted?"

"Oh, it's a book of poetry—a long poem called *The Faerie Queene*. I want to look up a reference very urgently."

"No problem," said Cheryl; and to Persse's astonishment she reached under the counter and pulled out a thick library edition of *The Faerie Queene*.

"God love you!" he exclaimed. "That's what I call service! I'll write to British Airways. I'll get you promoted."

"I shouldn't do that," said Cheryl. "It's my own book, for reading at slack times. We're not supposed to."

Persse, searching his pockets for the piece of paper with the reference on it, glanced at Cheryl with surprise. "*Your* book? I thought you went more for the Bills and Moon type of romance." He seemed to have lost the precious bit of paper. Damn.

"I used to," Cheryl agreed. "But I've grown out of that sort of book. They're all rubbish really, aren't they? Read one and you've read them all."

"Is that right?" Persse murmured abstractedly. He tried to recall the details of the reference written in Angelica's neat italic script. It was stanza sixty-something, and he was fairly sure that it was Book Two—but which canto? He riffled his way through each canto of Book Two, while Cheryl prattled on.

"I mean, they're not really romances at all, are they? Not in the true sense of romance. They're just debased versions of the sentimental novel of courtship and marriage that started with Richardson's *Pamela*. A realistic setting, an ordinary heroine that the reader can identify with, a simple plot about finding a husband, endless worrying about how far you should go with a man before marriage. Titillating but moral."

"Mmm, mmm," Persse muttered absently, flicking the pages of *The Faerie Queene* with moistened fingers.

"Real romance is a pre-novelistic kind of narrative. It's full of adventure and coincidence and surprises and marvels, and has lots of characters who are lost or enchanted or wandering about looking for each other, or for the Grail, or something like that. Of course, they're often in love too..."

"Ah!" Persse exclaimed, coming upon the episode of the Bower of Blisse, for he remembered Angelica mentioning to Morris Zapp the two girls whom Sir Guyon sees bathing in the fountain. His eyes zoomed in on stanza 66, and two words leapt off the page at him:

> *The wanton Maidens him espying stood*
> *Gazing a while at his unwonted guise;*
> *Then th'one her selfe low ducked in the flood*
> *Abash't that her a straunger did avise:*
> *But th'other rather higher did arise,*
> *And her two lily paps aloft displayed,*
> *And all, that might his melting hart entise*
> *To her delights, she unto him bewrayd:*
> *The rest hid underneath, him more desirous made.*

"Lily Papps!" Persse shouted joyfully. "There are two girls, not one. Lily and Angelica! They must be sisters—twins. A modest one and a bold one." He leaned across the counter and, cupping Cheryl's head between his two hands, stifled her still-continuing monologue with a smacking kiss.

"God bless you, Cheryl!" he said fervently. "For being in the right place at the right time with the right book. This is a great day for me, I can tell you."

Cheryl blushed deeply. Her squint increased and she seemed to experience some difficulty in breathing. In spite of these symptoms of stress, she managed to complete the sentence on which she was embarked before Persse interrupted her:

"... in psychoanalytical terms, romance is the quest of a libido or desiring self for a fulfilment that will deliver it from the anxieties of reality but will still contain that reality. Would you agree with that?"

Persse now registered a long-overdue astonishment. He stared into Cheryl's eyes, which were a remarkably pretty shade of blue. "Cheryl—have you been going to night-school since I first met you?"

Cheryl blushed even more deeply, and dropped her eyes. "No," she said huskily.

"You're never telling me that those are your own ideas about romance and the sentimental novel and the desiring self?"

"The desiring self is Northrop Frye," she admitted.

"*You* have read Northrop *Frye*?" his voice rose in pitch like a jet engine.

"Well, not read, exactly. Somebody told me about it."

"Somebody? Who?" Persse felt a fresh quickening of inner excitement, the premonitory vibrations of another discovery. Who in the world was most likely to engage airline staff in casual conversation about the generic characteristics of romance?

"A customer. Her flight was delayed and we got chatting. She noticed I was reading a Bills and Moon romance under the counter, and she said what are you reading that rubbish for, well, not in so many words, she wasn't rude about it, but she started to tell me about the old romances, and how much more exciting and interesting they were. So I got her to write down the names of some books for me, to get from the library. *The Faerie Queene* was one of them. To be honest, I'm not getting on with it very well. I preferred *Orlando Furioso,* it's more amusing. She knew ever such a lot about books. I think she was in the same line of business as you."

Persse had scarcely dared to breathe in the course of this narrative. "A young woman, was she?" he said coaxingly.

"Yes, dark, good-looking, lovely long hair. A foreign sort of name, though you wouldn't have said so to hear her speak."

"Pabst, was it—the name?"

It was Cheryl's turn to look astonished. "That's right, it was."

"When was it that you were talking to her?"

"Just the other day. Monday."

"Do you remember where she was going?"

"She was flying to Geneva, but she said she was going on to Lausanne. Do you know her then?"

"Know her? I love her!" Persse exclaimed. "When is the next plane to Geneva?"

"I don't know," said Cheryl, who had now gone very pale.

"Look it up for me, there's a good girl. She didn't happen to mention where she was staying in Lausanne? The name of a hotel?"

Cheryl shook her head. It seemed to take her a long time to find the flight information. "Come on, Cheryl, you found *The Faerie Queene* for me quicker than this," Persse teased. Then to his astonishment, a tear rolled down her cheek and splashed on to the page of the open timetable. "What's the matter, for the love of God?"

Cheryl blew her nose on a paper tissue, straightened her shoulders and smiled at him professionally. "Nothing," she said. "Our next flight to Geneva is at 19.30. But there's a Swissair flight at 15.45 which you might catch if you run."

He ran.

Persse had scarcely recovered his breath before the Swissair Boeing 727 was airborne. He blessed the impulse that had made him apply for the American Express card, which made flying almost as simple as catching a bus. He could recall the elaborate preparations for his first flight, not so many years ago, from Dublin to Heathrow, entailing the withdrawal of a thick roll of banknotes from his Post Office savings account, and the paying over of the same across the counter of the Aer Lingus office in O'Connell Street weeks before the date of his departure. Now he had only to wave the little green and white plastic rectangle in the air to be wafted to Switzerland at five minutes' notice.

At Geneva airport, Persse changed the money he had on him into francs, and took the bus into the centre of the city, where he transferred immediately onto an electric train to Lausanne. It was a warm, breathless evening. The train ran out along the shores of the lake, its surface smooth and pearl-pink, like stretched satin, in the glow of the setting sun, which struck rosily on the peaks of distant mountains on the other side of the water. Fatigued by the long day's travelling, and all its emotional excitements, rocked gently by the swaying motion of the train, Persse fell asleep.

He woke suddenly to find the train halted on the outskirts of a large town. It was quite dark, and there was a full moon reflected on the surface of Lac Léman, some distance below the railway track. Persse had no idea where he was, and his compartment was empty of other passengers whom he might have asked. After about five minutes, the train moved slowly forward and pulled into a station. Loudspeakers whispered the name, "*Lausanne, Lausanne.*" He alighted, apparently the only person to do so, and climbed the steps to the station entrance. He paused in its colonnaded portico for a moment to take his bearings. Before him was a forecourt, with taxis drawn up. A driver cocked an interrogative eyebrow. Persse shook his head. He would have a better chance of spotting Angelica, or being spotted by her, if he explored the town on foot.

There was an air of excitement and gaiety on the streets of Lausanne this evening that surprised Persse, who had always thought of the Swiss as a rather disciplined and decorous people. The pavements were thronged with strollers, many of whom were dressed rather theatrically in the fashions of yesteryear. An early twenties' look seemed to be all the rage in Lausanne this season: tailored, long-skirted costumes for the women, suits with waistcoats and small, narrow lapels for the men. Smiling faces turned outwards from café terraces beneath strings of coloured lights. Hands pointed and waved. A babble of multi-lingual conversation rose from the tables and mingled with the remarks of the parading pedestrians, so that to Persse's ears, pricked for a possible greeting from Angelica, the effect was rather like that of twisting the tuning knob of a powerful radio set at random, picking up snatches of one foreign station after another. "*Bin gar keine Russin, stamm' aus Litauen, echt deutsch . . . Et O ces voix d'enfants, chantant dans la coupole! . . . Poi s' ascose nel foco che gli affina . . .*" Though he was a poor linguist, and spoke only English and Irish with any fluency, these fragments of speech seemed strangely familiar to Persse's ears, as did the words of a song carrying from an open casement, rendered in an operatic tenor:

> *Frisch weht der Wind*
> *Der Heimat zu*
> *Mein Irisch Kind,*
> *Wo weilest du?*

Persse stopped under the window to listen. Somewhere in the neighbouring streets, a clock struck nine, with a dead sound on the final stroke, though by Persse's watch it was twenty-five minutes past the hour. A woman in long skirts, hanging on the arm of a man wearing a silk hat and opera cloak, brushed past him saying to her escort, "And when we were children, staying at the archduke, my cousin's, he took me out on a sled, and I was frightened." Persse wheeled round and stared after the couple, wondering if he was dreaming or delirious. A young man thrust a card into his hand: "*Madame Sosostris, Clairvoyante. Horoscope and Tarot. The Wisest Woman in Europe.*"

"Stetson!"

Persse looked up from his dazed inspection of the card to see a man dressed in the uniform of an officer in the First World War, Sam Browne and puttees, bearing down upon him, swagger-stick raised. "You who were with me in the ships at Mylae! That corpse you planted last year in your garden, has it begun to sprout?" Persse backed away in alarm. A group of people in a nearby beergarden, dressed in modern casual clothes, laughed and applauded. The madman in uniform rushed past Persse and lost himself in the crowd. Soon Persse heard him accosting someone else, crying "Stetson!" The clock struck nine again. A line of men dressed in identical striped business suits and bowler hats, and clasping rolled umbrellas, marched in step along the pavement, each man with his eyes fixed on the ground before his feet. They were followed by a laughing, jolly crowd of revellers in jeans and summer frocks who carried the bewildered Persse along with them until he found himself back near the station again. He saw a neon sign, "English Pub," and made towards it, but the place was so crowded that he couldn't even squeeze through the door. A poster

outside announced: "Beer at 1922 prices tonight, 8–10."
From within came, every few minutes, a gruff exclamation,
"HURRY UP PLEASE IT'S TIME!" followed by the groans and
pleas of those still waiting to be served. Persse felt the
pressure of a hand on his shoulder, and turned to confront a
brown, leathery countenance, hooded eyes and a reptilian
smile.

"Professor Tardieu!" he exclaimed, glad to see a familiar
face, even this one.

The other shook his head, still smiling. *"Je m'appelle
Eugenides,"* he said. *"Négotiant de Smyrne. Goûtez la
marchandise, je vous prie."* He withdrew his hand from his
jacket pocket and offered on his open palm a few shrivelled
currants.

"For the love of God," Persse pleaded, "tell me what is
going on here."

"I believe it is called street-theatre," said Tardieu, in his
immaculate English. "But you must have read about it in
the conference programme?"

"What conference?" said Persse. "I've only just arrived
here."

Tardieu stared at him for a moment, then burst into
prolonged laughter.

At Tardieu's suggestion, they took the funicular down to the
little port of Ouchy, and shared a snack of *perches du lac*
and dry white wine outside a harbourside tavern. From the
bar inside came the pleasant whining of a mandoline—for
the "Waste Land" happening extended this far.

"Every three years, the *T. S. Eliot Newsletter* organizes
an international conference on the poet's work in some
place with which he was associated," Tardieu explained.
"St Louis, London, Cambridge Mass.—last time it was
East Coker. I'm afraid we rather overwhelmed that charming little village. This year it is the turn of Lausanne. As you
undoubtedly know, Eliot composed the first draft of *The
Waste Land* here while recovering from a nervous breakdown in the winter of 1921–2."

" 'By the waters of Léman I sat down and wept.' " Persse
quoted.

"Just so. My own belief is that the crisis was precipitated by the poet's inability to accept his latent homosexuality . . . In principle I disapprove of this kind of insistence on the biographical origins of the literary text, but I was persuaded by some friends here to take in the conference on my way back from Vienna, and I must admit that the idea of acting out *The Waste Land* on the streets of Lausanne was very imaginative. Most diverting."

"Who are the performers?" asked Persse.

"Mostly students at the University here, with the addition of a few volunteers from among the conferees, like myself—and Fulvia Morgana over there." Michel Tardieu nodded in the direction of a tawny-haired, Roman-nosed lady in a clinging, sequin-studded black dress, sitting at a table with a small, slight, Jewish-looking man. " 'Belladonna, the Lady of Situations.' The man is Professor Gootblatt of Penn. He looks as if he wishes he were elsewhere, don't you think?"

The name "Fulvia" made Persse, for a reason he could not for the moment identify, think of Morris Zapp.

"Is Morris Zapp at this conference?"

"No. He was expected at the Vienna conference on Narrative last week, but he did not arrive. He was the subject of a narrative retardation as yet unexplained," said Tardieu. "But you, young man, what are you doing in Lausanne, if you did not know about the conference?"

"I'm looking for a girl."

"Ah, yes, I remember." Tardieu sighed reminiscently. "That was the trouble with my research assistant, Albert. He was always looking for a girl. Any girl, in his case. The ungrateful boy—I had to let him go. But I miss him."

"The girl I'm looking for must be at this conference," said Persse. "Where is it being held? What time is the first session tomorrow?"

"*Mais, c'est finie!*" Tardieu exclaimed. "The conference is over. The street theatre was the closing event. Tomorrow we all disperse."

"What!" Persse jumped to his feet, dismayed. "Then I must start looking for her at once. Where can I get a list of all the hotels in Lausanne?"

"But there are hundreds, my friend. You will never find her that way. What is the young lady's name?"

"You won't have heard of her, she's just a graduate student. Her name is Angelica Pabst."

"Oh course, I know her well."

"*You do?*" Persse sat down again.

"*Mais oui!* She attended my lectures last year at the Sorbonne."

"And *is* she attending the conference?"

"Indeed she is. Tonight she was the Hyacinth Girl. You remember:

> *You gave me hyacinths first a year ago;*
> *They called me the hyacinth girl.*"

"Yes, yes," Persse nodded impatiently. "I know the poem well. But where can I find her?"

"She was wandering about the streets, in a long white dress, with her arms full of hyacinths. Very charming, if one likes that dark, rather overripe kind of feminine beauty."

"I do," said Persse. "Have you any idea where she is staying?"

"Our Swiss hosts have, with characteristic efficiency, supplied a list of conferees' accommodations," said Tardieu, taking a folded paper from his breast pocket. He ran a long brown finger down a list. "Ah, yes, here it is. Pabst A., Mademoiselle. Pension Bellegarde, Rue de Grand-Saint-Jean."

"Where is that?"

"I will show you," said Tardieu, gesturing to a waiter for the bill. "It seems a modest lodging for one whose father is extremely rich."

"Is he?"

"I understand he is executive president of one of the American airlines."

"How well do you know Angelica?" Persse asked the French Professor, as the funicular drew them back to the town.

"Not very well. She came to the Sorbonne for a year, as an occasional postgraduate student. She used to sit in the front row at my lectures, gazing at me through thick-rimmed spectacles. She always had a notebook open and a pen in her hand, but I never saw her write anything. It piqued me, I must say. One day, as I was going out of the lecture theatre, I stopped in front of her and made a little joke. 'Excuse me, mademoiselle,' I said, 'but this is the seventh lecture of mine that you have attended and your notebook remains blank. Have I not uttered a single word that was worth recording?' Do you know what she said? 'Professor Tardieu, it is not what you say that impresses me most, it is what you are silent about: ideas, morality, love, death, things . . . This notebook'—she fluttered its vacant pages—'is the record of your profound silences. *Vos silences profonds.*' She speaks excellent French. I went away glowing with pride. Later I wondered whether she was mocking me. What do you think?''

''I wouldn't venture an opinion,'' said Persse, recalling one of Angelica's remarks at Rummidge: *''You have to treat these professors carefully. You have to flatter them a bit.''* He asked Tardieu if he had met Angelica's sister.

''Sister? No, is there a sister?''

''I'm pretty sure that there is.''

''This is the street.''

As they turned the corner, Persse suddenly panicked at the realization that he did not know what he was going to say to Angelica. That he loved her, of course—but she knew that already. That he had misjudged her? But she knew that as well, though he hoped she hadn't guessed how grievously. In all the excitement of pursuing her, or her double, across Europe, he had never thought to prepare himself with an appropriate speech for the moment of meeting. He almost hoped that she was still on the streets of Lausanne with her arms full of hyacinths, so that he would have time to sit in the pension's lounge and prepare himself before she returned.

Tardieu halted in front of a house with a small painted sign under a light over the door, *''Pension Bellegarde''.* ''Here you are,'' he said. ''I wish you goodnight—and success.''

''You won't come in?'' Persse found himself absurdly nervous of meeting Angelica alone.

''No, no, my presence would be superfluous,'' said Tardieu. ''I have performed my narrative function for tonight.''

"You've been most helpful," said Persse.

Tardieu smiled and shrugged. "If one is not a subject or an object, one must be a helper or an opponent. You I help. Professor Zapp I oppose."

"Why do you oppose him?"

"You have perhaps heard of a UNESCO chair in literary criticism?"

"Oh, that."

"Yes, that. *Au revoir*."

They shook hands, and Persse felt a small pellet-like object pressed into his palm. As the other walked away, Persse tilted his hand towards a streetlamp and discovered a solitary currant adhering to it. He nibbled the currant, turned, took a deep breath, and rang the doorbell of the pension.

A middle-aged woman in a neat, dark dress opened the door. *"Oui monsieur?"*

"Je cherche une jeune femme," Persse stammered. "Miss Papps. I mean, Miss Pabst. I understand that she is staying here."

"Ah! Mademoiselle Pabst!" The woman smiled, then frowned. "Alas, she has departed."

"Oh, no!" Persse groaned. "You mean she's gone for good?"

"Pardon?"

"She has checked out—left Lausanne?"

"Oui, m'sieu."

"When did she leave?"

"Half an hour ago."

"Did she say where she was going?"

"She asked about trains to Genève."

"Thanks." Persse turned and sprinted back down the street.

He ran all the way to the station, using the middle of the road, since the pavements were still crowded, cheered on by onlookers who evidently thought he was part of the street theatre, though he couldn't recall anyone actually running in *The Waste Land*—it was a rather ambulatory poem. He used such thoughts to distract himself from the stitch in his side and his chagrin at having missed Angelica by so small a margin. He dashed into the station and yelled at the first person he saw an interrogative *"Genève?"* The man pointed towards a staircase and Persse leapt down the stairs three at a time. But he had been misled, or mistaken: the train was drawn up beside the opposite platform, separated from him by another line. He heard doors slamming and a whistle shrilled. There was no time to retrace his steps—his only chance of catching the train was to cross the tracks and board it from this side. He glanced up and down the line to check that it was clear, but as he made to step down, a pair of uniformed arms closed around him and dragged him back from the brink.

"Non non, m'sieu! C'est défendu de traverser!"

Persse struggled momentarily, then, as the train moved smoothly out of the station, desisted. In one of the compartments he glimpsed the back of a girl's dark head that might have been Angelica. "Angelica!" he yelled despairingly, and futilely. The official released his grip on Persse and regarded him disapprovingly.

"When is the next train to Geneva?" Persse asked. *"A quelle heure le train prochain pour Genève?"*

"Demain," said the man with righteous satisfaction. *"A six heures et demi."*

As Persse came out into the station colonnade, a taxi driver cocked an interrogative eyebrow. This time he accepted the ride. "Pension Bellegarde," he said, and slumped back, exhausted, in the back seat.

The light over the front door of the pension was out, and the landlady took longer to answer Persse's ring. She looked surprised to see him back again.

"I'd like a room for the night, please."

She shook her head. "I am sorry, *m'sieu,* we are full."

"But you can't be!" Persse protested. "Miss Pabst has only just left. Can't I have the room she vacated?"

The woman pointed to her wristwatch. "It is late, *m'sieu.* The room must be cleaned, the linen changed. That cannot be done tonight."

"Madame," said Persse fervently, "let me have the room exactly as it is, and I'll pay you double."

The landlady was clearly suspicious of this offer from a

luggageless, wild-eyed, scruffy-looking foreigner, but when he explained that the young lady who had occupied the room was the object of his sentimental attachment, she smiled rosily and said he could have the room as it stood for half-price.

The room was under the steep eaves of the house, with a small dormer window that afforded a glimpse of the lake far below. The window was shut and the air inside the room heavy with the scent of a large bunch of hyacinths, crushed and wilting in the waste basket. The room showed all the signs of a recent hasty departure. Persse picked up a still-damp towel from the floor beneath the washbasin and held it to his cheek. He swallowed the dregs of water at the bottom of a glass tumbler as reverently as if it were communion wine. He carefully unfolded a crumpled paper tissue left on the dressing table, uncovering at its core the faint impression of a pair of red lips, to which he pressed his own. He slept naked between sheets that were still creased and wrinkled from contact with Angelica's lovely limbs, and inhaled from the pillow under his head the lingering fragrance of her shampoo. He fell asleep in a delirium of sweet sensation and poignant regret and physical exhaustion.

On waking the next morning, he made two precious discoveries underneath the hyacinths in the waste basket: a pair of nylon tights with a hole in one knee, which he tucked away into an inside pocket next to his heart, and a scrap of paper with a telephone number and "TAA 426 *Dep. 22.50 arr 06.20*" written on it in a neat italic hand, which he took immediately to the payphone in the hall downstairs. He dialled the number and was answered by a female voice.

"Transamerican Airways."

"Can you tell me the destination of your flight 426 that left Geneva at 22.50 last night?"

"Yes sir, flight 426 to New York and Los Angeles should have left at that time last night. But due to a technical problem the flight was postponed till this morning. We had to charter another plane."

"When did it leave?"

"It departs in one hour from now, at 09.30 hours, sir."

"Is there a vacant seat?"

"Plenty, sir, but you'd better hurry."

Persse thrust a generous quantity of francs into the hand of his bewildered landlady and ran down the hill to the taxi-rank in front of the station.

"Geneva airport," he gasped, collapsing into the back seat. "As fast as you can."

The route to the airport was mostly motorway, and the taxi passed everything on it. They arrived at the International Departures terminal at nine o'clock precisely. Persse gave all his remaining francs to the driver, who seemed well satisfied. He ran headlong at the automatic doors, which opened just in time to prevent him from crashing through their plate glass. Two Transamerican employees, a man and a girl, chatting idly behind the deserted check-in desk, looked up in surprise as Persse charged up to the counter.

"Do you have a passenger Pabst on Flight 426?" he demanded. "Miss Angelica Pabst?"

The man tapped on his computer terminal and confirmed that Miss Pabst had indeed checked in for the flight and was booked through to Los Angeles.

"Give me a ticket to Los Angeles, please, and a seat as near to Miss Pabst as possible."

Though the flight had technically closed, and the passengers were already boarding, the man got permission to issue Persse with a ticket—it helped that Persse had no luggage. The pair responded eagerly to the urgency of the transaction: while the man filled out the ticket and credit-card slip, the girl allocated him a seat. "You're in luck, sir," she said, studying her computer screen. "There's an empty seat right next to Miss Pabst."

"That's grand!" said Persse. He had a vision of himself, the last to board the plane, walking up the aisle and slipping into the seat next to Angelica while her head was turned to look out of the window, saying, quietly—saying what? *"Hallo. Long time no see. Going far? Did you [holding up the laddered tights] forget these?"* Or better still, saying nothing, just waiting to see how long it would take before she looked down and recognized his scuffed shoes, or the back of his hand on the seat arm between them, or simply felt the vibrations of excitement and expectancy flowing from his heart, and turned to look at him.

"Here's your Amex card, sir," said the man. "Could I see your passport?"

"Sure." Persse glanced at his watch. It was 9.15.

The man flicked open the passport, frowned, and thumbed through the pages very deliberately. "I can't find your visa, sir," he said at length.

Persse now knew, if he did not know before, what a cold sinking feeling was like. "Oh, Jaysus! Do I need a visa?"

"You can't fly to the United States without a visa, sir."

"I'm sorry, I didn't know."

The man sighed, and slowly tore Persse's ticket and American Express slip into small pieces.

Three

whhheeeeeeeeeeeeeEEEEEEEE! The scream of jet engines rises to a crescendo on the runways of the world. Every second, somewhere or other, a plane touches down, with a puff of smoke from scorched tyre rubber, or rises into the air, leaving a smear of black fumes dissolving in its wake. From space, the earth might look to a fanciful eye like a huge carousel, with planes instead of horses spinning round its circumference, up and down, up and down. *Whhheeee-eeeeeee!*

It's late July now, and schools as well as colleges and universities have begun their summer vacations. Conference-bound academics must compete for airspace with holidaymakers and package tourists. The airport lounges are congested, their floors are littered with paper cups, the ashtrays are overflowing and the bars have run out of ice. Everyone is on the move. In Europe, northerners head south for the shadeless beaches and polluted waters of the Mediterranean, while southerners flee to the chilly inlets and overcast mountains of Scotland and Scandinavia. Asians fly west and Americans fly east. Ours is a civilization of lightweight luggage, of permanent disjunction. Everybody seems to be departing or

307

returning from somewhere. Jerusalem, Athens, Alexandria, Vienna, London. Or Ajaccio, Palma, Tenerife, Faro, Miami.

At Gatwick, pale-faced travellers in neatly pressed frocks and safari suits, anxiously clutching their passports and airtickets, hurry from the Southern Region railway station to the Air Terminal, struggling against a tide of their sunburned and crumpled counterparts flowing in the opposite direction, festooned with wickerwork baskets, dolls in folk costume, straw sombreros and lethal quantities of duty-free cigarettes and liquor.

Persse McGarrigle is carried along by the departing current. It is nearly a week since the débâcle at Geneva airport, during which time he has flown home to Ireland, found a substitute for himself on the Celtic Twilight Summer School and got himself a visa to the United States. Now he is on his way to Los Angeles, to look for Angelica, by Skytrain, the walk-on, no-reservation service that posters all over London inform him is the cheapest way to travel to the States. But the Laker check-in counters are ominously deserted. Has he made a mistake about the departure time? No. Alas, the Skytrain has been suspended owing to the grounding of the DC-10, the Laker staff explain to Persse with regret, sympathy and a certain incredulity. Is it possible that there is anyone left in the entire world who hasn't heard about the grounding of the DC-10? I haven't been reading the papers lately, he says apologetically, I've been living in a cottage in Connemara, writing poetry. What's the quickest way for me to get to Los Angeles? Well, they say, you could take the helicopter to Heathrow, though it will cost you, and try the big nationals. Or you could go from here by Braniff to Dallas/Fort Worth, they have onward connections to LA. Persse gets the last standby seat on a Boeing 747 painted bright orange, which takes him to an airport so immense you cannot see its perimeter at under two thousand feet, baking like an enormous biscuit in a temperature of 104° Farenheit; shivers for three hours in a smoked-glass terminal building air-conditioned to the temperature of iced Coke; and flies on to California in a Western Airlines Boeing 707.

It is dark by the time they begin their descent to Los Angeles, and the city is an awe-inspiring sight from the

air—a glimmering gridiron of light from horizon to horizon—
but Persse, who has been travelling continuously for twenty-
two hours, is too tired to appreciate it. He has tried to sleep
on the two planes, but they kept waking him up to give him
meals. Long-distance flying, he decides, is rather like being
in hospital in that respect, and it wouldn't have surprised
him unduly if one of the hostesses had slipped a thermome-
ter into his mouth between meals. He had scarcely had the
strength to rip open the plastic envelope containing his
cutlery for the last dinner he was offered.

He staggers out of the terminal into the warm Californian
night, and stands dazedly on the pavement as cars and buses
sweep by in an endless procession. A man strides to the
edge of the kerb and waves down a minibus with *"Beverly
Hills Hotel"* emblazoned on its side, which promptly swerves
to a halt and springs open its door with a hiss of compressed
air. The man gets in and Persse follows. The ride is free, the
hotel room staggeringly expensive—clearly way out of Persse's
usual class of accommodation, but he is too tired to quibble
or to contemplate searching for a cheaper alternative. A
porter insists on taking his ridiculously small sports grip,
which is all the luggage he has, and leading him down long,
carpeted corridors decorated with a design of huge, slightly
sinister green leaves above the dado, and shows him into a
handsome suite with a bed as big as a football pitch. Persse
takes off his clothes and crawls into the bed, falls asleep
instantly, wakes up only three hours later, 2 a.m. local time
but 10 a.m. by his body clock, and tries to make himself
drowsy again by studying the entries under "Pabst" in the
Los Angeles telephone directory. There are twenty-seven of
them altogether and none of them is called Hermann.

But where is Morris Zapp? His non-appearance at Vienna
excited little interest—people often fail to show up at
conferences they have provisionally applied for. But at
Bellagio there is considerable concern. Morris Zapp never
returned from his jog in the woods that afternoon, after
writing his letter to Arthur Kingfisher. The letter is recovered
from the ongoing mailbox in the villa's lobby and confiscat-
ed by the police as a possible source of clues to his

disappearance; it is opened and perused and puzzled over and filed away and forgotten; it is never mailed and Arthur Kingfisher never knows that he was invited to the Jerusalem conference. Search parties are sent into the woods, and there is talk of dragging the lake.

A few days later, Désirèe, vacationing at Nice, gets a telephone call in her hotel room from the Paris *Herald-Tribune*. A young, rather breathless American male voice.

"Is that Mrs Désirée Zapp?"

"Not any longer."

"I beg your pardon ma'am?"

"I used to be Mrs Désirée Zapp. Now I'm Ms Désirée Byrd."

"The wife of Professor Morris Zapp?"

"The ex-wife."

"The author of *Difficult Days*?"

"Now you're talking."

"We just had a telephone call, Mrs Zapp—"

"Ms Byrd."

"Sorry, Ms Byrd. We just had an anonymous telephone call to say that your husband has been kidnapped."

"*Kidnapped?*"

"That's right ma'am. We've checked it out with the Italian police and it seems to be true. Professor Zapp went out jogging from a villa in Bellagio three days ago and never returned.'

"But why in God's name would anybody want to kidnap Morris?"

"Well, the kidnappers are demanding half a million dollars in ransom."

"*What?* Who do they think is going to pay that sort of money?"

"Well, *you* I guess, ma'am."

"They can go fuck themselves," says Désirée, putting down the phone.

Soon the young man is back on the line. "But isn't it true, Mrs Zapp—Ms Byrd—that you received half a million dollars for the film rights alone for *Difficult Days*?"

"Yeah, but I earned that money and I sure as hell didn't

earn it to buy back a husband I said good riddance to years ago.''

Désirée bangs down the phone. Almost immediately it rings again. ''I have nothing further to say,'' she snaps.

There is silence for a moment, then a heavily accented voice says, ''Ees dat Signora Zapp?''

Persse has breakfast in a pleasant room on the ground floor of the Beverly Hills called the Pool Lounge, which is full of people who look like film stars and who, it gradually dawns upon him, *are* film stars. The breakfast costs as much as a three-course dinner in the best restaurant in Limerick. His American Express Card will take care of the bill, but Persse is getting worried at the thought of the debits he is totting up on the Amex computer. A few days' living in this place would see off the remainder of his bank balance, but there's no point in checking out till noon. He goes back to his palatial suite and telephones the twenty-seven Pabsts in the directory without finding one who will admit to having a daughter called Angelica. Then, cursing himself for not having thought of the expedient earlier, he works his way through the head offices of the airlines in the Yellow Pages, asking for Mr Pabst, until, at last, the telephonist at Transamerican says, ''Just one moment, I'll put you through to Mr Pabst's secretary.''

''Mr Pabst's office,'' says a silky Californian voice.

''Oh, could I speak to Mr Pabst?''

''I'm sorry, he's in a meeting right now. Can I take a message?''

''Well, it's a rather personal matter. I really want to see him myself. Urgently.''

''I'm afraid that won't be possible today. Mr Pabst has meetings all the morning and he's flying to Washington this afternoon.''

''Oh dear, this is terrible. I've flown all the way from Ireland to see him.''

''Did you have an appointment, Mr . . .''

''McGarrigle. Persse McGarrigle. No, I don't have an appointment. But I must see him.'' Then, ''It's about his daughter,'' he risks.

"Which one?"

Which one! Persse clenches the fist of his free hand and punches the air in triumph. "Angelica," he says. "But Lily, too, in a way."

There is a thoughtful silence at the other end of the line. "Can I come back to you about this, Mr McGarrigle?"

"Yes, I'm staying at the Beverly Hills Hotel," says Persse.

"The Beverly Hills, right." The secretary sounds impressed. Ten minutes later the phone rings again. "Mr Pabst can see you for a few minutes at the airport, just before his plane leaves for Washington," she says. "Please be at the Red Carpet Club in the Transamerican terminal at 1.15 this afternoon."

"I'll be there," says Persse.

Morris Zapp hears the telephone ringing in the next room. He does not know where he is because he was knocked out with some sort of injection when they kidnapped him, and when he woke up, God knew how many hours later, he was blindfolded. From the sounds of birdsong and the absence of traffic noise beyond the walls of his room he deduces that he is in the country; from the coolness of the air around his legs, still clothed in red silk running shorts, that he is in the mountains. He complained bitterly about the blindfold until his captors explained that if he happened to see any of them they would be obliged to kill him. Since then, his main fear has been that his blindfold will slip down accidentally. He has asked them to knock on the door before they come into his room so that he can warn them of such an eventuality. They come in to give him his meals, untying his hands for this purpose or to lead him to the john. They will not allow him outdoors, so he has to exercise by walking up and down his small, narrow bedroom. Most of the time he spends lying on the bunk bed, racked by a monotonous cycle of rage, self-pity and fear. As the days have passed, his anxieties have become more basic. At first he was chiefly concerned about the arrangements for the Jerusalem conference. Later, about staying alive. Every time the telephone rings in the next room, he feels an irrational spasm of hope. It is the chief of police, the military, the US Marines. *"We know where you are, you are completely surrounded. Re-*

*lease your prisoner unharmed and come out with your
hands on your heads.''* He has no idea what the telephone
conversations are actually about, since they are conducted in
a low murmur of Italian.

One of Morris's guards, the one they call Carlo, speaks
English and from him Morris has gathered that he has been
kidnapped not by the Mafia, nor by the henchmen of some
rival contender for the UNESCO chair, such as von Turpitz,
but by a group of left-wing extremists out to combine
fund-raising with a demonstration of anti-American senti-
ment. The Rockefeller Villa and its affluent life-style evidently struck them as an arrogant flaunting of American
cultural imperialism (even though, as Morris pointed out, it
was used by scholars from all nations) and the kidnapping
of a well-connected resident as an effective form of protest
which would also have the advantage of subsidizing future
terrorist adventure. Somehow—Morris cannot imagine how,
and Carlo will not tell him—they traced the connection
between the American professor who went jogging at 5.30
every afternoon along the same path through the woods near
the Villa Serbelloni, and Désirée Byrd, the rich American
authoress reported in *Newsweek* as having earned over two
million dollars in royalties and subsidiary rights from her
novel *Difficult Days*. The only little mistake they made was
to suppose that Morris and Désirée were still married.
Morris's emphatic statement that they were divorced clearly
dismayed his captors.

"But she got plenty money, yeah?" Carlo said, anxiously.
"She don' wan' you to die, huh?"

"I wouldn't count on it," Morris said. That was Day
Two, when he was still capable of humour. Now it is Day
Five and he doesn't feel like laughing any more. It is taking
them a long time to locate Désirée, who is apparently no
longer to be found in Heidelberg.

The telephone conversation in the next room comes to an
end, and Morris hears footsteps approaching and a knock on
his door. "Come in," he croaks, fingering his blindfold.

"Well," says Carlo, "we finally located your wife."

"Ex-wife," Morris points out.

"She sure is some tough bitch."

"I told you," says Morris, his heart sinking. "What happened?"

"We put our ransom demand to her..." says Carlo.

"She refused to pay?"

"She said, 'How much do I have to pay to make you keep him?'"

Morris began to weep, quietly, making his blindfold damp. "I told you it was useless asking Désirée to ransom me. She hates my guts."

"We shall have to make her pity you."

"How are you going to do that?" says Morris anxiously.

"Perhaps if she receives some little memento of you. An ear. A finger..."

"For Christ's sake," Morris whimpers.

Carlo laughs. "A leetle joke. No, you must send her a message. You must appeal to her tender feelings."

"She hasn't got any tender feelings!"

"It will be a test of your eloquence. The supreme test."

"Yeah, there were two babies on that KLM flight, twin girls," says Hermann Pabst. "Nobody ever did discover how they were smuggled on board. All the women passengers were questioned on arrival at Amsterdam, and the stewardesses as well, of course. It was in all the papers, but you would have been too young to remember that."

"I was a baby myself at the time."

"Right," says Hermann Pabst. "I have some cuttings at home, I could let you have copies." He scribbles a note on a memo pad inside his wallet. He is a big, thickset man, with pale blond hair going white, and a face that has turned red rather than brown in the Californian sunshine. They are sitting in the bar of the Red Carpet Club, Pabst drinking Perrier water and Persse a beer. "I worked for KLM in those days, I was on duty the day the plane landed with those two little stowaways. They were parked in my office for a while, cute little things. Gertrude—my wife—and me, we had no children, not by choice, something to do with Gertrude's tubes" (he pronounces the word in the American way as "toobs"). "Now they can do an operation, but in those days... anyhow, I called her up, I said 'Gertrude, congratulations, you just had twins.' I decided to adopt those kids as soon as I set eyes on them. It seemed . . ." He gropes for a word.

"Providential?" Persse suggests.

"Right. Like they'd been sent from above. Which, in a way, they had. From 20,000 feet." He takes a swig of Perrier water and glances at his watch.

"What time does your plane leave?" Persse asks him.

"When I tell it to," says Hermann Pabst. "It's my own private jet. But I have to watch the time. I'm attending a reception at the White House this evening."

Persse looks suitably impressed. "It's very good of you to give me your time, sir. I can see that you are a very busy man."

"Yeah, I done pretty well since I came to the States. I gotta plane, a yacht, a ranch near Palm Springs. But let me tell you something, young man, ya can't buy love. That was where I went wrong with the girls. I spoiled them, smothered them with presents—toys, clothes, horses, vacations. They both rebelled against it in different ways, soon as they became teenagers. Lily ran wild. She discovered boys in a big way, then dope. She got in with a bad crowd at high school. I guess I handled it badly. She ran away from home at sixteen. Well there's nothing new about that, not in California. But it broke Gertrude's heart. Didn't do mine a lot of good either. I have high blood pressure, mustn't smoke, scarcely any drink"—he gestured to the Perrier water. "After a coupla years we traced Lily to San Francisco. She was living in some crummy commune, shacked up with some guy, or guys, making money by, would you believe, acting in blue movies. We brought her back home, tried to make a fresh start, sent her to a girls' college in the East with Angie, the best, but it didn't work out. Lily went to Europe for a vacation study programme and never came back. That was six years ago."

"And Angelica?"

"Oh, Angie," Hermann Pabst sighs. "She rebelled in a different way, the opposite way. She became an egghead. Spent all her time reading, never dated boys. Looked down at me and her mother because we weren't cultured—well, I admit it, I never did have much time for reading, apart from the *Wall Street Journal* and the aviation trade magazines. I tried to catch up with those *Reader's Digest* Condensed Books, but Angelica threw them in the trash can and gave me some others to read that I just couldn't make head or tail of. She got straight 'A's for every course she took at Vassar, and graduated Summa Cum Laude, then she insisted on going to England to do another Bachelor's course at Cambridge, then she told her mother and me she was going to Yale graduate school to do complete literature, or somethin'."

"Comp. Lit.? Comparative Literature?"

"That's it. Says she wants to be a college teacher. What a waste! I mean, there's a girl with looks, brains, everything. She could marry anybody she liked. Someone with power, money, ambition. Angie could be a President's wife."

"You're right, sir," says Persse. He has not thought it prudent to reveal his own matrimonial ambitions with respect to Angelica. Instead, he has represented himself to Mr Pabst as a writer researching a book on the behavioural patterns of identical twins, who happened to meet Angelica in England, and wanted to learn more of her fascinating history.

"What makes it worse, she refuses to let me pay her fees through graduate school. She insists on being independent. Earned her tuition by grading papers for her Professor at Yale—can you imagine it? When I make more money in a single week than he does in a year. There's only one thing she'll accept from me, and that's a card that gives her free travel on Transamerican airlines anywhere in the world."

"She seems to make good use of it," says Persse. "She goes to a lot of conferences."

"Conferences! You said it. She's a conference freak. I told her the other day, 'If you didn't spend so much time going to conferences, Angie, you would have gotten your doctorate by now, and put all this nonsense behind you.'"

"The other day? You saw Angelica the other day?" says Persse as casually as he can manage. "Is she here in Los Angeles, then?"

"Well, she was. She's in Honolulu right now."

"Honolulu?" Persse echoes him, dismayed. "Jaysus!"

"And I'll give you three guesses why she's there."

"Another conference?"

"Right. Some conference on John."

"John? John who?"

Pabst shrugs. "Angie didn't say. She just said she was going to a conference on John, University of Hawaii."

"Could it have been 'Genre'?"

"That's it." Pabst looked at his watch. "I'm sorry, McGarrigle, but I have to leave now. You can walk me to the plane if you have any more questions." He picks up his sleek burgundy leather briefcase, and Persse his scuffed sports bag. They walk out of the air-conditioned building into the smog-hazed sunshine.

"Does Angelica have any contact with her sister, these days?" Persse asks.

"Yeah, that's what she came home to tell me," says Mr Pabst. "She's been studying in Europe these last two years, on a Woodrow Wilson scholarship. Living in Paris, mostly, but travelling around, and always on the lookout for her sister. Finally tracked her down to some nightclub in London. Lily is working as some kind of exotic dancer, apparently. I suppose that means she takes her clothes off, but at least it's better than blue movies. Angie says Lily is happy. She works for some kind of international agency that sends her all over, to different jobs. Both my girls seem determined to see the world the hard way. I don't understand them. But then, why should I? They're not my flesh and blood, after all. I did my best for them, but somewhere along the line I blew it."

They walk out onto a tarmac parking area for private planes of every shape and size, from tiny one-engined, propeller-driven lightweights, fragile as gnats, to executive jets big as full-size airliners. A group of young men, squatting in the shade of a petrol tanker, rise to their feet expectantly as Hermann Pabst approaches, holding up handwritten signs that say "Denver", "Seattle", "St Louis", "Tulsa". "Sorry, boys," says Pabst, shaking his head.

"Who are they?" Persse asks.

"Hitchhikers."

Persse looks back wonderingly over his shoulder. "You mean they thumb rides in airplanes?"

"Yup. It's the modern way to hitchhike: hang about the executive jet parks."

Hermann Pabst's private plane is a Boeing 737 painted in the purple, orange and white livery of Transamerican Airlines. Its engines are already whining preparatory to departure, *whheeeeeeeeeeee*! They shake hands at the bottom of the mobile staircase that has been wheeled up to the side of the aircraft.

"Goodbye, Mr Pabst, you've been very kind."

"Goodbye, McGarrigle. And good luck with your study. It's a very interesting subject. People are surprisingly ignorant about twins. Why, Angelica gave me a novel to read once, that had identical twins of different sexes. I didn't have the patience to go on with it."

"I don't blame you," says Persse.

"Where shall I send those cuttings?"

"Oh—University College, Limerick."

"Right. So long."

Hermann Pabst strides up the steps, gives a final wave and disappears inside the aircraft. The steps are wheeled away from the plane and the door swings shut behind him. Persse puts his fingers in his ears as the engine noise rises in pitch and volume, and the plane slowly taxis towards the runway. *WHHHEEEEEEEEEEEEEE!* It disappears out of sight behind a hangar, then, a few minutes later, rises into the air and flies out over the sea before it banks and turns back towards the east. Persse picks up his grip and walks slowly back towards the little group squatting in the shade of the petrol tanker.

"Hi," says one of the young men.

"Hi," says Persse squatting down beside him. He takes a piece of foolscap from his bag and writes on it, in large letters, with a felt-tip pen, the word, "HONOLULU."

The telephone rings in Désirée's hotel room on the Promenade des Anglais. The man from Interpol sits up sharply, puts on his headphones, switches on his recording apparatus, and nods to Désirée. She picks up the phone.

"Ees dat Signora Zapp?"

"Speaking."

"I 'ave message for you, please."

After a pause and a crackle, Désirée hears Morris's voice. "Hallo, Désirée, this is Morris."

"Morris," she says, "where the hell are you? I've had just about . . ." But Morris is speaking on regardless, and it dawns on Désirée that she is listening to a tape-recording.

". . . I'm OK physically, I'm being well looked after, but these guys are serious and they're losing patience. I explained to them that we're not married anymore and as a special concession they've agreed to halve the ransom money to a quarter of a million dollars. Now, I know that's a lot of money, Désirée, and God knows you don't owe me anything, but you're the only person I know who can lay hands on that kind of dough. It says in *Newsweek* that you've made two million for *Difficult Days*—these guys clipped it. Get me out of this and I'll pay the quarter of a million back to you, if it takes me the rest of my life. At least I'll *have* a life.

"What you've got to do is this. If you agree to pay the ransom, put a small ad in the next issue of the Paris *Herald-Tribune*—you can phone it in, pay by credit card— saying *'The lady accepts'*, right? Got it? *'The lady accepts.'* Then arrange to draw from the bank a quarter of a million dollars in used, unmarked bills, and await instructions about handing them over. Needless to say, you mustn't bring the police into this. Any police involvement and the deal is off and my life will be in peril."

While Morris has been speaking, the telephone exchange has traced the call, and police cars are tearing through the streets of Nice, their sirens braying, to surround a call-box in the old town, in which they find the receiver off the hook and propped up in front of a cheap Japanese cassette recorder, from which the voice of Morris Zapp can still be heard plaintively pleading.

The next day, Désirée places a small ad in the Paris *Herald-Tribune*: *"The lady offers ten thousand dollars."*

"I think you're being very generous," says Alice Kauffman,

on the line from Manhattan to Nice, her voice gluey with the surreptitious mastication of cherry-liqueur chocolates.

"So do I," says Désirée, "but I figured ten grand is a sum Morris might just seriously attempt to pay back. And it might look bad if something happened to him without my lifting a finger."

"You're right, honey, you're so right," says Alice Kauffman, little kissing noises punctuating her words as she licks the tips of her fingers. "People are apt to get emotional about a situation like this, even women who are theoretically liberated. It might have an adverse effect on your sales if he died on you. Perhaps you should offer twenty grand."

"Would it be tax-deductible?" Désirée asks.

"What kind of woman is this?" Carlo demands of Morris. "Who ever heard of anybody bargaining with kidnappers?"

"I warned you," said Morris Zapp.

"And ten thousand dollars she offers! It's an insult."

"*You* feel insulted! How do you think *I* feel?"

"You will have to record another message."

"It's no use, unless you're prepared to lower your price. Suppose you come down to one hundred thousand?"

Blindfolded Morris hears a hiss of sharply intaken breath.

"I'll talk to the others about it," Carlo says. Ten minutes later he comes back with the tape recorder. "One hundred thousand dollars is our final offer," he says. "Tell her, and tell her good. Make sure she understands."

"It's not so simple," says Morris. "Every decoding is another encoding."

"What?"

"Never mind. Give me the tape recorder."

"Look at it this way, Désirée." Morris's voice crackles in the telephone while outside, beneath the balcony of her room overlooking the sea, police cars go hee-hawing along the Promenade des Anglais in search of the call-box it is coming from. "One hundred thousand dollars is less than one-twentieth of your royalties from *Difficult Days*, which incidentally I thought was an absolutely wonderful book, a knockout, truly—less than four per cent. Now, although I take absolutely no credit for that achievement, I mean it was entirely your own creative genius, it is nevertheless true, in a sense, that if I hadn't been such a lousy husband to you all these years you wouldn't have been able to write the book. I mean you wouldn't have had the pain to express. You could say I made you a feminist. I opened your eyes to the oppressed state of modern American women. Don't you think that, viewed in that light, I'm entitled to some consideration in the present circumstances? I mean, you pay your agent ten per cent for doing less.''

"The nerve," says Alice Kauffman, when Désirée recounts this new development on the transatlantic telephone. "I'd be inclined to let him rot. What are you going to do?"

"I'm offering twenty-five grand," says Désirée. "It's getting kind of interesting, like a Dutch auction. I wonder what the reserve is on Morris."

Persse sits on the narrow, crowded strip of beach in front of the Waikiki Sheraton, and tots up the sums on the pale blue American Express counterfoils that have accumulated in his wallet. He calculates that he has just about enough money in his bank account in Limerick to cover the total, but he will have to go into debt to get home. If he hadn't been lucky enough to get a free ride from Los Angeles to Honolulu on a plane chartered by a TV film crew, his finances would be in an even worse state.

It is hot, very hot, on the beach, in spite of the trade winds in which the palm trees sway and rustle overhead, and Persse feels unrefreshed by the swim he has just taken in an ocean that was like warm milk to the touch and almost as cloudy to the eye. The distant surf had tempted him, but he didn't like to leave his belongings unattended on the beach. He feels a distinct pang of nostalgia for the bracing, crystal-clear waters of Connemara, and its rock-strewn tidal beaches of firm-packed sand, where seabirds were often his only company earlier this summer. Here the sand is yielding and coarse-grained, and along the scarcely changing margin of the lukewarm sea plods an endless procession of humanity, in bikinis, trunks, Bermuda shorts and tank tops, the young and beautiful, the old and unlovely, the slim and the thin and the obese, the tanned and the freckled and the burned. Most of these people carry some form of food or drink in their hands—hamburgers, hot-dogs, ice-creams, soft drinks, even cocktails. The island is full of noises: twanging Hawaiian muzak from the hotel loudspeakers, rock music from toted transistor radios, the hum of air-conditioners and the thud of piledrivers laying the foundations for new hotels. Every two or three minutes, a jumbo jet rises into the air from the airport some miles to Persse's right and hangs, apparently almost motionless, above the bay, above the skyscraper hotels, the shimmying palms, the hired surf-boards and outrigged canoes, and shopping centres and the parking lots, before turning east or west; and from its windows those who are departing look down, with varying degrees of envy or relief, upon those who have just arrived.

When Persse himself arrived the previous evening, he took a taxi immediately to the University, but all the administrative buildings were closed, and he wandered round the campus, which resembled a large botanical garden with sculpture exhibits, asking people at random for the Genre Conference without success, until a security guard advised him to go home before he got mugged. He returned early next morning, after spending the night in a cheap lodging-house, only to be informed that the conference had ended the day before, and that all the participants had dispersed, including the organizers who might conceivably have known where Angelica had gone. All the University Information Office could offer him was a copy of the conference programme, which included a tantalizing reference to a paper on "Comic Epic Romance from Ariosto to Byron—Literature's Utopian Dream of Itself" which Angelica had apparently delivered, and to which an Italian Professor called Ernesto Morgana and a Japanese called Motokazu Umeda had responded. How he would have loved to hear that!

Clutching this useless souvenir of Angelica's passage, Persse took the bus down to Waikiki and, glimpsing a strip of blue sea between two huge hotels, made for the beach to relieve his frustration with some exercise, and to contemplate his next move. There doesn't seem to be any sensible alternative to returning home. Persse sighs and buttons his wallet back into the breast pocket of his shirt.

Then his attention is caught by a strikingly incongruous figure among the sun-oiled, half-naked vacationers paddling along at the edge of the water. It is an elderly lady wearing a sprigged blue muslin dress, the full skirt of which has been elegantly gathered up and dovetailed to expose a modest extent of bare white leg. She is carrying a matching parasol to shade her face. Persse leaps to his feet and runs forward to greet her.

"Miss Maiden! Fancy seeing you here!"

"Hallo, young man! The surprise is mutual, but a pleasant one I'm sure. Are you staying at the Sheraton?"

"Good heavens, no, but there seems to be no way of getting to the beach in this place without walking through some hotel lobby."

"I am staying at the Royal Hawaiian, which I am told is very exclusive, though what counts as vulgar in Honolulu I cannot imagine," says Miss Maiden. "Are you sitting somewhere? I feel the need of a rest and perhaps a drink. They have something called slush here which in spite of its name is rather refreshing."

"Are you here for the Genre Conference?" is Persse's first question, when they have seated themselves at the counter of the Sheraton's outdoor soda-fountain, with two gigantic paper cups full of raspberry-flavoured crushed ice before them.

"No, this is simply a holiday, pure indulgence without any self-improvement. It's a place I've always wanted to visit. 'Hawaii Five-O' is one of my favourite TV programmes. I'm afraid the reality is a little disappointing. It generally is, I find, since the invention of colour television. Are you on holiday here yourself, young man?"

"Not exactly. I'm looking for a girl."

"A natural ambition, but haven't you come rather a long way for that purpose?"

"It's a particular girl that I'm looking for—Angelica Pabst—perhaps you remember her at the Rummidge conference."

"But how very extraordinary! I met her just a few days ago."

"You met Angelica?"

"On this very beach. I recognized her, though I couldn't remember her name. I'm afraid I'm losing my memory for names as I get older. Your own, for instance, just this moment escapes me, Mr, er—"

"McGarrigle. Persse McGarrigle."

"Ah yes, she mentioned you."

"She did? Angelica? How?"

"Oh, fondly, fondly."

"What did she say?"

"I can't remember, exactly, I'm afraid."

"Please try," Persse begs her. "It's very important to me."

Miss Maiden frowns with concentration, sucking vigorously on her straw and making a gurgling sound in her paper cup. "It was something about names. When she reminded me that she was called Angelica Pabst, I ventured to say that she deserved a more euphonious second name, and she laughed and asked me if I thought 'McGarrigle' would sound any better."

"She did?" Persse is ecstatic. "Then she loves me!"

"Were you in any doubt about it?"

"Well, she's been running away from me ever since I first met her."

"Ah, a young woman likes to be wooed before she is won."

"But I can never get near enough to her to start wooing," says Persse.

"She's putting you to the test."

"She certainly is. I was on the point of giving up and going back to Connemara."

"No, you mustn't do that. Never give up."

"Like the Grail knights?"

"Oh, but they were such boobies," says Miss Maiden. "All they had to do was to ask a question at the right moment, and they generally muffed it."

"Did Angelica happen to tell you where she was going next? Back to Los Angeles?"

"I think it was Tokyo."

"Tokyo?" Persse wails. "Oh, Jaysus!"

"Or was it Hong Kong? One of those Far Eastern places, anyway. She was going to some conference or other."

"That goes without saying," sighs Persse. "The question is, which conference?"

"If I were you, I should go to Tokyo and look for her."

"There are a lot of people in Tokyo, Miss Maiden."

"But they are very *little* people, are they not? Miss Pabst would stand out in the crowd, head and shoulders above everybody else. What a magnificent figure of a gal!"

"Indeed she is," Persse agreed ardently.

"I'm afraid she must have thought me very rude—I just couldn't keep my eyes off her as she was towelling herself. She had been swimming, you see—I met her wading out of the sea, wearing a two-piece bathing suit, her hair wet and her limbs gleaming."

"Like Venus," Persse breathes, closing his eyes to picture the scene more vividly.

"Quite so, the analogy struck me also. She has the most beautiful tan, which is very becoming with dark hair and eyes I always think. I observe that you have the same fair skin as myself, which burns and peels at the slightest exposure—your nose, if you will excuse my mentioning it, is already looking rather red; I would advise you to get yourself a hat—but Miss Pabst has skin like brown silk, a flawless, even tan. Except for a birthmark rather high up on the left thigh—have you noticed that? Shaped rather like an inverted comma."

"I have not had," says Persse, blushing, "the privilege of seeing Angelica in a bathing costume. I'm not sure I could bear it. I should be tempted to fight every man on the beach who looked at her."

"Well, you would certainly have had your work cut out that day. She was being ogled from all sides."

"Don't tell me," Persse begs. "There was a time when I thought she was a striptease dancer—it nearly broke my heart."

"That charming young woman a striptease dancer? How could that be?"

"It was a case of mistaken identity. It turned out to be her sister."

"Oh? Has she a sister?"

"Her twin sister, Lily, it was." How long ago it seems that he pursued Angelica's shadow through the stews of London and Amsterdam. The memory of Girls Unlimited makes him think of Bernadette and reminds him that he is still carrying around, undelivered, the document signed by Maxwell. In all the excitement of getting back onto Angelica's trail, he has forgotten all about Bernadette. How was that? He traces it back to the encounter with Cheryl Summerbee at Heathrow—Cheryl, whom he last saw inexplicably weeping over her timetable of flights to Geneva. What strange, unpredictable creatures women are!

And now, here is Miss Maiden surprising him with an unwonted sign of feminine fragility. She looks pale and sways on her stool as if about to faint. "Are you all right, Miss Maiden?" he asks anxiously, steadying her with his hand on her arm.

"The heat," she murmurs. "I'm afraid it is too much for me in the middle of the day. If you would give me your arm, I think I will go back to my hotel and lie down."

By chance, Fulvia and Ernesto Morgana fly into Milan airport at about the same time, she from Geneva, he from Honolulu. They meet in the baggage hall and embrace with style, kissing on both cheeks.

"Oh!" exclaims Fulvia. "You are very bristly, *carissimo*!"

"*Scusi*, my dearest, but it was a long flight and you know I don't like to shave on aeroplanes, in case of sudden turbulence."

"Of course, my love," Fulvia assures him. Ernesto uses an old-fashioned cut-throat razor. "Did you have a good conference?" she asks.

"Very enjoyable, thank you. Honolulu is extraordinary. The post-industrial society at play. You must go some time. And you?"

"The Narrative Conference was boring but Vienna was charming. At Lausanne it was the other way round. Oh, there are my bags coming—quick!"

Fulvia has left her bronze Maserati in the airport carpark, and drives them both home in it. "Did you meet anyone interesting?" she asks, pulling into the fast lane and flashing her headlights at a laggard Fiat.

"Well, the Signorina Pabst, to whose paper I was responding, turned out to be amazingly young and amazingly beautiful, as well as a most acute critic of Ariosto."

"Did you sleep with her?"

"Unfortunately her interest in me was purely professional. Was Professor Zapp at Vienna?"

"He was expected, but did not arrive, for some reason. I met a friend of his called Sy Gootblatt."

"Did you sleep with him?"

Fulvia smiles. "If you did not sleep with Miss Pabst, I did not sleep with Mr Gootblatt."

"But I really didn't sleep with her!" Ernesto protests. "She's not that kind of girl."

"Are there still girls who are not that kind of girl? All right, I believe you. So who did you sleep with?"

Ernesto shrugs. "Just a couple of whores."

"How banal, Ernesto."

"Two at the same time," he says defensively. "So how was Mr Gootblatt?"

"Mr Gootblatt looked promising, but proved to lack both imagination and stamina. Unfortunately it turned out that we were both going on from Vienna to Lausanne, so we had to keep up pretences for another week. I did not invite him to visit us."

Ernesto nods as if this is all he wanted to know.

When they are indoors, and have showered and changed their clothes, they exchange gifts. Ernesto has bought Fulvia earrings and a brooch decorated with uncultured pearls, and Fulvia has bought Ernesto a silver-mounted riding crop. He mixes a dry martini for both of them, and they sit facing each other in the off-white drawing-room, Ernesto sorting through the mail which has accumulated in their absence, and Fulvia with a stack of neatly folded newspapers and magazines at her side. "It is a relief to ignore the news while one is away," she observes, "but there is such a lot of catching up to do when one returns home." She peels the top paper from the pile and scans the headlines. Her mouth falls open and her eyes stare. "Ernesto," she says in a quiet but steely tone.

"Yes, my love," he replies absently, ripping open envelopes with a paper knife.

"Did you by any chance tell any of our political friends about Morris Zapp? I mean about his being married to Désirée Byrd, the novelist?"

Ernesto, startled by his wife's tone of voice, looks up. "I might have mentioned it to Carlo, I suppose. Why do you ask?"

"Carlo is a young fool," says Fulvia, leaping to her feet and flinging the newspaper into Ernesto's lap. "He will get us all thrown into jail if you don't act at once. Morris Zapp has been kidnapped!"

They burst into Morris's bedroom in the middle of the night, waking him up. The blankets are ripped from the bed and he is jerked to his feet. Hands adjust and tighten his blindfold. Somebody roughly forces his feet into his Adidas. "Where are we going?" he quavers. "Shut up," says Carlo. "Has Désirée paid up?" "Quiet." Carlo sounds angry. Morris is shaking. He knows that this is it: either deliverance or death. Someone is rolling his sleeve up and dabbing at his forearm with a wet swab. "Don't move, or you'll get hurt." Surely they don't bother to give people an anaesthetic before bumping them off? It must be deliverance. Unless of course it's a lethal injection. He feels the prick of a needle. "Are you—" he begins, but before he can finish the sentence everything goes black.

The next sensation he becomes aware of is of a sharp rock digging into his right buttock, and cool air round his knees. Then the sound of birdsong. His hands are free. He pulls off his blindfold and blinks in a light that seems dazzling, but which, as his eyes accommodate, he perceives to be a delicate pink dawn sky, latticed with pine branches. He is lying on rough ground at the foot of a tall, straight tree. He sits up, and puts a hand to his throbbing head. His pale legs, protruding from the red silk running shorts, seem a long way off, and hardly to belong to him, but they bend at the knee when he wills them to, and, turning to lean against the tree for support, he struggles to his feet. He draws deep, intoxicating breaths of the pure, pine-scented air into his lungs. Free! Alive! God bless Désirée! His eyes begin to focus properly. He is in a forest, on a hillside. Through the trees he can see a grey strip of road. He stumbles down the hil towards it, grasping at tree trunks for support, falling once and grazing his leg.

The road is narrow and badly paved. It does not look as if much traffic passes on it. Morris hobbles across to the other side and stands on the grass verge, looking over a low wall into a deep valley between mountains. He can see the road ribboning beneath him for miles in long parallel loops. There is not a sign of human habitation.

Morris begins to limp slowly downhill. After a few minutes, he stops. Behind the birdsong, from far, far below, there comes a sweet mechanical sound, the faint burr of a distant vehicle. He looks over the edge of the road again, and sees a small dot climbing up the winding road towards him, moving rapidly along the straights and slowing to take the hairpin bends, occasionally disappearing behind at clump of trees, and shooting into visiblity again, a faint squeal of tyres now accompanying the growl of the engine. It is a powerful GT coupé, driven with skill and verve. When it reaches the stretch of road directly beneath him, Morris identifies it as a bronze Maserati.

As the car comes round the final bend, Morris steps into the road and waves it down. The Maserati sprints towards him, then stops abruptly, spraying gravel from its tyres. A deeply tinted window sinks into the door on the driver's side, and the head of Fulvia Morgana, her tawny hair held in a silk scarf, appears in the aperture. Her eyebrows are arched in astonishment above her Roman nose.

"Why, Morris!" she says. "What are you doing here? People have been looking all over for you."

In Japanese language no articles. No *"a"*, no *"the"*. In Japanese inn (*ryokan*) where Persse takes room (because cheaper than Western-style hotel) not many articles either.

No chair, no bed. Just matting, one cushion and small low table. At night maid lays out bedding on floor. Walls and doors are made of paper pasted on wood. No lock on sliding door. Maid brings meals to room, kneels to serve Persse seated on cushion before table. Noise of slurping audible through paper walls on all sides. In Japan polite to make noise when eating—signifies enjoyment. Communal bathroom where naked men soap and rinse themselves squatting on dwarf milking stools before climbing into large common bathtub to soak, floating languidly in steaming water, backs of heads resting on tiled rim of bath. Toilets like bidets hooded at one end and raised on plinth with footrests at each side: easy to pee in but other job trickier.

Persse wanders round Tokyo in a daze, not quite sure whether he is suffering more from culture shock or jet lag. He flew by night from Honolulu to Tokyo, crossed the international date line and lost a whole day of his life. One minute it was 11.15 p.m. on Tuesday, the next it was 11.16 p.m. on Wednesday. When he arrived in Tokyo it was still night. The night seemed to go on for ever. It is hot in Tokyo, hotter than Honolulu and without the mitigation of the trade winds. As soon as Persse goes out into the street he breaks out in sweat and feels it trickling down his torso from under his arms. The Japanese, however, seem unperturbed and unperspiring, waiting patiently at the intersections for the traffic lights to change, or pressed uncomplainingly together in the subway train.

Persse travels back and forth across Tokyo on his quest. He enquires from the British Council and the United States Information Service and the Japanese Cultural Ministry about conferences being held in Tokyo at this time, and though there are several, on subjects as various as cybernetics, fish farming, Zen Buddhism, and economic forecasting, none of them seems likely to be of interest to Angelica. He has great hopes of a congress of science-fiction writers in Yokohama, but on investigation its membership turns out to be exclusively Asian and male.

To make up for this last disappointment, Persse treats himself to a steak dinner in a restaurant in the centre of Tokyo—a luxury he can ill afford, but he feels less dejected

after consuming it with a few bottles of beer. Later he
wanders through the streets off the Ginza, lined with small
bars, whose pavements are crowded with harmlessly drunk
Japanese businessmen evidently celebrating the fact that it is
Friday. The night is close and humid, and suddenly it begins
to rain. Persse dodges into the first bar he comes to, an
establishment calling itself simply "*Pub*", and descends the
stairs towards the sound of pop music of nineteen-sixties
vintage, Simon and Garfunkel. Oriental faces turn and smile
genially at him as he comes into a small L-shaped bar. He is
the only Westerner present. A hostess shows him to a seat,
takes his order for beer and puts a bowl of salted nuts in
front of him. In the middle of the room two Japanese men in
business suits are singing "Mrs Robinson" in English into a
microphone, a phenomenon which puzzles Persse for several reasons one of which he cannot instantly identify. The
two men conclude their performance, receive friendly applause from the customers, and sit down among them. The
chief puzzle, Persse realizes, is that they managed to produce a very creditable imitation of Simon and Garfunkel's
guitar-playing without the advantage of possessing any visible instruments.

The hostess brings Persse his drink in a litre-sized bottle,
and a large album full of pop song lyrics in various
languages, all numbered. She motions him to choose one,
and he points at random at number 77, "Hey Jude!" and
returns the album to her, sitting back in the expectation of
having his request performed by the two cabaret artists. But
the hostess smiles, shakes her head, and gives the book
back to him. She calls something to the barman and motions
Persse to stand up, chattering to him in Japanese. "Sorry, I
don't understand," says Persse. "Can't they sing, 'Hey
Jude'? I don't mind—'A Hard Day's Night' will do." He
points to song number 78. She calls out something to the
barman again, he returns the book, she pushes it back into
his hands. "Sorry, I don't understand," he says, embarrassed.
The hostess gestures to him to sit down, to relax, not to
worry, and she goes across to a group of men at a table in
the opposite corner of the room. She returns with a youngish
man dressed in a neat sports shirt with an Arnold Palmer

monogram on the chest, and holding a small glass of liquor.
He bows and smiles toothily.

"Are you American? British?" he says.

"Irish."

"Irish? That is very interesting. May I interpret for you?
Which song do you wish to sing?"

"I don't wish to sing at all!" Persse protests. "I just
came in here for a quiet drink."

The Japanese beams toothily and sits down beside him.
"But this is *karaoke* bar," he says. "Everybody sings in
karaoke bar."

Hesitantly, Persse repeats the word. "*Karaoke*—what does
that mean?"

"Literally *karaoke* means 'empty orchestra.' You see, the
barman provides the orhestra," he gestures towards the bar,
at the back of which Persse now sees that there is a long
shelf of music cassettes and a cassette deck, "And you
provide the voice"—he gestures to the microphone.

"Oh, I see!" says Persse laughing and slapping his thigh.
The Japanese laughs too and calls something across to his
friends, who also laugh. "So which song, please?" he says,
turning back to Persse.

"Oh, I'll have to have a lot of beers before you get me up
to that mike," he says.

"I sing with you," says the man, who has evidently had
quite a few drinks himself this evening. "I also like Beatle
songs. What is your name, please?"

"Persse McGarrigle. And what is yours?"

"I am Akira Sakazaki." He takes a card from his breast
pocket and gives it to Persse. It is printed in Japanese on
one side and in English on the other. Underneath his name
there are two addresses, one that of a university English
Department.

"Now I understand why you speak English so well,"
Persse says. "I'm a university teacher myself."

"Yes?" Akira Sakazaki's smile seems to fill his entire
face with teeth. "Where do you teach?"

"Limerick. I'm afraid I haven't got a card to give you."

"Please write," says Akira, taking a ball pen from his
pocket and putting a paper napkin in front of Persse. "Your

name is very difficult for Japanese." When Persse obliges, Akira takes the paper napkin to the microphone and says into it, "Ladies and gentlemen, Professor Persse McGarrigle of University College, Limerick, Ireland, will now sing, 'Hey Jude'."

"No he won't," says Persse, signalling to the barman for another beer.

Akira evidently translates his announcement into Japanese, for there is a volley of applause from the other customers, and smiles of encouragement in Persse's direction. He begins to weaken. "Have you any Dylan songs in that book?" he asks.

They have some of the most popular ones, "Tambourine Man" and "Blowin' in the Wind" and "Lay, Lady, Lay". Persse doesn't really need the album with the lyrics, since he knows these songs off by heart, and frequently sings them in the bath, but undoubtedly his performance is enhanced by having the original backing tracks as accompaniment. He sings "Tambourine Man," nervously at first, but gradually warming to the task, and putting on a plausible imitation of Dylan's nasal whine. The applause is rapturous. He sings "Blowin' in the Wind" and "Lay, Lady, Lay" as encores. At Akira's earnest request, he sings "Hey Jude" in duet with him. They yield the floor at last to a young girl who sings, shyly, but with perfect timing, Diana Ross's version of "Baby Love".

Akira introduces Persse to his circle of friends, explaining that they are all translators, who meet once a month in this bar, "to let the hair down and put the knees up." The Japanese beams proudly as he displays these idioms to Persse. All the translators give him their cards except one who is asleep or drunk in the corner. Most of them are technical and commercial translators, but, learning that Persse is a teacher of English literature, they politely make literary conversation. The man sitting on Persse's left, who translates maintenance manuals for Honda motorcycles, volunteers the information that he recently saw a play by Shakespere performed by a Japanese company, entitled, "The Strange Affair of the Flesh and the Bosom."

"I don't think I know that one," says Persse politely.

"He means, *The Merchant of Venice*," Akira explains.

"Is that what it's called in Japan?" says Persse with delight.

"Some of the older translations of Shakespeare in our country were rather free," says Akira apologetically.

"Do you know any other good ones?"

"Good ones?" Akira looks puzzled.

"Funny ones."

"Oh!" Akira beams. It seems not to have occurred to him before that "The Strange Affair of the Flesh and the Bosom" is amusing. He ponders. "There is, 'Lust and Dream of the Transitory World,' " he says. "That is—"

"No, don't tell me—let me guess," says Persse. "*Anthony and Cleopatra*?"

"*Romeo and Juliet*," says Akira. "And 'Swords of Freedom' . . ."

"*Julius Caesar*?"

"Correct."

"You know," says Persse, "there's the makings of a good parlour game here. You could make up your own . . . like, 'The Mystery of the Missing Handkerchief' for *Othello*, or 'A Sad Case of Early Retirement' for *Lear*." He calls for another round of drinks.

"When I translate English books," says Akira, "I always try to get as close as possible to the original titles. But sometimes it is difficult, especially when there is a pun. For example, Ronald Frobisher's *Any Road*—"

"Ronald Frobisher—have you translated him?"

"I am presently translating his novel, *Could Try Harder*. Do you know it?"

"Know it? I know *him*."

"Really? You know Mr Frobisher? But that is wonderful! You must tell me all about him. What kind of man is he?"

"Well," says Persse. "He's very nice. But rather irascible."

"Irascible? That is a new word to me."

"It means, easily angered."

"Oh yes, of course, he was Angry Young Man." Akira nods delightedly, and calls the attention of his friends to the fact that Persse is acquainted with the distinguished British novelist whose work he is translating. Persse recounts how

Frobisher set the London *literati* adrift on the Thames, a story received with great pleasure by all, though they seem a little disappointed that the ship did not actually float out to sea and sink.

"You must know a lot of English writers," says Akira.

"No, Ronald Frobisher is the only one," says Persse. "Do you translate many?"

"No, only Mr Frobisher," says Akira.

"Well," says Persse. "It's a small world. Do you have that saying in Japan?"

"Narrow world," says Akira. "We say, 'It's a narrow world.'"

At this point, the man who was asleep in the corner wakes up, and is introduced to Persse as Professor Motokazu Umeda, a colleague of Akira's. "He is translator of Sir Philip Sidney," says Akira. "He will know more of the old Shakespeare titles."

Professor Umeda yawns, rubs his eyes, accepts a whisky, and when Persse's interest has been explained to him, comes up with "The Mirror of Sincerity" (*Pericles*), "The Oar Well-Accustomed to the Water" (*All's Well That Ends Well*) and "The Flower in the Mirror and the Moon on the Water" (*The Comedy of Errors*).

"Oh, that one beats them all!" exclaims Persse. "That's really beautiful."

"It is a set phrase," Akira explains. "It means, that which can be seen but cannot be grasped."

"Ah," says Persse with a pang, suddenly reminded of Angelica. That which can be seen but which cannot be grasped. His euphoria begins rapidly to ebb away.

"Excuse me," says Professor Motokazu Umeda, offering Persse his card, printed in Japanese on one side and English on the other. Persse stares at the name, which now rings a distant, or not so distant, bell.

"Were you by any chance at a conference in Honolulu recently?" he asks.

"Morris called me as soon as he got back to the villa," says Désirée. "At first he was hysterical with gratitude, it was like being licked all over your face by your dog when you

get back home from a trip, I could almost hear his tail wagging on the other end of the line. Then when it sank in that I hadn't paid over any money, he turned very nasty, more like the Morris I remembered, accused me of being mean and callous and putting his life in jeopardy.''

"Tsk, tsk," says Alice Kauffman on the other end of the telephone line, a sound like the rustling of empty chocolate wrappers.

"I told him, I was prepared to pay up to forty thousand dollars for his release, I was already collecting the notes together and stashing them away right here in the hotel safe, and it wasn't my fault if the kidnappers decided to let him go for nothing.''

"Did they?"

"Apparently. They must have got scared that the police would find them, or something. The police are all on my side, incidentally, they think I broke down the kidnappers' morale by bargaining with them. I'm getting a very good press here. 'The Novelist with Nerves of Steel', they call me in the magazines. I told Morris that, and it didn't make him any sweeter . . . Anyway, I'm going to put the whole story into my book. It's a wonderful inversion of the normal power relationships between men and women, the man finding himself totally dependent on the generosity of the woman. I might change the ending.''

"Yeah, let the sonofabitch die," says Alice Kauffman. "Where is he now, anyway?"

"Jerusalem. Some conference or other he's organizing. Another thing he's sore about is that a fink called Howard Ringbaum whom Morris specifically excluded from the conference took advantage of his temporary disappearance to get himself accepted by the other organizer. You'd think Morris would have better things to think about, wouldn't you, a man back from the edge of the grave, you might say?"

"That's men for you, honey," says Alice Kauffman. "Speaking of which, how's the book coming along?"

"I'm hoping this new idea will get it moving again," says Désirée.

*   *   *

According to Motokazu Umeda, who responded to her paper at Honolulu, Angelica intended to travel on to Seoul, via Tokyo, to attend a conference on Critical Theory and Comparative Literature to which, it was rumoured, various big Parisian guns had been lured by the promise of a free trip to the Orient. Persse, now beyond all thoughts of prudent budgeting, waves his magic green-and-white card again, and takes wing to Seoul by Japanese Airlines. On the plane he meets another Helper, a beautiful Korean girl in the adjacent seat, who is drinking vodka and smoking Pall Malls as if her life depends on consuming as much duty free as possible for the duration of the flight. The vodka makes her loquacious and she explains to Persse that she is going home from the States for her annual visit to her family and will not be able to indulge in alcohol or tobacco for the next two weeks. "Korea is a modern country on the surface," she says, "but underneath it's very traditional and conservative, especially as regards social behaviour. I can tell you, when I first went to the States I couldn't believe my eyes—kids being cheeky to their parents, young people kissing in public—the first time I saw that I fainted. Then smoking and drinking—at home it's considered insulting for a young unmarried woman to smoke in front of her elders. If my parents knew that I was not only smoking in front of my elders, but living with one of them, I guess they'd disown me. So I have to play the part of the good little Korean girl for the next two weeks, not smoking, refusing strong drink, speaking only when spoken to." She reaches up and presses the service button above her head to order another vodka. "Now my parents want me to come home and get married to a guy they have lined up for me—yes, we still have arranged marriages in Korea, believe it or not. My father can't understand why I keep putting him off. 'You want to get married, don't you?' he says 'Settle down, have children?' What can I tell him?"

"That you're already engaged?" Persse suggests.

"Ah, but I'm not," says the girl sadly. Her name is Song-Mi Lee, and she seems, to judge from the names she casually lets drop, to move in high academic circles in the United States. She tells him that the conference on Critical

Theory and Comparative Literature will almost certainly be held at the Korean Academy of Sciences, a purpose-built conference and study centre just outside Seoul. He can take a taxi from the city centre, but must be sure to agree the fare first and should refuse to pay more than 700 won. Later, after they have landed, he sees her in the Arrivals hall of the airport, demurely smiling and amazingly sober, being greeted with bouquets by proud parents in tailored Western clothes.

It is the monsoon season in Korea, and Seoul is wet and humid, a concrete wilderness of indistinguishable suburbs ringing a city centre whose inhabitants are apparently so terrorized by the traffic that they have decided to live under the ground in a complex of subways lined with brightly lit shops. Persse takes a taxi to the Korean Academy of Sciences, a complex of buildings in oriental-modernist style set at the feet of low wooded hills, but the conference on Critical Theory and Comparative Literature has, he is hardly surprised to learn, finished and its participants have dispersed— some on a sight-seeing tour of the south. So Persse takes a train which trundles through a sopping and unrelievedly green landscape of paddy fields and tree-topped hills swathed in mist, to the resort town of Kyong-ju, site of many ancient monuments, temples and modern hotels, and an artificial lake on which floats, like a gigantic bathtoy, a fibreglass pleasure-boat in the shape of a white duck, disembarking from which Persse meets, not Anglica, but Professor Michel Tardieu, in the company of three smiling Korean professors, all called Kim. Angelica, he learns from Tardieu, was indeed at the conference, but did not join the sightseeing tour. Tardieu seems to remember that she was going on to another conference, in Hong Kong.

Now it is mid-August, and Morris Zapp's conference on the Future of Criticism in Jerusalam is in full swing. Almost everybody involved agrees that it is the best conference they have ever attended. Morris is smug. The secret of his success is very simple: the formal proceedings of the conference are kept to a bare minimum. There is just one paper a day actually delivered by its author, early in the morning. All the other papers are circulated in Xeroxed form, and the

remainder of the day is allocated to "unstructured discussion" of the issues raised in these documents, or, in other words, to swimming and sunbathing at the Hilton pool, sightseeing in the Old City, shopping in the bazaar, eating out in ethnic restaurants, and making expeditions to Jericho, the Jordan valley, and Galilee.

The Israeli scholars, a highly professional and fiercely competitive group, are disgruntled with this arrangement, since they have been looking forward to attacking each other in the presence of a distinguished international audience, and the tourist attractions of Jerusalem and environs naturally have less novelty for them. But everybody else is delighted, with the exception of Rodney Wainwright, who still has not finished his paper. The only finished paper he has in his luggage is one by Sandra Dix, submitted to him just before he left Australia as part of her assessment in English 351. It is entitled "Matthew Arnold's Theory of Culture," and it begins:

> *According to Matthew Arnold culture was getting to know, on the matters that most concerned you, the best people. Matthew Arnold was a famous headmaster who wrote "Tom Brown's Schooldays" and invented the game of Rugby as well as the Theory of Culture. If I don't get a good grade for this course I will tell your wife that we had sex in your office three times this semester, and you wouldn't let me out when there was a fire drill in case somebody saw us leaving the room together . . .*

Rodney Wainwright goes hot and cold every time he thinks of this term-paper, to which he awarded a straight "A" without a moment's hesitation, and which he has brought with him to Israel in case Bev or some colleague should happen to go through his desk drawers while he is away and find it. But he goes even hotter and colder when he thinks of his own conference paper, still stalled at, *"The question is, therefore, how can literary criticism . . ."* If only he had completed it in time! Then it could have been photocopied and circulated like most of the other contributions to the conference, and it wouldn't have mattered if it had been unconvincing, or even unintelligible, because nobody is

seriously reading the papers anyway—you keep coming
across them in the Hilton waste baskets . . . But because he
hadn't a finished text to give Morris Zapp when he arrived,
Rodney Wainwright has been allocated one of the "live",
formal sessions—yes, he has been accorded the privilege of
delivering his paper in person, on, in fact, the penultimate
morning of the conference, for he was obliged to ask for as
much grace as possible.

It's not surprising, therefore, that Rodney Wainwright is
unable to throw himself enthusiastically into the giddy round
of pleasure that his fellow-conferees are enjoying. While
they are at the poolside, or at the bar, or within the walls of
the Old City, or in the air-conditioned bus, he is sitting at
his desk behind drawn blinds in his room at the Hilton,
sweating and groaning over his paper—or if he is not, he is
guiltily aware that he ought to be. His colleagues' carefree
high spirits add gall to his own misery, and as the week passes
with no progress on his paper, and professional humiliation
looming ever nearer, his resentment of their euphoric mood
focuses upon one man in particular: Philip Swallow. Philip
Swallow, with his theatrical silver beard and his braying
Pommie voice and his unaccountably dishy mistress. What
does she see in him? It must be the randy old goat's appetite
for sex, because they seem to have a lot of that: Rodney
Wainwright happens to occupy the room next to theirs and
is not infrequently disturbed, working on his paper in the
watches of the night, or in the middle of the afternoon, by
muffled cries of pleasure audible when he presses his ear to
the party wall; and if he should go out onto his balcony in
the cool of the evening to stretch his cramped limbs, the
chances are that Philip Swallow and his Joy will be on the
adjacent balcony, clasped tenderly together, Joy rhapsodiz-
ing about the sunset reflected on the roofs and domes of the
Old City, while Philip fondles her tits under her négligé.
Rodney surprised Joy sunbathing topless on her balcony one
morning when she evidently expected him to be at the
formal paper session, and he has to admit that the tits would
be well worth fondling. Not quite as spectacular as Sandra
Dix's, perhaps, but then Sandra Dix seemed to derive little
pleasure from having them fondled by Rodney Wainwright,

or indeed, from any aspect of his sexual performance, insisting on chewing gum throughout intercourse, and breaking silence only to ask if he wasn't finished yet. For such meagre erotic reward has he risked domestic catastrophe in Cooktown, which makes it all the more aggravating to face professional disgrace in Jerusalem to the accompaniment of loudly voiced orgasmic bliss from the next room.

How does Philip Swallow do it? After screwing his blonde bird into the small hours, he is up bright and early for a swim in the hotel pool, never misses the morning lecture, is always first on his feet with a question when the speaker sits down, and signs up unfailingly for every sightseeing excursion on offer. It is as if the man has been given ten days to live and is determined to pack every instant with sensation, sublime or gross. No sooner have they all returned from retracing the Way of the Cross or inspecting the Dome of the Rock or visiting the Wailing Wall, than Philip Swallow is organizing a party to eat stuffed quail at an Arab restaurant hidden away in some crooked alley of the Old City which has been particularly recommended to him by one of the Israelis, setting off afterwards in a taxi with Joy and other dedicated hedonists to find a discothèque that is functioning clandestinely on the Sabbath. Yes, while Jerusalem is hushed in holy silence, the streets deserted and the shops all shut, Philip Swallow is bopping away under the strobe lights to the sound of the Bee Gees, his silver beard beaded with perspiration, his eyes fixed on Joy's nipples bouncing under her cheesecloth blouse as she twitches to the same rhythm. Rodney Wainwright knows because he squeezed into the taxi himself at the last moment, rather than return to the solitary contemplation of his unfinished paper, though he does not dance, and sits goomily on the edge of the dancefloor all evening, drinking overpriced beer and also watching Joy's nipples bounce.

The next morning, Rodney does not hear Philip Swallow go whistling down the corridor for his early morning swim, so perhaps at last his excesses are taking their toll. But after breakfast he is down in the lobby with Joy, looking only a little pale and drawn under his tan, all ready for the day's outing—it is a free day (free, that is, from even a single formal lecture) and an excursion has been arranged to the Dead Sea and Masada.

Rodney Wainwright knows that he ought to give this outing a miss, because his paper is due to be delivered the next morning, and it is still no further forward than when he arrived. He ought to spend the day alone in his room at the Hilton, with a carafe of iced water, working on it. But he knows all to well that he will fritter the day away, tearing up one draft after another, distracted by envious speculation about the fun the others will be having, especially Philip Swallow. Rodney Wainwright accordingly constructs a cunning plot against himself, whereby he will leave the composition of his paper to the last possible moment, viz., tonight, and thus force himself to finish it by the sheer, inexorable pressure of diminishing time.

The sun blazes down out of a cloudless blue sky on the brown, barren landscape. Even inside the air-conditioned bus it is warm. When they step down onto the parking lot of a bathing station on the shore of the Dead Sea, the heat is like the breath of a furnace. They change into their swimming costumes and float—it is impossible to swim—in a dense liquid—you could hardly call it water—the temperature and consistency of soup, so highly seasoned with chemicals that it burns your tongue and throat if you happen to swallow a drop. Afterwards, they are urged by their guide, Sam Singerman, the resident Israeli professor, to cover themselves with the black mud on the beach, which allegedly has health-giving properties; but of the party only Philip and Joy, followed by Morris Zapp and Thelma Ringbaum, have the nerve to do so, daubing each other hilariously with handfuls of the black goo, which dries rapidly in the sun so that they resemble naked aborigines. They rinse the mud off under the shower heads at the back of the beach and Rodney Wainwright follows them into the hot spring baths, which are so agreeable that they keep the others waiting in the bus while they dry and change, a delay for which Thelma Ringbaum is bitterly reproached by her husband.

Masada is, if it is possible, even hotter. After lunch in the inevitable cafeteria, a form of catering that Israel seems to have made its own, they take the cable car up to the ruined fortifications on the heights where the Jewish army of Eleazar committed collective suicide rather than surrender to the Romans in 73 A.D. "I'd rather commit suicide myself than come up here again," remarks an irreverent visitor, passing into the cable car that Rodney is leaving. The air is certainly no cooler up here—the cable car seems only to have brought them closer to the sun, which beats down relentlessly on the rock and rubble. The tourists stagger about in the heat, barely able to lift their cameras to eye level, looking for scraps of shade behind broken escarpments. Philip Swallow and Joy, hand-in-hand, descend some steps carved in the rock, which curve round the western face of the mountain to a little observation platform that is out of the sun. As they stand at the parapet, looking out over an immense panorama of stony hills and waterless valley, Philip slides his arm round Joy's waist. My God, even in this heat he's still thinking about sex, Rodney says to himself, wiping the perspiration from his face with his rolled-up sleeve. Then Philip Swallow happens to turn in his direction and frowns.

"Enjoying yourself?" he says in a distinctly challenging tone.

"What? Eh?" says Rodney Wainwright, startled. He has hardly exchanged a word with the Englishman all the conference.

"Having a good look? Or should I say, wank?"

"Philip," Joy murmurs protestingly.

Rodney feels himself blushing hectically. "I don't know what you're talking about," he blusters.

"I'm just about sick and tired of being followed about by you wherever we go," says Philip Swallow.

Joy makes to move off, but Philip detains her, tightening his grip around her waist. "No," he says, "I want to have it out with Mr Wainwright. You told me yourself he spied on you at the hotel the other day."

"I know," says Joy, "but I hate scenes."

"It's the heat," says Rodney to Joy, tapping his own forehead illustratively. "He doesn't know what he's saying."

"I bloody well do know," says Philip Swallow. "I'm saying you're some kind of pervert. A voyeur."

"'Ullo, our Dad!"

They all turn round to face a bronzed young man wearing jeans, tee-shirt and a gold stud in one ear, who has approached them by the staircase on the far side of the platform. Now it is Philip Swallow's turn to look embarrassed. He springs apart from Joy as if he had been burned. "Matthew!" he exclaims. "What in God's name are you doing here?"

"Working in a kibbutz further up the Jordan," says the young man. "I hitched out here as soon as I finished me A-Levels, didn't I?"

"Oh yes," says Philip, "it comes back to me now."

"Haven't been quite with it this summer, have you, Dad?" says the young man, looking curiously at Joy.

"Won't you introduce me, Philip?" she says.

"What? Oh, yes, of course," says Philip Swallow, plainly flustered. "This is my son, Matthew. This is, er, Mrs Simpson, she's at the conference I'm attending."

"Oh, uh," says Matthew.

Joy extends her hand. "How d'you do, Matthew?"

"Perhaps you would like to go back to the cable car with Mr Wainwright, Mrs Simpson," says Philip Swallow quickly. "While I catch up with my son's news."

Joy Simpson looks stunned, as if she had received an unexpected slap in the face. She stares at Philip Swallow, opens her mouth to speak, closes it again, and walks away in silence, followed by Rodney Wainwright grinning insanely to himself. He catches her up at the top of the steps. "Do you want to look in at the Museum or go straight back down?" he says.

"I can find my own way back, thank you very much," she says coldly, standing aside to let him pass.

Philip Swallow seems to go into shock after this episode. As the party boards the bus to return home he complains in Rodney Wainwright's hearing of feeling feverish, and spends the entire journey with his eyes closed and an expression of suffering on his face, but Joy is silent and unsympathetic, sitting beside him with her own eyes inscrutable behind dark glasses. In the evening Philip does not come down to join the others, who, showered and changed into clean clothes, are gathering in the lobby to go off to a barbecue in Sam Singerman's garden. Rodney hears Joy telling Morris Zapp that Philip has a temperature. "Heat stroke, I wouldn't be surprised," he says. "It sure was hot as hell out there. Too bad he'll miss the barbecue. You wanna come on your own?" "Why not?" says Joy. Morris Zapp catches Rodney Wainwright's eye as he hovers a few years away. "You coming, Wainwright?" Rodney gives a sickly grin: "No, I think I'll stay in and look over my paper for tomorrow."

All two and three-quarter pages of it, he thinks bitterly, going off to the elevator, *Schadenfreude* at Philip Swallow's discomfiture and indisposition overshadowed by his own approaching ordeal. Tonight is the night. Make or break. Finish the paper or bust. He lets himself into his room and turns on the desk lamp. He takes out his three dog-eared, sweat-stained pages of typescript and reads them through for the ninety-fourth time. They are good pages. The prolegomena moves smoothly, confidently, to define the point at issue. *"The question is, therefore, how can literary criticism . . ."* Then there is nothing: blank page, white space—or a black hole which seems to have swallowed up his capacity for constructive thought.

The trouble is that Rodney Wainwright's imaginative projection of himself stepping up to the lectern the next morning with only two and three-quarter pages of typescript to last him for fifty minutes, is so vivid, so particular in every psychosomatic symptom of terror, that it hypnotizes him, it paralyses thought, it renders him less capable than ever of continuing with the composition of his paper. He sees himself pausing at the end of his two and three-quarter pages, taking a sip of water, looking at his audience, their faces upturned patiently, expectantly curiously, restlessly, impatiently, angrily, pityingly . . .

In desperation, he helps himself to an extravagantly priced miniature bottle of whisky from the refrigerator in his room, and thus stimulated, begins to write something, anything, using a blue ballpen and sheets of Hilton notepaper. Fuelled by more miniatures, of gin, vodka, and cognac, his hand flies across the page with a will of its own.

He begins to feel more optimistic. He chuckles to himself, twisting the tops off miniatures of Benedictine, Cointreau, Drambuie, with one hand, while the other writes on. He hears Joy Simpson return from the barbecue and let herself into the nextdoor room. He breaks off from composition for a moment to press his ear against the party wall. Silence. "No shagging tonight, eh, sport?" he shouts hilariously at the wall, as he staggers back to his desk, and snatches up a fresh sheet of paper.

Rodney Wainwright wakes in the morning to find his throbbing head reposing on top of the desk amid a litter of empty miniatures and sheets of paper covered with illegible gibberish. He sweeps the bottles and the paper into the waste basket. He showers, shaves, and dresses carefully, in his lightweight suit, a clean shirt, and tie. Then he kneels down beside his bed and prays. It is the only resource left to him now. He needs a miracle: the inspiration to extemporize a lecture on the Future of Criticism for forty-five of the fifty minutes allocated to him. Rodney Wainwright, never a deeply religious man, who has not in fact raised his mind and heart to God since he was nine, kneels in the holy city of Jerusalem, and prays, diplomatically, to Jehovah, Allah and Jesus Christ, to save him from disgrace and ruin.

The lecture is due to begin at 9.30. At 9.25, Rodney presents himself in the conference room. Outwardly he appears calm. The only sign of the stress within is that he cannot stop smiling. People remark on how cheerful he looks. He shakes his head and smiles, smiles. His cheek muscles are aching from the strain, but he cannot relax them. Morris Zapp, who is to chair his lecture, is anxiously conferring with Joy Simpson. Philip Swallow is apparently worse—his temperature won't go down, he has pains in his joints, and is gasping for breath. She has called a doctor to see him. Morris Zapp nods sympathetically, frowning, concerned. Rodney, overhearing this intelligence, beams at them both. They stare back at him. "I'm going back to our room to see if the doctor has come," says Joy.

"Right, let's get this show on the road," says Morris to Rodney.

Rodney sits grinning at the audience while Morris Zapp

introduces him. Still smiling broadly, he takes his three typewritten pages to the lectern, smooths them down and squares them off. With lips curled in an expression of barely suppressed mirth, he begins to speak. The audience, inferring from his countenance that his discourse is supposed to be witty, titter politely. Rodney turns over to page three, and glimpses the abyss of white space at the foot of it. His smile stretches a millimetre wider.

At that moment there is a disturbance at the back of the room. Rodney Wainwright glances up from his script: Joy Simpson has returned, and is in whispered consultation with Sam Singerman in the back row. Other heads in their vicinity are turned, and talking to each other, wearing worried expressions. Rodney Wainwright falters in his delivery, goes back to the beginning of the sentence—his last sentence. *"The question is, therefore, how can literary criticism..."* The hum of conversation in the audience swells. A few people are leaving the room. Rodney stops and looks enquiringly at Morris Zapp, who frowns and raps on the table with his pen.

"Could we please have some quiet in the audience so that Dr Wainwright can continue with his paper?"

Sam Singerman stands up in the back row. "I'm sorry, Morris, but we've had some rather disturbing information. It seems that Philip Swallow has suspected Legionnaire's Disease."

Somewhere in the audience a woman screams and faints. Everyone else is on their feet, pale, aghast, tightlipped with fear, or shouting for attention. Legionnaire's Disease! That dreaded and mysterious plague, still not fully understood by the medical profession, that struck down a congress of the American Legion at the Bellevue Stratford hotel in Philadelphia three years ago, killing one in six of its victims. It is what every conferee these days secretly fears, it is the VD of conference-going, the wages of sin, retribution for all that travelling away from home and duty, staying in swanky hotels, ego-tripping, partying, generally overindulging. Legionnaire's Disease!

"I don't know about anyone else," says Howard Ringbaum,

in the front row, "but I'm checking out of this hotel right now. Come on, Thelma."

Thelma Ringbaum does not stir, but everybody else does—indeed there is something of a stampede to the exit. Morris turns to Rodney and spreads his hands apologetically. "It looks like we'll have to abandon the lecture. I'm very sorry."

"It can't be helped," says Rodney Wainwright, who has at last been able to stop smiling.

"It must be really disappointing, after all the work you've put into it."

"Oh well," says Rodney, with a philosophical shrug of his shoulders.

"We could try and fix another time later today," says Morris Zapp, taking out a fat cigar and lighting it, "but somehow I think this is curtains for the conference."

"Yes, I'm afraid so," says Rodney, slipping his three typewritten sheets back into their file cover.

Thelma Ringbaum comes up to the platform. "Do you think it's really Legionnaire's Disease, Morris?" she asks anxiously.

"No, I think that it's heat-stroke and the doctor's being paid by the Sheraton," say Morris Zapp. Thelma Ringbaum stares at him in wonder, then giggles. "Oh, Morris," she says, "you make a joke of everything. But aren't you a teeny bit worried?"

"A man who has been through what I've been through recently has no room left for fear," says Morris Zapp, with a flourish of his cigar.

This doesn't seem to be true of the rest of the conferees, however. Within an hour, most of them are in the hotel lobby with their bags packed, waiting for a bus that has been hired to take them to Tel Aviv, where they will catch their return flights. Rodney Wainwright mingles with the throng, receiving their condolences for having had his lecture interrupted. "Oh well," he says, shrugging his shoulders philosophically. "What about Philip?" he overhears Morris Zapp asking Joy Simpson, who also has her bags packed. "Who's going to look after him?"

"I can't risk staying," she says. "I have to think of my children."

"You're abandoning him?" says Morris Zapp, his eyebrows arched above his cigar.

"No, I phoned his wife. She's flying out by the next plane."

Morris Zapp's eyebrows arch ever higher. "Hilary? Was that a good idea?"

"It was Philip's idea," says Joy Simpson. "He asked me to phone her. So I did.'

Morris Zapp carefully inspects the end of his cigar. "I see," he says at length.

Immediately, there is another diversion (it is only eleven a.m., but already it is easily the most eventful day of Rodney Wainwright's life). A tall, athletic young man, with a mop of red, curly hair, a round freckled face and a snub nose peeling from sunburn, wearing dusty blue jeans and carrying a canvas sports bag, comes into the Hilton lobby under the disapproving stare of the doorman, and greets Morris Zapp.

"Percy!" Morris exclaims, grasping the newcomer by his shoulders and giving him a welcoming shake. "How are you? What are you doing in Jerusalem? You're just too late for the conference, Philip Swallow has caught the Black Death and we're all running away."

The young man looks round the lobby. "Is Angelica here?"

"Al Pabst? No, she isn't. Why?"

The young man's shoulders slump. "Oh, Jaysus, I was sure I'd find her here."

"She never signed up for this conference, as far as I know."

"It must be the only one, then," says the young man bitterly. "I've pursued that girl around the world from one country to another. Europe, America, Asia. I've spent all my savings and had my American Express card withdrawn for non-payment of arrears. I had to work my passage from Hong Kong to Aden, and hitchhiked across the desert and nearly died of thirst. And never a sight nor sound of her have I had since she gave me the slip at Rummidge."

Morris Zapp sucks on his cigar. "I didn't realize you were so interested in the girl," he says. "Why don't you just write to her?"

"Because nobody knows where she lives! She's always moving on from one conference to another."

Morris Zapp ponders. "Don't despair, Percy. I'll tell you what to do: come to the next MLA. Anybody who's a conference freak is sure to be at the MLA."

"When is that?"

"December. In New York."

"Jaysus," wails the young man. "Must I wait that long?"

Rodney Wainwright leans forward and touches him on the arm. "Excuse me, young man," he says, "but would you mind very much not taking the Lord's name in vain?"

At the University of Darlington, it is deep summer vacation. The campus is largely deserted. The lecture rooms are silent save for the flies that buzz at the windows; the common rooms and corridors are empty and eerily clean. The rooms of the faculty are locked, and in the Departmental offices underemployed secretaries knit and gossip and bluetack to the walls brightly coloured picture postcards sent to them from Cornwall or Corfu by their more fortunate friends. Only in the Computer Centre has nothing changed since the summer term ended and the vacation began. There sit the two men in their familiar attitudes, like cat and mouse, spider and fly, the one crouched over his computer console, the other watching from his glass cubicle, his hand moving rhythmically from a bag of potato chips to his mouth and back again.

Robin Dempsey seems to have grown old in his swivel seat—Persse McGarrigle would scarcely recognize the thickset, broadshouldered, vigorous man who had accosted him at the Rummidge sherry party. These shoulders are hunched now, the blue suit hangs limply from them over a wasted torso, the jaw sags rather than thrusts, and the small eyes seem even smaller, set even closer together, than before. The atmosphere is charged. There is a tension in the room, like static electricity, a sense of things moving to a crisis. The only sounds are the tapping of Robin Dempsey's fingers on the keyboard of his computer terminal, and the crunching of Josh Collins's potato chips.

Josh Collins screws up the empty bag and tosses it into the waste basket, without taking his eyes off Robin Dempsey. Now there is only one sound in the room. Very quietly, stealthily, Josh Collins leaves his glass cubicle and tiptoes towards the hunched, frenziedly typing figure of Robin Dempsey. Robin Dempsey suddenly stops typing, and John Collins freezes in unison, but he is close enough to read what is printed on the screen:

I CAN'T GO ON LIKE THIS I'M OBSESSED WITH PHILIP SWAL-
LOW MORNING NOON AND NIGHT ALL I CAN THINK ABOUT
IS HIM GETTING THE UNESCO CHAIR I CAN'T BEAR THE
THOUGHT OF IT BUT I CAN'T STOP THINKING ABOUT IT
THE WHOLE WORLD SEEMS TO CONSPIRE AGAINST ME IF I
FORGET HIM FOR A MOMENT I'M SURE TO OPEN A JOUR-
NAL AND SEE SOME SYCOPHANTIC REVIEW OF HIS BLOODY
BOOK OR AN ADVERTISEMENT FOR IT FULL OF QUOTA-
TIONS SAYING IT'S THE GREATEST THING SINCE BREAD
AND THIS MORNING I GOT A LETTER FROM MY SON
DESMOND HE'S IN ISRAEL WORKING ON A KIBBUTZ HE
SAID MATTHEW SWALLOW THAT'S SWALLOW'S BOY IS
OUT HERE WITH ME YESTERDAY HE MET HIS DAD WITH
HIS ARM ROUND A GOODLOOKING BLONDE BIRD HE WAS
AT SOME CONFERENCE IN JERUSALEM AT LEAST THAT
WAS HIS STORY YOU SEE WHAT I MEAN SWALLOW IS
HAVING IT ALL WAYS SEX AND FAME AND FOREIGN
TRAVEL ITS NOT FAIR I CAN'T STAND IT I'M GOING
CRAZY WHAT SHALL I DO

Robin Dempsey pauses, hesitates for a moment, then presses the query key:

?

Instantly ELIZA replies:

SHOOT YOURSELF.

Robin Dempsey stares, gapes, trembles, whimpers, covers his face with his hands. Then he hears from behind him a snigger, a splutter of suppressed laughter, and swivels round on his seat to find Josh Collins grinning at him. Robin

Dempsey looks from the grinning face to the computer's screen, and back again.

"You—" he says in a choked voice.

"Just a little joke," says Josh Collins, raising his hands in a pacifying gesture.

"You've been tampering with ELIZA," says Robin Dempsey, getting slowly to his feet.

"Now, now," says Josh Collins, backing away. "Keep calm."

"*You* made ELIZA say Swallow would get the UNESCO chair."

"You provoked me," says Josh Collins. "It's your own fault."

With a cry of rage, Robin Dempsey hurls himself upon Josh Collins. The two men grapple with each other, lurching round the room and banging into the equipment. They fall to the ground and roll across the floor, shouting and screaming abuse. One of the machines, jolted by a flying elbow or knee, stutters into life and begins to disgorge reams of printout which unfurls itself and becomes entangled in the wrestler's flailing limbs. The printout consists of one word, endlessly repeated:

ERROR ERROR ERROR ERROR ERROR ERROR ERROR ERROR
ERROR ERROR ERROR ERROR ERROR ERROR ERROR ERROR
ERROR ERROR ERROR ERROR ERROR ERROR ERROR ERROR
ERROR ERROR ERROR ERROR ERROR ERROR ERROR ERROR
ERROR ERROR ERROR ERROR ERROR ERROR ERROR ERROR
ERROR ERROR ERROR ERROR

PART V

THE MODERN LANGUAGE ASSOCIATION OF AMERICA is not, to British ears at any rate, a very appropriately named organization. It is as concerned with literature as with language, and with English as well as with those Continental European languages conventionally designated "modern". Indeed, making up by far the largest single group in the membership of the MLA are teachers of English and American literature in colleges and universities. The MLA is a professional association, which has some influence over conditions of employment, recruitment, curriculum development, *etc.*, in American higher education. It also publishes a fat quarterly, closely printed in double columns, devoted to scholarly research, known as *PMLA,* and a widely-used annual bibliography of work published in book or periodical form in all of the many subject areas that come within its purview. But to its members the MLA is best known, and loved, or hated, for its annual convention. Indeed, if you pronounce the acronym "MLA" to an American academic, he will naturally assume that you are referring not to the Association as such, nor to its journal or its bibliography, but to its convention. This is always held

over three days in the week between Christmas and New
Year, either in New York or in some other big American
city. The participants are mostly, but not exclusively American, since the Association has funds to bring distinguished
foreign scholars and creative writers to take part, and less
distinguished ones can sometimes persuade their own universities to pay their fares, or may be spending the year in
the United States anyway. In recent years, the average attendance at this event has been around ten thousand.

The MLA is the Big Daddy of conferences. A megacon-
ference. A three-ring circus of the literary intelligentsia.
This year it is meeting in New York, in two adjacent
skyscraper hotels, the Hilton and the Americana, which,
enormous as they are, cannot actually sleep all the delegates, who spill over into neighbouring hotels, or beg
accommodation from their friends in the big city. Imagine
ten thousand highly-educated, articulate, ambitious, competitive men and women converging on mid-Manhattan on
the 27th of December, to meet and to lecture and to question
and to discuss and to gossip and to plot and to philander and
to party and to hire or to be hired. For the MLA is a market
as well as a circus, it is a place where young scholars fresh
from graduate school look hopefully for their first jobs, and
more seasoned academics sniff the air for better ones. The
bedrooms of the Hilton and the Americana are the scene not
only of rest and dalliance but of hard bargaining and
rigorous interviewing, as chairmen of departments from
every state in the Union, from Texas to Maine, from the
Carolinas to California, strive to fill the vacancies on their
faculty rolls with the best talent available. In the present
acute job shortage, it's a buyer's market, and some of these
chairmen have such long lists of candidates to interview that
they never get outside their hotel rooms for the duration of
the convention. For them and for the desperate candidates
kicking their heels and smoking in the corridors, waiting
their turn to be scrutinized, the MLA is no kind of fun; but
for the rest of the members it's a ball, especially if you like
listening to lectures and panel discussions on every conceivable literary subject from "Readability and Reliability in the
Epistolary Novel of England, France and Germany" to

"Death, Resurrection and Redemption in the Works of Pirandello," from "Old English Riddles" to "Faulkner Concordances", from "Rationalismus und Irrationalismus im 18. Jahrhundert" to "Nueva Narrativa Hispanoamericana," from "Lesbian-Feminist Teaching and Learning" to "Problems of Cultural Distortion in Translating Expletives in the work of Cortazar, Sender, Baudelaire and Flaubert."

There are no less than six hundred separate sessions listed in the official programme, which is as thick as a telephone directory of a small town, and at least thirty to choose from at any hour of the day from 8.30 a.m. to 10.15 p.m., some of them catering to small groups of devoted specialists, others, featuring the most distinguished names in academic life, attracting enough auditors to fill the hotels' biggest ballrooms. The audiences are, however, restless and migratory: people stroll in and out of the conference rooms, listen a while, ask a question, and move on to another session while speakers are still speaking; for there is always the feeling that you may be missing the best show of the day, and a roar of laughter or applause from one room is quite likely to empty the one next door. And if you get tired of listening to lectures and papers and panel discussions, there is plenty else to do. You can attend the cocktail party organized by the Gay Caucus for the Modern Languages, or the Reception Sponsored by the American Association of Professors of Yiddish, or the Cash Bar Arranged in Conjunction with the Special Session on Methodological Problems in Monolingual and Bilingual Lexicography, or the Annual Dinner of the American Milton Society, or the Executive Council of the American Boccaccio Association, or the meetings of the Marxist Literary Group, the Coalition of Women in German, the Conference on Christianity and Literature, the Byron Society, the G. K. Chesterton Society, the Nathaniel Hawthorne Society, the Hazlitt Society, the D. H. Lawrence Society, the John Updike Society, and many others. Or you can just stand in the lobby of the Hilton and meet, sooner or later, everyone you ever knew in the academic world.

Persse McGarrigle is standing there, on the third morning of the conference, rubbing the warmth back into his hands, half-frozen by the bitterly cold wind blowing down the Avenue of the Americas, when he is greeted by Morris Zapp.

"Hi, Percy! How are ya liking the MLA?"

"It's . . . I can't find a word for it."

Morris Zapp chuckles expansively. He is wearing his loudest check sports jacket, and toting a huge cigar. He is obviously in his element. Every few seconds somebody comes up and slaps him on the shoulder or shakes his hand or kisses him on his cheek. "Morris, how *are* you? What are you working on? Where are you staying? Let's have a drink some time, let's have dinner, let's have breakfast." Morris shouts, waves, kisses, signals with his eyebrows, scribbles appointments in his diary, while contriving to advise Persse on which lectures to catch and which to avoid, and to ask him if he has seen any sign of Al Pabst.

"No," sighs Persse dejectedly. "She's not listed in the programme."

"That doesn't mean a thing, lots of people sign up after the programme has gone to press."

"The Convention Office doesn't have her name among the late registrations," says Persse. "I'm afraid she hasn't come."

"Don't despair, Percy, some people sneak in without registering, to save the fee."

"That's my own case," Persse confesses. He is still paying off the cost of his trip round the world, and it has been a struggle to raise the money to get here; how he is going to get home is a problem he hasn't yet faced.

"You want to cruise around the various meetings, looking out for the subjects that are likely to interest her."

"That's what I've been doing."

"Whatever you do, don't miss the forum on 'The Function of Criticism', 2.15 this afternoon in the Grand Ballroom."

"Are you speaking?"

"How did you guess? This is the big one, Percy. Arthur Kingfisher is moderator. The buzz is that he's going to decide who is his favoured candidate for the UNESCO Chair today. Sam Textel is here, ready to take the good news back to Paris. This forum is like a TV debate for Presidential candidates.''

"Who else is speaking?"

"Michel Tardieu, von Turpitz, Fulvia Morgana and Philip Swallow.''

Persse registers surprise. "Is Professor Swallow in the same league as the rest of you?''

"Well, originally they invited Rudyard Parkinson, but he missed his plane—we just got a call from London. He was trying to put us in our place by only turning up for the last day of the Convention. Serves him right. Philip Swallow was here for the Hazlit Society, so they drafted him in as a substitute for Parkinson. He was born lucky, Philip. He always seems to fall on his feet.''

"He didn't have Legionnaire's Disease after all, then?''

"Nuh. As I thought, it was just heat-stroke. He'd been reading an article about Legionnaire's Disease in *Time* magazine and frightened himself into reproducing the symptoms. Hilary flew out to Israel to look after him quite unnecessarily. However, it had the effect of bringing them together again. Philip decided he was getting to the age when he needed a mother more than a mistress. Or maybe Joy did. But you didn't know Joy, did you?''

"No," says Persse. "Who was she?''

"It's a long story, and I must get my head together for the forum this afternoon. Look, the MLA executive are giving a party tonight, in the penthouse suite. If you wanna go, come along to my room at about ten tonight, OK? Room 956. *Ciao!*''

An immense audience was gathered in the Grand Ballroom to hear the forum on "The Function of Criticism". There must have been well over a thousand people sitting on the rows of gilt-painted, plush-upholstered chairs, and hundreds more standing at the back and along the sides of the vast, chandelier-hung room, attracted not only by the interest of the subject and the distinction of the speakers, but also by the rumoured involvement of the event in the matter of the UNESCO Chair. Persse, sitting near the front, and twisting round in his seat to scrutinize the audience for a sign of

Angelica, was confronted by a sea of faces turned expectantly towards the platform where the five speakers and their chairman sat, each with a microphone and a glass of water before them. A roar of conversation rose to the gold and white ceiling, until Arthur Kingfisher, lean, dark-eyed, hook-nosed, white-maned, silenced the crowd with a tap of his pencil on his microphone. He introduced the speakers: Philip Swallow, who, Persse noted with surprise, had shaved off his beard, and seemed to regret it, fingering his weak chin with nervous fingers like an amputee groping for a missing limb; Michel Tardieu, pouchy and wrinkled, in a scaly brown leather jacket that was like some extrusion of his own skin; von Turpitz, scowling under his skullcap of pale, limp hair, dressed in a dark business suit and starched shirt; Fulvia Morgana, sensational in black velvet dungarees worn over a long-sleeved tee-shirt of silver lamé, her fiery hair lifted from her haughty brow by a black velvet sweatband studded with pearls; Morris Zapp in his grossly checked sports jacket and roll-neck sweater, chewing a fat cigar.

Philip Swallow was the first to speak. He said the function of criticism was to assist in the function of literature itself, which Dr Johnson had famously defined as enabling us better to enjoy life, or better to endure it. The great writers were men and women of exceptional wisdom, insight, and understanding. Their novels, plays and poems were inexhaustible reservoirs of values, ideas, images, which, when properly understood and appreciated, allowed us to live more fully, more finely, more intensely. But literary conventions changed, history changed, language changed, and these treasures too easily became locked away in libraries, covered with dust, neglected and forgotten. It was the job of the critic to unlock the drawers, blow away the dust, bring out the treasures into the light of day. Of course, he needed certain specialist skills to do this: a knowledge of history, a knowledge of philology, of generic convention and textual editing. But above all he needed enthusiasm, the love of books. It was by the demonstration of this enthusiasm in action that the critic forged a bridge between the great writers and the general reader.

Michel Tardieu said that the function of criticism was not to add new interpretations and appreciations of *Hamlet or Le Misanthrope* or *Madame Bovary* or *Wuthering Heights* to the hundreds that already existed in print or the thousands that had been uttered in classrooms and lecture theatres, but to uncover the fundamental laws that enabled such works to be produced and understood. If literary criticism was supposed to be knowledge, it could not be founded on interpretation, since interpretation was endless, subjective, unverifiable, unfalsifiable. What was permanent, reliable, accessible to scientific study, once we ignored the distracting surface of actual texts, were the deep structural principles and binary oppositions that underlay all texts that had ever been written and that ever would be written: paradigm and syntagm, metaphor and metonymy, mimesis and diegesis, stressed and unstressed, subject and object, culture and nature.

Siegfried von Turpitz said that, while he sympathized with the scientific spirit in which his French colleague approached the difficult question of defining the essential function of criticism in both its ontological and teleological aspects, he was obliged to point out that the attempt to derive such a definition from the formal properties of the literary art-object as such was doomed to failure, since such art-objects enjoyed only an as it were virtual existence until they were realized in the mind of a reader. (When he reached the word "reader" he thumped the table with his black-gloved fist.)

Fulvia Morgana said that the function of criticism was to wage undying war on the very concept of "literature" itself, which was nothing more than an instrument of bourgeois hegemony, a fetichistic reification of so-called aesthetic values erected and maintained through an élitist educational system in order to conceal the brutal facts of class oppression under industrial capitalism.

Morris Zapp said more or less what he had said at the Rummidge conference.

While they were speaking, Arthur Kingfisher looked more and more depressed, slumped lower and lower in his chair, and seemed to be almost asleep by the time Morris had finished. He roused himself from this lethargy to ask if there were any questions or comments from the floor. Microphones had been placed at strategic intervals in the aisles to allow members of the vast audience to make themselves heard, and several delegates who had not been able to insinuate themselves into any other session of the convention took this opportunity to deliver prepared diatribes on the function of criticism. The speakers made predictable rejoinders. Kingfisher yawned and glanced at his watch. "I think we have time for one more question," he said.

Persse was aware of himself, as if he were quite another person, getting to his feet and stepping into the aisle and up to a microphone placed directly under the platform. "I have a question for all the members of the panel," he said. Von Turpitz glared at him and turned to Kingfisher. "Is this man entitled to speak?" he demanded. "He is not wearing an identification badge." Arthur Kingfisher brushed the objection aside with a wave of his hand. "What's your question, young man?" he said.

"I would like to ask each of the speakers," said Persse, "what follows if everybody agrees with you?" He turned and went back to his seat.

Arthur Kingfisher looked up and down the table to invite a reply. The panel members however avoided his eye. They glanced instead at each other, with grimaces and gesticulations expressive of bafflement and suspicion. "What follows is the Revolution," Fulvia Morgana was heard to mutter; Philip Swallow, "Is it some sort of trick question?" and von Turpitz, "It's a fool's question." A buzz of excited conversation rose from the audience, which Arthur Kingfisher silenced with an amplified tap of his pencil. He leaned forward in his seat and fixed Persse with a beady eye. "The members of the forum don't seem to understand your question, sir. Could you re-phrase it?"

Persse got to his feet again and padded back to the microphone in a huge, expectant silence. "What I mean is," he said, "what do you *do* if everybody agrees with you?"

"Ah." Arthur Kingfisher flashed a sudden smile that was like sunshine breaking through cloud. His long, olive-complexioned face, worn by study down to the fine bone, peered over the edge of the table at Persse with a keen regard. "That is a very good question. A very in-ter-est-ing question. I do not remember that question being asked before." He nodded to himself. "You imply, of course, that what matters in the field of critical practice is not truth but difference. If everybody were convinced by your arguments, they would have to do the same as you and then there would be no satisfaction in doing it. To win is to lose the game. Am I right?"

"It sounds plausible," said Persse from the floor. "I don't have an answer myself, just the question."

"And a very good question too," chuckled Arthur Kingfisher. "Thank you, ladies and gentlemen, our time is up."

The room erupted with a storm of applause and excited conversation. People jumped to their feet and began arguing with each other, and those at the back stood on their chairs to get a glimpse of the young man who had asked the question that had confounded the contenders for the UNESCO Chair and roused Arthur Kingfisher from his long lethargy. "Who is he?" was the question now on every tongue. Persse, blushing, dazed, astonished at his own temerity, put his head down and made for the exit. The crowd at the doors parted respectfully to let him through, though some conferees patted his back and shoulders as he passed— gentle, almost timid pats, more like touching for luck, or for a cure, than congratulations.

That afternoon there was a brief but astonishing change in the Manhattan weather, unprecedented in the city's meteorological history. The icy wind that had been blowing straight from the Arctic down the skyscraper canyons, numbing the faces and freezing the fingers of pedestrians and streetvendors, suddenly dropped, and turned round into the gentlest warm southern breeze. The clouds disappeared and the sun came out. The temperature shot up. The hardpacked dirty snow piled high at the edge of the sidewalks began to thaw and trickle into the gutters. In Central Park squirrels came out of hibernation and lovers held hands without the impediment of gloves. There was a rush on sunglasses at Bloomingdales.

People waiting in line for buses smiled at each other, and cab-drivers gave way to private cars at intersections. Members of the MLA Convention leaving the Hilton to walk to the Americana, cringing in anticipation of the cold blast on the other side of the revolving doors, sniffed the warm, limpid air increduously, threw open their parkas, unwound their scarves and snatched off their woolly hats. Fifty-nine different people consciously misquoted T. S. Eliot's "East Coker", declaiming *"What is the late December doing/With the disturbance of the spring?"* in the hearing of the Americana's bell captain, to his considerable puzzlement.

In Arthur Kingfisher's suite at the Hilton, whither he repaired with Song-Mi Lee to rest after the forum, the central heating was stifling. "I'm going to open the goddam window," he said. Song-Mi Lee was doubtful. "We'll freeze," she said.

"No, it's a lovely day. Look—there are people on the sidewalk down there without topcoats." He struggled with the window fastenings: they were stiff, because seldom used, but eventually he got a pane open. Sweet fresh air gently billowed the net drapes. Arthur Kingfisher took deep breaths down into his lungs. "Hey, how d'you like this? The air is like wine. Come over here and breathe." Song-Mi came to his side and he put his arm round her. "You know something? It's like the halcyon days."

"What are they, Arthur?"

"A period of calm weather in the middle of winter. The ancients used to call them the halcyon days, when the kingfisher was supposed to hatch its eggs. Remember Milton— *'The birds sit brooding on the calmèd wave'*? The bird was a kingfisher. That's what 'halcyon' means in Greek, Song-Mi: kingfisher. The halcyon days were kingfisher days. My days. Our days." Song-Mi leaned her head against his shoulder and made a small, inarticulate noise of happiness and agreement. He was suddenly filled with an inexpressible tenderness towards her. He took her in his arms and kissed her, pressing her supple slender body against his own.

"Hey," he whispered as their lips parted. "Can you feel what I feel?"

With tears in her eyes, Song-Mi smiled and nodded.

* * *

Meanwhile, in other rooms, windowless and air-conditioned, the convention ground on remorselessly, and Persse paced the corridors and rode the elevators in search of Angelica, slipping into the back of lectures on "Time in Modern American Poetry" and "Blake's Conquest of Self" and "Golden Age Spanish Drama", putting his head round the door of seminars on "The Romantic Rediscovery of the Daemon", "Speech Act Theory" and "Neoplatonic Iconography". He was walking away in a state of terminal disappointment from a forum on "The Question of Postmodernism", when he passed a door to which a handwritten notice hastily scrawled on a sheet of lined notepaper had been thumbtacked. It said: *"Ad Hoc Forum on Romance."* He pushed open the door and went in.

And there she was. Sitting behind a table at the far end of the room, reading in a clear, deliberate voice from a sheaf of typewritten pages to an audience of about twenty-five people scattered over the dozen rows of chairs, and to three young men seated beside her at the table. Persse slipped into a seat in the back row. God, how beautiful she was! She wore the severe, scholarly look that he remembered from the lecture-room at Rummidge—heavy, dark-rimmed glasses, her hair drawn back severely into a bun, a tailored jacket and white blouse her only visible clothing. When she glanced up from her script, she seemed to be looking straight at him, and he smiled tentatively, his heart pounding, but she continued without a change of tone or expression. Of course, he recollected, with her reading glasses on he would be just a vague blur to her.

It was some time before Persse became sufficiently calm to attend to what Angelica was saying.

"Jacques Derrida has coined the term 'invagination' to describe the complex relationship between inside and outside in discursive practices. What we think of as the meaning or 'inside' of a text is in fact nothing more than its externality folded in to create a pocket which is both secret and therefore desired and at the same time empty and therefore impossible to possess. I want to appropriate this term and apply it, in a very specific sense of my own, to romance. If epic is a phallic genre, which can hardly be denied, and tragedy the genre of castration (we are none of us, I suppose, deceived by the self-blinding of Oedipus as to the true nature of the wound he is impelled to inflict upon himself, or likely to overlook the symbolic equivalence between eyeballs and testicles) then surely there is no doubt that romance is a supremely invaginated mode of narrative.

"Roland Barthes has taught us the close connection between narrative and sexuality, between the pleasure of the body and the 'pleasure of the text', but in spite of his own sexual ambivalence, he developed this analogy in an overly masculine fashion. The pleasure of the classic text, in Barthe's system, is all foreplay. It consists in the constant titillation and deferred satisfaction of the reader's curiosity and desire—desire for the solution of enigma, the completion of an action, the reward of virtue and the punishment of vice. The paradox of our pleasure in narrative, according to this model, is that while the need to 'know' is what impels us through a narrative, the satisfaction of that need brings pleasure to an end, just as in psychosexual life the possession of the Other kills Desire. Epic and tragedy move inexorably to what we call, and by no acident, a 'climax' —and it is, in terms of sexual metaphor, an essentially *male* climax—a single, explosive discharge of accumulated tension.

"Romance, in contrast, is not structured in this way. It has not one climax but many, the pleasure of this text comes and comes and comes again. No sooner is one crisis in the fortunes of the hero averted than a new one presents itself; no sooner has one mystery been solved than another is raised; no sooner has one adventure been concluded than another begins. The narrative questions open and close, open and close, like the contractions of the vaginal muscles in intercourse, and this process is in principle endless. The greatest and most characteristic romances are often unfinished— they end only with the author's exhaustion, as a woman's capacity for orgasm is limited only by her physical stamina. Romance is a multiple orgasm."

Persse listened to this stream of filth flowing from be-

tween Angelica's exquisite lips and pearly teeth with growing astonishment and burning cheeks, but no one else in the
audience seemed to find anything remarkable or disturbing
about her presentation. The young men seated at the table
beside her nodded thoughtfully, and fiddled with their pipes,
and made little notes on their scratchpads. One of them,
wearing a sports jacket of Donegal tweed, and with a soft
voice that seemed to match it, thanked Angelica for her talk
and asked if there were any questions.

"Most impressive, didn't you think?" whispered a female voice into Persse's ear. He turned to find a familiar
white-coiffed figure beside him.

"Miss Maiden! Fancy meeting you here!"

"You know I can't resist conferences, young man. But
wasn't that a brilliant performance? If only Jessie Weston
could have heard it."

"I can understand that it would appeal to you," said
Persse. "It was a bit too near the knuckle for my taste."
Somebody in the audience was asking Angelica if she would
agree that the novel, as a distinct genre, was born when
Epic, as it were, fucked the romance. She gave the suggestion careful consideration. "You know who she is, don't
you?" he whispered to Miss Maiden.

"Of course I know, she's Miss Pabst, your young lady."

"No, I mean who she *was*. As a baby."

"As a baby?" Miss Maiden looked at him with a queer
expression, at once fearful and expectant. One of the young
men at the table said, if the organ of epic was the phallus,
of tragedy the testicles, and of romance the vagina, what
was the organ of comedy? Oh, the anus, Angelic replied
instantly, with a bright smile. Think of Rabelais . . .

"You remember those twin girls, six weeks old, who
were found in an airplane in 1954?" Persse hissed.

"Why should I remember them?"

"Because you found them, Miss Maiden." He took from
his wallet a folded photocopy of a newspaper cutting sent to
him by Hermann Pabst. "Look, *'Twin girls found in KLM
Stratocruiser'*—and here's your name: *'discovered in the
plane's toilet by Miss Sybil Maiden of Girton College.'* You

could have knocked me down with a feather when I saw that."

The cutting seemed to have the same effect on Miss Maiden, for she toppled off her chair in a dead faint. Persse caught her just before she hit the ground. "Help!" he cried. People hurried to his assistance. By the time Miss Maiden had recovered, Angelica had disappeared.

Persse ran distractedly through the Hilton lobby, took the slow and express lifts at random to various floors, prowled along the carpeted corridors, searched the bars and restaurants and shops. After nearly an hour, he found her, changed into a flowing dress of red silk, with her hair, freshly washed, all loose and shining about her shoulders. She was about to step into an elevator on the seventeenth floor as its doors slid open to let him out.

This time there was no hesitation in his actions. This time she would not escape. Without a word, he took her in his arms and kissed her long and passionately. For a moment she stiffened and resisted, but then she suddenly relaxed and yielded to his fierce embrace. He felt the long, soft line of her body from bosom to thigh moulding itself to his. They seemed to melt and fuse together. Time held its breath. He was dimly aware of the lift doors opening and closing again, of people stepping in and out. Then, when the landing was empty and silent once more, he drew his lips away from hers.

"At last I've found you!" he panted.

"So it seems," she gasped.

"I love you!" he cried. "I need you! I want you!"

"Okay!" she laughed. "All *right*! Your room or mine?"

"I haven't got a room," he said.

Angelica hung a *Do Not Disturb* sign on the outside of the door before locking and chaining it from inside. It was now late afternoon and already dark. She switched on a single, heavily-shaded table lamp which shed a soft golden glow on the bed, and drew the curtains across the window. Her dress sank with a whisper to the floor. She stepped out of it, and put her hands behind her back to release the catch of her brassiere. He breasts poured out like honey. They swung and trembled as she stooped to strip off tights and briefs. The beauty of her bosom moved him almost to tears; the bold bush of black hair at her crotch startled and roused him. He turned away modestly to take off his own clothes, but she came up behind him and ran her cool soft fingers down his chest and belly, brushing his rigid, rampant sex. "Don't, for the love of God," he groaned, "or I won't answer for the consequences." She chuckled, and led him by the hand to the bed. She lay down on her back, with her knees slightly raised, and smiled at him with her dark peat-pool eyes. He parted her thighs like the leaves of a book, and stared into the crack, the crevice, the deep romantic chasm that was the ultimate goal of his quest.

Like most young men's first experience of sexual intercourse, Persse's was as short as it was sweet. As soon as he was invaginated, he came, tumultuously. With Angelica's assistance and encouragement, however, he came twice more in the hours that followed, less precipitately, and in two quite different attitudes; and when he could come no more, when he was only a dry, straining erection, with no seed to expel, Angelica impaled herself upon him and came again and again and again, until she toppled off, exhausted. They lay sprawled across the bed, sweating and panting.

Persse felt ten years older, and wiser. He had fed on honey-dew and drunk the milk of paradise. Nothing could be the same again. Was it possible that in due course they could put on their clothes and go out of the room and behave like ordinary people again, after what had passed between them? It must always be so between lovers, he concluded: their knowledge of each other's nightside was a secret bond between them. "You'll have to marry me now, Angelica," he said.

"I'm not Angelica, I'm Lily," murmured the girl beside him.

He whipped over on to all fours, crouched above her, stared into her face. "You're joking. Don't joke with me, Angelica."

She shook her head. "No joke."

"You're Angelica."

"Lily."

He stared at her until his eyes bulged. The dreadful fact was that he had no idea whether she was Angelica or Lily telling the truth.

"There's only one way to tell the diffeence between us," she said. "We both have a birth mark on the thigh, like an inverted comma. Angie's is on the left thigh, mine on the right." She turned on to her side to point out the small blemish, pale against her tan, on her right thigh. "When we stand hip to hip in our bikinis, it looks like we're inside quotation marks. Have you seen Angelica's birthmark?"

"No," he said bitterly. "But I've heard about it." He felt suddenly ashamed of his nakedness, rolled off the bed, and hurriedly put on his underpants and trousers. "Why?" he said. "Why did you deceive me?"

"I never could resist a guy who was really hungry for it," said Lily.

"You mean, if any total stranger comes up and kisses you, you immediately drop everything and jump into bed with him?"

"Probably. But I figured who you were. Angie has talked to me about you. Why do you feel so sore about it, anyway? We made it together beautifully."

"I thought you were the girl I love," said Persse. "I wouldn't have made love to you otherwise."

"You mean, you were saving yourself for Angie?"

"If you like. You stole something that didn't belong to you."

"You're wasting your time, Persse, Angie is the archetypal pricktease."

"That's a despicable thing to say about your sister!"

"Oh, she admits it. Just like I admit I'm a slut at heart."

"That I won't attempt to deny," he said sarcastically.

"Oh, really?"

"Yes, really. The things you did."

"You seemed to dig them."

"I should have realized. No decent girl would have even conceived of them."

"Oh Persse—don't say that!" she suddenly cried, in a tone of real dismay.

"Why?" He went hot and cold.

"Because I *am* joking. I *am* Angelica!"

He flew to the bed. "Darling, I didn't mean it! It was beautiful, what we did, I—" He broke off. "What are you grinning at?"

"What about the birthmark? You forgot the birthmark." She twitched her right hip cheekily.

"You mean, you are Lily after all?"

"What do you think, Persse?"

He sank down on to a seat and covered his face with his hands. "I think you're trying to drive me mad, whoever you are."

He was aware of the girl pulling a coverlet from the bed and wrapping herself in it. She shuffled over and put a bare arm around his shoulder. "Persse, I'm trying to tell you that you're not really in love with Angelica. If you can't be sure whether the girl you just screwed is Angelica or not, how can you be in love with her? You were in love with a dream."

"Why do you want to tell me that?" he mumbled.

"Because Angie loves somebody else," she said.

Persse dropped his hands from his face. "Who?"

"A guy called Peter, they're getting married in the spring. He's associate professor at Harvard, very bright according to Angie. They met at some conference in Hawaii. She's hoping to get a college job in the Boston area, and Peter fixed it so she could give a paper at this convention to show off her paces. Angie heard that you were here looking for her, and she felt bad about it because she played some trick on you in England, right? She asked me to break it to you gently that she was already engaged. I did my best, Persse. Sorry if it lacked subtlety."

Persse went to the window, pulled back the curtain, and stared down at the brightly lit avenue below, and the cars and buses stopping and starting and turning at the intersection with 54th Street. He leaned his forehead against the cool glass. He was silent for several minutes. The he said: "I feel hungry."

"That's more like it," said Lily. "I'll call room service. What would you like to eat?"

Persse glanced at his watch. "I'm going to a party, I'll get some grub there."

"The penthouse party? I'll see you there," said Lily. "Peter is taking Angie and me. This is their room, actually. I was just using it to change in."

Persse unchained the door of the room. "Does Peter know what you do for a living?" he asked. "I saw your photograph in Amsterdam once. Also in London."

"I've retired from that," she said. "I decided to go back to school, after all. Columbia. I live in New York, now."

"When you used to work for Girls Unlimited," said Persse, "did you come across a girl called Bernadette? Her professional name was Marlene."

Lily reflected for a moment, then shook her head. "No. It was a big organization."

"If you should ever come across her, tell her to get in touch with me."

Persse took the elevator down the the ninth floor and found the door of room 956 open. Inside, Morris Zapp was sitting on the bed, eating nuts and drinking bourbon and watching television. "Hi, Percy, come in," he said. "All ready for the party?"

"I could do with a shower," said Persse. "Could I possibly use your bathroom?"

"Sure, but there's somebody in there right now. Sit down and fix yourself a drink. That was a real curveball of a question you threw at us this afternoon."

"I didn't mean to make things difficult for you," said Persse apologetically, helping himself to the bourbon. "I don't know what came over me, to tell you the truth."

"It didn't make any difference. It was very obvious that Kingfisher wasn't interested in what I was saying."

"Are you disappointed?" Persse sat down on a chair from which he had an oblique view of the TV screen. A naked couple who might have been himself and Lily an hour earlier were twisting and writhing on a bed.

"Nuh, I think I finally kicked the ambition habit. Ever since I was kidnapped, just being alive has seemed enough." Suddenly the screen went blank, and a legend appeared: *"Dial 3 to order the movie of your choice."* Another film, this time about cowboys, commenced. "They give you five minutes of a movie for free, to get you interested," Morris explained. "Then if you want to watch the whole thing, you call and have them pipe it in to your room and charge it."

"Everything on tap," said Persse shaking his head. "Oh brave new world!"

"Right, you can get anything you want by telephone in this city: Chinese food, massage, yoga lessons, acupuncture. You can even call up girls who will talk dirty to you for so much a minute. You pay by credit card. But if you're into deconstruction, you can just watch all these trailers in a row as if it was one, free, avant-garde movie. Mind you," he added pensively, "I've rather lost faith in deconstruction. I guess it showed this afternoon."

"You mean every decoding is not another encoding after all?"

"Oh it is, it is. But the deferral of meaning isn't infinite as far as the individual is concerned."

"I thought deconstructionists didn't believe in the individual."

"They don't. But death is the one concept you can't deconstruct. Work back from there and you end up with the old idea of an autonomous self. I can die, therefore I am. I realized that when those wop radicals threatened to deconstruct *me*."

The bathroom door opened and out came a lady in a towelling bathrobe and a cloud of fragrant steam. "Oh!" she exclaimed, surprised at seeing Persse.

"Good evening, Mrs Ringbaum," he said, getting to his feet.

"Have we met before?"

"At a party on the Thames last spring. The *Annabel Lee*."

"I don't remember much about that party," said Mrs Ringbaum, "except that Howard got into a fight with Ronald Frobisher, and the boat started drifting down the river."

"It was Ronald Frobisher who set it adrift, as a matter of fact," said Persse.

"*Was* it? I'll tackle him about that this evening."

"Is Ronald Frobisher here—at the MLA?" exclaimed Persse.

"Everybody is at the MLA," said Morris Zapp. "Everybody you ever knew." He was now watching a film about boxing.

"Everybody except Howard," said Thelma, with her head inside the wardrobe. "Howard is stuck in Illinois because he's been barred for life by the airlines for soliciting sex in flight from a hostess."

"I'm sorry to hear that," said Persse.

"It doesn't bother me," said Thelma with a chuckle. "I left that fink back in September, the best thing I ever did." She shook out a black cocktail dress and held it up in front of herself, standing before a full-length mirror. "Shall I wear this tonight, honey?"

"Sure," said Morris, without taking his eyes off the TV. "It looks great."

"Shall I go to the bathroom to put it on, or is this young man going to do the decent thing and wait in the hall?"

"Percy, go take that shower while Thelma is dressing," said Morris. "Borrow my electric razor if you need a shave. And by the way, in case your Irish Catholic conscience is shocked by the set-up here, I should tell you that Thelma and I are thinking of getting married."

"Congratulations," said Persse.

"Our romance started in Jerusalem," Thelma confided, smiling findly at Morris. "Howard never even noticed. He was too busy plotting to have sex with me in one of those cable cars at Masada."

When Persse had showered and shaved, the three of them took an express elevator to the highest public floor in the hotel, and then a man with a key admitted them to a small private lift that took them up to the penthouse suite. This was a huge, magical, split-level, glassed-in space which afforded breathtaking views of Manhattan at night. It was already crowded and loud with chatter, but the mood of the company was relaxed and euphoric. It helped that the only drink available was champagne. Arthur Kingfisher had donated a dozen cases. "He must have something really important to celebrate," commented Ronald Frobisher, who had commandeered one of the cases. He filled Persse's glass and introduced him to a lean, shrewd-eyed, red-haired woman in a green trouser-suit. "Désirée Byrd, Section 409, 'New Directions in Women's Writing,'" he said. "I'm Section 351, 'Tradition and Innovation in Postwar British Fiction'. Strictly speaking I'm just the Tradition bit. We were talking about that extraordinary spell of fine weather this afternoon."

"I'm afraid I missed it," said Persse, "I was indoors the whole afternoon."

"It was amazing," said Désirée Byrd. "I was in my agent's apartment talking about my new book. I was really depressed about it—I mean, it's virtually finished, but I'd completely lost faith in it. I way saying to Alice, 'Alice, I've decided I'm not a real writer after all. *Difficult Days* was a fluke, this new book is just a mess,' and she was saying, 'No, no, you mustn't say that,' and I said, 'Just let me read you some bits and you'll see what I mean,' and she said 'OK, but I'm going to open the window for a minute, it's so hot in here.' So she opens the window—imagine opening a window in Manhattan in the middle of winter, I thought she must be crazy—and suddenly this extraordinarily sweet warm air comes drifting into the room, and I started to read at random from my manuscript. 'Well,' I said after a page or two, 'that isn't too bad, actually.' 'It's tremendous,' said Alice. I said, 'It's not all that bad.' And, you know—it wasn't. It really wasn't. Well, you can guess what happened. The more I looked for lousy passages, the more enthusiastic Alice became, and the more I came to believe that *Men* is perhaps quite a good book after all."

"Marvellous," said Ronald Frobisher. "I had a similar experience. I was sitting in Washington Square at the same time, thinking about Henry James and basking in this extraordinary sunshine, when suddenly the first sentence of a novel came into my head."

"Which novel?" said Désirée.

"My next novel," said Ronald Frobisher. "I'm going to write a new novel."

"What's it going to be about?"

"I don't know yet, but I feel somehow that I've got my style back. I can sense it in the rhythm of that sentence."

"By the way," said Persse, "I met your Japanese translator last summer."

"Akira Sakazaki? He just sent me his translation of *Could Try Harder*—it looks like a bride's prayerbook. Bound in white, with a mauve silk marker." He refilled Persse's glass.

"I'd better get some grub inside me before I drink any more of this," said Persse. "Excuse me."

He was helping himself to the splended buffet supper spread out along one wall when a long arm, encased in a charcoal-grey worsted sleeve, very greasy around the wrist, reached over his shoulder and twitched the last remaining slice of smoked salmon away from the platter under his nose. Persse turned round indignantly to find Felix Skinner's yellow fangs grinning at him. "Sorry, old man, but I've a fatal weakness for this stuff." He dropped the slice of smoked salmon on to a plate already heaped with assorted foods. "What are you doing at the MLA?"

"I might ask you the same question," said Persse coolly.

"Oh, scouting for talent, testing the market, you know. Did you get my letter, by the way?"

"No," said Persse.

Felix Skinner sighed. "That's Gloria, she'll have to go . . . Well, we got a second opinion on your proposal, and we've decided to commission the book after all."

"That's marvellous!" exclaimed Persse. "Will there be an advance?"

"Oh, yes," said Felix Skinner. "Well, a small one," he added cautiously.

"Could I have it now?" said Persse.

"Now? Here?" Felix Skinner looked taken aback. "It's not normal practice. We haven't even signed a contract."

"I need two hundred dollars to get back to London," said Persse.

"I suppose I could give you that on account," said Felix Skinner grudgingly. "I happened to go to the bank this afternoon." He took two $100 bills from his wallet and passed them to Persse.

"Thanks a million," said Persse. "Your good health." He drained his glass, which was refilled in an absent-minded fashion by a shortish dark-haired man standing nearby with a bottle of champagne in his hand, talking to a tallish dark-haired man smoking a pipe. "If I can have Eastern Europe," the tallish man was saying in an English accent, "you can have the rest of the world." "All right," said the shortish man, "but I daresay people will still get us mixed up."

"Are they publishers too?" Persse whispered.

"No, novelists," said Felix Skinner. "Ah, Rudyard!" he cried, turning to greet a new arrival. "So you got here at last. You know young McGarrigle, I think. You were sadly missed at the forum this afternoon. What happened?"

"A disgraceful incident," said Rudyard Parkinson, puffing out his muttonchop whiskers so that he resembled an angry baboon. "I was just going through passport control at Heathrow—I was already late because I'd had a row with some impertinent chit at the check-in desk—when I was whisked off into a room by two thugs and subjected to a humiliating body-search and a third-degree grilling. I missed my plane in consequence."

"Good Lord, whatever did they do that for?" said Felix Skinner.

"They claimed it was mistaken identity. No excuse whatever, of course. Do I look like a smuggler? I made an official complaint. I shall very probably sue."

"I don't blame you," said Felix Skinner. "But was it worth coming so late?"

Parkinson began to mutter something about there being some people whom he wanted to meet, Kingfisher, Textel of UNESCO, and so on. Persse scarcely attended. Into his mind at the mention of "Heathrow" had swum the image of Cheryl Summerbee as he had last seen her, crying over her timetable; and it darted through him with the speed of an arrow, that Cheryl loved him. Only his infatuation with Angelica had prevented him from perceiving it earlier. As the consciousness of this fact sank in, Cheryl became endowed, to his mind's eye, with an aura of infinite desirability. He must go to her at once. He would take her in his arms, and wipe away her tears, and whisper in her ear that he loved her too. He turned away from Skinner and

Parkinson, spilling some of his champagne in the process, only to confront Angelica and Lily, each hanging on to an arm of the dark young man in the Donegal tweed jacket who had chaired the forum on Romance. He identified Lily by her red silk dress. Angelica was still wearing her tailored jacket and white blouse. "Hallo, Persse," she said. "I'd like you to meet my fiancé."

"Glad to meet you," said the young man, smiling, "Peter McGarrigle."

"No, it's *Persse* McGarrigle," he said. "*You're* Peter something."

"McGarrigle," the young man laughed. "I've the same name as you. We're probably related somehow."

"Were you ever at Trinity?" said Persse.

"Indeed I was."

"I'm afraid I did you out of a job once, then," said Persse. "When they appointed me at Limerick, they thought they were appointing you. It's been on my conscience ever since."

"It was the best day's work anyone ever did for me," said Peter. "I came to the States in consequence, and I've done very well here." He smiled fondly at Angelica, and she squeezed his arm.

"No hard feelings, Persse?" she said.

"No hard feelings."

"I heard you were at my paper this afternoon. What did you think of it?" She looked at him anxiously, as though his opinion really mattered.

He was saved from having to reply by the sound of someone rapping on a table nearby. The party hubbub subsided. A man in a sleek pale grey suit was making a speech from halfway up the flight of stairs that connected the two levels of the penthouse suite. "Who is it?" Felix Skinner could be heard enquiring. "Jacques Textel," Rudyard Parkinson hissed in his ear.

"As most of you know," Jacques Textel was saying, "UNESCO intends to found a new chair of literary criticism tenable anywhere in the world, and I think it's no secret that we have been seeking the advice of the doyen of the subject, Arthur Kingfisher, as to how to fill this post. Well, ladies and gentlemen, I have news for you." Textel paused, teasingly, and Persse looked round the room, picking out the faces, tense and expectant, of Morris Zapp, Philip Swallow, Michel Tardieu, Fulvia Morgana and Siegfried von Turpitz. "Arthur has just told me," said Jacques Textel, "that he is prepared to come out of retirement and allow his own name to go forward for the chair."

There was a collective gasp from the listeners, and a storm of applause, mingled with some expressions of a cynical and disapproving nature.

"Of course," said Textel, "I can't speak for the appointing committee, of which I am merely the chairman. But I should be surprised if there is any serious rival candidate to Arthur."

More applause. Arthur Kingfisher, standing just below Textel, held up his hands. "Thank you, friends," he said. "I know that some people might say that it is unusual for an assessor to put himself forward for the post on which he is advising; but when I agreed to act I thought I was finished as a creative thinker. Today I feel as if I have been given a new lease of life, which I would like to put at the service of the international scholarly community, through the good offices of UNESCO.

"To those friends and colleagues who may have been thinking that their claims to this chair are as good as mine, I will only say that in three years' time it will be up for grabs again." More applause, mingled with laughter, some hollow. "Finally, I would like to share with you a particular personal happiness. Song-Mi?" Arthur Kingfisher reached out and took the hand of Song-Mi Lee, gently pulling her up onto the step with himself. "This afternoon, ladies and gentlemen, this beautiful young lady, my companion and secretary for many years, agreed to become my wife." Cheers, shrieks, whistles, applause. Arthur Kingfisher beams. Song-Mi Lee smiles shyly. He kisses her. More applause.

But who is this little white-haired old lady who steps primly forward to confront the great literary theorist?

"Congratulations, Arthur," she says.

He stares, recognizes, starts back. "Sybil!" he exclaims,

amazed. "Where have you come from? Where have you been ? It must be thirty years . . ."

"Twenty-seven, Arthur," she says. "Just the age of your daughters."

"Daughters—what daughters?" says Arthur Kingfisher, loosening his necktie as if he is choking.

"Those lovely twin girls—there." She points dramatically to Angelica and Lily, who look at each other in amazement. Pandemonium among the audience. Sybil Maiden raises her voice above the hubbub. "Yes, Arthur, you remember when you took my long-preserved virginity during that summer school at Aspen, Colorado, in the summer of 'fifty-three? I thought I was too old to conceive children, but it proved otherwise." Now there is a breathless hush in the room, as all ears are strained to catch every word of this astonishing story. "A few weeks after we had parted, I discovered that I was pregnant—I, a respectable middle-aged spinster, fellow of Girton College, pregnant—and by a married man, for your wife was still alive then. What could I do but try to conceal the truth? Luckily I was starting a year's sabbatical in America. I was supposed to be working at the Huntington. Instead, I hid myself in the wilds of New Mexico, gave birth to the twins in the spring of 'fifty-four, smuggled them aboard a plane to Europe in a Gladstone bag—I travelled first class to get extra cabin baggage allowance, and there were no luggage searches and X-rays in those days—took the bag to the toilet as soon as we were airborne, and claimed to have found the babies there. Naturally, no one suspected that I, a supremely respectable spinster aged forty-six, could have been their mother. For twenty-seven years I have been carrying this guilty secret around with me. In vain have I tried to distract myself with travel. In the end it was through travel that I was brought face to face with my own grown-up children. Girls—can you ever forgive your mother for abandoning you?" She throws a piteous look in the direction of Angelica and Lily, who run to her side, and sweep her on to Arthur Kingfisher. "Mother!" "Daddy!" "My babies!" "My girls!" Poor Song-Mi Lee is in danger of being brushed aside, until Angelica

stretches out a hand and pulls her into the reunited family circle.
"Our second step-mother," she says, embracing her.

Everybody in the room, it seems, is embracing, laughing,
crying, shouting. Désirée and Morris Zapp are kissing each
other on both cheeks. Ronald Frobisher is shaking hands
with Rudyard Parkinson. Only Siegfried von Turpitz looks
cross and sulky. Persse grabs his hand and pumps it up and
down. "No hard feelings," he says, "Lecky, Windrush and
Bernstein are going to publish my book after all." The
German pulls his hand away irritably, but Persse has not
finished shaking it, and the black glove comes off, revealing
a perfectly normal, healthy-looking hand underneath. Von
Turpitz goes pale, hisses, and seems to shrivel in stature,
plunges his hand in his jacket pocket, and slinks from the
room, never to be seen at an international conference
again.

Lily came across to Persse. "We're all going on somewhere
we can dance," she said. "You want to come?"

"No thanks," said Persse.

"We could just go back to the room, if you like," she
said. "You and me."

"Thanks," said Persse, "but I ought to be on my
way."

He left the party a few minutes later, at the same time as
Philip Swallow. The Englishman's eye was moist. "I know
what it's like to discover that you have a child you never
dreamt existed," he said, as they waited for the main
elevator. "I found I had a daughter like that, once. Then I
lost her again." The lift doors opened and they entered
it.

"How was that?"

"It's a long story," said Philip Swallow. "Basically I
failed in the role of romantic hero. I thought I wasn't too
old for it, but I was. My nerve failed me at a crucial
moment."

"That's a pity," said Persse politely.

"I wasn't equal to the woman in the case."

"Joy?"

"Yes, Joy," said Philip Swallow with a sigh. He didn't
seem surprised that Persse knew the name. "I had a Christmas

card from her, she said she's getting married again. Hilary said, 'Joy? Do we know someone called Joy?' I said, 'Just someone I met on my travels.' "

"Hilary is your wife?"

"Yes. She's a marriage counsellor. Jolly good at it, too. She helped the Dempseys get back together. Do you remember Robin Dempsey—he was at the Rummidge conference."

"I'm glad to hear that," said Persse. "He didn't seem very contented when I met him."

"Had some kind of a breakdown last summer, I understand. Janet took pity on him. This is my floor, I think. Goodnight."

"Goodnight."

Persse watched Philip Swallow walking down the corridor, swaying a little with fatigue or drink, until the lift doors closed.

Persse walked through the Hilton lobby and out into the cold, crisp night. The temperature had returned to normal, and a raw biting wind was blowing down the Avenue of the Americas again. He began to walk in the direction of the YMCA. A black youth sped towards him a few inches above the broad sidewalk. But what Persse had at first taken for winged feet turned out to be attached to roller skates, and what looked like a helmet was a woolly hat worn over a transistor radio headset. Persse, mindful of New York mugging stories, and of the fact that he was carrying two hundred dollars in cash, stopped and tensed in readiness to defend himself. The young man, however, wore a friendly aspect. He smiled to himself and rolled his eyes up into his head; his movements had a rhythmic, choreographed quality, and his approach to Persse was delayed by many loops and arabesques on the broad pavement. He was clearly dancing to the unheard melodies in his earphones. He held a sheaf of leaflets, and as he passed he deftly thrust one into Persse's hand. Persse read it by the light of a shop window.

"Loneley? Horny? Tired of TV? We have the answers," it proclaimed. *"Girls Unlimited offers a comprehensive service for the out-of-town visitor to the Big Apple. Escorts,*

masseuses, playmates. Visit our Paradise Island Club. Take a jacuzzi bath with the bathmate of your choice. Have her give you a relaxing massage afterwards. Let it all hang out at our nude discothèque. Too lazy to leave your hotel room? Our masseuses will come to you. Or perhaps you just want some spicy pillow talk to get yourself off . . . to sleep. Dial 74321 and share your wildest fantasies with . . ."

Persse ran back to the Hilton lobby and pressed a dime into the nearest payphone. He dialed the number and a familiar voice said, somewhat listlessly: "Hallo, naughty boy, this is Marlene. What's on your mind?"

"Bernadette," said Persse. "I've got some important information for you."

ON the last day of the year, Persse McGarrigle flew into Heathrow on a British Airways jumbo jet. Having only hand-baggage with him, his scuffed and shabby canvas grip, he was one of the first of the passengers to pass through customs and passport control. He went straight to the nearest British Airways Information desk. The girl sitting behind it was not Cheryl. "Yes?" she said. "Can I help you?"

"You can indeed," he said. "I'm looking for a girl called Cheryl. Cheryl Summerbee. She works for British Airways. Can you tell me where I can find her?"

"We're not supposed to answer that sort of question," said the girl.

"Please," said Persse. "It's important." He put all a lover's urgency into his voice.

The girl sighed. "Well, I'll see what I can do," she said. She pushed the buttons on her telephone and waited silently for an answer. "Oh, hallo Frank," she said at length. "Is Cheryl Summerbee on shift this morning? Eh? *What*? No, I didn't. Oh. You don't? I see. All right, then. No, nothing. 'Bye." She put the phone down and looked at Persse,

384

curiously and with a certain compassion. "Apparently she got the sack yesterday," she said.

"What!" Persse exclaimed. "Whatever for?"

The girl shrugged. "Apparently she tried to get her own back on some bolshie passenger by marking his boarding card 'S', for suspected smuggler. The Excise boys did him over and he complained."

"Where is she, then? How can I find out her address?"

"Frank said she's gone abroad."

"Abroad?"

"She said she was fed up with the job anyway and this was her chance to travel. She'd been saving up apparently. That's what Frank said."

"Did she say where she was going?"

"No," said the girl. "She didn't. Can I help you, madam?" She turned aside to help another enquirer.

Persse walked slowly away from the Information desk and stood in front of the huge Departures flutterboard, with his hands in his pockets and his bag at his feet. New York, Ottawa, Johannesburg, Cairo, Nairobi, Moscow, Bangkok, Wellington, Mexico City, Buenos Aires, Baghdad, Calcutta, Sidney . . . The day's destinations filled four columns. Every few minutes the board twitched into life, and the names flickered and chattered and tumbled and rotated before his eyes, like the components of some complicated mechanical game of chance, a gigantic geographical fruit machine, until they came to rest once more. On to the surface of the board, as on to a cinema screen, he projected his memory of Cheryl's face and figure—the blonde, shoulder-length hair, the high-stepping gait, the starry, unfocused look of her blue eyes—and he wondered where in all the small, narrow world he should begin to look for her.